CRYSTAL LAKE VOLUME 1 BOOKS 1-3

CRYSTAL LAKE SERIES

LAURA SCOTT

READSCAPE PUBLISHING, LLC

HEALING HER HEART

CRYSTAL LAKE SERIES

Healing Her Heart

A Soldier's Promise

Coming Home by Laura Scott

Books 1-3 in the Crystal Lake Series

Please Note

Thank You

❀ Created with Vellum

OTHER BOOKS BY LAURA SCOTT:

Callahan Confidential

Shielding His Christmas Witness

The Only Witness

Christmas Amnesia

Shattered Lullaby

Primary Suspect

Protecting His Secret Son

The McNallys

To Love

To Cherish

To Laugh

To Honor

To Believe

To Promise

1

"Larissa, I put a new patient in room four for you," Merry Haines, the Hope County Hospital ER charge nurse, called out.

"Okay." Larissa Brockman finished documenting on her recent discharge and then pushed away from the computer. The hour was well past midnight, but the ER remained incredibly busy on this Memorial Day Friday night. Or rather, Saturday morning.

She crossed over to room four but then stopped abruptly in the doorway as she saw the familiar face of her patient. Annie Hinkle, a fifty-year-old woman looking a decade older than she should, was seated on the gurney cradling her right arm against her chest.

No. Not again. The tiny hairs lifted on the back of her neck in alarm. This was the second time Annie had been here over the past month. The last time was for a black eye that she swore was not caused by her husband, Kurt's, fist.

What would be her story this time? Larissa took a deep breath and let it out slowly before entering the room. "Hello, Annie."

"Hi." Annie's gaze barely met hers before skittering away.

"What did you do to your arm?" Larissa asked, keeping her voice gentle as she approached. She had the distinct impression the woman was on the edge and wouldn't hesitate to flee if cornered.

"I fell off the front porch—you know how klutzy I am." Annie refused to meet her gaze but kept staring down at her arm as if the injury might heal itself if she concentrated hard enough.

"I don't think you're klutzy at all," Larissa murmured. "Show me where it hurts."

"Right here," Annie said, removing her left hand to reveal a darkly mottled bruise encircling her wrist. Larissa felt a little sick looking at the injury, knowing there was no possible way this had happened from a fall. She could clearly envision a man's large hand squeezing hard enough to cause this. She'd be surprised if there weren't a few broken bones hidden beneath the horribly discolored skin.

"Okay, I'm going to get you a cold pack for that, and I'm sure the doctor will want X-rays, too." She kept her voice calm with an effort. "Do you need something for pain?"

Annie lifted her shoulder in a half-hearted shrug. "Maybe a pain pill would help."

Larissa nodded, thinking the poor woman needed far more than a pain pill. She batted a wave of helplessness aside. "Are you hurt anywhere else?" she asked. "Maybe you hit your head? Or your ribs?"

"No, just my wrist."

"All right, I'm going to check in with Dr. Allen, and then I'll be right back."

"Sure." Annie's gaze jerked away, causing Larissa's stomach to knot painfully.

She recognized the signs and symptoms of abuse. Only too well. Dark memories from the past threatened to overwhelm her, and she fought them back with an effort. Struggling to keep her emotions under control, she grabbed an ice pack from the supply rack and then went searching for Dr. Gabe Allen, the physician in charge of the patients on her team.

He was on the phone talking to the inpatient hospitalist about a patient he wanted admitted. She hovered nearby, waiting until he finished his call. He hung up the phone and flashed a warm smile. "Hi, Larissa, what's up?"

His smile was far too attractive, an effect she'd been fighting for months now. So far, she thought she was hiding her feelings pretty well. "I need you to examine my patient in room four," she said in a soft tone in a voice. "I'm convinced she's being physically abused."

Gabe's smile faded. "Are you sure?"

She'd only been a nurse here at the Hope County Hospital for six months, but she'd thought she'd proved her competence by now. She scowled. "Trust me, I'm sure."

Gabe gave a terse nod. "All right, let me finish up this inpatient admission, and I'll be right over."

"Thanks." She hurried back over to Annie's bedside, squeezing the disposable ice pack between her hands to activate the chemical reaction inside. "Here, place this around your wrist, okay?" she instructed. "Dr. Allen will be here shortly."

Annie winced but didn't say anything as she placed the cold pack over her wrist.

Larissa struggled to find the right words that might break through the woman's wall of denial. "Annie, you don't have to put up with anyone hurting you. We have programs that can help keep you safe."

"No one's hurting me," Annie swiftly denied. "I told you I fell off the porch." Her voice rose with indignation, and instinctively, Larissa knew she needed to back off or the woman might bolt.

"Okay, I'm sorry. I just don't like the idea of anyone hurting you." She forced a reassuring smile. "You're such a nice woman, and you certainly deserve to be treated as such. Oh, look, here comes Dr. Allen now."

"How are you, Mrs. Hinkle?" he asked. "I understand you may have broken your wrist."

"I fell off the porch," Annie said, repeating her story like a parrot.

"Hmmm," Gabe murmured as he removed the ice pack from her wrist. His eyebrows pulled together in a dark frown when he saw the extent of the injury. He probed the skin gently, his expression serious. "We're going to need several X-rays of this wrist," he said.

Larissa swiftly logged on to the computer. "AP and lateral views?" she asked as she entered the order.

"Yes." Gabe replaced the ice pack and gave Annie a stern look. "You know this didn't happen from a fall," he said bluntly.

"Yes, yes, it did." Annie's voice was beginning to sound desperate. "I'm klutzy and I fell off the porch."

Gabe's frustrated gaze locked on Larissa's, and she knew exactly what he was thinking. She gave him a tiny nod, acknowledging their dilemma, and then turned toward Annie. "Okay, just relax for now. The radiology tech will be here shortly to take you over to get the X-rays. Dr. Allen, do you think she could have a dose of Percocet for the pain?"

"Of course."

"Great, I'll be right back." Larissa walked over to the automated drug-dispensing machine and punched in her password along with Annie's name and ID number. The Percocet drawer popped open, and she removed one dose before closing it up again. When she spun around, she nearly bumped into Gabe.

"We have to notify the sheriff's department," he said in a low voice.

"I know." The Wisconsin state statutes were pretty clear regarding cases of suspected abuse. Still, she knew that doing the right thing could also backfire in a big way. "But you heard her. There's no way she's going to press charges against her husband. And I'm afraid that he'll only get angrier once the deputy questions him. What if he takes that anger out on her?"

Gabe thrust his fingers through his dark brown hair. "You could be right, but what choice do we have?"

"I don't know," she admitted, hating the feeling of help-lessness. The system was supposed to work for victims, but more often than not, it created a vicious cycle, one that couldn't be broken unless the victim took a stance. But too many of those victims didn't. "Let me talk to the social worker first, okay?"

"Okay, but giving her pamphlets on domestic violence isn't going to help," Gabe said with a dark frown. "We have to call the authorities."

She nodded, knowing with a sinking heart that he was right. She could only hope that the police could get through to Annie better than she and Gabe had been able to.

She closed her eyes and prayed that Annie wouldn't end up back in the ER with injuries that were far worse than a black eye or a broken wrist.

Please, Lord, keep Annie safe!

. . .

GABE STARED at the deputy in disbelief. "You're telling me there's nothing you can do?"

Deputy Armbruster held up his palms in a helpless gesture. "What do you want me to say? I could haul Kurt Hinkle down to jail, but if she doesn't press charges, he'll be out by morning."

That couldn't be right. "Surely there's enough evidence there to charge him with abuse even without her testimony?"

"Look, maybe he admits he grabbed her too hard, and she jerked away and oops? Look what happened?" The deputy sighed heavily. "Without Annie testifying against him, this could be made to look like some sort of accident rather than an intentional act of abuse. With no priors, he'll walk."

Gabe sensed Larissa beside him, and he was annoyed that he'd recognized her vanilla scent. Regardless, he kept his attention focused on the problem at hand. He just couldn't believe there wasn't something that could be done legally to prevent Kurt from hurting his wife. Again.

"What about the black eye from a few weeks ago?" she asked.

Gabe scowled. "I don't remember that."

"You weren't working that shift," Larissa pointed out. "I was on with Dr. Gardener."

Deputy Armbruster pursed his lips. "We could maybe argue that it's a pattern, but again, not likely. I got a black eye myself playing softball with my girls." He smiled grimly. "My daughter Elise has a good arm."

Gabe understood what the deputy was saying, but that didn't mean he had to like it. "So what can we do?"

"Look, I can go chat with Kurt if you want me to. At least he'll know that we're on to him and—"

"No," Larissa interrupted harshly. "Don't."

"What?" Gabe glared at her. "Why not?"

"Because he'll be mad and take his anger out on her, that's why." Larissa turned toward Deputy Armbruster. "If you can't arrest him, then just leave it alone."

Gabe couldn't believe what he was hearing. What was she doing? Why wasn't Larissa standing up for their patient? "I think it would do Kurt good to know we're on to him."

"Why?" Larissa asked, her green eyes sparking fire. "So next time he can hurt her where the bruises won't show?"

What? He took a step back. "No, of course not."

"Leave it alone," she pleaded. "I'll talk to Annie, okay? Maybe I can help in ways the police can't."

Deputy Armbruster shrugged. "Okay, let me know if anything changes."

"Gabe? We need your help over here," Merry called. "This patient's breathing is getting worse."

"Go ahead, I'll talk to Annie," Larissa said.

Reluctantly, he nodded and hurried over to where Merry was standing beside another patient who was clearly in distress. The beeping oxygen-saturation monitor showed numbers that were steadily declining. "Get me an intubation tray now."

All thoughts regarding his other patients vanished as he quickly focused on saving this gentleman's life. He placed the breathing tube and then quickly connected the oxygen supply, giving him several slow, deep breaths.

"O2 sat up to 90 percent," Merry announced with satisfaction.

The respiratory therapist came over to secure the tube. Gabe kept an eye on the guy's vital signs, reassured that he was holding his own, at least for the moment. "All right, call up to the ICU and let them know we have a patient for them."

"Will do," Merry promised.

Gabe did a quick visual check on the other patients under his care before heading back over to where Larissa was sitting beside Annie Hinkle. Annie was staring down at the cast he'd ordered to be placed on her wrist after determining that indeed she'd suffered two minor fractures.

Which could have easily been far worse. The good news was that she wouldn't need surgery.

The bad news was that he'd have to discharge her home. Back to her abusive husband.

He paused outside the doorway, listening as Larissa spoke softly to Annie. "Here's my name and phone number," Larissa said, pressing a small, folded piece of paper into Annie's uninjured hand. "Call me if you feel afraid, or if you just want to talk. I'd be happy to help in any way I can."

"Thank you," Annie whispered. "But really, I'm fine. Just a bit klutzy."

"Remember what I told you?" Larissa asked.

Annie slowly lifted her gaze to meet Larissa's. Her softly spoken "yes" sounded almost like an admission.

"Call me anytime," Larissa repeated.

"I will."

Gabe stood there for a long moment, wishing he'd heard the entire conversation between the two women. He'd sensed right from the start that Larissa had identified with Annie on a level that he couldn't possibly imagine.

Because of her previous ER experiences? Or from something more personal? He was surprised by the flash of anger at the thought of someone hurting Larissa.

He signed Annie's discharge orders, unable to get the thought out of his mind. From the moment he'd first met

Larissa, they'd connected on some sort of subliminal level. He was attracted to her, not just because of her pretty face and soft, wavy, blonde hair. But because they were both extremely dedicated to their patients and shared the same interests, like running. He'd caught sight of her several times when he took to the running trails, always giving her a nod of recognition but never stopping to chat.

He'd had to work hard to keep his distance from her. Romance and work did not mix, a lesson he'd learned the hard way.

He'd come to Crystal Lake a year ago, his pride battered and his reputation tarnished. After a year, he'd gained the respect he'd so desperately needed. Soon, he hoped to win the position of medical director for emergency medicine, putting his painful past away once and for all.

He refused to even consider a personal relationship, especially with one of the nurses.

But as he watched Larissa give Annie a brief hug and escort her out the door, he couldn't help wishing that he'd met Larissa under different circumstances. That she wasn't a nurse working in the ER with him.

Because he liked her, far too much.

2

L arissa finished off the rest of her twelve-hour night shift, grateful when the steady stream of patients slowed to a mere trickle. Between her deep concerns over Annie Hinkle and her ridiculous awareness of Gabe, she was physically and mentally exhausted.

Outside, she paused to stare in awe at the rising sun sliding up the horizon in the east. The beautiful sight helped restore her sense of peace.

Church services would be nice, too, even though it was Saturday she knew Crystal Lake Church always held an early morning service. She slid into her car and headed in the direction of the small, beautiful, white church steeple clearly visible between the leaves of the trees. She was glad it was Memorial Day weekend as she had the next two days off before she had to return to work. As painful as the twelve-hour shifts were to endure, the extra days off were wonderful.

At the stoplight, she yawned so wide her jaw popped. Her eyelids became unbearably heavy, and she pried her eyes open with an effort. Maybe it was better to forgo church services and head home since she was likely to fall asleep anyway. Her apartment was only a few miles away. Thankfully, she made it home without a problem.

Inside, she set her alarm to go off in five hours, so she could try to get back on a day-shift schedule. The worst part about working nights was switching back to day shifts on her days off.

When her alarm blared five hours later, she groaned and staggered over to shut it off. Every cell in her body craved more sleep, but she forced herself to stay upright.

A cup of coffee and a light breakfast helped clear away the lingering fog hovering along the edges of her mind. She stared outside at the bright sunlight. What she needed was a good rush of adrenalin. She tugged her running gear on, pulled her wavy hair back into a ponytail to keep it off her neck. A visor helped block the harsh rays from the sun as she headed outside.

The first half mile was the hardest, but once she hit her stride and wound her way along the jogging trail, shaded by towering trees, she felt every one of her muscles relax into an exhilarating rhythm. Other than being in church, these were the times she felt the closest to God, and she silently recited a prayer as she ran.

Distant sounds of laughter wafted up from the lake, where locals and tourists were enjoying the water. She lived in a small apartment building outside of town without direct access to the lake, although buying a small house on the water was one of her goals.

Maybe next year, she thought with a smile. She'd come to Crystal Lake to escape a bad relationship and to get far away from the high crime rate of Chicago. The night the cops busted up a drug deal going down in the apartment across the hall from hers had pushed her over the edge.

So far, she absolutely loved it here in Crystal Lake.

Her peaceful run was abruptly interrupted by the harsh roar of a motorbike. She hugged the side of the trail, peering over her shoulder to make sure she saw the cyclist before he came upon her unexpectedly.

The growl of the engine became louder, and she stifled a sliver of unease. One wrong move on this dirt-packed, hilly trail could result in disaster.

The motorbike abruptly crested the hill, heading straight toward her. She leaped off the trail to get out of harm's way. But she landed off balance, her foot slipping on loose rocks and branches. She went down hard. The motorbike swerved around a curve, the driver letting out a loud whoop.

"Idiot," she muttered, assessing for injuries. Her knees and the palms of her hands were scraped raw from her tumble, but it could have been worse.

She stood, and her right ankle zinged with pain. Great. Just what she needed—a sprained ankle roughly two and a half miles from home.

The sound of the motorbike grew louder again, and she stared at the trail, unable to believe the guy had the nerve to come back after the reckless stunt he'd pulled. Sure enough, he was riding down the trail, once again headed straight for her.

For a split second, she had the distinct impression that he was purposely trying to run her down. She scrambled out of the way, grasping the trunk of a tree for support as the motorbike whizzed by, so close that she could feel the heat from the engine blasting against her legs.

She clung to the tree for several long moments, afraid the motorcyclist was going to come back for a third time. She sent up a silent prayer, thanking God for her safety, before she finally let go of the tree and hobbled back onto the trail. She limped as pain reverberated up her leg with every step. Finding a thick tree branch, she improvised, using it as a walking stick.

The soft thud of footsteps on the trail made her tense. She forced herself to relax; there was no reason the driver of the motorbike would decide to come back on foot. It wasn't unusual to pass other joggers on the trail.

Sure enough, a runner came into view. A tall man, wearing a sweaty orange T-shirt and navy blue shorts, with ear buds tucked into his ears blocking out the noise. Personally, she didn't get why anyone would want to listen to music while running when the peace and quiet was so much more soothing. But to each his own.

As the jogger approached, she grimaced when she recognized Gabe Allen. She shouldn't have been surprised; she'd passed him on the running trails before, and they'd exchanged brief greetings before heading their separate ways.

When he caught sight of her, he frowned and immediately slowed down, tugging the ear buds from his ears. "Larissa, are you all right? What happened?"

She willed her heart rate not to jump as he stepped closer, concern darkening his warm, brown eyes. She cleared her throat and strove for a light tone. "Did a hotshot on a motorbike fly past you?" she asked wryly. "Because he ran me off the trail—twice."

"Yeah, I saw him." Gabe dropped down to a crouch to examine the scrapes on her knees before he gently prodded her ankle. She sucked in a swift breath, and he glanced up at her. "This looks like a bad sprain."

"Thanks for the diagnosis, doc," she said lightly. "I

realize I'm just a nurse, but I kinda figured that out all by myself."

Gabe didn't take offense but sent her a lopsided smile. "You should probably get an MRI to rule out ligament damage."

She shrugged. "Yeah, but I can't do that until the swelling goes down, anyway, right?"

"Right. You'll get a better picture if you wait a few days," he agreed, rising to his feet. "Come on, lean on me, and I'll help you get home."

"What?" His offer was so unexpected she nearly lost her balance. The last thing she needed was to cozy up to Gabe for two and a half long miles. "There's no need for you to cut your run short because of me. I have my trusty walking stick. I'll be fine."

"Don't be ridiculous. I'm not leaving you here like this. Leaning on me is way better than using a stick, and my place isn't that far, just a mile and a quarter from here."

A mile and a quarter still seemed like a long way, but it was better than going all the way to her apartment. She reluctantly nodded. "All right. But I'm hot and sweaty," she warned as he wrapped his arm firmly around her waist.

"Me, too," he said easily, shortening his stride to match hers.

Their progress was still awkward, and she was far too aware of being so close to Gabe. "I wish I knew who that motorbike driver was," she muttered in an attempt to distract herself from his nearness. "I'd report him to the police. He's a menace on these trails."

"I'm pretty sure that was Tommy Hinkle," Gabe said. "I've taken care of him a few times in the ER."

"Annie's son?" The knowledge almost made her feel sorry for him. "Do you think his father hits him, too?"

Gabe was silent for several moments. "Actually, I think the kid is probably too much like his father," he said finally. "The last time Tommy was in the ER was because he was under arrest for driving under the influence. He bragged that his dad would bail him out, no problem. I got the impression his dad lets him do whatever he wants. Maybe even encourages him."

She sighed and shook her head. "Poor Annie. I'm getting the feeling it's two against one in that household."

"Yeah, I'm afraid so." They walked along in silence for a few minutes. Then Gabe's arm tightened around her waist, drawing her to a halt. "There, see between the trees? That's my place. Think you can make it that far?"

"Yes, I can make it," she assured him, even though in truth, her right ankle still throbbed like crazy. Not to mention, being this close to him was wreaking havoc on her hard-won control.

Larissa knew she couldn't afford to let her guard down with Gabe. No matter how much she wanted to.

GABE GRIMLY PACED off the distance to his place as they made their way along the trail. He couldn't, in good conscience, leave Larissa to hobble along on her own, but holding on to her like this hadn't been the brightest idea he'd ever had.

She fit against his side perfectly, her slight frame hiding a strength he couldn't help but admire. Her ankle looked terrible, but she didn't whine or complain. In fact, if he hadn't offered to help her, he knew she would have continued on her way without asking for assistance.

He had to remind himself for the tenth time that she was an ER nurse, which meant she was off-limits. Permanently.

Knowing that Tommy Hinkle was the one who'd run her off the trail made him grit his teeth in anger. Larissa was right, the kid was a menace, but he suspected that there wouldn't be much the police could do about it now.

"Gabe? Is something wrong?" Larissa asked.

He glanced down in surprise. "No, why?"

"Your arm around my waist is getting tighter and tighter," she admitted. "You might want to lighten up a bit."

He mentally smacked himself. "Sorry about that," he said, relaxing his grip. "I was getting mad thinking about Tommy. How's your ankle holding up?"

"Just peachy," she said in a wry tone. "I'm trying to take heart in the fact that your house is slowly getting closer."

"We'll be there soon, and then you can relax," he promised. His modest, wood-sided A-frame overlooking the lake was his private sanctuary, and while he wasn't accustomed to having women over, it wasn't as if he could drag Larissa all the way to town on foot. He knew she lived in the same apartment complex that Merry Haines and several of the other staff lived in because he'd overheard the nurses comparing notes one day about an exceptionally noisy neighbor.

"Your home looks very rustic," she said as they finally approached the driveway. Only ninety more feet to go. "Somehow I expected something more...flashy."

"Flashy?" He grasped his chest as if wounded. "Do I really look like the type that goes for flashy?"

She chuckled. "No, but doctors generally live a much higher lifestyle than the rest of us."

He hid a stab of disappointment regarding her observation. Was she like so many of the other nurses? The ones who set their sights on marrying a doctor? And when they didn't get what they wanted, stooped so low as to tell lies, not caring that they destroyed a man's reputation?

"It's so beautiful," she murmured. "You must love the peace and quiet."

"I do," he agreed, refusing to waste any time thinking about Rebecca. She was out of his life, for good. Three more feet and they were up to his front stoop. "Can you navigate the step all right? Or should I carry you?"

"I can do it," she responded quickly.

He held the door open for her, and she limped inside, heading for the closest chair. "Thanks," she said with a sigh. "Feels good to sit down for a moment. I hate to ask for any more favors, but I'd appreciate a ride home."

"I'll drive you home as soon as we clean up those wounds." Didn't she realize there was blood oozing out from the dirt filled abrasions? "Sit tight, I'll be right back."

"Wait, you don't have to—" she began, but he ignored her. He went to rummage through his bathroom cabinet, finding everything he needed: dressings, tape, antibiotic ointment. When he returned, he discovered she'd made her way into the kitchen.

"I don't want to bleed on your carpet," she said with a hint of defensiveness. "And I washed the scrapes on my hands with soap and water."

He set the supplies on the table and then went over to fill up a bowl with soapy water. He brought it over and knelt beside her. "This might hurt," he warned as he took a soft washcloth and began cleaning her knees.

The abrasions weren't too bad, and she didn't say a word as he cleaned them up. "What's the matter?" he asked when he finished putting fresh dressings in place. "Did you think a measly doctor wouldn't know how to dress a wound?"

"No, you did a fine job," she said in a low voice. She

avoided his gaze. "Thanks so much. It's a good thing I'm off work for the next two days. A bit of rest and I'll be as good as new."

"You might want to see your doctor. He'll write you an excuse to stay off work longer if needed."

"I'll be fine," she repeated. "I'm sure you want to get back to your run, so if you could just drive me home, I'll get out of your hair."

She was acting a bit strange, and he thought she might be having more pain than she'd let on. He loosened her running shoe. "First, let's wrap up this ankle." The swelling hadn't gotten too much worse, which was a good sign since she'd been walking on it for the past twenty minutes. Maybe there wasn't any ligament damage. "Better?" he asked when he'd finished wrapping it snuggly.

"Much." Her voice sounded strained. "Thanks. Again."

He stared at her for a moment, trying to gauge her mood. He rose to his feet and crossed over to the fridge. He pulled out a bottle of water and handed it to her. After taking a swig of his own water, he took a bag of frozen peas out of the freezer. "Here, use this as an ice pack," he said, draping the bag over her ankle.

She let out an unexpected chuckle. "Too funny. I have a bag of frozen peas that I use as an ice pack, too."

He couldn't help but return her smile. "I bet every runner has a bag of peas in their freezer."

"Maybe," she agreed. She took a long drink of water before recapping the bottle. "So, is there anything else you think you need to fix, Dr. Allen? Or should we get going?"

He had the insane urge to offer to make her dinner but stopped himself just in time. "I'll drive you home. Here, lean on me. My car is in the garage."

"No problem." She held on to the peas and the water

bottle with one hand and held him around the waist with the other. It was a short distance, but he found he missed her touch once she was safely tucked into the passenger seat.

Larissa kept glancing out her window on the ride home, and he got the sense she was avoiding him for some reason. After about ten minutes, he pulled up to her apartment complex.

He insisted on helping her up to her apartment despite her protests that she'd be fine. "Do you need anything else?" he asked after she unlocked the door.

"Nope, but thanks again. See you later," she barely got out before she shut the door firmly between them.

He stared at the closed door for several long seconds before turning to make his way back outside to his car. The thought that she'd been so anxious to get rid of him didn't sit well.

And much like the way she'd interrupted his run— granted, through no fault of her own—she annoyingly infiltrated his thoughts for the remainder of the day.

3

Larissa slid behind the wheel of her car, intending to attend Sunday morning church services. However using her right foot to drive proved nearly impossible. After several jerky attempts at driving with her left foot, she let out a frustrated groan, turned off the car, and awkwardly climbed back out from behind the wheel. No way was that going to work. She was more likely to hit something than not.

She stared up at the cloudless sky, fighting a wave of helplessness. This stupid ankle was going to ruin her few days off work if she couldn't manage to drive a car. She propped herself against the vehicle, enjoying the cool breeze as she tried to figure out what to do next.

Less than one day and she was already heartily sick of being stuck in her apartment. Maybe she could manage to hobble down to Rose's Café? Josie would keep her company at least for a while. There was nothing the café owner liked more than gossip.

"Larissa!"

She turned when she heard her name, surprise

widening her eyes when she caught sight of Gabe Allen walking toward her. He'd parked his car a few spaces down from hers.

"Hi, Gabe." She was glad that this time she didn't smell like sweat and was dressed in a flowery skirt and a matching pink, short-sleeved top. She tried not to fidget with her clothing. "What are you doing here?"

"I brought over a pair of crutches in case you needed some help getting around." He gazed at her attire and lifted his brow. "Are you headed somewhere special?"

She blushed and wished she could stop this ridiculous reaction to him. "I planned on attending church services, but driving is apparently not an option." Had he mentioned crutches? She brightened with the possibility. "I bet I could walk to church, though, if you're serious about allowing me to borrow those crutches." Church and then Rose's café. Much better than sitting around and staring at the four walls of her apartment.

"I think it would be better if I drove you to church," Gabe said slowly. "Crutch walking isn't easy for long distances."

"Oh." She was flabbergasted by his willingness to take her to church because she'd never seen him attend services in the past. "That's very kind, but I don't want to take you out of your way."

"It's no problem. Here, lean on me, and we'll get you over to my car."

She found it unsettling to realize she was standing close to Gabe with his arm anchored around her waist for the second time in less than twenty-four hours. She had no idea why God kept sending this man into her path, but for right now, she couldn't think of an excuse not to go along with his offer. Other than the obvious one, that spending time with Gabe wasn't smart.

But she breathed a little easier when she was safely seated in the passenger seat of his car. She waited until he slid into the driver's seat before glancing at him. "You know, I wouldn't mind if you dropped me off at church and came back in an hour if you don't want to go in with me."

Gabe looked past her, over his shoulder as he backed out of the parking space. "Is that a polite way of saying I'm not welcome?" he asked.

"No! Of course not." She was horrified that he would think that. "I guess I just never noticed you attending church services before."

A smile bloomed across his features. "Isn't it the job of a good Christian to convince us non-goers to attend church and to rediscover our faith?" he asked in a teasing tone. "At least that's what my sister always tries to do."

She relaxed after hearing his sister was a Christian. "Yes, you're right about that. I would love for you to come to church, but I can't force you to believe in God. You have to come to that realization on your own."

Gabe was silent for a moment. "I have to be honest with you. I haven't been to church in well over a year."

She wondered what had happened to cause his lapse in faith. And given what he'd just told her, she had no idea why he'd even offered to come with her in the first place. But she didn't want to pry into his personal life by asking. She, better than anyone, understood the need for privacy. "Well, I have to tell you that out of all the church services I've attended in my lifetime, Pastor John gives one of the best," she said lightly. "He's down to earth and yet always helps remind us what God would want us to do. Maybe I'm being presumptuous, but I think you'll like him."

Gabe made a noncommittal noise but didn't say anything more as he pulled up to the parking lot of the church. She struggled to get out of the car, which wasn't easy, but within moments, Gabe was there, helping her.

"Thanks," she murmured, hoping he wouldn't notice the breathlessness in her tone.

"Stay there," he told her. "I'll get the crutches."

He pulled the aluminum crutches out of the backseat and set them next to her. "Try these. I set them up for your height based on memory, but I might have the measurements wrong."

She took the crutches and propped them beneath her armpits, not surprised to discover they were perfect. "They're great. Thanks so much."

"I broke my foot once, so trust me, I know what you're going through," he confided. "It's not as easy to crutch walk as it looks."

She flashed him a smile and made her way over toward the sidewalk leading up to the front door of the church. Gabe stayed right beside her, his hand hovering on the small of her back, as if he was worried she might fall.

There weren't many parishioners in attendance as it was the holiday, but those who were there greeted her by name. She didn't know if she should introduce Gabe, and if so, as what? Her friend? A colleague? One of the doctors she worked with? She couldn't bring herself to use any of those options, so she decided not to say anything at all.

Gabe was likely regretting his offer to bring her, based on the knowing looks being flashed their way. Did Gabe realize the power of small-town gossip? She could feel her cheeks turning red and ducked her head, hoping no one would notice.

She told herself not to worry what anyone else thought.

If this was what Gabe needed to bring him back to the church, then the minor discomfort was well worth it.

Closing her eyes, she sent up a small prayer. *Please, Lord, show Gabe the way home.*

GABE STOOD beside Larissa in church, wondering why on earth he'd agreed to this. She'd given him an out, had offered to be dropped off and picked up in an hour when the service was over. Honestly, that was exactly what he'd considered before she mentioned it.

But he hadn't taken the chance to skip out. Instead, here he was, attending church in the first time in over a year. His sister had dragged him to services whenever possible back in Madison, but after moving to Crystal Lake, he hadn't bothered.

When Larissa had mentioned that she couldn't force him to believe in God, he'd relaxed his guard. He loved his sister, Kimberly, but she was constantly preaching at him, trying to get him to buy into every one of her beliefs. Instinctively, the more she pushed, the more he'd backed off.

He picked up the hymnal and found the opening hymn. One thing he'd rather liked about the church services was the music. It occurred to him now just how much he'd missed it.

As the organist began to play, they rose to their feet and began to sing along. His baritone was a bit rusty, but he soon got into the rhythm.

He caught Larissa's pleased smile as she joined him in singing along. Her arm lightly brushed his, and he kept his eyes centered on the hymnal, pretending not to notice.

Even though he did.

The pastor was younger than he'd anticipated. Gabe hadn't expected to enjoy the service, despite Larissa's glowing praise of Pastor John Gorman, but since the theme of the sermon today was forgiveness, he found his attention riveted on the pastor's words.

Pastor John paused for a moment and then read, "*And whenever you stand praying, if you have anything against anyone, forgive him, that your Father in heaven may also forgive you your trespasses (Mark 11:25).*"

The passage struck a chord deep within. He'd remained so angry with Rebecca after the way she'd destroyed his reputation at the University Hospital in Madison. Telling his boss and the hospital leadership that he'd sexually harassed her when, in fact, she was simply upset because he'd broken off their relationship. She'd cost him his job. No matter how much he'd tried to deny her allegations, he knew there was no way to recover from the stigma.

It was her word against his, and he'd lost. Big time.

Shaking off the past, he focused on the pastor's sermon. According to Pastor John, if he wanted to find peace, he first had to cleanse his soul. And that meant forgiving Rebecca.

Could he really do that? He knew he should, but saying and doing were two different things.

The organist began the closing hymn before he'd even realized the service was nearly over. And he was even more surprised that he hadn't been watching the clock, the way he used to. In fact, he'd enjoyed the service.

"Thanks for bringing me, Gabe," Larissa said softly. "That was exactly what I needed this morning."

"My pleasure," he responded. "Don't tell my sister, but I liked it, too."

She laughed, and the sound reminded him of picnics at the beach. Or maybe that was just the last time he could remember being happy. Odd that he felt more lighthearted and relaxed around Larissa.

"How would you like to go out on my boat this afternoon?" he offered. "I know the lake will be busy considering it's the Memorial Day holiday, but we can still have fun."

Her blue eyes glowed with excitement and surprise. "Oh, I'd love to do that. You have no idea how horrible it is sitting inside the apartment while everyone else is out having a good time."

"Great. How about we grab some lunch and then head over to my place. Unless you need to go home first for some reason?"

"No, I'm fine." She blushed. "And I was thinking of stopping at Rose's Café, anyway."

"Rose's Café it is." He was glad she'd agreed to come with him, even though he wasn't exactly sure why he'd brought the idea up in the first place.

Nothing had changed. Larissa was still a nurse at Hope County Hospital, and he was still vying for the medical director position. He couldn't afford to get emotionally involved with someone he worked with. Yet he could relate to where she was coming from. Sitting at home alone didn't hold a lot of appeal for him, either.

He would just have to make sure that spending the day with Larissa was about being friends and nothing more.

LARISSA TOLD herself that being out on Gabe's boat didn't mean anything. Even though Josie had wagged her eyebrows when she'd noticed Larissa and Gabe together. Larissa tipped her face to the sun and tried to calm her racing heart. Maybe this wasn't the best idea she'd ever had.

So why had she said yes?

The logical answer was that she'd been bored and hadn't wanted to sit around in her apartment. But the real reason was that she liked Gabe. As a person, not just as a physician she worked with.

And she hadn't liked a man in a really long time.

For the first time, she realized that she'd been running away from her past. As much as she learned to love Crystal Lake, the fact of the matter was that she would have worked anywhere that wasn't Chicago Central.

Gabe wasn't Rolland. She'd made one bad decision, but did she have to live with that one bad decision forever? Maybe it was time to forgive herself. Wasn't that what Pastor John had suggested?

"I brought you here to relax, not to be stressed out," Gabe said as he slowed the boat, banking gently around a curve.

She hadn't realized that her distress had been so evident and cleared her features. "Sorry about that. I guess I was wallowing in the past. You're right that being out on the water like this is very relaxing. You must come out here whenever you have a day off, weather permitting."

"I don't come out often enough," he admitted. "I tend to lose myself in running instead."

She grinned. "Yes, I know."

He was silent for a long moment. "I've been working hard to let go of the past as well," he finally said. "So I understand how it can creep up on you at the worst time."

She lifted a brow, surprised he'd admitted that much. "We should be able to let go, right? Considering how nice and peaceful it is here."

He nodded as he glanced around. "Yeah, nothing like the city, that's for sure." He lifted his brow. "It's a bit ironic that we're both relatively new to the area."

She remembered her first few weeks here and suppressed a shudder. "At least you were a Wisconsinite." She'd heard he'd moved here from Madison. "I came from Chicago, and let me tell you, that was a huge hurdle to overcome."

He laughed. "I can only imagine."

She smiled in spite of herself. "Thankfully, Julie Crain befriended me, and since she grew up here, the locals finally stopped treating me like an outsider." Julie was working this weekend or she would have had someone to hang out with.

Someone other than Gabe Allen.

Not that she was complaining or anything.

"I bet if we asked around, we'd find more transplant residents than those who were born here," Gabe confided.

The thought of people who were born and raised here made her think of poor Annie Hinkle. According to Julie, the Hinkles had been here as long as she had. Her smile faded. "You might be right," she agreed.

Her cell phone rang, surprising her. She stared at the screen for a moment, tempted to let the call go to voice mail as she didn't recognize the number. Reluctant curiosity compelled her to press the green button to answer. "Hello?"

"Larissa? It's me, Annie." The woman was speaking so softly she could barely hear her.

A shiver of apprehension rippled down her spine. "Annie? What's wrong? Are you okay?"

There was a loud crash followed by nothing but silence.

Annie had hung up.

4

"Was that Annie Hinkle?" Gabe asked, every sense on alert. When she nodded, he tried to remain calm. "What happened?"

Larissa's tortured gaze met his. "I don't know, but I think we should call the police."

He quickly turned the boat back toward his pier. "Are you sure? Maybe she just didn't want anyone to know she was calling you."

"She was talking really softly, as if she didn't want anyone to hear her. But then I heard a crash and then— nothing. I'm worried something terrible has happened to her."

He understood where she was coming from. The dark bruise around Annie's wrist had revealed an ugly story despite her claims of falling off the porch. He'd seen his share of domestic violence cases when he'd been in Madison, but he couldn't figure out why the women didn't just get out. He knew being a victim was part of the cycle, believing the guy was going to change, thinking that next time the same thing wouldn't happen, but it was still frustrating.

"Call 911 and send the deputies over there just in case."

He could hear Larissa on the phone, speaking to Deputy Thomas, explaining Annie's abrupt call and the crash she'd heard. After she finished, she turned back toward him. "They said they'd send a squad out to check things out."

"That's good," he said as he pulled up next to his pier. "Wait for me to help you," he cautioned. He made quick work of tying up the boat before giving her a helping hand.

She crutch-walked up the front lawn at a fast pace. He followed close behind. "Do you know where Annie and Kurt live?" she asked as they rounded the house.

He had a bad feeling about where this was going. "Yes. They live in a small house in the woods. They don't have access to the lake, but their house is tucked into the trees. I think Kurt likes his privacy." Privacy that gave him plenty of opportunity to hit his wife without anyone overhearing.

"Will you drive me there?"

He didn't want to because he was worried about her safety. Both Kurt and Tommy could be unpredictable. Yet how could he refuse? If anything, Larissa might be able to calm Annie down if she was upset since she'd established a good rapport with the patient during her last visit.

"I'll drive you there," he agreed. "But we're not going inside until the cops show up."

Larissa looked like she wanted to protest, but she didn't say anything as she slid into the passenger seat. He took the crutches, stuffed them in the back, and then jogged around to the driver's side.

"Hurry," Larissa urged.

He was already pushing the speed limit, but he nudged the gas pedal a bit more. "Try calling Annie back, see if she answers."

Larissa did as he suggested, but apparently no one

answered because she dropped the phone into her lap. "I don't like it," she murmured. "Something's not right."

As he approached the south side of the lake, he heard the wail of sirens getting louder. The squad sped past them, kicking up dust and gravel, and he couldn't help feeling a sense of relief.

He could only hope and pray the deputies had gotten there in time.

When he approached the long, winding driveway, he pulled off on the side of the road and cut the engine.

"What are you doing?" she asked, her tone laced with impatience. "We have to check on Annie."

"Larissa, the police are there. We can't just barge up the driveway into the middle of what could be a bad situation. For all we know, Annie could be a hostage. There could be weapons involved." And from what he'd heard about Kurt, the guy was an avid hunter, so for sure he owned at least one gun, if not more. "Let's just sit here for a minute and wait."

Larissa's expression betrayed her frustration, but when she bowed her head to pray, he reached over to take her hand in his. "Dear Lord, we ask that You please keep Annie safe in Your care," he murmured.

"Amen," Larissa whispered.

LARISSA STARED THROUGH THE WINDSHIELD, searching for some sign of either Annie or the police. Both windows were down, too, but they couldn't hear anything, and she wasn't sure if that was a good thing or not. At least there wasn't any shouting or gunfire. But what if everyone was already dead? She couldn't bear the thought.

Usually prayer helped keep her calm, but she couldn't deny an acute sense of urgency. She was pleased that Gabe had prayed with her, and if the situation wasn't so tense, she might have asked him more about what had caused him to stray from his faith.

The sound of muted voices reached her ears, and she grabbed Gabe's hand. "Did you hear that?" she whispered.

He nodded. "Maybe there's nothing to worry about," he suggested.

As much as she wanted to believe that, she knew too well it wasn't likely. Abusive men didn't just turn over a new leaf. They always wanted to prove that they were in control, no matter what it took. And the abuse was always the victim's fault.

You're so stupid! How could you do something so stupid? Whack! Maybe next time, you'll think before you open up your mouth! Smack!

Larissa shivered despite the warm air as memories of the past came rushing forward. Her stepfather had beat her mother on a regular basis, but it wasn't until her stepfather started beating Larissa that her mother had finally escaped.

"Hey, what's wrong?" Gabe whispered. "You suddenly got very pale."

She needed to pull herself together. "Nothing. I'm fine."

The sound of a car motor startled her, and she held her breath until the squad car came into view. The two deputies inside looked grim.

"What happened?" Gabe asked through his open window. "Is Annie all right?"

The two deputies exchanged a long look. "Apparently everything is all right. Annie claims she knocked a pot of hot water off the stove and that her burns are superficial. She's refusing medical care. And Kurt has promised to take care of her."

Larissa shook her head, knowing that there was way

more to the story. But what could they do? If Annie wouldn't come forward to testify against her husband or come in to get medical care, they couldn't take any action against him.

"Sorry we bothered you," Gabe said.

"It's no bother," Deputy Thomas said with a dark frown. "But it is frustrating. At the moment, our hands are tied. Let us know if you hear anything more."

"Thanks," Larissa murmured, feeling sick to her stomach. She didn't say anything as Gabe started up the car and drove away. She knew it would only be a matter of time until Annie was hurt again.

The only question remaining was whether or not she'd survive the next attack.

GABE GLANCED OVER AT LARISSA, who'd been unusually quiet during the ride back to his place. "How about some steaks on the grill?" he offered.

Her eyebrows rose in surprise, and he mentally braced himself for rejection. "Actually," she said slowly, "that sounds wonderful."

Despite his intent to keep Larissa in the friendship category, he was thrilled that they'd be spending the evening together. He assumed that Larissa didn't want to be alone, and he couldn't blame her, especially since he knew she was as depressed as he was about Annie's situation.

But he was glad all the same.

"I hope you don't mind if I stop at a grocery store," he said. "I need to pick up something to go along with the steaks."

"Sounds good. I'd be happy to pay for salad fixings," she offered.

"I'll pay for the salads," he said firmly as he executed a

U-turn in the road to head back toward town. A few minutes later, he pulled into the parking lot of the local grocery store.

He helped her out of the car, once again distracted by her vanilla scent. He quickly pulled her crutches out of the back seat and handed them to her. "Ready?" he asked.

"Of course," she said, swinging into a crutch walk like a pro.

He grabbed a basket and followed her to the produce section. "Oooh, the tomatoes look delicious," she gushed.

He grimaced. "If you like tomatoes."

Her jaw dropped in mock horror. "You don't like tomatoes? How is that possible? Everyone likes tomatoes!"

"I don't," he said with a wry grin. "But help yourself. Do you like cucumbers?"

"Of course, what's not to like?"

"What about salad dressing?" he asked when they'd filled the basket with veggies. "I have ranch dressing at home, but if you want something else, that's fine."

"I love ranch dressing, so I'm good."

Ridiculous to be pleased that they had some tastes in common. They made their way over to the checkout lines, and he I ignored the surprised glances in his direction as he paid for the groceries. It was a little late now to be worried about the gossip mill, considering he'd already attended church with Larissa.

After the way Rebecca had ruined his reputation at Madison, he'd tried to avoid attracting attention here in Crystal Lake. He hadn't been seen with a woman before now.

But there was no denying that he'd been living a lonely existence. And what was the harm of picking up veggies for dinner with Larissa? He didn't care what people said about him outside the hospital. As long as his reputation within the Emergency Department remained untarnished, he was fine.

The drive back to his house didn't take long. Once inside, Larissa took over the kitchen. "I'll make the salads," she said, running the veggies under water to clean them. "You can grill the steaks."

"Yes, ma'am," he teased as he pulled the steaks out of the fridge, where he'd been marinating them all afternoon. The fact that he'd planned on having dinner with Larissa all along made him pause for a moment.

Was he really considering breaking his cardinal rule against dating co-workers?

No, he wasn't. He couldn't afford to do anything that might jeopardize his career. They were friends, that's all. And friends could certainly share dinner on occasion. Not a big deal.

He glanced up from the grill when Larissa came out through the patio doors, his breath catching in his throat at the pretty sight she made with her flowery skirt, her pink top and the soft smile that tugged at her mouth as she dropped into one of the deck chairs. "Salads are ready whenever you are," she announced. "And don't worry, nary a tomato to be found in yours. Mine, of course, is loaded with them."

His response was strangled in his throat, and he had to pull himself together with an effort. "Sounds great," he finally managed. "And how do you like your steak?" he asked, trying to find his balance even as his thoughts raced. How had this suddenly turned into a date?

"Medium-rare," she said. "And let me guess, you're the kind of guy who likes your meat to moo at you."

He couldn't help but laugh. "Not me, I like my steaks medium-rare, too."

They ate out on his deck, overlooking the lake, and he couldn't remember ever enjoying a meal more. When the sun set over the horizon and the mosquitoes came out, they reluctantly went inside. Since Larissa was on crutches, he brought all the dirty dishes in and set them on the counter. She tried to start the dishes, but he shooed her away. "I have a dishwashing machine, there's no reason for you to do them."

"All right," she agreed. "It's time for me to head home, anyway. Thanks for dinner, Gabe."

"You're very welcome," he said huskily. As much as he didn't want her to leave, he knew that it would be best for him if she did. He was already far too aware of her. And far too comfortable around her. "Do you need help getting out to the car?"

"Hey, I'm a pro with these things by now," she said, propping the crutches beneath her arms. "Although you were right about the fact that crutch walking isn't as easy as it looks. My arms are already tired and sore from one measly day."

He knew exactly what she meant. "You'll get used to it after a few days."

"I hope so."

He held the door open for her so she could make her way outside. The ride back to her apartment didn't take long, another novelty of living in Crystal Lake compared to Madison. All the streets in Madison led to the capitol, which made traffic a total nightmare every day.

"Are you working tomorrow?" Larissa asked, breaking into his thoughts.

"Yes, are you?"

"No, I'm off one more day." Was that a flash of disappointment in her features? It was difficult to tell in the dim light. For a moment, he considered asking one of his colleagues to cover for him so they could spend another day together.

Bad idea, he told himself. Really bad idea. Besides, he'd see her the following night.

He tried to find a neutral topic. "If your ankle isn't better, get in to see your doctor. I still think you might need that MRI."

"I will," she promised.

He pulled into the parking lot of her apartment building and shut off the car so he could help her out. Of course, being Larissa, she was already trying to get out on her own.

Trying not to roll his eyes, he hurried around to assist. She attempted to pivot on one foot and teetered to the side.

"I've got you," he said, catching her before she could fall against the door. Her small frame fit into his arms perfectly, and suddenly, he didn't want to let her go.

"Thanks," she said breathlessly, her face buried against his chest.

He stood, fighting against the desire to wrap his arms around her, drawing her even closer. But then she pulled back a bit and tipped her head to look up at him. And he couldn't seem to help himself.

He lowered his mouth to capture hers in a tender kiss.

5

L arissa melted against Gabe, lost in his kiss. It wasn't until there was a loud bang from someone slamming a car door nearby that she finally regained her senses.

She pulled away, struggling to catch her breath. Why had he kissed her?

Why had she kissed him back?

"Larissa," he began, and she immediately knew he was about to apologize.

"It's okay," she said quickly, cutting him off. "I really need to get going. Thanks again for everything," she said, desperately wishing she could just walk away.

But of course, she couldn't walk anywhere, not without the crutches.

"Can you get the crutches out for me?" she asked when he didn't say anything.

"Sure." He stepped back, opened the door, and pulled them out. "I'll walk you inside," he said.

"No!" The word came out much harsher than she'd intended. Couldn't he see she was hanging on by a thread?

"Goodnight, Gabe."

She tucked the crutches beneath her already-sore armpits and made her way up the sidewalk. Of course, Gabe didn't just let her go inside by herself; in fact, he rushed ahead to open the door for her.

Keeping her gaze averted, she made her way toward the elevator. "Thanks, but I've got it from here," she said with a bright smile. "Have a great day at work tomorrow," she added as the elevator doors opened. She swung inside and jabbed the button to close the doors.

It wasn't until the doors closed and the elevator starting moving that she sagged against the wall in relief. The trembling in her legs had nothing to do with the exertion of crutches and everything to do with Gabe's kiss.

What had just happened? A better question might be— why had that happened?

She'd heard about Gabe's aloof reputation on her very first day. All the nurses talked about the fact that the good-looking ER doctor didn't date nurses. Not even ones who worked elsewhere in the hospital.

But that wasn't the only reason she'd been fighting her attraction to him. She didn't want or need the complication of a man in her life. She was here getting over a bad relationship, not to jump into a new one.

Still, she couldn't help lightly touching her tingling lips. Gabe's kiss hadn't just barreled against the walls she'd built around her heart, it had broken straight through.

She closed her eyes and prayed for strength.

LARISSA'S ANKLE felt much better the next morning, so much so that she decided against going to an urgent care, her only option on the Memorial Day holiday. The swelling had come down to the point she probably didn't really need the crutches, but she used them anyway just to rest the ankle a bit more, especially since she was scheduled for another twelve-hour shift the next day. At least she was scheduled for the night shift, so she'd have the entire day to rest it.

Summer clouds darkened the sky, making it a great day to stay inside doing chores. Getting her laundry done was tricky, but she managed to scoot the basket into the elevator to get down into the basement.

As the day wore on, she couldn't seem to stop thinking about Gabe. Which was ridiculous, because she'd already decided that she needed to keep her distance from him. Yet she must have checked her phone a dozen times, wondering if she'd missed his call.

Or a call from Annie.

She thought about the poor woman as she placed the frozen bag of peas over her ankle. She'd called Annie's number several times, but the calls went straight to voice mail. Either Annie's phone was turned off or Kurt had destroyed it.

She shivered, hoping that Annie had managed to keep the phone hidden. If not, the poor woman had no way of calling for help. Not that she'd called the police so far.

Larissa had sensed Gabe's frustration yesterday when Annie had refused to press charges. She understood all too well what was going on in Annie's mind.

How many times had she begged her mother to leave George? Too many to count. Her mother always had an excuse —either she was afraid she wouldn't be able to find a job, or she was afraid George would come after her, or she was afraid George would actually leave her alone. She'd tried to tell her mother they were better off without him, but it wasn't until he'd attacked Larissa that her mother had sneaked away in the dead of the night, going straight to a women's shelter, one of the many Larissa had tried to convince her to go to in the past.

The years after George had been rough on both of them. Her mother had been depressed, and the only job she'd been able to get was that of a waitress, which hadn't brought in much money. Larissa had gotten a job as soon as she'd turned sixteen to help with the household expenses. When she was seventeen, she took the nursing assistant program through her high school and had gotten a decent-paying job at a local nursing home. She enjoyed working with patients and had decided to go into nursing.

Ironically, once she'd headed off to college, her mother had found a new man, one that didn't hit her or abuse her in any way. He was significantly older, but as long as her mother was happy, she didn't care. In talking to Annie in the ER, she'd tried to explain to Annie that she could do the same.

But after the incident last evening, she could only assume her words had fallen on deaf ears. Well, maybe not completely deaf, as Annie had tried to call her.

Shaking off her depressing thoughts, she finished her laundry and then settled in for a movie marathon. She had a secret weakness for the old Star Wars movies and watched one after another, staying up as late as possible so she could sleep in before her next night shift.

The next afternoon, her ankle felt even better. She stayed off of it until she needed to get dressed for work. Even then, she wrapped it snuggly for extra support.

Dark storm clouds obscured the sun, streaks of lightening flashing across the sky as she headed to the hospital. She hurried, trying to beat the rain, making it inside the hospital with mere seconds to spare before the sky opened up and rain pelted the earth.

She grinned at her friend Julie. "I thought for sure you'd be off today. Didn't you work the past two days?"

"Tonight is my last of three shifts in a row, and then I'm off for four glorious days," Julie responded. "Can't wait!"

Julie was lucky to have purchased a townhouse on the lake. She'd gotten a decent price because one side had suffered a kitchen fire. If Larissa had managed to save more money, she might have put in a bid for the place herself. Although she was glad her friend had gotten it. Next year, she silently promised. Next year she'd have enough money for a down payment.

"Are you in the trauma room tonight?" Larissa asked as they made their way over to the desk. Debra was the charge nurse, and she looked harassed as they approached.

"I don't know," Julie said with a wry smile. "Guess we'll find out."

"I'm glad you're both here," Debra said. "We're short staffed tonight, so I'll need both of you to take a team and help cover the trauma room," she instructed. "Larissa, you're team one, and Julie, you're team two. I have Jessica covering team three, and I'll pitch in as needed."

Larissa exchanged a wince with Julie before nodding. "Okay."

"This is going to be a long night," Julie muttered as they walked away to their respective teams. "I bet this storm is going to bring a bunch of trauma cases in. We'll be running for sure."

"You're probably right," Larissa agreed. Too late now to wish she'd gotten a doctor's excuse. Although to be fair, she was glad she hadn't called in, otherwise she would have left Debra, Julie, and Jessica to handle the ER alone.

For the next three hours, Larissa dealt with a steady stream of patients, and thankfully, only two trauma patients had come in. She'd taken the first one, and Julie had taken the second.

"Tag, you're it," Julie had joked as they passed in the hallway like ships in the night.

"I know, I know," Larissa muttered. They were to take turns with the traumas unless there were two at the same time, and then Debra would come and assist.

Gabe walked into the ER at quarter to eleven, and she realized he was also assigned the night shift. The doctors worked eight-hour shifts instead of twelve, and she hadn't really thought about Gabe at all until now.

Memories of their heated kiss made her blush, and she kept her gaze focused on the computer screen as he went over to the main census board.

"Okay, Mr. Harris, you're all set for discharge," she said, walking into her patient's room. "Remember you have to follow up with your doctor first thing tomorrow morning, okay?"

"I'll remember," the elderly patient said as he stood. Mr. Clarence Harris had congestive heart failure and often forgot to take his medications, which then caused him to become short of breath. In reading his chart, it sounded like his son wanted him to go to a nursing home, but the older man kept refusing.

"All right, take care, then." She helped him out to a wheelchair. Rick, one of their techs, came over to escort the patient outside.

"Hi, Larissa, I'm surprised to see you here." Gabe's voice broke into her thoughts. "How's your ankle?"

She took a deep breath before turning to face him. "It's a

lot better, thanks. I have the crutches in my car if you want them back."

"No rush," he said with a shrug. The way he stood there with his hands stuffed into the pockets of his lab coat, she sensed there was more he wanted to say, but just then, their trauma pagers went off.

"Car versus pedestrian just off Highway Z," Gabe said out loud as he read his pager. "Victim is a fifty-year-old woman, and her vitals are bad. It doesn't sound good."

Her stomach clenched with dread as she read the same message. Annie was fifty years old and lived near Highway Z. Granted, that didn't mean she was the victim. Still, she sent up a quick prayer for Annie's safekeeping.

"We should call a chopper, in case she needs to get to Madison," she suggested as she followed Gabe into the trauma bay. They were only a level-two trauma center, and if this patient was really bad, they'd need to stabilize her and get her transferred as soon as possible.

"Good idea."

She'd barely made the call when the ambulance bay burst open revealing a bevy of paramedics surrounding a gurney. The moment she saw the victim, she knew it was Annie despite the massive amount of blood.

"Fifty-year-old woman with serious head injury, unconscious at the scene. Vitals reflect hypovolemic shock. We have fluids running wide open."

"Is there another victim?" Gabe asked.

"No, apparently this was a hit and run."

Larissa concentrated on taking care of Annie, but deep down, she felt certain Kurt was the one behind the wheel of the car that had hit his wife.

And she suspected he'd intended to kill Annie.

. . .

LARISSA AND GABE worked on Annie for a solid hour before they deemed her stable enough to transfer. Larissa watched the flight team wheel Annie away and silently prayed.

Dear Lord, please keep Annie safe in Your care.

"Larissa?" Gabe's low voice broke into her prayer. "Are you all right?"

Suddenly, she wasn't. She had to get away, just for a few minutes. "Excuse me," she murmured, slipping away.

She stepped outside, staying beneath the overhang so that she didn't get drenched by the rain. What had happened to Annie? Had she tried to escape Kurt on foot? Had she been on the road, helpless as he drove directly at her?

Squeezing her eyes shut didn't help erase the image she could see so clearly in her mind. Maybe it wasn't Kurt, she tried to tell herself. Maybe Annie had been running from her husband and dashed onto the road, directly in the path of an on-coming car.

She took several deep breaths, trying to calm her ragged nerves. There wasn't anything she could do to help Annie right now. She and Gabe had done their best, placing a breathing tube and a central venous catheter before pumping several units of blood into her system.

The rest was up to the trauma team in Madison and God.

Feeling calmer, she turned to go back inside, shivering when a blast of cold rain hit her back, soaking through the thin fabric of her scrubs. The trauma bay was empty now and had already been cleaned up, which made her feel guilty. It was almost four in the morning, the most difficult part of the night shift, and she realized she must have stayed outside longer than she intended.

Time to stop worrying about Annie and to focus her

attention on the handful of patients who still needed care on her team.

She was about to head through the trauma bay when suddenly the ambulance bay doors opened behind her, letting in a blast of cool air. She jumped around in surprise and nearly tripped over her feet when she saw a disheveled man standing there holding a gun.

"This is all your fault," he said in a harsh tone, waving the gun in her general direction. "Annie's gone, and it's all your fault!"

Kurt Hinkle. Was he intoxicated? He certainly acted like it; his eyes were bloodshot and his gait unsteady. She swallowed hard and tried to edge behind one of the metal bedside tables, not much protection against a bullet. When Kurt came farther in the room, she fought a rising panic.

Where was everyone? Couldn't they hear Kurt?

"Don't move!" he threatened. He took a step toward her, and she couldn't help shrinking backward, dragging the metal bedside table with her.

And this time when he raised the gun and pointed it directly at her, his hand was far too steady.

6

Gabe glanced impatiently at the clock on the wall. Where was Larissa? It wasn't like her to take such a long break in the middle of her shift like this. He'd always been impressed by what a hard worker she was.

But he also knew just how upset she was at seeing the extent of Annie's injuries. The burn from two nights ago had been weeping and was covered in dirt and grime from the highway. Annie had also sustained several broken bones, a head injury, and a potential ruptured spleen. It had been a long time since he'd seen anyone so badly hurt. And knowing Larissa, she was likely blaming herself even though there was absolutely nothing she could have done to prevent what had happened.

Still, he couldn't help sending up a quick prayer for Annie's recovery. And then shook his head in mild disbelief when he realized he'd prayed more since attending church with Larissa than he had in the year his sister had hounded him to go.

Not that he planned on telling Kimberly that.

Julie came abruptly around the corner and barreled

right into him. He steadied her with his hands on her shoulders. "Whoa, take it easy."

"Sorry," she said with a sigh, taking a step back. "It's been so crazy busy." She frowned. "Have you seen Larissa? One of her patients needs something for pain."

"I'll find her," he promised. "Just get her patient the pain meds for now, okay?"

"Okay." Julie disappeared, and he swung around to head back to the trauma bay.

He slowed to a stop when he heard a familiar voice.

"Annie's not here, Kurt. Why don't you put the gun down and have a seat so I can arrange for you to go and see her?"

Kurt? Gun? Ice crawled down his spine, and he sprinted toward the nearest phone and punched in 911. "Kurt Hinkle is armed with a gun and is in the trauma bay with Larissa," he said in a low, terse tone to Grace, the sheriff's department dispatcher. "Hurry."

He hung up the phone, swung around, and quickly flagged down Debra, the charge nurse. "Keep everyone out of the trauma bay, do you understand?" he said as quietly as possible.

"What's going on?"

"Kurt Hinkle is in there with a gun, but the police are on their way. Keep everyone out and far away from this area," he repeated, moving toward the door.

"You can't go in there," Debra protested, grabbing his arm.

"Yes, I can. Just keep everyone out here, okay?" He shook off her hand and edged toward the door leading to the trauma bay. He didn't want to barge in there in case he startled Kurt into shooting.

But he couldn't bear the thought of Larissa facing someone as unstable as Kurt alone, either.

Dear Lord, please give me strength.

He cracked the door open and peered inside. The ice on his spine turned glacier when he saw how close Kurt was to Larissa, just six feet away, with his gun leveled directly at the center of her chest. Larissa stared up at Kurt with wide, frightened eyes with nothing but a small metal bedside table between them.

There was no way he was waiting for the sheriff's deputies. He shoved open the door and stepped into the room. "Put down the gun, Kurt."

The older man swung around to face him, the gun bobbing up and down in his hand. "Stay out of this, doc. This is between her and me."

"Put the gun away," he repeated, projecting a calmness he didn't feel. "Don't make this worse than it already is."

"Get outta here!" Kurt shouted, his face turning red.

From the corner of his eye, he noticed Larissa was edging farther away from Kurt, exactly the way he'd hoped. The trauma bay was big and open; there weren't any places to hide or much to use as a barrier against a gun.

"Why are you threatening Larissa?" he asked, striving for a conversational tone. "She hasn't done anything to you."

Mentioning Larissa was a mistake as Kurt immediately swung back toward her. "You should have stayed away from Annie," he accused. "You shouldn't have filled her head with ideas of leaving me. It's your fault she got hurt. If she wouldn't have left, she'd be fine right now."

Gabe couldn't believe Kurt's twisted logic, but then again, he didn't understand why any man would physically abuse his wife, either. Kurt was so far beyond rational that Gabe didn't have a clue how to get through to him.

"I was trying to help Annie," Larissa said with a note of defiance. "You're the one who keeps hurting her, not me."

Gabe silently urged Larissa to be quiet. There was no sense in making the guy mad.

"What do you want, Kurt?" Gabe asked, desperate to get the man's attention focused back on him instead of on Larissa. "I can't help you if I don't know what you want."

"I want you to get out of here," Kurt shouted. "If you don't, I'll start shooting!"

Gabe glanced helplessly at Larissa, trying to think of a way to stall. Kurt might be drunk, but considering his hunting background he didn't dare bank on the fact that Kurt might not hit his target. Especially considering Larissa was in close range.

Where were the sheriff's deputies? Shouldn't they have been here by now? What was taking them so long?

"Now!" Kurt said, firing the gun for emphasis, the sound echoing through the trauma bay.

"Get down," Gabe shouted to Larissa as he dropped to the floor. He rolled and then came up in a small crouch, ready for the next gunshot.

Larissa must have sensed what was about to happen, because when he glanced over, she was hunkered down in the corner of the room holding the small metal bedside table turned sideways so that the tray protected her chest. He didn't see any blood, so he hoped and prayed that meant she wasn't hit. Thankfully, she had some cover.

"Kurtis Hinkle! Drop your gun and come out with your hands up!"

Kurt spun around toward the doors leading in from the ambulance bay, where the sheriff's deputies were located. Gabe took advantage of Kurt's momentary distraction to dive toward Larissa. She clutched at him, and he held her tight for a fraction of a second before he shoved her behind him.

"Stay down," he whispered. A bullet could still go through him to get to her, so he used the metal bedside table as a shield while hoping for the best. He took heart in the fact that he could see a deputy standing just outside the door he'd come through earlier.

The cops had Kurt and the trauma bay surrounded. But the danger was far from over.

"Go away or I'll kill them both!" Kurt shouted.

"What do you want, Kurt?" one of the deputies shouted. "Do you want to see Annie?"

"Annie's dead!" Kurt screamed, his face mottled with anger.

"Annie's not dead," Gabe said and hoped he wasn't lying. "She's at a hospital in Madison. The deputies can arrange for you to see her."

"You're lying!"

Gabe probably was lying since he doubted the deputies would take him anywhere near Annie. It was clear they believed Kurt was the one who'd run Annie down. But they needed to get Kurt to surrender his gun before anyone got hurt.

"Do you want to see your son, Tommy?" the deputy asked from outside the ambulance bay doors.

"Leave my son out of this!" Kurt grew even more agitated, pacing back and forth in front of the ambulance bay doors. "Stay away from him, do you hear me?"

Gabe realized that Tommy was a lever they could use, and hopefully the deputies knew that, too. Because right now there wasn't much between him and Larissa and the madman with a gun.

And Kurt could easily shoot them both before the deputies would have a chance to stop him.

. . .

LARISSA HAD PRAYED ALMOST non-stop since Kurt had cornered her in the trauma bay. And the fact that Gabe was here, too, made her feel even worse.

She didn't doubt for a minute that Kurt had been driving the car that slammed into his wife. Annie had clearly been trying to get away from him. Hadn't Kurt admitted that much already?

This was her fault, Kurt was right about that. She should have spent more time with Annie the night she'd come in for her broken wrist. She should have convinced Annie to get away from Kurt right then and there. She could have taken Annie to a safe house, at least for the night.

But she hadn't. And now she and Gabe were both in danger. Trapped in a corner where Kurt could easily kill them. The fact that Kurt hadn't shot either of them yet was nothing short of a miracle. Maybe his being intoxicated was actually working in their favor. He didn't seem to be thinking too clearly.

The door leading in from the trauma bay was slowly opening about an inch or so, and she realized one of the sheriff's deputies was standing there. From the angle of the door, he wouldn't have a good shot at Kurt, but just knowing the deputy was there helped steady her nerves.

"It's not too late, Kurt. Put down your gun and come outside. We understand this is all just a big understanding." The voice outside sounded like Deputy Armbruster. "Come out while you still can."

"No! If you come in here, I'll kill them both!"

The door from the main part of the ER opened even wider, and Larissa tensed as she saw Deputy Thomas kneeling there, wearing full SWAT gear. Despite the awkward position, he pointed his handgun at Kurt. She thought she was prepared for the sound of gunfire, but the blast made her jump.

Kurt screamed and swung around, shooting wildly before he went down hard. The next few seconds passed in a blur, but suddenly the gunfire stopped and the nightmare was over.

"I have him," Deputy Thomas said as he stood over Kurt, who was bleeding profusely onto the floor. Kurt's gun was on the other side of the room far out of reach.

"Get him up on a gurney," Gabe said. He shoved the metal tray aside and rose to his feet, pulling her up, too. "Are you all right?" he asked in a low tone, his warm, brown eyes gazing down at her.

"I think so." Her hands were still trembling, so she clutched them together.

Thank you for saving us, Lord!

"Run and get Julie to come and help me with Kurt," he said, moving away. "He needs medical attention. You can cover the patients on the teams until we've finished."

She could barely wrap her mind around the fact that Gabe was going to help fix Kurt's gunshot wound. But then she realized they simply couldn't let him die, no matter how much he might have deserved it. So if Gabe could do it, so could she. "I'll help you."

"You don't need this, get Julie," Gabe repeated, heading over to where the sheriff's deputies were handcuffing Kurt Hinkle to a gurney. There was so much blood that she knew there wasn't time to waste.

She went over and grabbed IV supplies, knowing that they'd need access in order to give badly needed blood and fluids. The rest of the ER staff poured in to assist once the deputies had given the all clear. Soon she and Julie were working as a team, pumping four units of O-neg blood in at a time through a rapid infuser.

"Call the trauma surgeon on call," Gabe ordered. He stared down with obvious concern at the open wound on Kurt's lower abdomen where Deputy Thomas's bullet had penetrated deeply into his flesh. "I can't stop the bleeding, and he needs to get to the OR stat!"

A nicked artery certainly explained the massive blood loss. Larissa didn't allow herself to think about anything that happened before, focusing solely on saving Kurt's life. Even though she knew he'd end up in jail if they managed to succeed.

She heard Julie making the call to the surgeon. "Dr. Rausch is on his way in."

Gabe grimaced and began packing the wound. "I hope he gets here in time."

"Do you need a suture tray?" Larissa asked after she finished hanging four more units of blood. Kurt's vitals were low but stable, at least for now.

Gabe gave her a grim nod. "I'll try my best to patch him up at least until he can get to the OR."

She pulled a sterile vascular tray off the shelf on the back wall and quickly opened it up as Gabe pulled on a new set of sterile gloves. The vascular tray wasn't really equipped for a large-vascular injury, but it was better than nothing.

Larissa handed Gabe instruments and lap sponges as he worked to stem the bleeding enough to see what he was doing. He placed a few sutures, and the blood gushing out slowed to a trickle. He put more sutures in and then stepped back. "That's all I can do for now."

Fifteen minutes later, Dr. Rausch strode in and took command of the situation. Within moments, she and the transporter wheeled Kurt over to the OR. Deputy

Armbruster followed alongside, unwilling to let his prisoner out of sight.

"I'm afraid you can't go in there," she warned, putting a hand on the deputy's arm. She wasn't sterile, either, and neither one of them would be allowed any farther. "You'll have to stay out here if you really want to wait."

"You can be sure I'll wait for him," Deputy Armbruster muttered. "Although, frankly, it's a waste of time patching him up since he'll be spending the rest of his life in jail."

She didn't have an answer for that and was ashamed to admit she'd had the same thought earlier. But the source of the injuries didn't matter; as health care professionals, they were obligated to save lives to the best of their ability. Even Kurt's. "There's a coffee machine over there. Help yourself," she murmured.

"Thanks. I'll have to take your statement later, okay?"

"I'll hang around after my shift is over," she promised.

"Tell the doc I'll need to talk to him, too."

She nodded to indicate she'd pass the message. "Take care." She turned and made her way back to the ER. She felt bad that Julie and Debra had been covering her patients all this time. But when she glanced up at the clock, she stared for a moment, unable to believe that only an hour had passed since Kurt had trapped her in the trauma bay.

The rest of her shift passed by in a blur. After she gave report to the oncoming nurse, she headed outside, surprised to see the bright sun. The rain from the night before had passed, giving way to a new day.

As much as she wanted to go home, she knew the police still wanted to talk to her and to Gabe.

Just then, Gabe joined her outside. Wordlessly, he crossed over and pulled her into his embrace. She leaned against him, relieved and glad to be alive.

"I've never been so afraid in my whole life," he murmured in her ear. "I'm thankful you weren't hurt."

"Me, too," she said, her voice muffled by his shirt. "I mean, I was terrified he was going to shoot you."

"Deputy Thomas saved the day."

She couldn't argue that one.

The parking lot began filling with cars, members of the hospital leadership team and the public relations department arriving to take charge of the situation. As they streamed past, she felt distinctly self-conscious and tried to pull away, knowing Gabe wouldn't want to be seen hugging her like this in public.

But he refused to let her go. His arms tightened around her, and when she glanced up at him questioningly, he simply smiled, lowered his head, and kissed her in full view of anyone who cared to watch.

And she reveled in the sweetness of his kiss.

7

G abe barely noticed the various pairs of eyes boring into him as he kissed Larissa. Only when he needed to breathe did he break away and lower his forehead to rest on hers. His pulse thundered in his ear, and he realized he didn't want to let her go.

"I prayed for your safety," he confessed in a low voice. "And God answered my prayers."

"Me, too," she admitted. "I prayed for us and for Annie."

"At least Annie is safe from Kurt now," he said. "Kurt will be stuck behind bars for a long time."

"I know." Larissa ducked her head and leaned back as if trying to put more distance between them. "Gabe, we're attracting too much attention."

"I don't care." And he was surprised to realize he truly didn't care. Larissa wasn't Rebecca, and no matter what happened, he knew Larissa would never spread lies about him. It was ridiculous it took him this long to realize that. Or maybe he was just hiding behind the idea because it was a good excuse. "I care about you, and I don't mind if the whole world knows it."

Her green eyes widened in surprise. "But Gabe, you never date any of the ER nurses. Ever."

He couldn't help but smile. "Until you."

She looked flabbergasted by his response, but Deputy Thomas interrupted them. "Dr. Allen? Larissa? Do you have time to give your statements?"

"Of course," Larissa said.

He didn't want to let her go but had to be content with holding her hand. "Could we sit down somewhere? It was a long night, and I'm sure Larissa is exhausted."

"No problem. Let's head over to the patio outside the dining room."

Once they were seated at the picnic table, Deputy Thomas took out his notebook and pen. "Larissa, why don't you start at the beginning?"

"After we transferred Annie to Madison, I needed a moment alone, so I went outside and stood beneath the overhang just outside the ambulance doors. I guess I must have been out there longer than I thought, because when I came back in, the trauma bay was already clean, and everyone was gone. I was about to head back to my team of patients when Kurt came in."

"Did you see him outside?" Deputy Thomas asked.

"No, but I probably wasn't paying attention. I will admit I thought he was the one who drove into his wife, but I never expected that he'd come looking for me armed with a gun."

Gabe couldn't bear the fear underlying her tone, and he gave her hand a reassuring squeeze.

"Then what happened?"

"I tried to talk him into putting the gun down, but he just kept coming closer and closer. I didn't have a way to call for help, but then the door leading from the arena opened, and I saw Gabe standing there."

"And you went inside?" Deputy Thomas asked, a deep frown furrowing his brow. "You're lucky he didn't kill you."

"I couldn't just stand there while he took a shot at her," Gabe said. "Besides, I figured I could get him to talk. I needed to try and stall long enough for you and your guys to get there."

Deputy Thomas didn't look happy, but he spared Gabe a lecture, asking a few more questions before he closed his notebook. "I appreciate your time. Thanks."

"That's all you need?" Larissa brightened. "We can go home?"

"Yes, you're free to go home."

Deputy Thomas walked away, and Gabe glanced at Larissa. "How about I drive you home?" he suggested. "We'll pick up your car later."

"I'd rather just drive my car home now, if you don't mind." Larissa tucked her hair behind her ear and avoided his direct gaze. "But thanks again, Gabe. For everything."

He didn't want to let her go, but he couldn't very well force her to allow him to stay, either. He frowned as she walked to the parking lot alone.

Why was she was pushing him away?

Maybe after everything that had happened, she needed some time alone. So he'd give her a few hours to sleep and to recharge.

Then he was going to make his feelings known by asking her out on a proper date. And he could only hope and pray she wouldn't say no.

LARISSA DRAGGED herself out of bed after five hours of sleep, determined to get back on a regular schedule since she had day shifts scheduled after her day off. Her ankle was a little sore, so running was out of the question.

A boat ride would have been great, but she quickly veered away from thoughts of Gabe. She was still struggling with everything that had happened with Kurt. The way he'd accused and threatened her brought back terrible memories of life with George.

She hadn't told anyone about the abuse her mother had suffered. Larissa hadn't mentioned the time George had broken her arm, either, since that one injury had been nothing compared to everything George had put her mother through.

She'd prayed for the strength to forgive George, but seeing Kurt in the trauma bay made her realize she really hadn't forgiven George. Or Kurt. Or Rolland, who hadn't hurt her physically but who'd tried to control her just the same.

And she needed to forgive all of them.

Or she'd never be able to move on from her past.

When her buzzer went off, she dragged herself over to the intercom. "Yes?"

"Larissa? It's Gabe. Can I come up?"

She hesitated but then acquiesced. "Sure."

The apartment wasn't too messy, and she smoothed her hair back, wishing she'd put on a touch of make-up. When Gabe knocked at her door, she took a deep breath and opened it.

"Hi." Did he look nervous or was she just imagining it? "I wasn't sure if you'd be up yet."

"I like to try and get back on a day schedule if I can." She closed the door and followed him into the living room. "Can I get you a soft drink?"

"No, thanks." Yep, he definitely looked nervous. "Larissa, would you go out to dinner with me tonight?"

His abrupt question caught her by surprise. "What made you change your mind about dating colleagues?" she asked.

Gabe nodded. "You're right, you deserve an explanation." He paused for a minute. "I dated Rebecca, one of the nurses I worked with in Madison. I quickly figured out that we didn't have anything in common; in fact, she made it clear the best thing she liked about me was my title."

"Your title?" She frowned, not quite following.

"Doctor." He lifted a shoulder in a half-hearted shrug. "You must know the type, the ones who only want to marry a doctor because they think we rake in the big bucks. Rebecca didn't even like being a nurse; she complained about it all the time. I broke things off, and that's when everything turned ugly."

"Oh, Gabe," she murmured. Unfortunately, she did know there were nurses out there who were only interested in marrying a doctor.

"She alleged I sexually harassed her, that I made unwanted advances toward her. There was a huge investigation, and I thought for sure I'd be vindicated, but a few of her friends lied for her, and pretty soon it was her word against mine. So I left and came here, to Hope County Hospital."

"I don't blame you for keeping your distance," she assured him. "That's a terrible thing for her to do to you."

"Thanks, but I think I've had it easy compared to others." Gabe held out his hand, and she couldn't resist taking it and moving closer to him. "I understand now that the reason you related so well to Annie is because you went through something similar, didn't you?"

She shouldn't have been surprised that he'd figured it

out. "My mother was married to an abusive man," she admitted in a low voice. "I saw the vicious cycle first-hand, and no matter how hard I tried, I couldn't seem to stop it."

His hand tightened on hers, and when she met his gaze, his concern was obvious. "How did you escape?"

"My mother only cared about the abuse when George started hitting me. The night he broke my arm, she took me to the hospital, and from there, we went to a women's shelter."

Gabe groaned and pulled her close, wrapping his arm around her shoulder. "I'm sorry you had to go through that again last night. Thankfully, God was watching over you. Over both of us."

Her eyes pricked with tears. He was being too nice; she didn't deserve his kindness. Here she'd convinced Gabe to go to church, and she was the one who was at a crossroad in her faith. "I can't seem to find a way to forgive him," she whispered. "I thought I had, but last night after Kurt was shot, I immediately thought he deserved to die."

"A perfectly natural reaction," Gabe pointed out. He leaned back, put his finger beneath her chin, and forced her to meet his gaze. "I thought the same thing."

"But Gabe, don't you see? God expects us to forgive our enemies."

"Yes, He does." Gabe's gaze was intense. "But He also promises to help us learn how to forgive our enemies. He doesn't necessarily make us figure it out on our own."

She wanted to believe him, but really, there was no way of knowing if she'd ever be able to forgive George for what he did to her mother, or forgive Kurt for what he did to Annie. And how could she find peace and love if she didn't?

"Larissa, I'm falling in love with you."

Gabe's declaration stole her breath, and she instinctively shook her head. "I don't know that I'm ready for that."

"I'll give you all the time you need, as long as you give me a chance. Don't shut me out, Larissa."

She pulled away and rose to her feet, threading her fingers through her hair. "I'll try, but I can't make any promises," she said finally.

"That's all I can ask," he said. "So will you have dinner with me tonight? I'll pick you up at six."

A reluctant smile tugged at her mouth. "All right, dinner at six."

"Great. See you soon." Gabe left, and within minutes, she was second-guessing her decision.

Restless, she paced the apartment. Remembering the news vans that had been parked outside the hospital, she called her mother, who answered on the first ring. "Larissa? I heard about what happened at the hospital on the news. Are you all right?"

"I'm fine, Mom. Perfectly fine." She winced, realizing she should have called her mother sooner. "How are you doing? How are things with Ed?"

"Ed's fine, he's always good to me, Larissa. You're the one I'm worried about."

She stared out the front window for a long moment. "Mom, I have a question for you. Have you forgiven George for everything he's done?"

"Of course I have," her mother responded. "In fact, I feel sorry for him."

She nearly choked at that. "Feel sorry for him? Why?"

"Because he'll never have true love the way you and I will. He'll never know God's love either. I pray for his soul every day."

Humbled, Larissa thought her mother was far smarter

than she'd ever given her credit for. "You're right, Mom," she said. "George deserves our prayers."

And so did Kurt. Maybe if she kept thinking about it from her mother's perspective, she could really find a way to forgive them both.

LARISSA WAS DRESSED and ready to go well before six, so she didn't mind when Gabe showed up ten minutes early.

"Larissa, you look absolutely beautiful."

She reached up to give him a quick hug. "You don't look half bad, yourself."

He looked surprised yet pleased at her warm embrace. He gave her a quick kiss on the cheek and then held the door open for her. "After you."

He drove to a very nice restaurant that was perched high on a hill overlooking the lake. As fancy as the place was, she decided she preferred the meal they'd shared on his deck.

"I bet their steaks aren't nearly as good as yours," she said in a low tone.

He grinned. "But their lobster is amazing."

"I still like dining on your deck better," she insisted, leaning back to peruse the menu. The lobster was listed as market value so she skipped that one, looking for something more reasonable.

"Have whatever you like," he said as if reading her mind. "After last night, we deserve to splurge."

She didn't want him to think she was anything like Rebecca, so she settled on a more reasonable shrimp dish.

After the server took their order, Gabe reached across the table to take her hand. "You look happier tonight than you did this afternoon."

She couldn't deny the truth. "I am happy."

"So you must have heard that Annie is still in the ICU but her vitals are stable."

"No, I hadn't heard, but I'm glad to hear she's hanging on." She took a sip of water. "And how's Kurt doing?"

"He survived, too, and is listed as critical but stable in the ICU."

She was surprised by the lack of resentment she felt about that news. "Actually, I talked to my mother, and she made me look at men like Kurt and George differently."

"Oh yeah? How?"

She repeated what her mother had told her. "I think I can see now why God asks us to forgive our enemies. Because He knows that we have His love and they don't. And really, what more could we ask for?"

"You're a very special lady, Larissa," Gabe said, his hand tightening around hers. "I'm lucky to have found you."

She couldn't deny what was in her heart. "I think you're pretty great yourself, Gabe."

A wide grin split his face, and he stood and came around the table, drawing her up to her feet. "Does this mean we're officially dating, Ms. Brockman?" he asked in a teasing tone, sliding his arms around her waist.

"I believe it does, Dr. Allen," she agreed, reaching up to wind her arms around his neck.

The playfulness vanished as he stared deeply into her eyes. "I love you, Larissa."

Her heart swelled to the point she feared it might burst with joy. "I love you, too."

When he kissed her, the entire restaurant burst into applause, and she found she didn't mind one bit.

Thank you, Lord!

Dear Reader,

When I was a young girl my parents used to take us "up north" to stay in a cabin on Fish Lake. I always remember those trips fondly, learning how to swim and water ski on the lake. So when it came time to write a mini-series I wanted to create a setting that reminded me of the fun times I had as a young girl.

I created this fictional town of Crystal Lake a few years ago and the town and its characters drew me back to tell more stories about it. This Novella is to introduce my new Crystal Lake series. If you enjoyed this story I hope you consider reading A Soldier's Promise which is Julie Crain's story. The first chapter is after this letter if you want to give it a try.

I love to hear from my readers and you can find me on Facebook under LauraScottBooks, on Twitter @laurascottbooks or my website www.laurascottbooks.com.

Yours in faith,

Laura Scott

A SOLDIER'S PROMISE

A SOLDIER'S PROMISE

Book 2 in the Crystal Lake Series
Amazon Kindle Edition

Copyright © 2013 by Readscape Publishing, LLC

Cover art by The Killion Group, Inc.
Digital Formatting by Author E.M.S.

Please Note

1

"Hey, Jules—we have two trauma patients on the way, ETA less than five minutes."

ER nurse Julie Crain stifled a groan. She'd just returned from taking her previous patient down to the morgue, and she was emotionally drained from dealing with his grieving family. She forced her exhaustion aside. "Okay, what's the story?" she asked, glancing up at Merry Haines, the ER charge nurse at Hope County Hospital.

"A two-vehicle crash, T-bone on the driver side. From what I hear, the drunk driver who ran a red light and caused the crash wasn't hurt-but the guy in the SUV and his young daughter are being brought in."

Julie caught her breath as her heart thumped painfully in her chest. Oh, no. Not a young child. She couldn't handle an injured child. She closed her eyes and prayed.

Please God, keep the little girl safe. And her father, too.

"I hope they lock up the drunk driver and throw away the key," Merry muttered.

She understood where Merry was coming from.

Working in the ER, they'd both seen more than their fair share of alcohol- or drug-related injuries and deaths.

Dr. Gabe Allen came into the room in time to catch the last part of their conversation. "The driver was Tommy Hinkle," he said with a dark scowl. "So yeah, I think that scenario is highly likely."

Not a tourist then, but one of their own. Tommy Hinkle was the Crystal Lake troublemaker, picking up where his father had left off. At nineteen, he wasn't even legal to drink at all, much less drink and drive.

Tommy would end up in jail this time, for sure. Just like his father. The only good thing was that his mother, Annie Hinkle was still recovering in a Madison rehab center from a terrible car crash and wasn't here to see her son behind bars.

Before she could check over their supplies, the doors from the ambulance bay burst open, and a bevy of paramedics wheeled in two gurneys.

Julie was relieved to be in position to take the first patient, which happened to be the father.

"Thirty-year-old Derek Ryerson, suffered loss of consciousness at the scene," the paramedic announced. "We placed two eighteen-gauge PIV's and gave a liter of fluid so far. His vitals remained stable throughout transfer."

She quickly connected the heart monitor leads to his chest, reassured by the steady beat of his heart. She leaned over to perform a neurological assessment, noting an abrasion on the side of Derek Ryerson's left temple that was easily seen, considering his military-short dark hair. Concerned about a possible head injury, she carefully lifted his eyelids and peered at his pupils. She flashed her penlight, grateful to note they were both equal and reactive.

She continued her assessment, listening to his heart and his lungs. The right side of his lungs didn't sound as clear as his left side, and there was an angry red band across his chest from where the seatbelt had held him in place, likely preventing additional and more serious injuries. When she brushed a hand over the right side of his ribcage, he let out a low groan.

Bruised or broken ribs? Or something worse? She glanced up again at the heart monitor, but his vitals continued to be stable.

Before she could call over to Dr. Allen, a large hand reached out to grab her wrist. She gasped, her gaze clashing with his as he stared at her intently. His hard, blue, uncompromising gaze caused a spurt of fear.

"My daughter. Lexi," he said hoarsely. His pain-glazed eyes bored into hers, and his grip on her wrist tightened painfully. "Where's Lexi?"

The flash of fear faded when she realized he was concerned about his daughter. She glanced over to where Merry and Gabe were examining the young girl. "Don't worry. Lexi is right here in the gurney beside you. My name is Julie and I'm your nurse. Merry and Dr. Allen are taking good care of your daughter."

Lexi must have heard her father's voice, because up until now, the silent child created a sudden commotion from the gurney next door as she struggled to get away from where Merry was trying to hold her down. "Daddy! Let me up! I wanna see my daddy!"

"Lexi." Derek dropped Julie's wrist and struggled to push himself upright as if intending to go to his daughter. He didn't get far before he let out a harsh sound and grabbed the right side of his chest, swaying dangerously. His face went pale, beads of sweat popping out on his forehead.

"Take it easy. You're going to hurt yourself more," Julie told him, trying to keep calm, knowing she didn't have the strength to hold him down if he chose to get up. Derek Ryerson was a big man, at least six feet tall and broad shouldered—his entire body was solid muscle. Whatever he did for a living, he kept in shape. "You have a couple of bruised or broken ribs, and we haven't cleared your spine yet, either. We also need to make sure you don't have a head injury."

For a moment, he stared into her eyes, as if trying to decide whether or not to believe her. Considering the strength with which he'd grabbed her wrist, she thought he couldn't be too badly injured. She waited, simply looking back at him, secretly amazed at how brilliant his blue eyes were.

Good thing she was immune to good-looking men.

After what seemed like a long time, he dragged his gaze from hers. "Lexi, listen to what the doctors and nurses are telling you to do, okay, honey? They're only trying to help. I'm right here next to you. I promise I won't leave without you."

"Daddy, I want my daddy," the girl cried out between heartbreaking sobs, repeating herself over and over again, seemingly inconsolable. The poor child must be traumatized from the accident.

"Gabe? I might need a chest X-ray here," she called out, doing her best not to be distracted by Lexi's sobbing mantra, even though she wanted nothing more than to cross over to offer comfort.

Gabe walked to her side. "His vitals, along with his oxygen saturation, are stable, so let's do a CT scan of his head, neck, chest, and abdomen. That way we'll have the big picture."

"Sounds good." She picked up the phone and called over to radiology to put in the request for the CT scan. When she finished, she turned back to Derek. "How does your head feel?"

"Fine," he said through gritted teeth. The lines bracketing his mouth indicated suppressed pain, but whether from just his ribs or his head, too, she couldn't say for sure. He closed his eyes, as if he couldn't stand the bright lights. "I'm fine, just take care of my daughter."

She frowned. Was his head injury worse than she thought? Hadn't she already told him that his daughter was being cared for? "Merry and Dr. Allen are taking good care of Lexi, remember? Does your back hurt anywhere? I need you to be honest with me, because if you have a cracked spine that goes undiagnosed, you could become paralyzed."

He opened his eyes and glared at her, but she refused to back down. She couldn't understand why he was downplaying his injuries. "No, my back doesn't hurt. My neck is sore, and my head hurts a bit, too. The right side of my chest feels like it's on fire, but nothing hurts as much as listening to Lexi cry."

She smiled gently, feeling bad for him. She could only imagine how difficult it would be to stay on a gurney if her niece had been injured. "I know, and I'm sorry. But the best thing you can do for your daughter is to make sure you're all right. She needs you."

"I'm fine, nothing a little aspirin won't cure. Bruised and battered from the airbag and the crash, but fine."

There was no point in arguing. She glanced over at the next gurney, where Gabe and Merry where in deep conversation.

"I don't see any sign of serious injury," she heard Merry saying to Gabe. "The paramedics believe she was likely in a proper booster seat in the back on the passenger side, opposite from the point of impact. When they arrived, they found her out of the seat and clinging to her father. Apparently, they had a heck of a time getting her away from him, and they had to give her a mild dose of Versed to get her onto the gurney. She's probably fine, but we should get a chest and abdominal CT scan, just to be sure there is no internal bleeding from the straps of her car seat."

Julie waited until Merry finished. "Since they both need CT scans, I should take them down the hall to radiology together. I think Lexi will be calmer if she can be with her father."

"She can't go into the scanner with him," Gabe pointed out with a frown.

"No, but I could sit with her in the viewing room, behind the lead glass," she argued. "And once Lexi sees her father going through the scanner, maybe she'll cooperate when it's her turn."

Gabe and Merry looked at each other and shrugged. "Fine with me," Gabe finally agreed.

Satisfied, Julie waited for Gabe to finish his exam of Derek and then entered the necessary radiology orders for both patients into their respective charts.

She made the arrangements and then quietly told Derek the plan. "I'm going to put Lexi in a wheelchair and have her sit with me in the viewing room to watch you go through the scanner first. The machine makes some loud noises, which can be scary. I want to reassure her it doesn't hurt."

His expression was guarded. "Are you sure she's well enough to sit in a wheelchair?"

His protectiveness for his daughter made her smile. "Amazingly, Lexi doesn't seem to have any injuries at all," she assured him. "But we'd like to get a body scan just in case there's some internal bleeding. Kids aren't always good about being specific with their aches and pains. Or maybe she gets that streak of stubbornness from you."

For a moment, a flicker of grim amusement flashed in his eyes in response to her gentle teasing, and he subtly relaxed. "All right," he agreed. "If you think it will help. Can I talk to her while I'm in there?"

"Not while they're scanning. You'll need to stay still and hold your breath when they tell you to. You can talk to her before and after, though."

"Okay." He lifted his hand and gingerly rubbed the right side of his chest.

"Show me exactly where it hurts," she said, noticing the gesture.

The stubborn look came back into his eyes, and she feared he was going to deny any pain at all, but he gently fingered the area where his lowest ribs were. "Right here, mostly. You were probably right about the cracked ribs."

"Maybe. Or you could have some damage to the lower lobe of your lung or damage to your spleen." She figured blunt honesty was best, so he would understand the seriousness of his situation. "Your breath sounds were a bit diminished on the right side, but the CT scan will tell us everything we need to know."

He reached out to grasp her wrist again. "If they have to take me to surgery, I need you to promise you'll look after Lexi."

Stunned, she gaped at him. Look after Lexi? What on earth did he mean? "Is there someone I can call for you? Her mother? Grandparents? Friends?"

"There's no one to call," he said flatly. "Lexi and I are on our own."

She swallowed hard and nodded, desperate to reassure him. "All right, but try not to worry. I'm sure you'll be fine."

He didn't let it go. "Promise me. If something happens, I want you to look after her. Don't let strangers take her away. Promise!"

────────

DEREK KNEW he probably sounded like a lunatic, but he didn't care. The pain along the right side of his chest was bad, far worse than he'd let on, and after what the petite brunette nurse had said about the possible damage to his lung, he was very much afraid that, once they'd completed the scan, they'd whisk him off to surgery.

He'd downplayed his injuries because he didn't want to stay overnight in the hospital, unless, of course, Lexi needed to be observed. No matter what, he was not going to leave his daughter. Lexi had already been through so much, more than any six-year-old should have to handle. With her mother dead and buried, she needed him now, more than ever.

If only he'd stopped for something to eat earlier, he wouldn't have been driving through the intersection at the same moment as the idiot who'd run a red light, slamming into them.

"Daddy?"

He turned his head, hiding a wince, to look at his daughter. True to her word, the pretty nurse—what in the world was her name?—had gotten Lexi into a wheelchair and brought her over to the side of his gurney. He forced a broad, reassuring smile. "Hey Lexi, how are you feeling?"

Her solemn gaze didn't waver from his. "Fine," she whispered. "Can we leave now?"

If only they could. He'd been all set to leave without the scans until the nurse had mentioned the possibility of a cracked spine. At this point, he needed to know exactly what he was dealing with. Besides, he needed to be sure Lexi was all right, and if that meant getting a scan first, so his daughter could see it wouldn't hurt, then that's exactly what he'd do. He held his daughter's gaze, holding his smile in place. "Afraid not, baby-doll, first we have to get checked out by the kitty-cat machine." Lexi wasn't easily distracted, especially when she wanted something. But that didn't stop him from trying.

"I don't want to stay here." Lexi's eyes, blue like his, revealed a hint of fear. "It's scary."

The pretty nurse, he couldn't read her name on her ID badge because his vision was blurry, another tidbit he hadn't fessed up to, came over. "Lexi, we need to make sure your daddy's not seriously hurt. So we're going to take him for a CT scan, but you can watch from behind the glass the whole time, all right?"

Lexi barely spared the nurse a glance. He wanted to apologize for his daughter's behavior, but there was no point, since Lexi had no idea she was being rude.

"Okay, let's go," the woman said in a cheerful voice. She went behind Lexi's wheelchair to push her forward, while his gurney was maneuvered by a tall guy who was likely some sort of orderly. When the gurney went over a bump, he had to clench his teeth against a surge of pain. He focused on the nurse, who was talking to Lexi.

"We'll be finished with these scans in a half hour, Lexi," she was saying in that same cheery tone. "See the clock on the wall up there? It's seven o'clock in the evening. Do you know how to tell time?"

Derek was surprised when Lexi's head moved in a barely

discernible nod. His daughter was listening, even if she didn't appear to be paying attention.

"The big hand is on the twelve, and we'll be all finished before the big hand gets down to the six."

Lexi glanced at the clock but said nothing more. The lack of response didn't stop the nurse's rather one-sided conversation, and he was grateful she didn't pass judgment on his daughter the way so many others had.

The way Lexi's grandparents had.

The CT scan didn't take long, and as soon as they were finished looking into his head, he talked briefly to Lexi, reassuring her. Then he had to stay quiet until the rest of the scan was completed. When the scan was complete, he heard the nurse encouraging Lexi to take her turn.

His daughter, bless her stubborn heart, wasn't too keen on the idea. When he saw Lexi's wheelchair come closer, he turned his head toward her. "Lexi, we can't leave until I know you're safe and healthy. The kitty-cat machine doesn't hurt. All you have to do is to close your eyes and let them take pictures. Once I know you're fine, we'll leave."

He could see the instant flare of protest in the nurse's eyes at his rash promise, but he glared at her, silently threatening her not to contradict him. She pressed her lips together firmly but didn't say anything.

Lexi finally agreed to the scan, and he watched protectively as the nurse allowed his daughter to climb down from the wheelchair and up onto the CT table by herself. He had to give the woman points for being astute—she seemed to instinctively know that Lexi wouldn't tolerate being touched or carried by a stranger.

After the orderly came back to push his gurney out of the way, his nurse crossed over. She locked her gaze on his and spoke in a low tone. "Derek, the lower lobe of your right lung has collapsed. Dr. Allen needs to put a small catheter in between your ribs to re-inflate your lung."

"Can he do that right here? Or do I have to go to the operating room?" he asked, dreading the answer.

"He can do that right here, but it's going to hurt." Her large chocolate-brown eyes held sympathy.

"Let's get it done fast, then, before Lexi is out of the scanner."

"That's what I thought, too," she confessed. When she leaned closer, her nametag came into focus. Julie. He remembered now, her name was Julie. The pretty name somehow fit her dainty frame and cheerful personality. "I need to prep the side of your chest, first, okay?"

"Go for it," he said. "Just hurry."

She hadn't been kidding about the pain, but surprisingly, once the procedure was over, the fire in his chest felt better. The pain wasn't gone, not by a long shot, but breathing was certainly was easier.

"Now just a quick X-ray of your arm and your chest to make sure your lung has re-inflated, and you'll be set for a while," Julie informed him.

"No other internal bleeding?" he asked. Even though he had no plans of staying, he wanted to know exactly what he was dealing with.

"You have a hard head, but luckily, no sign of intracranial bleeding, although you do have a small concussion. You also have two cracked ribs and a bruised spleen, but no other internal bleeding was found. And Lexi's scan is complete too. Rick, our orderly, is bringing her back here momentarily. Her scan was completely clear. You and your daughter are very lucky to have escaped serious injury."

"Great." The relief was nearly overwhelming. Once he would have thanked God, but not anymore. Not that he thought God would listen to him anyway, considering the way he'd taken Lexi and bolted out of St. Louis in the dead of night. But no matter what, he wasn't going to take Lexi back.

The urge to keep moving was strong. They couldn't afford to stay in one place for too long.

He focused his gaze on Julie. "We are lucky, but we're finished here. I suggest you get our discharge paperwork started, because we're leaving as soon as possible."

2

Derek watched Julie's brown eyes widen in horror. "What? You can't leave, not with a chest catheter in place. We want to keep you overnight, to make sure your concussion doesn't get worse." Her distress was obvious. And maybe, if circumstances had been different, he might have considered staying.

But he needed to protect Lexi.

No matter what.

"I'm not staying here overnight." Slowly, he sat upright on the gurney, mentally prepared this time for the pain slicing through his chest. He swung his legs over the side, hiding the stab of pain the best he could. "Since Lexi's fine, we're leaving. We missed dinner, and I'm sure she's hungry."

To his amazement, Julie planted her hands on her slim hips and stood directly in front of him, staring him down. "Oh, really? And how do you plan on leaving here? On wings? Because from what I heard of the crash, your vehicle isn't drivable."

He momentarily closed his eyes, belatedly remembering that inescapable fact. Okay, so they couldn't drive off to another town, but that didn't mean they had to stay at the hospital. He opened his eyes and focused on Julie. "Where's the nearest motel?"

"Mr. Ryerson, the closest motel is in Crystal Lake, about ten miles away, but it's the height of the tourist season, not to mention Friday night of a holiday weekend. Why don't you just stay here at the hospital for one night? That way, we'll know for sure you're stable enough to leave."

He shook his head. "No thanks. I know my rights—you can't keep me here against my will. I need some clothes. And would you mind if I borrowed your phone? I'd like to call the motel, regardless. Maybe they had a cancellation." The alternative—staying here—was almost too much to bear. He didn't want Lexi to end up in the child welfare system, or worse, with her grandparents again. His daughter was staying with him, end of story.

Julie let out a heavy sigh. "It's easy to see where your daughter gets her stubborn streak."

He ignored the jab, keeping an eye on his daughter, who was staring at him with her usual unblinking gaze. "Lexi, we're going to leave as soon as we sign off on some paperwork, okay?"

She gave another of her tiny nods.

"I have to let Dr. Allen know you're planning to leave AMA," Julie muttered. At his questioning glance, she added, "Against medical advice."

Julie left, and he stayed sitting upright at the edge of the gurney, although he wanted nothing more than to lie back down, because now his head was throbbing in sync with his ribs.

"Daddy." Lexi reached out and put her small hand on his bare knee. "You're hurt."

Sometimes he forgot just how smart his daughter was,

when she hid behind her wall of silence. "Not that bad, baby-doll. I'll be fine, don't worry."

The doctor came into the cubicle, a frown furrowed between his brows. "I hear you're planning to leave AMA."

"Look, Doc, I don't have insurance, and with my daughter here depending on me, I can't afford to stay. So cut me a little slack, would you? Surely it's safe to discharge me."

"Did you forget about the catheter we left between your ribs to keep your lung inflated?" the doctor asked dryly.

Well, yeah, maybe he had. He bit back a surge of impatience. "Okay, how long does the catheter need to stay in?" he asked. "As a former soldier, I know a little about field medicine. I'll pull it out myself in a couple of days."

The doctor scowled but then relented. "Look, I'll agree to discharge you, but on the condition you come back tomorrow, so I can at least look you over one more time. If your lung is good, I'll take the catheter out. No charge," he added hastily when Derek opened his mouth to argue. "A free follow-up visit isn't too much to ask, is it?"

Since Lexi was still watching him with her eerie, unblinking stare, he nodded in agreement, more for her benefit than his. "Sure Doc, no problem. Whatever you say."

"Good." The doctor stared at him for a moment, as if unsure whether or not to trust him. "I'll give you twenty-four hours' worth of narcotics, to hold you over until you can get the prescription filled. Julie will be back soon with your scripts and your discharge paperwork."

He hoped she'd also bring scrubs and a phone, too. He nodded even though all this movement was making his head hurt worse, but he had no intention of giving them any reason to keep him here. If they knew how bad he really felt, they'd prevent him from putting one foot out the door.

Julie didn't come back for a good ten minutes, and when she did, her smile was strained. "There's a deputy who wants to see you before you leave." She set a clean pair of scrubs on the gurney next to him. "Once you're finished with the police, I'll be back with my phone."

Police? He froze, trying to think rationally. The last thing he wanted to do was to talk to the cops. What if they knew about Lexi and hauled him to jail? He didn't have to talk to them, did he? Before he could say anything, Julie disappeared, and a cop strode in.

"Mr. Ryerson? My name is Deputy Thomas. How are you and your daughter feeling?" The deputy looked young, not even close to his thirty, and he found himself hoping that the guy's youth might work in his favor.

"We're fine. Just a bit bruised. What happened to the driver of the pickup truck?"

The deputy scowled. "He's been arrested. I need to ask you a few questions so I can finish up the accident report."

His gut tightened at the thought of answering a bunch of questions. How long before Claire's parents found him? Did they already have an AMBER alert out for Lexi? No, surely not. He was Lexi's legal guardian.

For now.

"I see from your registration that you're from St. Louis, Missouri," Deputy Thomas said. "Whatcha doing way up here in Crystal Lake, Wisconsin?"

He could feel beads of sweat rolling down his spine. "Taking a summer vacation with my daughter," he answered easily. He sensed Lexi moving closer to him, and he put his arms around her slim shoulders. "Friend of mine recommended Crystal Lake."

"Really? Who's your friend?"

He swallowed hard. "Jake Strawn. He lives in Chicago,

and he spent some time up here a few years ago." Jake Strawn had been a soldier in his platoon, and he did live in Chicago. The rest was a slight stretch of the truth.

Deputy Thomas scrunched up his forehead. "Name doesn't ring a bell," he said slowly. For a moment, Derek thought the deputy would see right through him. "But then again, we get lots of tourists up here from Northern Illinois. Probably a good thing his name doesn't sound familiar, right?"

A wave of overwhelming relief almost caused him to fall off the gurney. It took a moment before he could speak. "Can I get a copy of the accident report for my insurance company?"

"Sure, just give us a few days to get everything processed. Might be ready by Monday."

"Thank you." Derek smiled and hoped Deputy Thomas would leave. Soon. Like now.

"Anything else you need?" Thomas asked.

For a moment, he was tempted to ask for a ride but decided it wasn't worth the risk. For all he knew, Claire's parents had already put out the alert. "No, I'm fine."

"Okay, then, take care."

"I will." He held his breath until the deputy had gone. For a moment, he closed his eyes, tempted to say a tiny prayer of thanks.

Except he didn't pray anymore.

"Are you okay?" Julie had returned and was looking at him with concern. He forced another smile, hoping he didn't look nearly as bad as he felt.

"I'm fine."

She held out a slim device. "Here's my mobile phone. I have the number for the Crystal Lake Motel programmed in if you want to call them, but I can already tell you they're booked. And so is every other motel and bed and breakfast within a twenty-mile radius. The Fourth of July is Tuesday, and lots of people are making a long weekend out of the summer holiday."

His heart sank as he took the cell phone. He made the call even though he knew she hadn't been kidding. No vacancies. Within a twenty-mile radius. And he had no car. Maybe he should have taken a ride from the deputy? His shoulders slumped as he tried to figure out their next best option.

Too bad he was all out of ideas.

"Look, Mr. Ryerson," she started.

"Call me Derek," he interrupted.

"Ah, okay, Derek. Please reconsider staying overnight here."

"No can do." He slid off the gurney and reached for the scrubs. "We'll figure out something," he said with more confidence than he felt.

Julie turned away, her expression grim. Abruptly, she spun back to face him. "Look, I own a side-by-side town-house. I live on one side, and the other side is undergoing major remodeling. But the good news is that the bedrooms are fine; it's the kitchen and living rooms that are pretty much gutted, so you won't be able to cook. But you and your daughter are welcome to stay there, if you don't mind spending the night in the middle of a construction zone."

Was she serious? With a flare of hope, Derek pinned her with an intense gaze. It was then he noticed the slender cross she wore around her neck. She was a Christian, and offering a place to stay for a family in need was exactly something a Christian would do.

His relief was short-lived as he tried not to think about how sweet Julie would turn her back on him in a heartbeat if she knew he was on the run with his daughter. Claire's parents had filed a court order to take custody away from him, and he feared they had the power and the money to succeed. Would Claire's parents file a police report about Lexi missing? Based on the Deputy's response, he thought maybe they hadn't gone to the police, at least not yet. Maybe they would use a private investigator, to keep things quiet.

Either way, Lexi's grandparents wouldn't stop until they got what they wanted. They were rich and entirely too used to getting their own way.

But there would be plenty of time to worry about them in the morning. Right now, he was grateful to know he and Lexi had a safe place to stay. Surely he'd feel better in the morning. "Thanks very much, we'd love to take you up on your generous offer, wouldn't we, Lexi?"

His daughter, as usual, didn't reply but simply stared at him, her bright blue eyes full of concern and a hint of fear.

His gut clenched, and he knew he'd do anything necessary to remove the last remnants of fear from his daughter's eyes.

Anything.

FOR A MOMENT, Julie wished she could take back the impulsive offer. You'd think she'd have learned her lesson about getting too involved with a patient after the fiasco with Andrew, but no, here she was putting herself in the middle of Derek's situation. But what else could she do? There really wasn't anywhere else for him to go, and truly, she'd made the offer in the first place for Lexi's sake.

Because of Amelia.

She couldn't, in good conscience, simply let Derek and Lexi walk out the door without a vehicle or a place to stay. She'd just have to make sure she kept her distance emotionally.

She forced a smile. "Okay, give me a few minutes, and we can leave. My shift ended well over an hour ago, so this won't take long. If you need help getting the scrubs on, let me know." She hoped he didn't notice her blush.

"Thanks," he said again. And the genuine sincerity reflected on his face knocked her off balance.

Last year, after the painful disintegration of her engagement, she'd made a conscious effort to avoid men. Which hadn't been too difficult, since there wasn't an overabundance of single men in Crystal Lake.

A fact that had suited her just fine.

Derek Ryerson was a patient, just like Andrew had been. But Derek was different in that he was a father with a young daughter. As soon as Derek was healthy, they'd be on their way to wherever they were headed. Hardly anyone came to Crystal Lake with the intention of staying.

Soon enough, things would go back to normal.

Ignoring her aching feet, she walked to the computer to finish up her charting. Thankfully, Merry had taken care of Lexi's discharge note before she'd left for the evening, so all she had to do was to finish Derek's. After five minutes, she sat back, satisfied she'd completed all the required documentation, and logged off the computer.

When she returned to Derek's room, she noticed he'd managed to get the scrub pants on and the scrub top, too, although he'd hacked at it with a scissor, cutting it down the front so that he didn't have to lift his arms over his head.

The wallet he'd tucked into the front pocket of the scrubs made the fabric hang crooked.

Why his resourcefulness made her want to smile, she had no idea. "Are you both ready?" she asked.

"Sure." He reached over to take Lexi's hand, and she recognized the quick flash of pain that he tried to hide.

"Why don't you both wait out front for me, and I'll drive my car up to the door," she offered. "Save you some walking."

She almost expected him to argue, but he nodded. "Okay. What kind of car do you have?"

"An old green Honda." She left Derek and his daughter standing outside in the cool, summer night and jogged to her car, trying to ignore the screaming protest of the soles of her feet. She reminded herself that her aches and pains were nothing compared to how Derek must feel.

She drove up to the main emergency entrance and found Derek holding Lexi's hand and leaning heavily on a cement pillar. She'd suspected he was hurt far worse than he'd let on.

At least with him staying at her townhouse, she could keep an eye on him. And help take care of his daughter at the same time.

"I don't have a booster seat for Lexi," she pointed out apologetically, opening both the front and back passenger doors. "Luckily, my townhouse isn't far, just ten to fifteen minutes away. She should be fine in the backseat."

"I'll sit in back with her," Derek said, making Lexi scoot over while he carefully lowered himself into the backseat. She noticed that he looked like he was still in pain, but didn't say anything. He'd refused to stay at the hospital, and there was no reason to keep harping on him about it.

She shut the doors and then ran around to the driver's

seat. The silence from the back was a little uncomfortable, so she found herself chatting idly as she headed toward home. "Crystal Lake is a spring-fed lake, about six miles wide and nine miles long. It's very peaceful at night, but during the day there's lots of activity—boaters, water-skiers, wave runners, and inner-tubers."

She glanced in the rearview mirror, not entirely surprised to find Derek with his head back against the seat and his eyes closed. Lexi was wide awake, though, staring straight ahead, possibly listening, although she didn't say anything.

"I don't know if you've ever been inner-tubing, Lexi, but it's great fun. You sit in the middle of an inner tube, and a boat pulls you around the lake. If you and your dad plan on staying for a few days, maybe we can try it."

Lexi blinked and gave a tiny nod. Julie frowned, thinking the young girl was unusually quiet for a six-year-old. Amelia had talked nonstop, asking dozens of questions, ever curious.

Until a rare form of leukemia had taken her young life.

Her chest constricted, and she shoved thoughts of her niece out of her mind. Even after eighteen months, the memories sneaked up on her, blindsiding her with their potency.

"Your dad mentioned something about food. We can stop for a pizza on the way home," she offered. "Do you like pizza? Or do you want something else?"

There was a long pause, and this time Lexi answered in a soft voice. "Pizza."

Derek roused himself, giving his daughter a nudge. "What do you say, Lexi?"

There was a slight pause. "Please."

"Okay, pizza it is." She smiled at Derek in the rearview mirror. "I thought you were asleep."

"No, just resting."

Belatedly, she remembered the prescription for pain medication. "I should stop at the pharmacy first, so we can get your prescription filled."

"No need. The doc gave me a few samples. I should be fine until tomorrow."

She wasn't surprised Gabe had given him some free meds, since he'd mentioned Derek's lack of health insurance. She wondered if Derek had enough money to get the prescription filled.

There was a pizza place in town that sold pre-made cheese pizzas for five bucks each. She bought two and then headed home.

Her townhouse was on the outskirts of town, overlooking the lake. The place had been partially destroyed by a kitchen fire, and the former owners, who lived in Illinois, had sold it to her at a steep discount. Julie was hoping she could eventually fix it up and either rent out the one half for a little additional income or potentially sell it, depending on what happened with the real estate market.

After almost two years, though, she wasn't nearly as far along on the remodeling as she'd hoped to be. Partially because sinks, commodes, counters, and cabinets cost far more than she ever would have imagined. And she'd also have to pay someone to help her install the new items, which would cut deeply into her meager savings.

She'd spent most of the first year making her side more livable and had only recently started on the other side.

"Here we are," she said brightly, as she pulled into the driveway of the unoccupied side of the townhouse. The layouts of the two townhouses were mirror images of each other. In the back, there were patio doors from both kitchens leading out to a cement slab, where she had some secondhand patio furniture. "Lexi, will you carry the pizzas while I help your dad?"

The girl wordlessly took the boxes she gently placed in her arms, while Derek tried to maneuver his way out of the backseat on his own.

"Stubborn man," she muttered half under her breath as she went around to the passenger side to give a helping hand. "Let me help," she advised. "If you pass out on me, I'll never get you inside by myself."

"I won't pass out," he said, his voice low and raw with pain and determination.

She didn't bother to point out the obvious, that he might not have much choice in the matter. She ducked her head inside the car and hooked her left arm beneath his right armpit. "Grab on to the car frame with your good arm," she directed. "On the count of three, we're going to swing you out. Ready?" He nodded, and she braced herself with her right arm on the car the best she could, as well. "One, two, *three!*"

They both pulled, hauling him to his feet. Derek groaned, sagging against the car as if his legs wouldn't hold him up. She held on to him, pressing him back against the car, hoping he wouldn't fall.

"Are you all right?" she asked, glancing up at his face, which was disconcertingly close.

"Yes." His voice sounded weak, thready. "Give me...a...minute."

"Take as much time as you need." He was too big, too heavy for her to do much else. She needed him to be able to get into the house under his own power. She glanced over at Lexi, who was staring at them both with her wide eyes. "Are you hungry, Lexi? Because I sure am, and that pizza smells really good."

Derek opened his eyes and straightened, as she suspected he would the moment she mentioned Lexi. Derek's strength when it came to his daughter was nothing short of amazing. "I'm hungry, too," he said in a forced tone. "Let's get settled inside so we can eat."

Once she ascertained he was actually supporting his own weight, she slowly moved away. She went around and opened the front door, using her key. She flipped on the living room lights, wincing a little at how awful the walls looked. In some areas, the blackened drywall was still in place, and in others, the drywall had been stripped away, revealing bare studs and electrical wires. She held the door open for Lexi and Derek.

"I told you it was under construction," she said defensively when he glanced around curiously.

"It's fine," he said gruffly. "Are there beds, or are we sleeping on the floor?"

She was impressed he'd even considered sleeping on the floor, considering his cracked ribs. "There are twin beds in the first bedroom, but I'll have to run over to get sheets. I'll pick up some paper plates and napkins, too. The water still works in the bathrooms but not in the kitchen. I'll turn up the hot water heater for you. And there isn't a stove or fridge." She knew it was ridiculous, but she felt bad she didn't have more to offer him. She was almost tempted to give him her side, but even though he was injured, he was a stranger. And besides, she could just as easily provide them some meals without giving up her personal space.

"This is perfect," Derek said as he made his way down the hall to the closest bedroom. He went straight toward the side of the bed and eased his weight on the edge of the mattress. It was as if he'd read her mind when he continued, "I can't thank you enough for providing us a place to sleep."

She flashed a small smile, trying to convince herself she was not making the same mistakes she'd made with Andrew, as she took the pizza boxes from Lexi and set them on the small bedside table between the two beds. "I'll be right back," she promised.

Out in the kitchen, she opened the patio doors and went over to her side of the townhouse. She didn't bother to lock her patio doors as there was hardly any crime in Crystal Lake.

She found two sets of sheets, two lightweight blankets, and a couple of spare pillows in her linen closet. Back in the kitchen, her heart jumped into her throat when she found Lexi standing there, staring at her.

"Did you come to help?" she asked, even though she knew by now not to expect an answer. "Here, you can carry the paper plates, paper cups, and napkins, okay?"

Lexi obediently took the items and then went back out through the patio doors to return to the side where her father waited. Julie followed more slowly, stepping carefully since she couldn't see very well around the bundle of bedding in her arms.

While Derek stood up, she quickly made the beds, working as fast as possible so he could sit back down. He didn't eat much, but Lexi devoured her pizza, betraying the depth of her hunger.

Derek's face was pale, and she suspected he was staying upright by sheer stubborn will. Chatting with Lexi, Julie cleaned up the napkins and paper plates and then picked up the leftover pizza. "I'll keep this in my fridge. If you need anything, I'm right next door, okay?" The nurse in her didn't want to leave, and suddenly she was worried about Lexi. "Maybe Lexi should stay with me?" she offered.

Lexi moved closer to her father, and Derek put his arm around her shoulders. "We'll be just fine, won't we, Lexi?"

"All right," she agreed, knowing that rest would likely help Derek more than anything else. "Take your medicine, okay?"

"I already did. Thank you," Derek said again.

She nodded and slipped out of the townhouse through the patio doors in the demolished kitchen, leaving father and daughter alone.

The hour wasn't all that late, just nine fifteen, but she was exhausted, so she didn't waste any time heading to bed. When a strange sound woke her up, she gasped and peered through the darkness. It took a moment to realize the small face peering at her belonged to Lexi.

"What's wrong?" she asked.

"Help my daddy," Lexi said, her gaze intense. "Please, help my daddy!"

3

D erek groaned under his breath and pulled himself across the hallway floor, beads of sweat rolling freely down his face, burning his eyes.

The plank-wood floor had plenty of splintered edges, but he ignored the minor irritation. He knew he'd frightened Lexi, and his mission right now was to get back into the bedroom, where he could possibly use the bed frame as leverage to get back up.

Get up, soldier! Now! No excuses! You're a soldier, so you'd better start acting like one!

Derek used his legs and his good arm to propel his body across the floor, inch by agonizing inch, finally crossing the threshold into the bedroom. The fire was back in his chest, worse than before, and he suspected that he'd inadvertently displaced the catheter they'd stuck in his chest to re-inflate his lung.

"Lexi?" he called out, unsure where his daughter had gone. "I'm here and I'm fine. I'm going to get into bed, now, see?"

Actually, he couldn't see a thing through the red haze of pain that shrouded his vision.

He grasped the lower bed frame and tried to figure out how to pull himself upright. He closed his eyes, thinking it would be easier to stay on the floor. He'd ask Lexi to give him a pillow, and he'd be fine until morning.

"Derek, are you okay?"

He recognized that soft, female voice. Julie. The nurse. He forced his eyelids open.

Nothing worse than feeling helpless, especially when he realized Lexi had woken her up. Because of him.

"Derek? What happened?" she asked.

She touched his shoulder, and he shoved his lame pride aside to answer. He couldn't read the expression on her face with the hallway light on behind her. "Sneezed. Woke up on the bathroom floor."

"You passed out?" Instantly, she dropped to her knees, bringing her face closer to his. "Did you hit your head again?"

"No." At least he didn't think so. The pain in his head was about the same; it was his chest that was killing him. He didn't like being dependent on her for help. Didn't like being dependent on anyone other than himself. "Toss me a pillow and a blanket. I'll rest here until morning."

"Don't be ridiculous," she said, and he heard the distinct note of impatience in her tone. "You're not sleeping on the floor. If I can't help you up, I'll call an ambulance."

"No ambulance." Since she was obviously going to be difficult about this, he rolled onto his injured side and grabbed on to the bed frame with his uninjured left arm. "I'll get up."

She muttered something under her breath that he

couldn't quite make out. It sounded like stubborn as an ox, but he couldn't bring himself to care. She put her arm under his right armpit again. "Try just sitting first. Your legs are strong. Once we get you into a sitting position, you should be able to stand."

Easy for her to say—her rib cage wasn't engulfed in fire. His lungs felt like two strips of sandpaper rubbing together with every breath. But complaining didn't get the job done, so he concentrated on pushing off the bed frame. With Julie adding her strength and supporting his injured side, he suddenly found himself sitting upright, his side pressed against the bed.

"Thanks," he grunted, trying to catch his breath. But it was no use. That stupid catheter wasn't keeping his lung inflated, and the last thing he wanted to do was to go back to the hospital. For sure, they'd keep him.

And he didn't think he had the strength to leave AMA a second time.

"Rest for a minute, and then I'll help you get up on your feet," she said, her voice close to his ear.

He had the absurd thought that, with Julie's support, he could do anything.

He glanced over at Lexi, who stood silently, her eyes wide and her face pale. He forced himself to smile for her benefit. "I'm proud of you, Lexi. You were smart to get help."

His words didn't seem to reassure his daughter, so he decided the only thing that was going to make Lexi feel better was if he could get up on his feet and back on top of the bed.

"Use the strength in your legs as much as you can," Julie advised when she felt him shift. "I'll give you as much leverage as I can manage."

Considering she was all of five foot three inches on a good day and weighed, in his estimation, less than a hundred and twenty pounds, he couldn't imagine she'd provide any leverage. Although she'd surprised him with her ability to get him out of the backseat of the car.

Maybe being close to God gave her an edge over everyone else. Right now, he'd use any advantage he could get.

He leaned against the bed frame, trying to get his legs into a good position. Between support from the bed frame and Julie's help, he somehow managed to get his feet under him, and finally, he was up and sitting on the edge of the bed.

The pressure on his chest didn't ease, and he struggled to breathe. Something so natural shouldn't be so difficult.

A cold, round circle was pressed against his side, and he realized Julie had a stethoscope in her ears, listening to his chest. "Your lung is down again," she said accusingly, as if he'd done the deed on purpose.

"I know," was all he could manage. What did she want him to say? The sneeze had caught him off guard, and the pain had been so intense he'd dropped like a stone.

"Stay sitting upright. I'm going to try something, okay?"

He nodded, since he wasn't in any shape to stop her anyway.

She bent down and sucked on the end of the pigtail catheter hanging out of his chest, like she was drinking a thick malt out of a straw. And suddenly, the fire eased, and he could breathe again.

"It worked," he said in amazement. He took another breath, just to make sure his imagination hadn't played tricks on him. "I can breathe easier."

"There's a valve in these catheters, which must have closed when you sneezed." She peered down at the dressing around the catheter, no doubt looking for signs of bleeding.

"Well, that settles it, no more sneezing for me," he said in an attempt to lighten the mood. He reached out a hand toward his daughter, who came over to huddle next to him. He hugged her reassuringly. "I'm fine, Lexi. Thanks to Julie, I'm going to be just fine."

Julie stared at him, clearly exasperated. "I suppose I'd be wasting my breath if I encouraged you to go back to the hospital."

For a moment, he almost felt guilty for disappointing her. "Yes, because there's no need to go back. I'm fine now. Thanks for your help. Again."

"Stop thanking me," she said suddenly, scrubbing her hands over her face. "This is my fault. I should have offered you my place to spend the night. I should have thought about the drywall dust making you sneeze."

The way she was beating herself up over something she couldn't control was ridiculous. "Don't, Julie. You've gone out of your way to offer us a place to stay. I'm very grateful. Besides, it probably wasn't the drywall dust that made me sneeze. I have allergies." A small stretch of the truth. He was only allergic to cats, and even though he hadn't seen any, it didn't mean she didn't have one tucked away somewhere.

She stared at him for a few minutes, as if she didn't believe in his allergies for one minute, before she finally turned away. "I'll get you another dose of pain medicine, and then you really need to try and get some rest."

"What time is it?" he asked when she brought over two pills and a glass of water. He didn't think he was due for more pain meds yet.

"One thirty in the morning. And don't worry, you can take the medication every four hours."

He gratefully swallowed the pills and then kissed the top of Lexi's head before easing himself down on the bed. "Okay, baby-doll, it's time to get some sleep."

Lexi obediently climbed into her twin bed but lay on her side, right near the edge, facing him. Her eyes were wide open, almost as if she were afraid to fall asleep.

His heart squeezed in his chest. His poor daughter had been through so much. He wanted desperately to give Lexi the solid foundation of love and support she needed.

That she deserved.

"Goodnight, Lexi. Goodnight, Derek," Julie said as she headed back out to the hall.

Before Derek could answer, he was shocked and stunned beyond words to hear his daughter reply in a soft voice, "Goodnight, Julie."

———

THE NEXT MORNING, Julie crawled out of bed far later than normal, thankful that she had the next three days off work.

Remembering her overnight guests staying next door spurred her into action. Derek hadn't eaten much pizza last night; he was undoubtedly hungry.

After she showered and dressed, she headed into the kitchen to prepare breakfast. Cooking for guests seemed strange. Not that Derek was really a guest. He was more like a patient.

Best to remember that fact. The sooner he felt better, the sooner he and Lexi would be on their way.

She needed to keep her distance from Derek and Lexi. Getting emotionally involved would only result in feeling hurt when it was time for them to move on. Yet she couldn't deny that Lexi's soft goodnight had touched her deep in her heart, the effect lingering long after she'd returned to her side of the townhouse.

Lexi reminded her of Amelia, even though the two girls were as different as night and day. Lexi was far too quiet, although maybe the trauma of being in a crash, on top of having her father injured, had been too much for the little girl to handle.

The summer heat was already making the interior of her kitchen stuffy, even with the open windows, so she made sure every ceiling fan was on to help circulate the air. By mid afternoon, she might have to use the air conditioner, although she'd rather not.

As she cooked a big batch of scrambled eggs, she wondered about Lexi's mother. Not once during their brief stay in the ER, or last night for that matter, did the little girl ask for her mother. Only her father.

Had Derek tragically lost his wife? Or were they divorced? Either option must have been a while ago, or surely Lexi would have called out for her mother when she arrived in the trauma bay.

She plunked the toast into the toaster then turned back to check the eggs and nearly shrieked when she saw Lexi hovering near the patio doors.

Obviously she'd been so preoccupied with thoughts of Derek that she hadn't heard the child come in.

Putting a hand over her racing heart, she forced a smile. "Good morning, Lexi. I'm cooking breakfast for you and your dad. Do you like scrambled eggs? If not, I have Cheerios and milk."

Lexi stared at her solemnly for so long Julie didn't think she'd answer. "Eggs."

"Great, scrambled eggs it is. Did you come over to help? That's very nice." Then she frowned. "Unless, there's something you need? Is your dad all right?"

Lexi did that tiny nod that, if Julie wasn't watching closely enough, she might have missed. "I'm hungry."

"Me too." The toast popped, so she spread a thin layer of butter over the crispy browned bread. "Do you want to help me carry this over to your dad?" She glanced at her kitchen table and abruptly changed her mind. "You know what, Lexi? It would be easier to eat in my kitchen. Let's ask your dad to come over here."

Lexi darted out the patio door without answering, and Julie had to assume that she'd gone to get her father. It was tempting to go over to offer Derek assistance, but she purposely held herself back.

If Derek wasn't able to stand and walk over here to sit at the kitchen table for a simple meal, then he needed to be taken back to the hospital, despite his protests.

But she needn't have worried. Lexi soon returned with her father on her heels. Wearing the same scrubs she'd given him last night, he moved slowly and gingerly but held himself straight and tall.

"Good morning," she greeted them both cheerfully, trying not to hover as Derek eased himself into a chair. "Hope scrambled eggs and toast is okay." Why the sudden rush of nervousness? She wasn't running a restaurant, and he was hardly in a position to argue about what she fed him.

The un-Christian thought shamed her.

"Sounds better than okay," Derek said quickly. For being injured, he seemed acutely aware of her emotions. Or maybe she just wasn't good at hiding them. "Lexi loves scrambled eggs, don't you, sweetheart?"

Lexi nodded and then ducked her head, swinging her legs back and forth in a steady rhythm. Julie gave Lexi the first plate of food, Derek the second, and then went back to get something for herself.

Once seated, she bowed her head and clasped her hands together. "Dear Lord, thank you for this plentiful meal we're about to eat. Please help Derek get better soon and guide us on Your chosen path as we begin our day. Amen."

A brief silence followed her prayer, and she could feel the intensity of Derek's curious gaze as she took a bite of her eggs. Hadn't he ever witnessed anyone praying before? Or prayed for him to get better? If not, his education was sorely lacking.

"How are you feeling today?" she asked, glancing at Derek.

"As good as can be expected," he admitted. "Surprisingly, the pain seems a bit better when I'm up and moving."

"Your muscles will become stiff and sore if you stay in one place too long. As difficult as I'm sure it must be, you need to keep moving."

He flashed a smile and nodded. "Good advice, Nurse Julie."

She could feel herself blushing and focused her attention on her food.

"Sure is peaceful around here," Derek said, staring through the screen to the concrete patio.

"Yes, I love the peace and quiet." She had a small television but didn't turn it on often. Sometimes she listened to the national news, but lately, the global turmoil was just too depressing. "Would you rather listen to the radio?"

"No." The force of his abrupt response surprised her. "I like the peace and quiet, too."

Such a small thing in common, yet it made her smile inside. "So, what are your plans for the day?"

He stared at his plate for a moment. "I have to find out the extent of the damage to my car. I'm not even sure it's fixable. And the doc wanted to check me over one more time." She was pleased he finished up his eggs and started on the toast. At least his appetite seemed to have returned. "I know I have no right to ask any more favors," he said in a low voice. "But would you mind giving us a ride? If you have the day off, that is."

"Yes, I have the next couple of days off. And of course I don't mind giving you a ride." She told herself that spending the day with Derek and Lexi was nothing like what had happened with Andrew, but it was. Andrew had needed her help, just like Derek. Her own fault for believing Andrew cared about her in return.

She'd just have to make sure she didn't get too emotionally involved with Derek and Lexi.

But even if she had thought things through last evening, she knew she would have made the same offer.

Where else would Derek and Lexi have gone?

"Thank you," Derek murmured. "If all the people here are as gracious and kind as you, Crystal Lake must be a wonderful place to live."

"Crystal Lake is a great place to live, and anyone here would have done the same thing I did." She stood and began stacking the dirty dishes to carry them over to the counter. "You'll have to give me a few minutes to clean up before I'll be ready to go."

He glanced at the dishes on the counter. "I'll help," he offered.

Whoever this stranger was, he was certainly polite. "Really, it's easier if I wash them myself." She couldn't explain why the thought of standing next to Derek, doing something as mundane as dishes, made her distinctly uncomfortable.

There was a brief pause, and then he capitulated. "All right, then. Come on Lexi, let's go over and make our beds, okay?"

When the screen door slammed behind them, she put her hands on the counter and momentarily closed her eyes.

Why was she so attracted to Derek? Okay, maybe Derek was strong, kind, gentle, and polite—seemingly everything Andrew had proved he wasn't. So what? She should be glad she'd offered her townhouse to a nice stranger.

Just as she was glad she'd found out about Andrew's lying and cheating before she'd vowed to love, honor, and cherish him.

Derek and Lexi were only passing through town. Or looking to spend some quiet time together. She refused to entertain the hope that Derek Ryerson and his young daughter would stay to make a home here in Crystal Lake.

DEREK FOUGHT a wave of guilt as he helped Lexi straighten the sheet and blanket on her bed. He knew he was taking advantage of Julie's sweet, Christian nature, but what choice did he have?

He was glad the news of his and Lexi's disappearance didn't seem to have made its way to the small town of Crystal Lake, Wisconsin. But how long did he have before the alarm went out? Thanks to the Fourth of July holiday on Tuesday, he likely had a couple of days to figure out their next steps before he had to go on the run again.

Claire's parents couldn't serve him a court order if they couldn't find him.

He tried to consider his options, but there weren't many. The last thing he wanted to do was to betray Julie by stealing her car. A fleeting thought that had crossed his mind. The problem was that he only had a couple of thousand in cash, and he couldn't afford to spend it all in one place.

He'd need something to tide them over until he could find a job. Especially with the economy as bad as it was. Most of his experience was as a soldier and even though he'd received an honorable discharge there was no guarantee he'd find something quickly or easily.

Once he and Lexi had made the twin beds, he wandered back into the half-demolished, open-concept kitchen and living area. There was a crowbar propped against the wall that still had some charred Sheetrock hanging.

Julie was clearly working on her remodeling project a little at a time. Pulling down old drywall didn't take a whole lot of finesse, but putting up new Sheetrock did. Luckily, he had some experience with construction work.

He lifted the crowbar, wincing as the muscles in his chest protested. Steeling himself against the pain, he drove the claw end of the crowbar into the seared drywall and pulled, bringing a big chunk of drywall crashing to the floor.

He sucked in a quick breath. Yeah, that hurt. But so what? As he lifted the crowbar, intending to take another chunk of the wall down, an idea burned in his mind.

Julie yanked open the screen door and glared at him.

"What's going on?" she demanded. "You scared me to death, making all that noise."

"Sorry," he said with a grimace. He leaned the crowbar back up against the wall and shifted to face her. "I found a way to repay you for your generosity." He lifted a hand, indicating the room. "I'll work on your remodeling project as payment for you allowing me and Lexi to stay here for the next few days."

4

J ulie stared at Derek in shock. His offer was generous, but really, she couldn't believe he was even considering doing physical work on her townhouse while having cracked ribs. The man was truly a glutton for punishment. "Derek, there's no need for you to worry about paying me back. You can't do construction work until you're medically cleared by the doctor."

His smile was pained. "I'm a former Army sergeant. I assure you I can work on the townhouse just fine. And don't worry, I know my limits. I won't overdo things. But I can still help out."

Had she ever met a more stubborn man? She bit back a surge of frustration. "Let's get to the hospital, okay? We have plenty of other things to do right now rather than wasting time arguing over this."

"Please," he said in a low voice.

Her annoyance faded at the softly spoken plea. She understood that being helpless and at other people's mercy was probably difficult for him. She wasn't surprised that he was former military, considering the short haircut and the way he carried himself so straight and tall. Once again, she found herself wondering about Lexi's mother. Derek said he and Lexi were alone, but she couldn't help wondering about the woman who'd given birth to Lexi. Not that Derek's loss was any of her business.

She glanced at Lexi, who stared at her with a steady gaze, identical to Derek's. She sighed, knowing she may as well give in since he'd try to do the work anyway. With any luck, he'd get tired quickly. "When you're able to work, I'd be more than happy to work out a deal with you. But first, we're going to see the doctor and check out your car."

"Thank you," he murmured, and she knew the battle had already been lost. Or in his case, won. Not that she planned on keeping score.

They headed outside to where she'd left her car in the driveway. She opened the driver's side door but then stopped when she realized Derek had remained standing over by the townhouse. "Shouldn't we lock the door?" he asked.

"This is Crystal Lake," she said dryly. "We don't lock our doors here."

He looked surprised, making her think that he was used to living in the city rather than in a small town. It made her a little uneasy that there was so much she didn't know about him.

"Would you mind if we went to find my truck first?" he asked as they made their way down the sidewalk to the car. "I'd like to get Lexi's booster seat. And if you're right about the lack of crime around here, maybe our luggage, my phone, and my tools are still inside."

"Sure." She was struck by how Derek always seemed to put his daughter first. He was still a stranger, but he seemed so genuine. Of course, she'd thought the best of Andrew, too, and he'd proved to be a lying, cheating jerk. Obviously she couldn't trust her instincts. At least, not when it came to men.

As before, Derek slid into the backseat to stay near his daughter. She felt like a taxi driver as she maneuvered her way through the small town. This time, Derek looked around curiously rather than being half out of it.

"How did you know my truck would be here?" Derek asked when she pulled up in front of Billy's garage.

"Because Billy's is the only towing service we have," she said, sliding out from behind the wheel. She knew Derek and Lexi followed as she walked over to the open garage door. "Henry! Are you here?"

"His name isn't Billy?" Derek asked, his blue eyes mirroring his confusion.

She laughed. "No, Henry bought the place about ten years ago from old Billy Colby and decided there was no reason to change the name."

"You've lived here a long time, then?" he asked.

Her smile faded. "Yes, I grew up here." Her parents had passed away several years ago, but she never had the urge to leave. Granted, staying on after breaking off her engagement was the hardest thing she'd ever done. At least now that a year had passed, the gossip had died down a bit. Andrew's decision to leave with his new fiancée had helped. She shook off the painful memories. "Henry!"

"I'm right here. Ya don't have to shout." Henry looked older than his forty-five years, thanks to years of smoking. He'd finally quit but constantly chomped on pieces of nicotine gum. He swiped his greasy hands on his coveralls and squinted at them. "Are ya here for the Blazer?"

"Yes. How much do I owe you for the tow?" Derek asked, stepping forward.

"A hundred even," Henry said. "I checked it out, and I gotta tell ya, there ain't no way to salvage it. Probably totaled."

"Where is the vehicle?" she asked as Derek pulled out his wallet. She'd been about to pay the fee herself, but clearly Derek had this covered.

"Around back," Henry said, gesturing with his thumb as he accepted the cash.

She followed the men around the corner and then sucked in a harsh breath, glad she'd lagged behind when she saw what was left of Derek's car.

It was a miracle he wasn't hurt worse. The entire driver's side of the car was nothing but mangled metal. She gave another silent prayer of thanks to God for keeping him safe.

Derek's expression was grim as he went over to the passenger side of the car and opened the door. When he pulled out Lexi's booster seat, she reached around to take it from him.

"I'll put this in my car," she said.

Derek nodded before turning back to the vehicle. She could have assured him that whatever he had in the truck was still there. Henry would never have considered stealing from one of his towed vehicles.

The people of Crystal Lake were generally law-abiding citizens. Especially now that Tommy Hinkle and his father, Kurt, were behind bars.

By the time she'd strapped Lexi's car seat into the backseat and returned to the mangled car, she discovered that Derek had pulled two suitcases out. The sight of his luggage brought her up short. Was she crazy to allow this man to stay with her? If Andrew were still around, he'd have a fit. But Andrew wasn't part of her life any longer, and despite her unease, she refused to go back on her word.

Hiding her attack of nerves, she picked up the larger of the two suitcases and carried it to her trunk.

Derek carried the smaller suitcase over and stored it beside the larger one. "I'm just going to get my tools," he said before striding back to his wrecked truck.

Within ten minutes, Derek had everything stashed in the back of her car. He went over and said something to Henry. The older man nodded and then shook Derek's hand.

She refrained from asking what transpired despite her curiosity. Derek helped Lexi get into the booster seat and then surprised her by climbing into the passenger seat beside her.

"Next stop, Hope County Hospital," she said cheerfully as she left Billy's garage.

Derek nodded but still looked upset about leaving his truck behind. He fiddled with his phone, sliding the charger into the port and making sure the device still worked.

"You might want to call your insurance company," she said. "The sooner you put them on notice, the sooner they'll cut you a check."

"Yeah." Derek scrubbed his hands over his face. "But I doubt they'll do much without the accident report."

He was right; she should have thought about that. "We can swing by after you've been seen at the hospital," she offered. "May as well get everything done in one trip."

"No need. The deputy told me the report wouldn't be done until Monday," he said.

"I have connections at the sheriff's department. Sheriff Torretti is a great guy and I know his wife Megan. I can ask for a rush on the report."

"Monday is fine," Derek said sharply. When she glanced at him in surprise, he seemed to backpedal. "It's not like anything is going to be processed over the weekend anyway."

She shrugged and let the matter drop. Maybe he was hurting more than he'd let on. Especially after the way he'd been hauling suitcases around.

The sooner Gabe Allen looked him over, the better.

————————

DEREK GRIPPED the armrest of the passenger door, hoping Julie wouldn't insist on stopping at the police station. He was thankful she didn't have the news on, but if Claire's parents had put out the alarm, the risk of being arrested was too high. Claire's parents had tons of money, and they'd made it clear that they'd take custody of Lexi away from him.

He tried to take deep, calming breaths, but it wasn't easy with sore ribs. When Julie pulled up in front of the hospital, he gave a tiny sigh of relief.

"Why don't you get out here, and I'll park the car?" she suggested.

"I can walk, you know," he muttered, getting really sick of being treated like an invalid. He supposed that being a nurse made her more conscientious than others, but still. He glanced back at Lexi. "Do you want to come with me?" he asked.

Lexi nodded. He was impressed at how well his daughter was handling all this, especially since she didn't normally warm up to strangers at all. He opened the back passenger door and helped her get out of the booster seat. He lifted Lexi out and then set her on her feet. Before closing the door, he caught Julie's gaze. "Ah, Dr. Allen, right?"

She smiled, and he was surprised at how much that small gesture transformed her features. Julie was really quite pretty in a girl-next-door kind of way. Not as classically beautiful as Claire, but then again, that hadn't worked so well for him, had it? Julie was attractive, but it didn't matter, since he had no plans to stay in Crystal Lake.

He figured he had a week at the most before he needed to be on the road again.

"Yes, Dr. Gabe Allen. Just keep in mind that you might have to wait if they're busy."

"I understand. Thanks again. Come on, Lexi." He took his daughter's hand and walked inside the emergency department. At least this time, he was walking in and not being wheeled in on a gurney.

He told the nurse at the front desk that he was here to see Dr. Allen. She placed the call and, within five minutes, waved him back. "You can go into room three," she directed.

At first, he'd assumed that the ER wasn't very busy since they'd taken him right away, but when he went back into the main arena, he was greeted by a cacophony of activity. Various patients were wailing in pain or yelling out for one reason or another. Monitors beeped, and there seemed to be a constant stream of chatter from the staff who scurried from one place to another.

Room three looked to be one of the few empty rooms, and he felt guilty for wasting the doctor's valuable time. He waited inside the doorway, thinking it might be better if he just left, since they were so busy. Only the thought of disappointing Julie kept him there.

Ten minutes later, Dr. Allen and a nurse rushed in. "So,

how did you survive the night?" the doctor asked without wasting time exchanging small talk.

"Fine," Derek said, lifting his arm so that the nurse could take down the dressing around the chest tube.

"He sneezed, and his lung deflated again," Julie said as she entered the room. "I applied negative pressure on the valve, and he seemed to be better after that."

"Hmmm." The doctor cocked an eyebrow at him questioningly so he reluctantly nodded.

"Yeah, that sounds right."

"We'll need to get another chest X-ray," Dr. Allen said to the nurse. "I'm tempted to leave the catheter in for another day, but we'll see how your X-ray looks."

He kept his mouth shut, sensing it would do no good to argue. When it came time to get the X-ray, he flashed Lexi a reassuring smile before following the nurse to the radiology area.

Five minutes later, he was back in the room. Dr. Allen pulled up the X-ray on the computer screen right in the room. "No sign of the pneumothorax," he muttered. "But I'd still like to keep the catheter in another day."

"I'll bring him back tomorrow after church," Julie said.

Dr. Allen nodded. "I'm not working, but maybe I can just stop by your place. How do your ribs feel?"

"Sore, but tolerable."

"All right, try not to do any more sneezing, and I'll see you tomorrow."

"Thanks Doc," he said, sincerely grateful to know he hadn't made anything worse last night. The pain had been scary, but he felt a hundred percent better today. Well, maybe that was a slight exaggeration. More like fifty percent better. "I appreciate the special treatment."

"No problem." Dr. Allen flashed them both a tired grin before leaving them alone.

Derek held Lexi's hand as he followed Julie back out to the parking lot. Getting in and out of the car still hurt, but he bit back a low groan when he slid inside.

Neither one of them said anything as Julie pulled out of the hospital parking lot.

"The drugstore is on the way home," she said, finally breaking the silence. "We can stop to get your prescription filled."

"I don't need more pain meds," he said quickly. He was afraid if she knew how low he was on cash, she'd insist on paying for them herself, and he was in debt to her enough already. "I still have a couple of the samples left, and I don't plan to use them unless I'm desperate."

"Like you were last night?" she asked. "I can't believe you weren't going to tell the doctor what happened."

He shrugged, feeling guilty for disappointing her when, really, he had far bigger issues to worry about. "You heard the doc, no sign of a pneumo-whatever, so I'm fine."

She didn't answer but tightened her fingers on the steering wheel as if she was struggling not to lose control. He felt bad for making her upset, but he couldn't explain how important it was that he stay out of the hospital at all cost. He didn't want Lexi to end up in the foster care system. And he for sure didn't want Claire's parents to get custody of Lexi again.

Lexi was...special. She didn't need that private super strict school that Claire's parents had picked out for her. Lexi hated it, and forcing her to go was making her worse instead of better. Claire's parents thought she needed struc- ture, but what Lexi needed was love and attention. What she needed was to be with her father and time to recuperate from losing her mother.

Now that he was honorably discharged from the Army, he could take better care of Lexi than a bunch of strangers, no matter how well intentioned.

He'd made a promise to Lexi and to Claire before she died, and he intended to keep it.

5

Julie stood in her kitchen, watching through the patio doors as Derek and Lexi walked down to the lake. Despite her protests, Derek had insisted on bringing in the luggage and his tools. They way he was moving slowly and carefully, favoring his right side, convinced her that he'd overexerted himself. Again. Yet no matter how many times she told him to rest, he ignored her and did what he wanted. Lexi instinctively stayed close to her father's side rather than running toward the water the way Amelia used to do.

Thoughts of her niece always brought the threat of tears, so she turned away, trying to think of other things. It was close to noon, and there was plenty of leftover pizza to eat for lunch, but she also needed something to make for dinner. She opened her freezer and stared at the meager contents.

Hamburgers on the grill sounded good, and best of all, she wouldn't have to turn on her oven. Thanks to her small garden, she even had the fixings for a salad. Tomorrow, after church, she'd have to make a run to the grocery store since she wasn't used to feeding three people.

The sound of boat engines and shrieking laughter filtered in off the lake. Her brother, Zack, left his boat here during the summer months, and she wondered if Derek and Lexi would like to take a spin out on the lake after they'd eaten.

Or maybe they just wanted to spend some time alone. After all, it wasn't her job to entertain them.

No matter how much she wanted to.

Since she was becoming far too fascinated with her unexpected houseguests, she busied herself with doing some bills and other paperwork until her stomach rumbled. Figuring Derek and Lexi must be hungry too, she pulled the leftover pizza out of the fridge and heated it up in her microwave. Then she piled paper plates and napkins on top of the pizza box before making her way outside.

"Are you guys hungry?" she called. "There's plenty of left-over pizza for lunch."

Derek looked up and flashed a smile, which somehow made him look about ten years younger. She wasn't at all happy that her pulse jumped in response. "I am," he said eagerly. "How about it, baby-doll?"

Lexi gave another of her short nods and readily walked back up to the townhouse with her father.

"Thanks, Julie, this looks great," Derek said, looking down at the food with appreciation.

She ducked her head, hoping he hadn't noticed her pink cheeks. Why was she reacting to Derek like this? Ridiculous. "It's nothing, just more leftovers than I could ever finish by myself."

Lexi scrambled up to sit on her knees so she could reach

the table, and Derek gingerly sank into a chair beside her. Julie took her seat and bowed her head to pray.

"Dear Lord, thank You for providing this food and for this fantastic summer day. Amen."

She opened her eyes and looked up, surprised to see that both Derek and Lexi had bowed their heads, too, while she'd prayed. All she knew about Derek was that he used to be in the military, and while he hadn't joined her in prayer, he hadn't scoffed at her faith, either.

And why did she care one way or the other? She had to stop thinking that Derek and Lexi would be here long enough for it to matter. She was simply helping him out of a jam—it wasn't as if this was some sort of long-term friendship or anything.

"Is that boat on the lift yours?" Derek asked before taking a healthy bite of his pizza. He truly looked so much better today that she could barely reconcile this man sitting across from her with the guy who'd been sprawled on the bedroom floor last night, pale and sweating in pain.

"It belongs to my brother, but I'd be happy to take you both out for a ride if you're interested."

Derek grinned with excitement. He cocked his head and glanced down at his daughter. "What do you think, Lexi? Do you want to go for a boat ride?"

Lexi's expression lit up. "Yes!" It was the most enthusiasm she'd seen from the girl since bringing them both home last night.

"Well then, sounds like a plan," Julie said, betraying her eagerness. She finished her slice of pizza and pushed away from the table. "You'll have to give me a few minutes to make sure everything is clean. I haven't had the boat out in two weeks."

"Sit down and finish your lunch, Julie," Derek said

firmly. "There's no rush. Lexi and I can help clean up the boat if needed."

The fact that he was supposed to be resting seemed to be lost on him, but she bit back her argument and sank back down, helping herself to another small slice of pizza. She gave up trying to lecture him, since it didn't do any good anyway.

After they finished the entire pizza, Derek making a much bigger dent than he had last night, she tossed the empty box in the garbage and then went back inside to fill a pail with warm, soapy water.

Derek and Lexi were waiting patiently for her out on the patio, and, of course, Derek took the pail of water from her before they walked down to the lake together. If his ribs were aching, he made sure the pain didn't show on his face.

She removed the boat cover, grimacing when she saw that the seats were lightly coated with dirt. But with all three of them working together, it didn't take long before the boat was sparkling clean.

She hauled out Amelia's life vest for Lexi and instructed the girl on how to put it on. Lexi didn't seem thrilled but, after a stern look from her father, didn't complain. Julie slid the key into the ignition and glanced over at Derek and Lexi. "Are you ready?"

Derek nodded. "Sure."

Knowing that bouncing over the waves might cause him pain, she started out at a slow pace. The lake was busy, so she had to carefully navigate the craft around the other boaters, making sure to keep an eye out for skiers and tubers. When she came upon an open stretch of lake, she pushed the throttle forward, kicking up some speed, and was rewarded by Lexi's laughter.

All too soon, she had to slow back down, carefully

turning around to head back toward her home. She glanced over at her passengers, glad to see Derek looked relaxed, with Lexi tucked close to his side.

"I don't suppose you'd let me drive?" he asked, capturing her gaze with his.

"Sure, why not?" she pulled the throttle back so that the boat was idling as they awkwardly switched seats. His arm brushed hers, and she had no business inhaling his masculine scent, especially since it went straight to her head. She moved away, taking a seat across from Lexi.

As Derek drove them leisurely around the lake, she could feel the curious stares from some of her friends and neighbors. The smile on her features dimmed as she realized what this little outing probably looked like to everyone else. As if she and Derek were seeing each other on a personal level.

She closed her eyes for a moment, dreading the thought of being the source of more rumors. The gossip had flown fast and furious after Andrew had left her. Being out in public like this would only encourage the small town tongues to start flapping all over again.

Leaving her to explain why Derek and Lexi had left, as she knew they would, right after the holiday.

———

DEREK ENJOYED BEING out on the boat, but as soon as he realized the three of them were becoming the center of attention, he turned the boat around to head back to Julie's place.

Stupid to forget, even for a moment, that he and Lexi needed to keep a low profile. As far as he knew, Julie hadn't so much as turned on a radio or a television since last night, but that didn't mean her neighbors hadn't. He'd already pushed his luck with Deputy Thomas.

Lexi was legally in his custody, but that didn't mean Claire's parents weren't still searching for them. And who knows what story they might have told the police?

After all, they had wealth and power on their side when all he had was love.

"Let's go again, Daddy," Lexi said with a rare pout.

"Sorry, baby-doll, but my ribs are still a little sore," he said. He wasn't lying, because his ribs did ache—not that he'd let a little pain get in the way of making Lexi happy.

Going to the private school that Claire's parents had forced upon her hadn't made her happy, either. Keeping her safe was more important. And the fear of being found by Claire's parents trumped another boat ride by far.

"We can go out again another day," Julie assured Lexi. "Maybe even tomorrow afternoon. I have to go to church in the morning and then stop at the grocery store, but then we have the rest of the day free."

He wasn't surprised that Julie planned to go to church since she'd mentioned that to the doc, but the flash of guilt caught him off guard. He ignored the emotion as he carefully pulled the speedboat into its docking station next to the pier. "Lexi, why don't you get your sketchbook? I bet Julie would appreciate a pretty picture of her lake."

"Oh, I'd love that," Julie agreed with enthusiasm. "Would you do that for me, Lexi? Please?"

His daughter gave another of her reserved, tiny nods, and he was relieved she'd allowed herself to be distracted from taking another trip around the lake. He shut off the motor and helped Lexi out of the boat first, before reaching down to help Julie with the cover.

"I'll get it. You need to rest those ribs," she said.

"I'm not an invalid," he muttered, his tone sharper than he intended. He knew she was reacting to the excuse he'd given to Lexi for going back home, which made him feel guilty again. Hadn't Julie noticed the way people stared at them?

"I know, but I can do this," she said. "Why don't you take Lexi back up to the house?"

Julie was avoiding his gaze, and he realized maybe she had noticed the curious stares and was embarrassed to be seen with him and Lexi. The thought bothered him, even though he knew Julie's personal life was none of his business.

For all he knew, she might be seeing someone, although she certainly hadn't mentioned it. He almost asked her but then gave himself a mental shake. "All right, let's go, Lexi."

He climbed off the boat and took his daughter's hand. Lexi seemed to hesitate, but after one last glance over her shoulder at Julie, she came along with him.

He didn't relax until they were back up at the patio outside the townhouse, away from the curious eyes of Julie's neighbors. He gingerly lowered himself into one of the patio chairs while Lexi ran inside the townhouse for her sketchbook.

His ribs were still sore, but the ache in his head seemed to be a bit better. Being out on the lake had been wonderful; for a few brief moments, it had been nice to forget all his worries and enjoy being out on the water. But then reality had crashed through his false sense of security.

He wasn't here to have fun. He needed to figure out where he could find a job and a place to live. Someplace where he could establish himself in a community, making it difficult for Claire's parents to take Lexi away from him. If that was even possible.

He closed his eyes for a moment, rubbing a hand along the right side of his chest. There was nothing worse than feeling useless. He wished he felt strong enough to start working on the half-gutted townhouse. The sooner he could pay Julie back for her hospitality, the better.

Lexi came back outside and climbed into the seat beside him. He opened his eyes, blinking against the bright sunlight. Thankfully, the umbrella overhead helped provide some shade, and he watched as Lexi pulled out her colored pencils and began to draw the lake.

"Would you like some iced tea or a soft drink?" Julie asked as she walked up.

"Sure. Tea would be great," he said, even though he knew that he was already imposing on Julie far more than he had a right to.

"Lexi, do you like root beer?" Julie asked.

His daughter nodded but didn't look up from her drawing. Once his daughter was preoccupied with something she liked to do, it was difficult to get her attention. He was about to apologize for Lexi's behavior, but Julie was already disappearing into her side of the townhouse, the screen door sliding shut behind her.

He allowed his eyes to drift closed, giving in to a wave of insidious fatigue. Why he should be so tired, he had no idea. It wasn't as if he'd done much. And if he was this exhausted just from running a few errands and going for a boat ride, then how in the world was he going to do the construction work on Julie's townhouse that needed to be done?

"Derek, why don't you go inside to lie down?"

He pried his eyes open and summoned a smile. "It's nice

being out here like this." He reached for the glass of ice-cold tea. "Thanks, again."

Julie gave him an exasperated look as she sat down beside him. "I don't know what you're trying to prove," she muttered. "It hasn't even been twenty-four hours since your accident."

He didn't want to think about the crash. "Does your brother live around here?"

"He lives about an hour away in Madison," she said. "Unfortunately, Zack doesn't get up here as much as he used to. Still, we've stayed close since our parents died."

There was a hint of sadness in her tone, but he held back from asking anything too personal. After all, it wasn't as if he wanted to reciprocate. Julie seemed like the type of woman who'd feel compelled to report him to the authorities if she knew the truth.

"This area looks like a nice place to live," he said instead. "How many people are there in Crystal Lake?"

"About fourteen hundred people live within Hope County, and over half of them live within a twenty-five mile radius to the lake. The people here either work at the medical center, for the government either in city hall or the sheriff's department, or in the service sector, which depends a lot on tourism to survive."

"No manufacturing jobs, huh?" he asked.

"No. We had a car manufacturing plant about thirty miles from here, but that closed down a few years ago, after the collapse of the economy."

He figured as much. Crystal Lake might be a great place to live, but he needed some sort of job that would support him and Lexi. He'd done some construction work prior to going into the service, but with the economy the way it was, no one was building new houses anymore.

Eight years in the Army hadn't exactly prepared him for the civilian job market. Of course, he'd planned to reenlist until Claire had told him about her cancer. The doctor had given her six months to live.

She'd only lasted four.

Seven years ago, when Claire had discovered she was pregnant, he'd asked her to marry him, but she'd refused. At least Claire had let him be a part of Lexi's life, and not only had he sent most of his money to Claire, he'd spent as much time as he could with Lexi. But after Claire had found out about her cancer, she'd asked him to come back to care for their daughter. He'd jumped through yards of red tape before he was granted his honorary discharge, but it was several weeks too late. Claire had passed away, and Lexi had ended up living with Claire's parents until he'd arrived stateside. Thankfully, Lexi hadn't forgotten him and had clung to his shoulders like a little monkey, as if she'd never let him go.

It had been his first inkling of what the child had gone through with her grandparents. Apparently, even when Claire was too weak to care for Lexi, her parents had taken over, enrolling her in that ridiculous private school where she was punished if she didn't act like the other kids.

Which had been most of the time.

He still saw red when he thought about what Lexi had been through, so he forced the images away. He was not about to let Claire's parents get custody of Lexi. In the few weeks they'd been together, Lexi had already begun to relax and trust him. Now more than ever, he believed he'd made the right decision to take her away. He and Lexi would make things work.

"Here, Julie, this is for you." His daughter's voice pulled

him away from his thoughts. He was surprised that Lexi had opened up even that much to a virtual stranger.

"Lexi, this is a beautiful picture," Julie said with awe. "The detail is absolutely amazing. I had no idea you were so talented."

Glancing over, he caught the shy smile his daughter flashed at Julie. The hero worship was clear in Lexi's bright blue eyes.

In that moment, the truth sucker punched him, stealing his breath.

Lexi was looking up to Julie like a surrogate mother.

And when it was time for them to leave, his daughter would be hurt all over again.

6

J ulie was truly stunned at how talented Lexi was and couldn't help staring at the lake drawing, marveling at the detail. She'd loved Amelia with all her heart, but her niece's pictures had been stick people and crude landmarks. Nothing like Lexi's precise drawing of the lake within which everything was amazingly to scale.

As silence hung heavily, she scrambled for something to talk about. "I thought we'd have burgers for dinner if that's okay with you," she offered, glancing over at Derek.

"Sounds good," he agreed.

She stared at him for a moment, feeling as if there might be something wrong, and not just because he was avoiding her gaze. The silence stretched between them, only not as relaxing as it had been earlier.

As the sun began its slow descent on the horizon, she took Lexi's drawing with her and went into the kitchen to begin making the hamburger patties. Through the window, she noticed Derek slowly rise to his feet and walk over to the grill.

She took the plate of raw burgers outside, and Derek

barely glanced at her as he took the plate. "I'll make them," he said.

"Thanks." She returned to the kitchen for the salad, wondering why there was this weird tension between them. Had she said something wrong? Or was he simply tired from being outside all day?

She took the salad bowl out and set it on the patio table. "Lexi, would you mind helping me bring out the plates, napkins, silverware, and condiments?"

Lexi nodded and readily slid down off the chair. Derek glanced over, and she hesitated, getting the impression that he was about to say something. But then he simply turned back to the grill, using the spatula to flip the burgers.

The rest of the meal was just as strained, despite her efforts to chat. It seemed that the easy camaraderie that had existed between them had disappeared without a trace. And she had no idea why. When the meal was over, Derek and Lexi helped her carry everything back inside but then disappeared into their side of the townhouse.

As she washed the dishes, she wondered if Derek's ribs were hurting him more than he'd let on. Certainly, she understood if he needed rest. But why did it seem that there was something more bothering him?

When she finished with dinner, she went back outside to sit on one of her patio chairs to watch the sun set over the lake, feeling a strange sense of loneliness without Derek and Lexi seated beside her.

———

THE NEXT MORNING, Julie ate a bowl of cold cereal before

getting dressed for church. She chose a flowery skirt and a matching blouse and then took the time to blow-dry her hair so that it was nice and straight. She headed over to the adjacent townhouse and knocked on the screen door. After a few minutes with no response, she called out, "Derek? Lexi?"

A dark shadow appeared, and she noticed with relief that Derek was standing on the other side of the screen.

"Good morning," Derek said quietly. His hair was damp from a recent shower, and he was dressed in a clean pair of jeans and a red T-shirt, an acute reminder that he had regular clothes rather than the scrubs. He appeared more rested than he had the day before, and she suspected that no one seeing him like this would believe he'd suffered a collapsed lung and bruised ribs less than forty-eight hours ago. Obviously, he was a quick healer.

"Good morning." She smoothed a hand over her skirt, feeling nervous. "Um...I have cold cereal for breakfast if you and Lexi are hungry. And I was wondering if you and Lexi wanted to attend church services with me this morning?"

"Cereal sounds fine, but I think we'll pass on the church services," he murmured. "Thanks anyway."

She did her best to keep the keen sense of disappointment from her features, even though she knew that if Derek and Lexi had come with her, the town gossips would have had a field day. Certainly it was better this way.

So why was she so upset?

"All right, I'll be heading out shortly, but please help yourself to whatever you need in the kitchen, okay?" She pasted a bright smile on her face with an effort. "I'll see you both later." Fighting tears, she turned away.

"Julie," he said in a low voice.

She stopped and took a deep breath before turning back to face him. "Yes?"

"Thank you, for everything."

Her mouth went dry, and for a wild moment, she thought he was saying goodbye. But how could Derek and Lexi possibly leave? As far as she knew, there weren't many places nearby to rent a car, especially on a Sunday.

"You're welcome," she managed. As she turned and walked back to her side of the townhouse, she paused in the kitchen, gripping the back of a kitchen chair, inwardly debating the idea of forgoing church services. Maybe if she stayed here, Derek and Lexi wouldn't leave. She'd find a way to convince them to stay, at least through the holiday.

But as soon as the thought crossed her mind, she knew she was being ridiculous. She still needed to go grocery shopping, or they'd all starve. And whether she liked it or not, Derek and Lexi had every right to leave her townhouse and Crystal Lake whenever they wanted to.

Her fault if she found that idea depressing.

Maybe praying would help her find peace. She straightened her shoulders and grabbed her purse and car keys before heading for the door. She would go to church, and she would go grocery shopping afterwards. And if Derek and Lexi were gone when she returned, then obviously, that was God's will.

If she could survive the scandal of Andrew's affair, she'd certainly survive Derek and Lexi leaving.

Better for her to remember her role here was simply to help a stranger and his daughter in need. Derek wasn't looking for anything more.

And she shouldn't be, either.

DEREK LEANED on the door frame, fighting the urge to call Julie back. The flash of disappointment in her eyes had cut deep, even though he knew he couldn't afford to be seen with Lexi in such a public place. For all he knew, Deputy Thomas would be there, or some of the other members of the town's law enforcement. If Claire's parents had sounded the alarm they may recognize him and arrest him.

He hadn't been to church in years, but surprisingly, he realized he'd have liked to go with Julie.

Lexi came up to stand beside him, and he forced himself to focus on his daughter. "Are you hungry, baby-doll?" he asked in a lighthearted tone.

"Yes," she said with a shy smile.

"All right, give me a few minutes to clean up first, and we'll find something to eat, okay?"

As he finished making their beds, he heard the sound of Julie's car driving away and winced at the flash of guilt. Julie had been nothing but kind to them, and he felt bad at the way he'd acted last night, putting distance between them.

But at the same time, he couldn't afford to cause his daughter any more pain.

Time to get himself back on track. He walked back into the main living area to find Lexi waiting impatiently. "Let's get some cereal, okay?"

She followed him next door, and he couldn't deny feeling like an intruder as he rummaged through Julie's kitchen. With Lexi's help, he found the box of cereal, bowls, spoons, and milk.

They ate at the kitchen table, overlooking the lake, which was surprisingly noisy with boaters and skiers making the most out of another glorious day. Apparently the tourists didn't bother attending church services either.

Lexi looked longingly out toward the water, and he knew she wanted to swim. He needed to get some work done on the townhouse as a way to repay Julie's kindness, but he didn't want to disappoint his daughter, either. Although he needed to get rid of the stupid catheter in his chest, too. If Dr. Allen didn't show up, he figured he could pull it out himself, no problem.

"I have to do some work first, Lexi, but when I'm finished, we can go down and swim, okay?"

She scowled and kicked her feet rhythmically under the table. He recognized the signs of her distress, but as much as he cherished his relationship with Lexi, she also needed to learn that she couldn't always have her way.

"Work first, then play," he repeated. He stood and took the bowls to the sink. Julie had left hers there as well, so he filled the sink with soapy water, washed and dried them before putting everything back where he'd found them. Lexi had stubbornly remained at the kitchen table, swinging her legs and rocking a bit, but he didn't say anything. Bringing attention to her behavior never helped. Something he'd tried to explain to Claire's parents, to no avail.

"I'll be right next door if you need something," he said, pretending he wasn't bothered by his daughter's silent motion as he slipped outside.

Back inside the gutted portion of the townhouse, he picked up the crowbar and began pulling down the remainder of the blackened drywall. Within ten minutes, he was covered with dust and sweat, but despite the throbbing pain across his ribs, he felt a keen satisfaction at his slow but methodical progress.

The patio doors opened, and Lexi came inside, and the

tension around his chest eased a bit. It was one thing to tell himself that it was best to leave Lexi alone when she got in one of her moods, but following his own advice was far from easy.

"Hey, baby-doll, stay back so you don't get hurt, okay?"

She gave a small nod and stayed near the patio doors as he continued to rip down the drywall. When Lexi put her hands over her ears in response to the noise, he stopped with a sigh.

He swiped the hem of his T-shirt across his forehead and set the crowbar aside. He crossed over to Lexi. "Why don't you sit outside on the patio for a bit?" he suggested. "I should be done here in about an hour, and then we can swim, okay?"

She stared at him for a long moment, dark reproach in her blue eyes, but he steeled his heart against giving in.

"Lexi, Julie has helped us a lot, hasn't she?" he asked.

His daughter's lips formed a pout, but she nodded her agreement.

"I'm doing this to help Julie. She's giving us food and a place to sleep. All I'm asking is for an hour or so to do some work for her." He didn't bother explaining that his sore ribs wouldn't tolerate much longer than that anyway. "Don't you think that's the right thing to do?"

Lexi scowled but gave another nod.

"Good girl," he said. "What would you rather do? Sit and read in your room? Play video games? Or sit outside and draw?"

"Draw," Lexi said promptly, and he grinned again, wondering why he'd bothered to ask. Lexi could easily spend hours drawing, which had been another problem with that private school Claire's parents had enrolled her in. The teachers there were all about learning, which was fine, but they didn't provide any time for Lexi's drawing. And they forced her to interact with the other kids, which Lexi found very distressing. And when she didn't socialize with the other kids or raise her hand in class, the teacher made her sit outside in the hall. The memory made his blood boil.

He forced the memories aside. "Okay. Let's get your sketchbook, okay?" He went over to find her book and her pencils and carried them outside. He glanced at the lake and then turned back to Lexi. "No swimming without me, all right?"

"I know," she said, barely casting him a glance as she reached for her pencil.

He sat down beside her, catching her gaze with his. "I mean it, Lexi. No swimming without me."

She must have recognized the seriousness of his tone, because she said, "I know, Daddy."

"Good." He stood and made his way back inside to finish pulling down the drywall. As he worked, he kept an eye on his daughter. But he needn't have worried. When Lexi concentrated on drawing, the rest of the world ceased to exist.

And for once he was glad for his daughter's single-minded focus.

———

JULIE TRIED to pay attention to the church services, but once the final hymn had been sung and she'd followed her fellow parishioners outside, she couldn't remember what the theme of the pastor's sermon had been.

She smiled and greeted people as she made her way to

her car, too preoccupied to notice that a few of them were looking at her with frank curiosity. No doubt, the rumors were already flying about how she'd been seen with the tall, dark stranger and his daughter.

The next stop was the grocery store, and she mentally reviewed her list as she pushed her cart up and down the rows, moving fast. Too fast, because then she forgot something and had to go back for it. It wasn't until she was in line at the register, tapping her foot impatiently, that she realized her stomach was knotted with anxiety.

A sensation that didn't ease as she transferred her groceries into the trunk of her car. After sliding behind the wheel, she had to remind herself not to speed through town as she headed home.

As she pulled into her driveway, she glanced around for any sign of Derek or Lexi. But even though the windows were open, she didn't hear a sound from their side of the townhouse.

Her heart lodged in her throat as she opened the trunk and walked around to pick up one bag of groceries. She practically raced inside and set the bag down on the kitchen table before crossing over to the patio doors.

The sound of Lexi's laughter stopped her, and she let out a sigh of relief when she saw two heads bobbing in the water near shore, evidence that Derek and Lexi were swimming in the lake.

They were still here.

Derek hadn't been telling her goodbye after all.

Every bit of apprehension that she'd felt since she left earlier that morning faded away as she watched father and daughter playing in the water.

Suddenly, she abruptly straightened. What in the world

was Derek thinking? He shouldn't be swimming! Not when he still had the catheter in his chest.

In a flash, she threw open the patio doors and ran down the grassy slope to the lakeshore. "Derek! Get out of the water! That catheter site is going to get infected!"

Derek stood and carried Lexi over to the shore. After he set his daughter on her feet, he swiped his wet hair from his face. "Calm down. Your friendly doctor Gabe Allen stopped by with his fiancée Larissa and took the catheter out."

She vaguely remembered Gabe offering to do that when they were in the hospital yesterday. She shouldn't have been surprised, Gabe was a great guy and this is exactly something he'd do. How had she missed seeing Gabe and Larissa at church? "Really?"

"Yes, and he gave me some water-proof dressings to put over the small incision while swimming. So you see? There's nothing to worry about."

She scowled and planted her hands on her hips. "I highly doubt he meant for you to swim in the lake. Those dressings are for showering with clean water."

"I promise, he really did say I could swim in the lake," Derek insisted.

"Okay, okay." Was she overreacting? Maybe. "If you don't mind, I'll take a look at the wound after lunch. Just in case." She turned and walked back up to the house, belatedly realizing that she'd left the rest of the groceries in the car. Never before had a man sent her from exasperated to happy within five minutes. Andrew had mostly made her sad. She shrugged and brought in another bag of groceries.

"Would you like some help?" Derek asked once he'd dried himself off with a towel.

"I'm fine," she said, knowing that Derek would only get in the way since he didn't know where everything went anyway. "I bought cold cuts and Italian bread to make sandwiches for lunch."

"Sounds good." Derek stood near the door, and the minute she'd emptied the last grocery bag, he took her hand. "Come on, I want to show you something."

Far too conscious of his hand wrapped around hers, she curiously followed him outside to the set of patio doors leading into the other side of the townhouse. And when she walked in, she gasped in surprise. All of the drywall had been taken down off the walls of the living room and kitchen area, while the floor had been swept clean.

"You did all this today?" she asked in awe.

He nodded. "I still need to do the ceiling, but taking old drywall down is a lot easier than putting new stuff up. Although I should be able to get to that in a couple of days."

"I...don't know what to say," she murmured, her cheeks pink with gratitude. All this time, she'd feared that Derek and Lexi were leaving, when in fact, he'd been working as a show of good faith in keeping up his end of the bargain.

And in that moment, she grimly realized that, despite her best efforts, she'd grown far too emotionally attached to Derek and Lexi.

A path that would surely lead to heartbreak.

7

As Julie fixed lunch, she couldn't help noticing how Derek was moving slowly and carefully again as he crossed the patio and sat down at the table. No doubt the physical work he'd done earlier, tearing down most of her old drywall, had been too much.

Granted, she very much appreciated the work he'd done, but at the same time, she didn't want him to hurt himself again, either.

She brought out the sandwiches and chips she'd picked up at the store and then went back inside for soft drinks. She chose iced tea for herself and Derek, and a tall glass of ice-cold milk for Lexi.

Both Derek and Lexi sat with their hands together, as if waiting for her to pray. Once she'd taken her seat, she bowed her head and took a deep breath, letting it out slowly. "Dear Lord, we thank You for the food You've provided for us today, and we ask for Your wisdom in guiding us on the path You want us to take, especially Derek, who seems intent on working too hard when he's still in pain. We ask this in the name of Christ the Lord. Amen."

She heard a choked laugh as she opened her eyes to find Derek fighting a smile. She pinned him with a stern look. "I'm not kidding," she muttered. "You need to listen to what your body is telling you."

"I know, but I'm fine."

"Yeah, I've heard that before," she said wryly. "You always say that, no matter how much pain you're in. And don't think I've forgotten about your dressing, because I haven't. As soon as we're finished here, I'm going to take a look at your catheter site."

"Yes, Nurse Julie," he responded lightly.

She smiled in spite of herself and glanced at Lexi, who was eating her sandwich with gusto. Julie was glad Lexi didn't seem to be a picky eater, the way Amelia had been. Finding foods that Amelia would eat, even before she'd started chemotherapy, had been a challenge. When the chemo had started, Amelia had lost several pounds, until the child was nothing but skin and bones.

"Julie, why are you sad?" Lexi asked.

She pulled her mind away from the painful memories. "I was thinking about my niece, Amelia," she said honestly. "Sometimes you remind me of her."

Lexi's blue eyes, mirror images of her father's, regarded her steadily. "And that makes you sad?"

"More happy than sad," she corrected. "So tell me how you enjoyed swimming in the lake. Did the seaweed bother you?"

Lexi wrinkled her nose. "A little, but my daddy held me up and kept me away from the weeds."

"That's great, Lexi," Julie said with a smile. "And I'm sure you'll get used to the seaweed."

Derek raised a brow, and she belatedly realized she'd done it again, assuming they'd be staying longer than a few days. What in the world was wrong with her? She needed to think of Derek as a patient, not as a single father. Or a handsome man.

As soon as they were finished with lunch, she jumped up and began carrying things inside. Derek and Lexi helped, so it didn't take long to put everything away. When they were finished, Lexi went back outside to her drawing. She stopped Derek from following his daughter, gesturing to the kitchen table.

"Sit down," she said to Derek in her best don't-mess-with-me tone. "I want to clean that wound."

He looked as if he might argue but then gingerly lowered himself onto one of the kitchen chairs as she went into the bathroom to get her first aid kit. When she returned, she noticed Derek was watching his daughter, who was engrossed in her drawing.

"She's quite the artist," she murmured as she opened the kit and set out the supplies.

"I know, and she can draw for hours if I let her," Derek agreed.

She filled a bowl with hot water and then brought over the bowl, a clean washcloth, and some mild soap. "At least it's better than playing video games."

"Trust me, she does that, too." Derek slid his arm out of his T-shirt and held his elbow up so she could look at the small puncture site.

"This might hurt a bit," she warned as she peeled the clear, transparent, waterproof dressing off. She was surprised to see that the skin beneath was nice and dry. The puncture site was small and seemed relatively clean.

"How bad does it look?" Derek asked.

"Not as bad as I expected," she grudgingly admitted. She did her best to focus her attention on the task at hand and not the masculine scent of Derek's skin. After dipping the washcloth in the hot water, she gently cleaned the wound. When she glanced up at Derek, she was disconcerted to find his face was mere inches from hers.

She stared into his eyes for a long moment before taking a step back. She glanced around for the antibiotic ointment, a bit flustered by his nearness. "I'll, um, just use a bit of this and cover it with gauze for now," she said, knowing she was babbling but unable to make herself stop. "We'll save those waterproof dressings for swimming and showering, okay?"

"Sounds good," he murmured.

Stop talking, she told herself as she taped the two-by-two square gauze over the small puncture site. She straightened, trying to hide shaking fingers. "All finished," she said in a breathless tone.

"Thanks, Julie," he said as he put his arm back through the sleeve of his T-shirt.

She gave a terse nod and leaned forward to gather up her supplies at the same instant Derek chose to stand, the movement causing them to bump into each other.

When Derek's hands lightly grasped her waist to steady her, her breath lodged in her throat, and her heart rate kicked into triple digits.

Overwhelmed by his nearness, she looked up at him at the same time he tipped his head down toward hers. His blue eyes were dark and intent, and when he lowered his mouth to hers, she didn't move. Didn't blink.

There was nothing she wanted more than Derek's kiss.

His mouth settled over hers, and she gently parted her lips, reveling in his taste, leaning against him when her knees went weak.

"Daddy?" Lexi's voice crashed the moment.

Derek pulled away so quickly she lost her balance and

had to grab on to the kitchen table for support as Derek hastened to put distance between them. "What's up, baby-doll?" he asked in a hoarse tone. She couldn't help being glad that he'd obviously been as affected as she was by their kiss.

"Do you want to see my drawing?" Lexi asked.

"Of course I do," he said, moving forward to escape through the patio doors. The spring door slid shut with a bang behind him.

Julie stayed where she was for several long moments, trying to rein in her rioting emotions.

Why had he kissed her? Why had she kissed him back? Well, she knew why she'd kissed him back, because really, what sane woman wouldn't? Derek was tall, dark and handsome, not to mention gentle and kind.

But she truly had no idea why he'd kissed her in the first place. Andrew had found her attractive at first but then had lost patience with her. He'd ended up getting back together with his old girlfriend. She'd be better off staying far away from Derek. But as she cleaned up the first aid supplies and dumped out the water in the sink, she couldn't stop wondering if or when Derek might kiss her again.

———

DEREK MENTALLY BERATED himself for being an idiot as he peered down at Lexi's drawing. Why had he kissed Julie like that? She was a beautiful, kind, Christian woman who had gone out of her way to help him and Lexi. And how had he thanked her? By giving in to the need to kiss her.

He'd be lucky if she didn't immediately demand they leave, after the stunt he'd pulled.

He forced himself to concentrate on Lexi's drawing. She'd chosen to do a picture of Julie's townhouse this time, rather than the lake, and he had to admit, his daughter had an eye for detail. She'd even included Julie's small vegetable garden.

"It's beautiful, Lexi," he said honestly. "Just like you."

"Will Julie like it?"

"Of course she will." He shouldn't have been surprised by Lexi's desire to make Julie happy, but he was. Since they'd left St. Louis, Lexi hadn't said a word about her mother's death or her grandparents. It was as if his daughter had pushed away all the bad memories of the past. He only hoped they wouldn't come out to haunt her when she least expected it.

"I'll give to Julie," Lexi said, picking up the drawing and heading toward the patio doors. When Lexi disappeared inside, he scrubbed his hands over his face.

Lexi hadn't mentioned seeing the two of them kissing, but then again, Lexi didn't have much use for conversation in general. He sincerely hoped his daughter hadn't noticed. The last thing he wanted to do was to hurt Lexi in any way. He took a deep breath and winced when his ribs protested.

The very idea that Julie might ask them to leave made him feel like a jerk. And for the first time in years, he offered up a silent prayer. *Please, Lord, give me the strength to do what is right for Julie and for Lexi.*

Surprisingly, he felt calmer after the prayer. Was it possible God was still listening to him? A soldier who'd sinned more times than he could count? Once, he'd believed in God's willingness to forgive, but he wasn't so sure that killing Afghani soldiers was something that God would condone. Not to mention the fact that he and Claire had created Lexi outside of the sanctity of marriage. So many sins. Too many sins.

But he could believe that Julie had God's protection, so maybe, just maybe, his prayer wouldn't fall on deaf ears.

Somehow, he had to find a way to keep his guard up around Julie. They could be friends, but nothing more. He headed toward the townhouse he was sharing with Lexi and picked up the crowbar again.

The best thing he could do for Julie was to repay her kindness—not by kissing the living daylights out of her, but by helping to finish up her construction project. So he climbed the small stepladder and ignored the stab of pain rippling across his chest as he began chipping away at the old drywall on the ceiling.

Julie deserved better than a jobless man on the run with his daughter, and the sooner he remembered that fact, the better.

―――――――

DEREK WORKED on the task of bringing down the rest of the drywall covering the ceiling until he was in so much pain he couldn't lift his arms anymore. He climbed down from the stepladder and propped the crowbar against one of the two-by-four studs, pressing a hand to his aching ribs. Assailed by a sudden wave of dizziness, he sank down to the floor and concentrated on not passing out cold.

He closed his eyes and tipped his head back against the two-by-four studs, taking one slow breath followed by another, willing the dizziness to recede. He knew very well he needed to pull himself together before Julie happened to show up to find him like this. She'd be disappointed again, maybe even angry enough to yell at him, rightfully so, although in a way, this was all her fault.

The hard work and subsequent pain had pushed thoughts of kissing her again right out of his mind.

A reluctant smile tugged at the corner of his mouth. Okay, maybe it was best not to mention that fact if she came looking for him.

After a few minutes, the room stopped spinning, and he opened his eyes, longing for a drink of ice-cold water or the sun tea Julie loved. But getting something to drink would require him to move, so he decided to stay right where he was for a little longer.

The throbbing of his ribs didn't ease much, telling him he'd overdone it big-time. But as he stared up at the ceiling, he was satisfied to realize he'd managed to get more than a quarter of the ceiling drywall down. Not too bad for a man who'd been in a car crash recently.

He estimated that he would have the rest of the drywall down by the Fourth of July, which would be perfect timing. He didn't dare stay in Hope County too long, even though it felt good to be doing something constructive rather than driving aimlessly, looking for a place that might be hiring.

He stared at the half-demolished kitchen and living room area and considered staying long enough to get the entire job finished. But as soon as the thought formed, he dismissed it.

For one thing, Julie might not have the money to purchase the necessary supplies. Drywall, cabinets, counters, and sinks had a way of adding up to a pretty penny. There were about five sheets of drywall propped in one corner, but that wouldn't be nearly enough to finish the open-concept room.

No, best that he complete as much of the work as possible before hitting the road with Lexi.

"Derek?"

Julie's voice came from outside, not from the patio but from the front yard.

"Coming," he called, forcing himself to move. Getting back on his feet was no easy task, and by the time he managed the feat, tiny beads of sweat were rolling down his temples.

For a long moment, he stood bracing himself against the wall, trying to gather the strength he'd need to face Julie without letting on how much pain he was in. She'd take it personally even though it was his own stupid fault for over-exerting himself.

"Derek? Come on, I want you to meet my brother, Zack," Julie called again, a note of impatience lacing her tone.

"I'm coming," he assured her. He used the hem of his T-shirt to swipe away the sweat and stepped carefully over the drywall debris littering the floor as he made his way across the room. He pasted a broad smile on his face in an attempt to hide his discomfort as he opened the front door.

"There you are," Julie exclaimed. She stood next to a tall man with medium-brown hair. "Derek, this is my brother, Zack Crain. Zack, this is Derek Ryerson, Lexi's father."

His greeting died in his throat when he stared in horror at the police car parked at the end of Julie's driveway. It took another second or two for his brain to register that Zack was dressed in uniform blue, complete with a shiny badge pinned to his chest and a gun nestled at his waist.

Why on earth hadn't Julie mentioned her brother was a cop?

8

Derek forced himself to approach Julie and her brother, ignoring the tight knot of anxiety twisting his gut. "Nice to meet you, Zack," he said, reluctantly holding out his hand. "Sorry about the dust and sweat."

Zack's gaze narrowed a bit, but he returned the greeting. "No problem. Good to meet you, too." The handshake was hard and brief.

Derek let his hand drop to his side and wondered how long it would take for Julie's brother to run a background check on him. Probably not long. Would he even wait to leave or run the check right now in his squad car?

His pulse jumped erratically, and he knew he should take Lexi and leave right away. But how? A rental car? Maybe he could afford a rental, at least until he got to a bus station. And then what?

Where would he go? What would he and Lexi do?

"Derek, are you all right?" Julie asked, pulling him from his panicked thoughts.

"Um, yeah. Sorry. What did you say?"

"I was telling Zack about the work you've been doing on the townhouse," she said. A hint of concern shadowed her eyes.

"Right. Actually, I just pulled more drywall off the ceiling, and it's a bit of a mess. Why don't you wait here while I clean things up?" He couldn't deny he was desperate to get away. Maybe he could convince Julie's brother that he was harmless. And then maybe, just maybe, her brother the cop wouldn't run a background check only to find Claire's parents had filed for custody.

But the shred of hope wasn't reassuring. Not when he knew that, if the situation were reversed, he'd be doing a background check on a stranger who was sharing a townhouse with his sister.

He turned and walked back inside, letting the screen door slam shut behind him, trying to act natural as he began sweeping up the debris littering the floor. When Julie, Zack, and Lexi came inside, he stopped and leaned on the broom, trying to look casual when in fact he feared his legs might buckle beneath him. "What do you think?" he asked, striving for a normal tone.

"Wow, looks great," Julie said in awe. Then she frowned. "Your ribs must be killing you. It can't be easy working on the ceiling."

He shrugged. "The results are worth it."

Zack stared at him, his gaze faintly accusatory. "How long are you planning to stay?"

"Until after the holiday," Derek murmured. "Hopefully by then, my car will be replaced and I'll be able to hit the road again."

"What? No. Knock it off, Zack," Julie said in a stern tone. "I'm thrilled to have Derek and Lexi here. And I told you, we have a mutually beneficial arrangement. He and Lexi get food and a roof over their heads, and in return, I get work done on the townhouse. It's a win-win for both of us."

"Yeah, that's what I'm afraid of," Zack muttered darkly.

Derek tried to control a flash of anger on Julie's behalf. "I don't like what you're insinuating," he said in a clipped tone. "Julie has been nothing but kind. Lexi and I are very grateful for her willingness to give us food and shelter. It's not my intent to take advantage of your sister. She's perfectly safe."

Lexi must have noticed some of the tension in the room because she came over to stand close to his side. He put a reassuring arm around his daughter, hugging her close.

Surprisingly, a spasm of pain flashed across Zack's features, and he rather abruptly turned away.

"Are you planning to stay for dinner, Zack?" Julie asked in an obvious effort to change the subject.

"No, I have to get back. Thanks anyway." Zack walked back outside and settled his police hat back on his head.

Derek's shoulders slumped with relief at the news her brother wasn't planning on staying, but that didn't change the fact that he needed to figure out a way to get out of town. And soon.

Before his luck ran out.

———

JULIE FOLLOWED her brother back to his squad car. "Zack, please consider staying for dinner," she murmured. "Derek is really a nice guy."

Zack shook his head, avoiding her gaze. "I can't. The way he looks with his daughter..." He sighed and scrubbed his hands over his face. "I just can't."

She knew how difficult losing Amelia had been for Zack. No parent should have to lose both his spouse and his daughter within a two-year timeframe. She wanted to help ease his pain, tried to convince him to hand his burdens over to God, but Zack refused.

Her brother hadn't stepped foot in a church since losing Emma and Amelia. Her heart ached for him. They'd grown closer over the years since losing their parents.

"Goodbye, Julie," Zack said as he slid into the driver's seat.

She forced a smile. "Bye, Zack. Stop by again soon."

He gave a terse nod as he twisted the key, bringing the engine to life. But he didn't back out of the driveway right away. Instead, he lowered the passenger window. "Are you sure you can trust this guy?"

"Absolutely," she said, as if she hadn't had the exact same fears just yesterday. But that was before the kiss. Interesting, because a normal woman might be more worried about her safety after a heated kiss.

Except she wanted to kiss him again.

She inwardly shook her head at her foolishness.

Zack grimaced and lifted his hand in a wave as he rolled backward out of the driveway. She stood on the lawn, shielding her eyes from the sun, her heart heavy and aching as she watched him drive away.

She felt something soft brush against her side and glanced down in surprise to see Lexi standing close, they way she usually stood next to her father. It was as if the little girl knew Julie was feeling sad again and wanted to offer comfort.

Her throat tightened with unshed tears, so she simply gave Lexi a hug. But when she glanced up, she noticed Derek was watching them with a frown.

She immediately released the little girl and stepped back, feeling as if she'd crossed a line. Why didn't Derek want her to be close to Lexi? Because they were leaving soon? Probably. She pulled herself together with an effort. "I better start dinner," she said in a low voice.

Derek didn't say anything as she went over to her side of the townhouse, closing the door firmly behind her.

She leaned weakly against the door, blinking back ridiculous tears. Why did she allow herself to get so emotionally involved? You would think she'd have learned her lesson with Andrew. She knew better than anyone how care and compassion did not lead to love.

Besides, she knew Derek and his daughter were only here for a brief stay. His unexpected kiss hadn't meant anything, except maybe to thank her.

After Andrew's betrayal, she'd refused to date. Well, to be fair, there hadn't been many available men to date. And she was afraid of making the same mistakes all over again.

Was she really willing to risk opening her heart to a man who'd made it clear he was just passing through?

No, she wasn't. With renewed strength and determination, she pushed away from the door and headed toward the fridge, where she'd stored the groceries she'd purchased that morning. She pulled out the chicken and searched for her skewer so she could make rotisserie chicken on the grill. Once the chicken was roasting away, she headed outside to her small garden to pick fresh lettuce, tomatoes, and cucumbers for the salad.

Puttering in her garden helped her to relax. Once she was sure she'd regained her composure, she went over to Derek and Lexi's side of the townhouse to see what they were up to and to let them know what time to expect dinner.

Her jaw dropped in surprise when she discovered Derek

was standing next to his packed suitcases while Lexi was rocking back and forth in the corner. "Where are you going?"

The flash of guilt in his eyes confirmed her worst fears. "Isn't it obvious? Your brother is worried about you, and I really don't blame him. I think it's best for everyone if Lexi and I move on."

"Why? How? You don't even have a car!"

"I know I've already imposed enough, but would you mind dropping us off at Billy's? Harold said he'd rent me a car cheap if needed. If you don't want to drive us, that's fine. We can walk. It's not that far."

"Don't go," she pleaded. "Not yet. Not until you're feeling better." Her earlier pep talk vanished in a puff of smoke now that she was faced with the reality of Derek's intent to leave. "Please?"

He hesitated, looking more worn out than ever before. "It's really best if we go."

It took all her willpower not to point out that leaving wasn't best for Lexi. The girl was rocking back and forth, staring at the floor, obviously upset. She wanted to go over and cuddle the girl close.

Was Lexi the reason Derek was so set on leaving? Because she was bonding too much with his daughter? She couldn't blame him for wanting to protect Lexi.

"If you really want to leave, it's best to wait until the morning. That way you'll have a whole day to travel, rather than just a few hours." Did she sound as desperate as she felt? Somehow she couldn't manage to drum up the energy to care. "And it's one less night you'll have to pay for a hotel room. Not to mention, I've already started dinner."

Derek stood indecisively, a deep frown furrowed in his brow as he rubbed a hand over his ribs. She imagined the pain was much worse now, considering the amount of work he'd done on the ceiling of her townhouse.

"Lexi, do you like chicken?" she asked. "Chicken roasted on the grill is one of my favorites. Dinner should be ready in less than a half hour."

"All right," Derek muttered with a sigh. "We'll stay one more night."

She felt relieved even though she knew the morning would be here soon enough. "Great. Do you need help putting the suitcases away?"

"No, but thanks," he said with a weary smile.

Since she still had the urge to comfort Lexi, she forced herself to turn around and leave. Derek had made his feelings known, leaving her little choice but to honor his wishes.

As she cleaned the vegetables from her garden, she couldn't help trying to think of a way to make Derek change his mind about leaving in the morning.

———————

DEREK ROLLED the suitcases back to the bedroom he shared with Lexi, wincing at how sore his muscles were. He hadn't felt this bad since waking up in the emergency department of Hope County Hospital.

And he'd hurt Julie's feelings too, but it couldn't be helped. Staying one more night wasn't smart, even if her logic made sense. Lexi's constant rocking was what had convinced him in the end. He couldn't bear to drag his daughter out of the townhouse kicking and screaming.

Hopefully Lexi would be better by tomorrow morning,

or he might not have a choice. Right now, he imagined Julie's cop brother was already running a check on him. Normally, he wouldn't be worried—after all, he didn't have a criminal record.

But Claire's parents were rather irrational in their quest for custody. They truly believed he was incapable of raising his own daughter. They'd demanded he hand Lexi over, and when he'd refused, things had turned ugly.

Threats, outrageous accusations—he'd been shocked at how bitterly angry they'd been.

He sank down on the edge of his bed and debated taking a pain pill. Working on the ceiling after finishing the walls had obviously been incredibly stupid. A hint of a smile tugged at his mouth as he remembered Julie calling him a stubborn ox.

Yeah, okay, so maybe he was a stubborn ox. Right now he was a hurting stubborn ox. But the last thing he wanted was for Julie to know how horrible he felt. She'd feel obligated to take him back to the hospital when all he really needed was a little rest. Or maybe a lot of rest.

Surely he could hang on long enough to eat dinner?

Of course he could. Soldiers could do anything.

"Daddy?" Lexi's fearful voice snapped him back into focus.

"Hey, baby-doll, what's up? Are you finished with your drawing?"

Lexi stared at him as if to ask who he was kidding. She'd been rocking since he'd explained how they needed to leave. Granted, he knew she might be sad to go, but he'd seriously underestimated her reaction.

For a moment, he doubted his ability to be a good father to Lexi. Maybe Claire's parents were right? Maybe she'd do better in the long run with more structure?

Maybe he was the idiot for thinking he knew what was best for Lexi?

"Hurts?" his daughter asked, coming close enough to put her tiny hand on his chest. He stared down at her for a long minute, choked up by her concern.

"Not too bad," he murmured. He reached up and tucked a glossy strand of hair behind her ear. "Are you still mad at me?"

Lexi shrugged and shook her head. "I love you, Daddy."

Her soft words arrowed straight into his heart. It was as if she knew exactly what he needed to hear.

"I love you too, baby-doll," he managed, drawing her close and gently resting his cheek on her hair. And suddenly, he knew that it was more than just Lexi knowing what he needed to hear.

It was God guiding him on the path he was supposed to take.

Feeling stronger, he pressed a kiss on top of Lexi's head and then struggled back to his feet, barely able to suppress a low groan. No doubt about it, he was going to be in a lot of pain tonight.

He forced himself to straighten his spine to walk down the hall into the gutted kitchen and living room. He held the patio door open for Lexi before following her outside to the patio.

Julie closed the hood of the grill and turned toward them. "I think I must have set the gas too high, because the chicken is just about done."

"I'm ready to eat whenever you are," he said as he lowered himself carefully into a chair. As much as he knew he should help Julie bring out the plates and silverware, he was afraid he'd only embarrass himself by falling flat on his face. "Lexi, would you please help Julie set the table?"

Lexi smiled and ran over to Julie. Soon they had the table set, complete with small salads.

Julie struggled a little with the roasted chicken, and he pushed himself up to help her. As they wrestled with the bird, Julie began to giggle. "This is why I don't do this more often," she said. "Too much work."

He carried the plate of roasted chicken out to the patio table. They all took their seats, but this time he decided to lead the prayer.

"Dear Lord, thank You for this wonderful food we're about to eat, and thank You for bringing Julie into our lives. Amen."

There was a half-second pause before Julie echoed, "Amen."

The food was delicious, but he must not have hidden the extent of his pain very well, because the moment they were finished, Julie jumped up. "Stay put, Derek. I'm going to get you some ibuprofen."

"Thanks." Maybe with the ibuprofen and the pain meds, he'd get some rest.

"Here you go," Julie said, dropping four tablets into the palm of his hand. The brush of her fingertips was so gentle he had the insane urge to kiss her again.

Bad idea, buddy, he told himself sternly. Really bad idea.

Lexi didn't have to be told to help Julie clear the table; she seemed actually eager for the task. Sitting and letting others do the work wasn't easy, but he stayed where he was, closing his eyes and hoping the ibuprofen would start to work.

Soon.

"Derek, why don't you go lie down?" Julie said. "You don't look comfortable sitting upright with your head tilted over to the side."

He grimaced and rubbed the crick in his neck. "It's too early for Lexi to go to bed."

"I know you don't want her to get too close to me," Julie said in a low voice, "but I thought we could light some sparklers tonight. I was saving them for the holiday, but if you're leaving in the morning, there's no point in waiting." Her sad smile made him feel even worse. "Get some rest, Derek. I'll bring Lexi in soon."

"Okay." He gritted his teeth and pushed himself upright. Julie slid her arm around his waist and helped keep him steady as he made his way inside.

"Take another pain pill," she ordered.

He was too sore to argue. "Thanks again," he murmured as he stretched out on the bed. Within minutes, he was sound asleep.

JULIE LIT SPARKLERS WITH LEXI, enjoying the way the little girl made sparkly circles by waving her arms. As they enjoyed the pre-holiday celebration, she tried not to dwell on the fact that Derek and Lexi were leaving in the morning.

Hearing Derek give the before-dinner prayer had been bittersweet. His gratitude had warmed her heart, even though she knew he was really just saying goodbye.

When Lexi began yawning, she put the sparklers away and gathered up the burnt sticks, making sure there weren't any glowing embers left over that might start a fire. The year before, they'd had a terrible drought, and the sheriff had put a ban on all fireworks, including sparklers. But this year had seen more snow and rain, allowing the citizens of Crystal

Lake to celebrate the Fourth of July holiday with all the usual fun and flair.

"Time for bed, Lexi," she said.

Surprisingly, the little girl didn't put up much of a fuss. Julie slid open the patio door so Lexi could step in.

The interior was dark, since there weren't any lights in the kitchen or living area. Julie felt along the wall to find the light switch.

"Brush your teeth and go to the bathroom, okay, Lexi?" she whispered.

"Okay." Lexi disappeared into the bathroom.

Julie leaned against the wall but then straightened when she heard a low groan. Derek? She walked farther down the hall until she reached the bedroom.

The door was ajar, and when she peeked in, she saw Derek writhing on the bed in pain, his hand on his chest as he fought against what looked to be a terrible muscle spasm.

9

Julie couldn't ignore his pain, so she pushed the door open and hurried into the room. "Easy now," she murmured, placing her hands on his chest and pressing down on the muscles. "Let me try to help."

Derek let out another low groan, and she knew that even though deep massage was the best way to ease the muscle spasm, it was also painful.

"I'm sorry," she whispered even as she continued pressing on his chest. His muscles felt rock hard beneath the palms of her hands, and she felt awful knowing she was hurting him. "Can you turn onto your side?"

He turned over so that his back was facing her, and she continued to massage the tense muscles for him. Lexi came up to stand beside her, looking anxiously at her father. Julie tried to flash a reassuring smile. "Your daddy will be fine in a few minutes. How about if you crawl into bed, okay, sweetie?"

Lexi didn't say much but did as Julie suggested. She knew Derek must be hurting very badly since he hadn't tried to reassure his daughter the way he had in the emergency room.

She ignored the straining in her arms and shoulders as she continued her massage. The minutes slipped endlessly by until she felt the muscles in Derek's body begin to loosen up. But still, she didn't stop, for fear the muscles might tighten up again.

Another fifteen minutes later, Derek's breathing evened out, telling her the worst was over. The muscles beneath her fingers were finally relaxed and supple. "You're amazing," he murmured.

A reluctant smile tugged at her mouth. "Hardly. I'm a nurse, remember?"

"And an excellent one, at that. Thanks, Julie," Derek said in a low voice. He rolled onto his back, gently taking her hands in his, giving them a quick squeeze. "I'm feeling much better now."

When he let go, she stepped back, gently flexing her own wrists and elbows. "Are you sure?"

"Yes." As if to prove his point, he rolled upright so that he was sitting on the edge of the bed. He gingerly ran his hand down his chest. "I was an idiot. You have every right to say 'I told you so,'" he muttered.

She let out a heavy sigh. "There's no point. You obviously figured that out the hard way."

"Yeah, that's true. Is Lexi okay?"

"Looks like she's asleep," she said, taking a step back so that he could see his daughter. "Do you want another pain pill before I go?"

"It's too soon. Besides, I'll be fine."

His evasive tone made her wonder if he even had any pain medicine left. But it was too late to go out now, especially on a Sunday. "We'll get your prescription filled tomorrow."

He grimaced and avoided her gaze. "I'll be fine," he repeated. "Goodnight, Julie. Thanks again for making me feel better."

She wanted to try and convince him not to leave in the morning, but it was getting late, and she didn't want to disturb Lexi's sleep, so she let it go. "Goodnight, Derek."

Julie tiptoed out of the room and gently closed the door behind her. She walked through the gutted kitchen and living area, thinking about how Derek had overworked himself earlier that afternoon. The night air was cool as she went outside. The quiet night soothed her soul, and she stopped for a moment and tipped her head back to gaze up at the stars.

Please, Lord, show Derek the path You want him to take. Amen.

———————

DEREK WOKE up to bright sunlight streaming in through the window, betraying the fact he'd overslept. For a moment, he was almost afraid to move, but his stomach rumbled, reminding him he hadn't eaten much the night before. He gingerly tested his muscles, noting that he was still a bit stiff and sore, although nothing like the agonizing pain of last night. He glanced over to find his daughter, but Lexi was already up and gone. No doubt, she'd gone over to eat breakfast with Julie.

Julie. For a moment, he closed his eyes, remembering

how she'd helped him out last night, easing his pain. He was indebted to her again. Big-time.

And how was he going to make it up to her? By leaving.

A wave of regret washed over him. He didn't want to leave. Didn't want to go back to driving through towns filled with strangers.

But if he stayed, he risked being discovered, either by her brother, Zack, doing a background check on him, or by the Hope County deputy who was likely filing his accident report today.

With a heavy heart, he climbed out of bed and headed into the bathroom. He found the waterproof dressings and realized a hot shower would help him feel better. At least physically, if not emotionally.

The steamy water did wonders for his sore muscles, but his mind still whirled with indecision. He was no closer to a solution as he dressed and headed over to find Lexi and hopefully some breakfast.

He found his daughter crouching in the garden next to Julie, listening intently as Julie showed her how to pull weeds. He blinked to make sure he wasn't hallucinating, but no, his daughter was actually doing something besides drawing and playing video games.

Because of Julie—not because of him.

The kernel of self-doubt he'd experienced the day before abruptly grew to astronomical proportions. Was he really doing the right thing for Lexi? Maybe he wasn't cut out to be a single father.

"Daddy!" Lexi caught sight of him and came over to wrap her arms around his waist. Her fingers were coated with dirt, but he didn't care as he hugged her back. "Better?" she asked, tipping her head back to look up at him.

"Much better, baby-doll. It's nice of you to help Julie with her garden."

"Tomatoes," Lexi said with a gleam in her eye. "I like tomatoes."

"They're my favorite, too," Julie said, swiping her hands down the sides of her jeans. Her smile didn't quite meet her eyes. "You're looking better, Derek. Are you hungry? We had French toast this morning."

"I am hungry, but you don't have to wait on me," he said in a rush. "I can make my own breakfast."

"I don't mind. Just give me a minute to wash up. Lexi? Come with me. You need to wash your hands, too."

Lexi gave a nod and skipped next to Julie as they went inside. He let out his breath in a heavy sigh and followed more slowly. He sank down into the closest kitchen chair and held his head in his hands.

Help me, Lord. Guide me. Show me the way.

"Derek? Are you all right?" Julie asked, putting her hand on his shoulder. He had to stop himself from taking her hand in his and pulling her close.

"Fine," he said gruffly. "Where's Lexi?"

"She went outside to draw." Her brow was pulled into a frown. "You don't look fine, Derek. You look like you're still in pain."

He was, but not the kind of pain she was talking about. "Really, I'm fine."

"I'll get you more ibuprofen, but you shouldn't take it on an empty stomach." Julie took her hand away and went back over to where she had the ingredients assembled for breakfast. "This won't take long."

"I'm not leaving." The words popped out of his mouth before he even realized he was going to say them.

She froze, looking a little ridiculous with the spatula hanging in mid-air. "You're not?"

A smile tugged at the corner of his mouth. "No, I'm not. Unless you want me to."

"I...no." For a moment, she gaped at him. "Why would you think I wanted you to leave?"

He didn't know why he had the insane urge to confide in Julie. He forced himself to hold back the instinct. "I thought maybe your brother might have talked you into it."

"No, of course not." She flipped the egg-coated bread on the sizzling grill. "We lost our parents several years ago, and Zack tends to be a bit on the overprotective side. But he's been more withdrawn and abrupt these days, ever since he lost his daughter to leukemia eighteen months ago."

His chest tightened with sympathy. He couldn't imagine losing Lexi to some horrible cancer. And now that he knew, he could understand why her brother had wanted to get far away yesterday. "That's tough. I can't say that I blame him."

"Yes, it's been difficult." Julie stared at the French toast, but he sensed she was really looking back into the past. "Amelia was a beautiful little girl. Constantly talking, constantly moving. Until she got sick..." Her voice trailed off.

He pushed to his feet. "I'm sorry, Julie. Why don't I take over here? You should sit down for a while."

"No, it's all right." Her smile was pathetic, but he gave her points for trying. "When I first saw Lexi, she reminded me a little of Amelia, but they're really very different."

He straightened, ready to come to Lexi's defense. But he needn't have worried.

"Lexi is so quiet and so talented. She's the complete opposite of Amelia. Every time Lexi draws another picture for me, I'm flabbergasted at how good she really is. You might want to consider getting her into an art program."

"I have thought about it," he agreed. Too bad art programs were expensive and he was currently unemployed. But he was determined not to be unemployed forever. And he ignored the tiny voice in his head telling him Claire's parents would be able to afford an art program. They believed that super-strict private school was best for Lexi. There was no way they'd even consider paying for an art program.

"Sit down, Derek, these will be ready shortly."

He reluctantly returned to the table, yet despite the seriousness of the conversation and his conflicting thoughts, he felt lighter, less apprehensive than he had when he'd first woken up.

Because he'd agreed to stay. A decision he'd made for himself as much as for his daughter.

JULIE WAS SECRETLY THRILLED Derek wasn't leaving, but she tried to hold her emotions in check. After all, he'd leave eventually.

Unless, of course, he found a reason to stay?

Ridiculous to allow her thoughts to wander down that path. She sensed Derek didn't have a lot of money, and the way he'd asked about any manufacturing jobs made her more convinced that he needed work of some sort.

He was doing a great job on her townhouse, but after he'd overexerted himself yesterday, she didn't want him anywhere near a crowbar or a hammer. If he would just give himself time to heal, they could probably come to some sort of arrangement.

So what was his hurry?

She had no idea. Unless he was walking the edge financially, which was a distinct possibility. At least his appetite had returned.

"I have to work a four-hour shift this afternoon," she said, crossing over to join him at the table. "Apparently, one of the nurses called in sick, so they've asked me to cover from three to seven-thirty."

"No problem," Derek said. "Lexi and I will be fine."

"Why don't we stop by and pick up your accident report?" she offered. "That way you can get your insurance company focused on getting your settlement ready."

Derek stared down at his plate for a moment, and she wondered if he resented the fact that she was poking her nose into his business. But really, it was silly of him to rent some car when the insurance company needed to pay him for the wrecked vehicle.

Unless he hadn't been telling the truth about having insurance?

"All right," Derek agreed.

She was surprised but pleased. "Great. We'll head out as soon as I'm finished."

"No, we'll head out as soon as I finish the dishes," he corrected. "You cooked, so it's my job to clean up."

She was about to protest but then realized that Derek probably needed to feel as if he were contributing at least in some way. And since working on the townhouse wasn't an option, doing the dishes was a dismal second. "All right, I'll see what Lexi is up to."

Lexi was drawing another picture of the lake, only this time, she focused more on the boats and skiers rather than on the trees and water. Julie sat down next to her. "Who taught you how to draw, Lexi?"

"Mommy," Lexi responded absently, barely looking up from her picture.

This was the first time Lexi had mentioned her mother, and Julie sensed she should tread lightly. "That's wonderful," she murmured.

"I miss my Mommy," Lexi said plaintively.

She didn't want to assume that Lexi's mother died, so she wrapped her arm around the little girl's shoulders in a soft hug. "What happened, sweetie?"

"My mommy died." Lexi abruptly dropped her pencil and turned to bury her face against her breast.

"Oh, sweetie, I'm sorry," she murmured, her heart aching for the child. "But I'm sure your mommy is up in heaven with God."

Lexi lifted her head, her tiny face intense as she absorbed the idea. "You mean like an angel?"

She nodded. "Yes, exactly like an angel. Every time you miss her, you should just close your eyes and talk to her. I'm sure she's an angel up in heaven listening to you."

"Really?" Lexi's voice held a hint of hope mixed with doubt.

"I promise," she murmured, tears welling in her eyes as she glanced over to see Derek hovering in the doorway. Would he be upset that she'd talked to Lexi about heaven and God? She hoped not.

"Julie is right, Lexi," he said as he walked outside. "Your mommy is up in heaven with God."

The little girl smiled and released Julie in favor of her father. Derek scooped her up and held her close as Julie discreetly swiped at her damp eyes.

"Are you ready to go?" Derek asked after he set Lexi back down.

"Sure." It was almost as if Derek wanted to get the

errand over with. Not that she could blame him. Maybe he thought that the sooner he put his insurance company on notice, the sooner he could get a replacement vehicle.

And the sooner he could leave, taking Lexi far away.

The ride to the sheriff's department took about fifteen minutes, and as she drove into the parking lot, Derek's expression grew grim, and she half-expected him to ask her to turn around.

They climbed out of the car and into the hot, humid air. The sun reflected off the blacktop parking lot as they made their way toward the building. The interior of the building was much cooler in comparison, the blast of air-conditioning causing her to feel chilled.

"Hi, Grace, how are you?" she greeted the older woman who sat behind the dispatch desk.

"Hanging in there," Grace responded with a grimace. She was a large woman, her dark hair liberally streaked with gray. "Stay back, Julie, I might have a touch of the flu. I've been feeling sick to my stomach, and my back's been hurting too. Gotta tell you, getting old sure ain't fun."

Now that Grace mentioned being in pain, Julie noticed that her skin was ashen with tiny brackets of pain lining her mouth. "Maybe you should have called in sick today," Julie suggested with a frown. "You look like you could use some rest."

"Carol had her baby last night," Grace said with a heavy sigh. "Leaves us only four dispatchers for a while, and we've gotta cover all three shifts. But that's enough about me. What can I do for you?"

She still didn't think Grace looked so good, but she introduced Derek. "Derek needs a copy of his accident report from Friday evening, so that he can get in touch with his insurance company."

"Oh yeah, heard all about that from Deputy Thomas, especially after he arrested that no-good Tommy Hinkle," Grace said. She struggled to her feet and then braced herself against the desk, as if she couldn't get her breath.

Something was definitely wrong. Julie hurried around through the open doorway to Grace. The woman was sweating profusely, and her skin had gone slate gray.

"Sit down, Grace." She glanced back at Derek. "She needs an ambulance. We need to call 911, but Grace is the one who usually takes those emergency calls." It was crazy to think that she couldn't get help for the dispatcher.

Derek had followed her inside the dispatch office. "I know how to use the radio," he said as he took over the controls.

"Grace, try to take slow, deep breaths," Julie said, suspecting the dispatcher was having a heart attack right before her eyes. "Do you have a baby aspirin in your purse?"

"No," Grace answered weakly.

She bit her lip and listened as Derek confidently put out the 911 call, praying help would arrive soon.

But then Grace slumped in her seat, and she knew there wasn't a moment to waste. "Help me get her to the floor," she said to Derek. "I need to start CPR."

10

As an ER nurse, this wasn't the first time she'd had to perform CPR, but providing life-saving measures in the middle of the dispatch office was much different than being in the emergency room where they had equipment readily available. What she wouldn't give for an oxygen tank, ambu mask, and meds.

"I can help," Derek murmured, kneeling on the opposite side of Grace's prone figure. He gently tipped her head back so he could provide rescue breaths as needed.

Julie was extremely grateful for Derek's support. She spared Lexi a quick glance, noting the little girl was off to the side, watching them with wide blue eyes. Julie's heart went out to the child, but she couldn't allow herself to be distracted.

"One and two and three and," she counted out loud for Derek's benefit. They worked in tandem through two rounds of CPR before Derek insisted they switch places.

Shortly after the switch, two Deputies came rushing in. "What happened to Grace?" Deputy Matson demanded.

"Heart attack. Where's the ambulance?" Julie asked. She recognized both deputies from working in the ER.

"On the way," Deputy Armbruster said. He swept his gaze around the interior of the office. "Poor Grace. We must have overworked her, and it's even worse now that Carol delivered her baby."

"Yeah," Deputy Matson agreed. "But we need to find someone to take her place, and quick." Even as he spoke, he leaned over to take a call.

"Derek knows how," she said before leaning down to give two rescue breaths.

"Really?" Deputy Armbruster asked hopefully.

Derek appeared to be concentrating on nothing more than doing good chest compressions. And doing an excellent job, based on the strength of Grace's pulse.

Please, take care of Grace, Lord!

The wailing sounds of the ambulance made her weak with relief. Within moments, the paramedics were inside the building, coming over with a gurney, heart monitor, and supplies. She'd never been so thankful for medical supplies.

Derek continued chest compressions, and Julie gave another two breaths before looking up at the paramedics. "I suspect she's having an acute myocardial infarction."

"What were her symptoms?" The first paramedic wore a nametag that said Sam. He nudged Derek aside in order to place large patches on Grace's chest. Within seconds, he had her hooked up to the portable cardiac monitor.

"Pale, sweating, complaints of back pain and nausea," she said as she watched Grace's heart rhythm. "She's in v-fib."

"All clear! Shocking at 200 joules," Sam said as he pushed the button on the machine.

She watched Sam give two more shocks, and then

suddenly, Grace's heart rhythm changed into what looked to be a normal sinus rhythm with depressed ST segments. Julie leaned forward to feel for a pulse. She felt a rush of relief when she found the thready beat. "We have a pulse."

"Let's give more oxygen and nitro so that we can get her packed up to roll," Sam said to the other paramedic. "We need to get to the hospital before we lose her again."

Julie rose to her feet and backed away, knowing there wasn't anything more she could do. She glanced over to find Derek hugging Lexi and wondered if seeing Grace had reminded the little girl about losing her mother.

She sent off another prayer for Grace, hoping the dispatcher would be all right. Now that the adrenalin rush was over, she felt shaky and weak.

After the paramedics left, there was a weird silence in the dispatch area as if no one knew what to say next. "Thanks for your help," Deputy Armbruster finally said. "I'm thankful you were both here for Grace. Your quick thinking made all the difference."

"Glad we could help," Derek murmured.

Julie tried to smile. "Derek saved the day. I wasn't sure how we were going to call for help, but he jumped right in."

The deputy nodded and then cleared his throat. "Were you serious about knowing how to do dispatch?"

Derek shrugged and nodded, still keeping his arm around Lexi. "Yeah, I learned in the Army."

"Would you consider a temporary job for the summer?" Armbruster asked. "Obviously, we could use some help around here. With both Grace and Carol on medical leave, we're really strapped for help. I can put in a good word with Sheriff Torretti once you fill out an application."

Julie held her breath, waiting for Derek's reply.

"I'd very much like a job, even a temporary one," Derek said. "If you're serious about hiring me."

She closed her eyes with relief. *Thank You, Lord!*

———————

DEREK KNEW he was crazy to even consider taking a job with the Hope County Sheriff's Department. The risk was too high. But the lure of paid employment was too much to ignore. Since no one had come to arrest him, he had to assume his background check had been fine. Claire's parents must not have sent the police after him, despite his fears. Or maybe hiring a private investigator was more their style, especially since he was Lexi's legal guardian.

For now.

He couldn't help thinking that this potential job was a sign from God. He'd considered settling down somewhere to establish himself as part of a community, so why not here in Crystal Lake? Wiping his damp palms on the sides of his jeans, he sat down in front of the computer.

"I'll pick up your police report while we're waiting," Julie said, her eyes bright with excitement. She took Lexi by the hand and went over to talk with Deputy Armbruster.

Calling himself all kinds of a fool for taking the risk, he began filling out the online application form. His longest work experience was the eight years in the Army, but he also put in the technical college degree and the construction work he'd done prior to that.

When it came to references, he stared blankly at the screen. Claire's parents were out of the question. After a long moment, he put in his CO's name and number, along with Jake Strawn, his Chicago buddy's name and number. Lastly, he put in Julie's name and then felt foolish when he realized he didn't have her number.

When he was finished, he pushed the send button and stood up. He glanced over to the two deputies. "I put in my cell number, and I'm staying in Julie Crain's rehabbed townhouse if you need to get in touch with me."

"Sounds good. Thanks again," Deputy Armstrong said, offering his hand.

It was surreal to shake the deputy's hand before walking outside to meet Julie and Lexi.

"Julie said we can get ice cream," Lexi announced. "Can I have chocolate, Daddy?"

"Ice cream, huh?" he asked, sending Julie a wry smile.

"Well, why not? We're celebrating, aren't we?" Julie asked cheerfully. "I called into the ER, and Grace has been taken straight to the cardiac cath lab. They told me she was critical but stable, and her chances look fairly good at this point. And you have a new job. Two very good reasons to celebrate."

"I haven't been offered the job yet," he reminded her. Although it surprised him how keenly he wanted it. He grinned at Lexi. "Yes, Lexi, chocolate ice cream sounds good to me, too."

They left Julie's car in the small parking lot and walked down the couple of blocks to Main Street. The summer sun was hot but not nearly as bad as what they'd suffered in Afghanistan. For a moment, he imagined himself back there, holding on to his rifle with a tight, sweaty grip as he stayed alert, searching for signs of Afghani soldiers. He shook his head to dislodge the painful memory and forced himself to glance around curiously. There were lots of cars and people crowding the street, which wasn't surprising since he'd been unable to find a hotel with a vacancy over the holiday weekend. Still, being surrounded by families made him acutely aware of the way he, Julie, and Lexi fit right in.

Don't go there, he warned himself. They were not a family. It would do well to remember Julie was being a friend to him, nothing more.

The ice cream parlor was packed, so they patiently waited their turn. They all three ended up with chocolate ice cream, but when Julie pulled out her purse, he stopped her with a hand on her arm. "I've got it."

When she looked as if she were about to protest, he narrowed his gaze, shook his head, and fished out his wallet. After he paid for the cones, they strolled back outside.

"There's a Fourth of July parade here tomorrow morning," Julie said. "I have to work a twelve-hour shift, but you and Lexi should come and watch."

"Would you like that, Lexi?" he asked, glancing down at his daughter's chocolate-smeared face.

She nodded vigorously, too preoccupied with her ice cream to say anything.

"If you want to borrow my car, you can drop me off at work in the morning," Julie continued. "Although I should warn you I need to be at the hospital by seven a.m."

"Not a problem," he murmured. He glanced around, wondering if this was real or little more than an incredible dream. He'd been on edge ever since leaving St. Louis, to the point he'd been unable to relax. Being here now, walking down Main Street with Julie and Lexi, he felt comfortable and at ease.

He told himself that he was taking the risk of staying here for Lexi's sake. Because his daughter seemed to be happy. And he couldn't bear the thought of hauling Lexi out of Julie's townhouse against her will.

But deep down, he suspected he was really staying for himself. As much as he liked the town of Crystal Lake, he liked Julie Crain even more.

———————

JULIE KNEW they were attracting some attention from the locals as they made their way through town but couldn't bring herself to care. Derek was staying. He and Lexi were staying!

She knew Derek would be offered a job with the sheriff's department and hoped and prayed he'd accept. Things were working out perfectly. It was almost as if coming in last night to find Derek's packed suitcases hadn't happened.

"Are you ready to head back?" she asked Derek as the crowds of people became suffocating. She understood the town depended on tourism to survive, but she preferred the quiet days when there weren't so many strangers around.

"Sure," Derek agreed.

She had some time yet before she had to go into work, and she found herself wishing she hadn't agreed to help out. At least she was only filling in for four hours, and the extra money would come in handy. Especially once Derek was ready to begin putting up new drywall.

The thought pulled her up short. There was no guarantee that Derek would stay with her once he was offered a dispatch job with the sheriff's department. He might insist on moving somewhere else. Although surely he'd still need her help to watch Lexi while he was working, wouldn't he? Her mind spun with the logistics.

Obviously, they needed to talk once the job offer came through, but for now, she decided to take each day one at a time.

When they arrived back at the townhouse, Lexi wanted to go back out on the boat.

Julie glanced at the clock. "Sure, we can go out for an hour or so before I have to leave for work."

"Yay!"

Julie smiled, glad to see Lexi jump from one foot to another with excitement. The shy little girl who'd come from the accident scene was slowly fading away.

"Okay, let's get your swimming suit," Derek said, taking Lexi by the hand.

"Don't forget your waterproof dressings," Julie added.

"I won't."

Within fifteen minutes, they were down on Zack's boat. Julie held out the keys for Derek. "Do you want to drive?"

"Sure." His eyes gleamed with anticipation, which made her laugh as she took a seat toward the front of the boat.

Dozens of other boaters were on the lake as well, but Derek did a fine job of steering clear of everyone else. "I should have inflated the inner tube for Lexi," Julie said with a wry glance over her shoulder at Derek. "I have everything beneath the seat cushion but didn't even think to use the pump to inflate the inner tube."

"Next time," he said easily.

She sat back against the seat, thinking about how happy she was to know there would be a next time. She tipped her face into the sun and thought about how wonderful it was to be outside like this.

But all too soon, it was time to head into shore. She

changed into her scrubs and then left for work with Derek's promise to have dinner ready by the time she came home ringing through her ears. She couldn't help the broad smile that seemed permanently grooved into her cheeks as she entered the busy ER.

"What is up with you?" Merry greeted her with a smile. "It's been a long time since I've seen you so happy."

Julie knew Merry was referring to her sorrow over losing Amelia and her broken engagement. It wasn't as if she'd tried to wallow in the past, but watching her young niece pass away had been the hardest thing she'd ever done. Much harder than suffering through the gossip of Andrew's affair. She'd leaned on God and prayer, but for some reason, it had taken being with Derek and Lexi to pull her back to normal. "I am happy," she responded lightly. "Have you been busy here?"

"You could say that," Merry said with a sigh. "If you could take team one and the trauma bay, I'd appreciate it."

"Sure thing. Fill me in on the patients who are in team one."

Within minutes, she was swept away into the controlled chaos of the emergency department. Her cell phone rang, but she was busy admitting another patient, so she ignored it. When she had a break, she noticed the call was from her brother and made a mental note to call him back when her shift was over.

"How's Grace Banner doing?" she asked Merry when they crossed paths.

"She's doing great. She had two cardiac stents put in but thankfully didn't need open-heart surgery."

"I'm so glad to hear that," Julie murmured. "I was really afraid she wouldn't do well."

"Everyone around here has been saying that Grace is

alive today because of you," Merry informed her. "If you hadn't been at the sheriff's department to start CPR, it's likely she wouldn't have made it."

Since Grace had been alone in the dispatch center, Julie knew Merry was probably right. "Derek is the true hero," she said. "He used the radio to call for help, and his chest compressions were far better than mine."

Merry raised a brow. "Derek, huh? Would that be Mr. Derek Ryerson and his adorable daughter, Lexi?"

She blushed and nodded. "You know very well that's him."

Merry reached out to put a gentle hand on Julie's arm. "Jules, be careful, okay? I know he seems like a nice guy, but after everything you've been through in the past year, I don't think it's wise to jump into anything."

The memory of Derek's kiss warmed her cheeks. "Don't worry, I'm not jumping into anything. We're friends, that's all. And I'm hoping to bring him back to the church."

Merry's eyes were shadowed with worry. "While getting him to come back to his faith is great, just remember you felt the same way about Andrew, and look how that ended up."

"I know." Andrew had also come through the ER after a waterskiing accident, which had broken his left tibia and fibula. She'd reached out to him and offered her help, which he'd gratefully accepted. They'd grown close over the next few months, and he'd even proposed marriage, which had thrilled her. But then she'd discovered his old girlfriend had come to town and that Rebecca had stayed overnight at his place for the weekend. When she'd confronted Andrew, he'd told her it was her fault because she wouldn't sleep with him. And he made it clear that he was only going along with her ideas of faith and attending church because that was what she'd wanted.

News of Andrew's affair and their broken engagement had rippled through the town to the point she couldn't go anywhere without someone offering her sympathy. Only after Andrew and Rebecca had returned to Madison did the wagging tongues die down.

She pulled herself back from the painful memories. "I know, Merry, but it's different this time. Derek isn't Andrew."

"Maybe not, but he is new in town just like Andrew was. And really, what do you know about Derek on a personal level?"

Merry sounded just like her brother, Zack, which caused a rare flash of temper. "I know he's a stubborn, hard-working guy and a very good father. And I know he used to serve our country in the Army, too. Honestly, Merry, he's been nothing but polite and respectful."

"What about faith?" Merry persisted. "Don't make the same mistake you made with Andrew."

"Granted, Derek didn't attend church with me, but he participates in prayer, so I think there's hope." When Merry opened her mouth again, Julie held up her hand. "Don't, Merry. Derek and I are friends, nothing more. So leave it alone, okay?"

"Okay," Merry agreed with a sigh. Her pager went off, and she read the message with a grimace. "Looks like another ambulance is on the way in."

Julie returned to work, glancing frequently at the clock as the last hour of her shift passed by with excruciating slowness. When her co-worker came in to relieve her, she headed out to the parking lot, happy to be going home.

To see Derek. And of course, Lexi.

True to his word, Derek had brats and hotdogs ready for

the grill when she arrived. "Smells delicious," she said as she stepped out on the patio.

"It's nothing fancy," Derek said. "Although I did make potato salad, too."

"Wow, a man who can cook," she said lightly, Merry's concern echoing in her mind. Was she reading too much into Derek's kindness? Was it possible this was all just a big act he was putting on for her benefit?

"Sit down. I'll bring the food over in a minute," Derek said. The relaxed smile on his face only emphasized his handsome looks. If this really was an act, the guy deserved an Academy Award.

Derek brought the tray of food over and set it in the center of the table. When they were all seated, Julie bowed her head to pray. "Dear Lord, thank You so much for providing us this food we are about to eat. Also, please keep watching over Grace as she heals in the hospital, as she very much needs Your strength and support. Amen."

"And please watch over Grandma and Grandpa, too," Lexi added. "Amen."

Grandma and Grandpa? Julie raised her head. The stricken expression on Derek's face confirmed he'd lied to her that night in the hospital about how he and Lexi were alone.

She felt sick to her stomach as she wondered what else he'd lied about.

11

Derek swallowed hard as Julie went pale, her gaze full of reproach as she stared at him. He couldn't very well chide Lexi for including her grandparents in their evening prayer, because for one thing, Claire's parents needed prayers in a big way. And for another, this abrupt revelation wasn't Lexi's fault.

It was his.

"I'll explain later," he murmured, trying to reassure Julie with a half-hearted smile.

Julie frowned but thankfully didn't say anything in front of Lexi. And he mentally kicked himself over and over again when Julie did little more than pick at her food.

He should have confided in her before now. Before she'd grown close to Lexi. Before they'd become friends.

Before he'd kissed her.

His own appetite vanished along with Julie's, but he made an effort for Lexi's sake. But no matter how hard he tried, there was no way to ease the strained atmosphere.

When they'd finally finished, he pushed his chair away from the table. "Lexi, help me clear the dishes," he said.

"I'll do it," Julie said abruptly, jumping to her feet. He sensed she wanted to get away and wished he could think of a way to make her realize...what? That he was sorry he'd led her to believe that he and Lexi were all alone in the world? That he hadn't intended to mislead her at all? That all he wanted was to help Lexi get out of that strict private school and recover from the shock of losing her mother?

For a moment, he dropped his head into his hands, feeling almost as helpless as the night Claire's parents had informed him they were going to take him to court in an attempt to gain custody of Lexi. He'd been completely alone then.

But somehow, he felt even worse now. Because despite everything Julie had done for them, he'd let her down.

Guide me through this, Lord. Show me the way.

When he felt Lexi's soft hand on his arm, he pulled himself together. His daughter's expression was troubled, and he wished more than anything for her to be happy again. The way she'd been on the boat ride or swimming in the lake. "I love you, Lexi," he said softly.

"I love you, too, Daddy." Instantly, Lexi was crawling into his lap, and he held her tightly, almost afraid to let her go.

After several long moments, he kissed the top of Lexi's head and eased away. "Come on, baby-doll, we need to help carry these dishes in for Julie." Since Julie hadn't returned after escaping inside, he figured it was the least they could do.

"Okay." Lexi grabbed the ketchup bottle with both hands as he stacked the rest of the dirty plates and they both went inside.

The kitchen was empty when he set the dirty dishes on the counter. Should he try to find Julie? Or give her the privacy she deserved?

As he went back outside to pick up the last of the dishes and condiments, his chest tightened with panic. What if Julie planned to ask him and Lexi to leave? She had every right to kick them out if she wanted to.

How much would her sweet, Christian nature tolerate? He suspected he'd already pushed her past the breaking point.

His thoughts whirled as he cleaned up the after-dinner mess. Since Julie was still nowhere to be found, he decided he should wash the dishes, too.

It was the least he could do to make amends.

Sensing he'd intruded enough, he left the dishes to air dry and made his way outside onto the patio. The sun was low on the horizon, and he wished Julie were here to share in the wonder of the beautiful sunset over the lake.

And then he saw her, sitting on the grassy bank of the lakeshore, hugging her knees to her chest. She must have gone out the front door and slipped down to the lake without his noticing.

He needed to talk to her even though it was too early to send Lexi to bed. Thankfully, his daughter happened to be preoccupied with a video game. "Stay here, okay, Lexi?"

She gave him a tiny nod.

Derek took a deep breath and let it out slowly as he walked down to talk to Julie.

———

JULIE HEARD Derek's footsteps swishing against the grass and mentally braced herself as he dropped down beside her.

"I'm sorry," he said in his deep, soft voice.

She didn't turn to look at him. "Your personal life is none of my business," she said in a frosty tone.

There was a brief pause, but she kept her gaze focused on the setting sun. She wasn't in the mood to talk, and hopefully, Derek would get the message and leave her alone.

"You already know Lexi's mother died about four months ago," he said. "I was still in Afghanistan, trying to fight through the red tape to return stateside when Claire told me she was diagnosed with pancreatic cancer. They gave her six months, but she didn't last that long. I missed her death by a full month, and by the time I returned, Claire's parents had taken over Lexi's care."

She couldn't pretend indifference to his story. "I'm sorry. That must have been awful for you."

He nodded and shrugged. "Even though I'd been gone for almost seven months, Lexi remembered me and latched onto me like I was her rock amidst the storm. Turns out that Claire's parents had very distinct ideas about childrearing, and in fact, they'd enrolled Lexi in a super-strict private school that she absolutely hated."

Her heart squeezed for the little girl. "At least there's no school in the summer," she murmured.

Derek let out a harsh laugh. "There was for Lexi. It was clear Claire's parents didn't want her underfoot all day, but when I took Lexi out of the program, they went nuts. Claimed I had no idea how to raise my own daughter. They were...so angry."

She glanced over, feeling sympathy for Derek and the awful situation he'd found himself in. "I'm sure they were just grieving their daughter," she said.

"Maybe," he allowed. "But you have to understand, they never liked me. Obviously because I was irresponsible enough to get their daughter pregnant but mostly because I was nothing more than a soldier in the Army. When I discovered Claire was pregnant, I begged her to marry me, but she refused. I'm sure the last thing her parents wanted was me as a son-in-law. I spent as much time with Lexi as I could and sent most of my paycheck to Claire to help pay for expenses. Right before I was deployed to Afghanistan, I thought Claire was softening toward me. That she might even give a more permanent relationship a try."

"What happened?"

"Four months into my deployment, she told me she had pancreatic cancer." Derek's expression was so bleak she longed to comfort him. "I couldn't believe it at first, because she seemed so healthy before I left."

She was all too familiar with the way cancer sneaked up and stole a life when you least expected it. "Pancreatic cancer is difficult to diagnose, and once you have symptoms, it's almost always too late."

Derek let out a heavy sigh. "Yeah, that's exactly what happened. Anyway, Claire begged me to look after Lexi when she was gone. She arranged for me to have custody and told me that Lexi needed her father more than ever now. I gave her my promise that I would."

"Oh, Derek," she murmured. "Of course you and Lexi belong together. I just don't understand why you didn't tell me this sooner?"

"You didn't let me finish," he said dryly. "I think Claire's parents expected me to drop Lexi into their laps and return to Afghanistan. When I told them I had custody of her, they were furious. Claire's parents are rich and prominent members of society. They're best friends with several judges. When they told me they would fight for custody and win, I believed them. So I cashed in what was left of my savings and took off with Lexi."

"Ohhh," she said as the picture became crystal clear. "So you're running away from Claire's parents."

"I'm protecting Lexi from Claire's parents," he corrected sharply. "They have this, I don't know, strange idea of what Lexi should be and are determined to mold her into their image of a perfect granddaughter. They buy her all kinds of frilly things and girl toys that Lexi could care less about. They just don't understand Lexi is perfect the way she is."

His defensiveness regarding Lexi made her want to smile. "Of course Lexi is perfect the way she is, but Derek, don't you think Claire's parents have a right to be a part of Lexi's life?"

"Not if they threaten to take her away from me," he muttered harshly.

She sighed and shook her head. "Derek, do you really think a judge, even one who might know Claire's parents, would take custody away from a child's biological father?"

"Yes, I do. Especially since the only job offer I had was from Claire's father, which, of course, magically disappeared when I took Lexi out of that ridiculous school." Anger shimmered in Derek's tone. "You can bet they'd take custody away from me in a heartbeat. Which is why I'm asking you to keep this quiet for now. I have to believe that Claire's parents didn't call the police on me yet, since Deputy Armbruster didn't seem at all suspicious. But I also think it's just a matter of time. And if I can get this job, then I'll be one step closer to keeping Lexi."

She had to admit his logic made sense. How could she deny him the opportunity to keep his daughter? Especially since she really didn't want him to leave.

For selfish reasons, not necessarily noble ones.

"I won't say anything," she promised.

Derek nodded and rose to his feet, still favoring his right

side as he placed a hand over the right side of his chest. "Thank you."

She watched him walk back to Lexi, hoping and praying that Derek wasn't still in love with Claire. Because she was already starting to care about him.

Far too much.

AFTER A RESTLESS NIGHT, Julie dragged herself out of bed to get ready for her twelve-hour shift in the ER. A quick shower made her feel a little better, although she desperately needed coffee to kick-start her brain.

When she trudged into the kitchen, she was brought up short by the sight of Derek and Lexi sitting at her kitchen table eating bowls of cold cereal.

She blinked owlishly at them. "Good morning."

"Good morning." Derek's voice was tentative, as if unsure if she was still upset with him or not. "I made coffee. Hope you don't mind."

She forced a smile. "I could use about a gallon," she said, making her way over to the steaming pot. "Thanks."

Several sips later, the rush of caffeine cleared her mind. When she turned back toward the table, she realized there was a bowl and spoon already set out for her.

"Um, is the offer of driving you to work still an option?" Derek asked hesitantly. "I thought it would be nice to take Lexi to the parade, but we can always walk if you'd prefer."

"No need to walk, you can use the car today," she assured him. It wasn't necessary for him to keep tiptoeing around her, but she wasn't sure how to get their former camaraderie back. "We'll have to leave in about fifteen minutes, though."

"No problem. Finish your breakfast and leave the dishes. I'll take care of them."

She nodded, feeling a little bit like she was taking advantage of him, but there wasn't time to do anything about it now. As soon as she finished her breakfast, she stood and grabbed her stethoscope. "I'm ready."

Lexi must have been tired because she didn't say much as Derek drove the ten miles to Hope County Hospital. When Derek finally pulled up to the front doors of the ER, she glanced over. "I should be finished by seven-thirty, but I'll call if I'm running late."

"Sounds good. See you then."

She climbed out of the car and waved goodbye. As she walked inside, she told herself there was no reason to worry about Derek and Lexi leaving town. Not today and certainly not on the Fourth of July holiday. After all, Derek was planning on taking Lexi to the parade.

So why did she have this nagging sense of impending doom?

She shrugged off the feeling and did her best to concentrate on the patients that were located on her team for the day. The hospital census was high, which unfortunately meant long wait times for patients who needed to be admitted. One thing she liked about working in the ER was that there was always a wide variety of patients—from minor injuries from burns, heatstroke, and alcohol intoxication to more serious injuries from a four-car motor vehicle crash on the interstate.

Her brother called several more times without leaving a message, so she called him back on her lunch break. He didn't answer, so she left him a message, explaining she was at work and she'd try to call him when she was finished. Guiltily, she remembered she hadn't called him last night, either.

She hoped Zack was doing all right and found herself worrying about her brother as her afternoon wore on. Zack had been in a rough place for a long time, but no matter how much she begged him, he'd refused to return to Crystal Lake.

Or to church.

Despite the high level of activity, her shift dragged on for what seemed like forever. There was a brief lull around dinnertime, which gave her hope that she'd actually get out on time.

She called Derek's mobile phone, relieved when he answered on the first ring. "Hi, how was the parade?"

"Great." His voice sounded strained. "What time do you want me to pick you up?"

"I should get out of here on time, so seven-thirty is fine. Is something wrong?"

"No, nothing's wrong. I cooked the pork chops you had in the freezer for dinner. Hope that's okay."

"Sure, that's fine." All her instincts were on alert. She couldn't shake the feeling that something bad had rattled Derek. Since she didn't really have time to talk, she didn't push the issue. "See you soon."

"Sounds good." Derek hung up before she could say anything more.

She punched out at seven-thirty, and as she walked outside to meet Derek, her brother called again. "Where have you been?" Zack demanded. "I've been trying to get a hold of you for the past two days."

"I was working. Why? What's going on?"

"We need to talk. Is that Ryerson guy still staying with you?"

"Yes, Zack, I already told you he was planning to stay through the holiday. Why?"

"I was running a search on him and discovered St. Louis has a court order out against him. He's bad news, Jules. You need to kick him out right away."

Derek drove up in her car, his expression looking grim. And she knew that her brother had interfered in Derek's personal business. "Where are you, Zack? Did you drive up here to talk to Derek?"

"Maybe I did drive up to serve the court order. So what? Just because he plans to slap up some drywall doesn't mean he can use you as a shield against a custody suit. He has seventy-two hours to bring his daughter back to St. Louis or they'll put out a warrant for his arrest."

"Look, I'll talk to Derek, okay? I have to go. I'll call you back in a little while." Her mind was racing as she disconnected from the call.

Derek's car accident was on Friday evening, and it must have been sometime after the weekend that Lexi's grandparents had gone to court to file the order demanding Derek bring Lexi back to St. Louis.

Yesterday was Monday, and frankly, she was surprised the court order had gone in so quickly. And equally shocked that the Hope County Sheriff's Department hadn't known about it yesterday when Derek had applied for the dispatch job.

Although maybe they wouldn't know until the seventy-two-hour timeframe had passed and the arrest warrant was issued. Her brother's butting into her business gave them the advance notice they needed.

She walked over to the car. "There's something you need to know," he said.

"I already heard from Zack," she interrupted. "I'm sorry he stuck his nose into your business, but don't you see? This is actually good news."

Derek's scowl deepened. "You're kidding, right?"

"No, just listen to me for a minute," she said. "At least you were given the court order right away, so there's plenty of time for us to take action."

"Take action?" he glanced over at her as he navigated the traffic around town. "Look, Julie, I appreciate everything you did for me and Lexi, but we need to hit the road. The sooner the better."

Hit the road? Was he crazy? "Derek, there's no point in running again. Don't you see? It's just a matter of time before the police find you. And by then, your reputation will be shot, which will only give Lexi's grandparents the upper hand."

"What choice do I have?" he asked.

She gave him an exasperated look. "You can go back to St. Louis and face Claire's parents. You can convince them to drop this ridiculous notion of fighting for custody."

12

"Going back to St. Louis is not an option," Derek said harshly. He gripped the steering wheel so hard his knuckles went white, and he had to bite back a flash of anger. Julie had no idea what she was talking about. Why had he thought she would take his side? Hadn't he known all along that her Christian conscience would force her into turning him over to the authorities?

If he was hurt by her unwillingness to go along with his plan, he had no one to blame but himself.

"Why is running away a better option?" she demanded.

"Keeping Lexi safe is the only option." He wasn't going to waste time arguing. Besides, he'd already heard all this and more from her brother, Zack, when he'd slapped the court order into his hand. He'd immediately jumped into action. His and Lexi's suitcases were packed and ready to go. He'd have already left town except for the fact that he hadn't been able to get in touch with Henry to snag one of his cheap rental cars. For some reason, he hadn't expected the old guy to close up on the holiday.

"Derek," she started, but he cut him off with a stern look.

"Not now." They'd already said far too much in front of Lexi. Glancing in the rearview mirror, he wasn't surprised to see Lexi rocking back and forth in her booster seat, a sure sign of distress. "How are you doing back there, baby-doll? Are you okay?" he asked in a cheerful tone.

Lexi didn't answer, and he battled another wave of helpless frustration. Why couldn't Claire's parents leave him alone? Lexi had been doing so well over the past few days. She'd even brought up her mother to Julie. He didn't like the thought of Lexi regressing back to her protective wall of silence, which he knew would happen once they left town.

He glanced over at Julie, who was staring straight ahead, her lips pressed together in a firm line. She wouldn't talk any more in front of Lexi, but he knew she didn't consider their discussion finished.

But it didn't matter what arguments she was likely formulating in her mind. She didn't know Claire's parents. Didn't have any idea what he was up against. What chance did an unemployed soldier have against a wealthy couple?

None whatsoever.

When he pulled into Julie's driveway, he was relieved to see that Zack's squad car was gone. Not that it really mattered, since the damage was done.

"Derek, be reasonable," Julie pleaded in a low tone after Lexi ran inside.

He raised his eyebrows in disbelief. "Me? You want me to be reasonable? Didn't you hear a word I told you last night about Claire's parents? They have judges on their side. What do I have? Nothing. Claire wasn't even my wife." He could barely hold back his frustration. The situation couldn't get much worse. He didn't even have enough money for a decent lawyer.

"We have God on our side, Derek," Julie said softly.

"We? You're not involved in this mess; it's just me and Lexi. I don't need your help or God's help, either. Excuse me," he muttered as he brushed past her to head inside.

He didn't see Lexi inside and knew she was probably hiding in the bedroom. For a moment, he stood there and stared at the packed suitcases he'd left standing in the center of the room. He really needed Henry to call him back because he wasn't going to get very far without a ride. And considering their recent argument, he didn't think Julie would be willing to drive him to the bus station in Madison.

He let out a heavy sigh as he scrubbed his hands over his face. Just a few hours ago, he'd been so full of hope that things were finally going in the right direction. He'd finished tearing down the drywall off the ceiling, leaving the bare studs ready to be covered with new Sheetrock. He felt a stab of remorse that he wouldn't be able to finish the job.

Small payment for everything Julie had done for him. He suspected she'd keep on giving if he let her, but enough was enough. He and Lexi would figure something out. They'd be fine.

But he couldn't deny he'd miss Crystal Lake once he was gone. And Julie.

Especially Julie.

———————

"Lexi?" Derek called as he walked down the hall toward the bedroom. He looked in the bathroom and both bedrooms, but Lexi was nowhere to be found.

Panic tightened his chest. Where was she? With Julie?

Derek strode outside and rapped lightly on the wood frame of Julie's patio door. "Julie? Is Lexi with you?"

Julie came over to meet him, a tiny frown furrowed in her brow. "No, Lexi isn't with me. I thought she was with you. She went into your side of the townhouse, didn't she?"

"Yes, but I can't find her. She might be hiding. Can we look around your place?"

"Of course." She opened the screen door and let him in.

Between the two of them, it didn't take long to validate the townhouse was empty. His stomach knotted with anxiety as he went back outside onto the patio. "Lexi!" he shouted. "Come home right now!"

"You don't think she went down to the lake by herself, do you?" Julie asked. She came outside still wearing her scrubs from work. "Maybe we should check the boat."

Derek was already jogging down toward the lakefront. "Lexi!" Sheer desperation laced his tone. "She's never done anything like this," he muttered.

Julie swallowed hard. "We shouldn't have said anything in front of her," she said softly.

"She was upset before I picked you up," he said, knowing full well this mess was his fault. "Your brother and I argued a bit, and then when I packed our suitcases, I could tell Lexi was distressed." Derek jumped onto the boat. "Lexi?" He looked around at all the places a six-year-old might use to hide, not that there were many.

But the boat was empty.

An overwhelming sense of helplessness hit hard. Where was his daughter?

Dear Lord, help me! Please help me find Lexi! Please keep her safe from harm!

JULIE FOLLOWED Derek down to the boat, raking her gaze over the lake to be sure the little girl hadn't fallen in the water. "Lexi!" she shouted, adding her voice to Derek's.

"Dear Lord, help me find her," Derek murmured as he jumped off the boat back on land.

She grasped his hand and held on tightly. "God will help us find her, Derek. She couldn't have gone far."

He squeezed her hand. "Let's split up. You check the front, and I'll keep looking here in the back."

"All right." She hurried back up to the house, making a sweep around Derek's side in case the little girl was crouched somewhere over there. But there was no sign of Lexi, even when she went around to the front. "Lexi!" she yelled, heading out to the street. The sun was low on the horizon, and it wouldn't take long for darkness to fall. They needed to find Lexi and fast.

Could she have walked down the road? Julie debated taking the car and driving around the area but didn't want to leave without telling Derek.

She darted inside the house to grab her car keys but then remembered Derek had been the one to drive home. She went back outside to find him. "Do you have my keys? I thought I'd take the car and look for her."

"Sure." He tugged the keys from his pocket. "Wait a minute, did you check the garden?"

"No." She followed Derek over to the far right side of the townhouse where her small garden was located. Relief whooshed out when she saw Lexi huddled between the house and the garden, rocking back and forth.

"Lexi, honey, you scared me," Derek said as he walked

over to crouch down beside his daughter. "Didn't you hear me calling you?"

"Don't want to go, don't want to go, don't want to go," Lexi repeated over and over again.

Julie's heart went out to the little girl as Derek gathered her into his arms and rose to his feet. She couldn't hear what he murmured, but the way he clutched her close, she knew he was trying to reassure her.

"Is there anything I can do?" she asked softly.

"Not really." Derek didn't show any signs of discomfort from his ribs as he carried Lexi back toward his side of the townhouse. "I guess we'll spend the night here, if that's okay with you."

"Of course it's okay," she responded. "It's too late to do anything more tonight, anyway."

"Thanks." He gave her a brief nod before disappearing inside.

Julie walked into her kitchen more slowly, wishing there was some way to convince Derek to face Lexi's grandparents. She understood that they were prominent members of the community, but surely a biological father had rights, too? She'd be more than happy to testify on his behalf if needed. Maybe she was being overly optimistic about his chances, but certainly he needed to try. Why couldn't he see that running away would only make things worse?

She went into the bathroom to wash up and then changed into a pair of comfy sweats, considering the air outside had turned a bit cool. She was too distracted to sleep, however, so she went back into the kitchen to make a cup of herbal tea to help her relax.

The plate of grilled pork chops and green beans Derek had thoughtfully left for her was still on the counter, but she wasn't a bit hungry. Just the thought of food made her stomach roll with nausea.

A shadow outside on the patio caught her eye. She froze but then relaxed when she realized Derek was sitting outside in the darkness, holding his head in his hands.

She told herself not to go outside, that Derek needed to work this through on his own. But her silent lecture didn't do any good. In less than two minutes, she found herself quietly sliding open the patio door and stepping outside.

He didn't look up when she approached, either, because he hadn't heard her or because he wanted to be alone.

Yet she couldn't just leave him out here. "Hey. Are you okay?" she asked, dropping into a chair beside him.

He lifted his head, but she couldn't read his expression in the darkness. "I've never been so scared," he murmured. "If anything had happened to her, I would have never forgiven myself."

"I know." She ached to comfort him. "But Lexi's okay."

"She's not okay," Derek muttered. "This has been rough on her."

There wasn't much she could say to that. "I'm sorry," she said helplessly.

He shook his head. "I've been sitting here praying for guidance, but so far the only answer seems to be to do what you suggested—go back to St. Louis and face Claire's parents."

Her heart filled with hope. "God knows what's best."

"I'm surprised He's listening to me," Derek confessed softly. "After everything that happened with Claire and the Afghani soldiers I've killed..." His voice trailed off.

"Derek, God is always there for us, especially during those times we need Him the most." She could only imagine what horrors he'd lived through in Afghanistan, and she understood a little better why he'd resisted going to church. "God would never turn against you. But maybe you gave up on Him?"

He let out a heavy sigh. "Maybe. It's hard to hang on to faith when you're watching your men dying around you. The Bible teaches us to turn the other cheek, but instead we're sent out there to kill the enemy. There were times I looked down at my hands and could only see the blood of the lives I'd taken."

She put her arm around his shoulders and gave him a hug. "Derek, I'm sorry you had to go through all that. But you need to know, God is still there for you. All you have to do is believe."

"You've helped remind me about that," he admitted. "I guess I've been lost for a while now."

"Or maybe you weren't lost at all. It could be that God intended for you to come here all along," she pointed out. "God often takes matters into His own hands."

The moonlight revealed a ghost of a smile. "You could be right about that."

She gave him another quick hug. "So does this mean you're going to head back to St. Louis?"

The smile faded. "Yes, but I don't know if facing Claire's parents will do any good." He abruptly pulled away and rose to his feet, pacing the small length of the patio. "What if I lose Lexi? I can't imagine a life without my daughter. She's all I have left in the world."

"They can't take her completely away," she reasoned, trying to use logic to cut through his fear. "You would still have some rights."

He let out a harsh sound. "What, visits every other weekend? While she struggles in that ridiculous school they forced on her? No, I can't do that. I won't do that."

She understood his angst. What Claire's parents were doing was so wrong, there just had to be a way to get through to them. "What can I do to help?" she asked. "There has to be a way to ensure that you don't lose custody of your daughter."

"I wish I knew," he said with a heavy sigh. He tipped his head back to gaze up at the stars. "I know I need to leave this in God's hands, but it isn't easy. She's my whole life."

There was a tiny part of her that wished she was part of his life, too. But of course, his daughter had to come first. "I'd like to come with you," she offered tentatively. She rose to walk over to his side. "You don't have to do this alone. Maybe I can help make Claire's parents see what a great father you've been. I'd even testify in court if necessary."

He went still, looking down at her. She wished she could see the expression in his eyes. "Julie, you've already given us so much, I can't possibly accept anything more. It's not right for me to take advantage of you."

"That's Zack talking," she said with a scowl. "I bet he's the one who said that to you, right?"

Derek shrugged, which was answer enough.

"Why can't you believe that I care about you and Lexi?" she asked. "I can't stand the thought of the court system tearing you apart."

"I don't deserve someone like you," he murmured. And when he reached out to draw her close, she didn't resist but went willingly into his arms.

He tipped her face up to kiss her, and she reveled in the gentle sweep of his mouth against hers. Their first kiss had been an accident, but this time, she knew he meant to kiss her.

And she absolutely meant to kiss him back.

All too soon, he broke off the kiss, tilting his head back

and taking several deep breaths, and she smiled when she felt the racing beat of his heart. "I think it's time for me to go," he said huskily.

She buried her face against his chest, holding on to him for a moment longer, wishing she didn't have to let go. But since they couldn't stand here like this all night, she forced herself to take a step back. "All right," she agreed reluctantly, trying to smile. "But you didn't answer my question."

"What question?" he asked wryly. "Apparently, my mind turns to mush around you."

She had to laugh. "About whether or not you'll let me come with you to St. Louis. I'm off tomorrow and can probably switch shifts for Thursday, too. If you'd like some moral support."

He was quiet for so long she thought he was going to insist on going alone. "I'd like that," he finally said softly. "If you're absolutely sure about going along."

"I'm sure." She hoped her relief wasn't too evident. "Goodnight, Derek."

"Goodnight, Julie."

She went inside to get ready for bed, thinking that she was already far too emotionally involved with Derek and Lexi.

What if he did succeed in maintaining custody of his daughter? He might decide to stay in St. Louis to be near Lexi's grandparents. They might even work out some sort of arrangement where Lexi would stay with her grandparents before and after school, which would help Derek out when he found a job.

She didn't have a right to be sad, but she couldn't ignore the distinct impression that helping Derek would only take him and Lexi away from her forever.

Leaving her alone again.

erek negotiated the heavy traffic of St. Louis with dread curling in his stomach. The entire trip had been far from smooth—getting Lexi to agree to get in the car at all had been a major feat in and of itself. She'd only given in when Julie agreed to sit in the backseat with her.

Now that they were close to their destination, tempers were running a big ragged. In the cold light of day, he was second-guessing his decision. He wasn't even sure what he was going to say to Claire's parents. Hi, how are you, and how dare you try to take my daughter away from me? Yeah, somehow he didn't think that line was going to work well for him.

"Maybe this wasn't a good idea," he murmured in a low voice, glancing over at Julie seated in the passenger seat. Once they'd stopped for lunch, Lexi had been a little better about letting Julie sit up front with him. "I'm worried about how Claire's parents are going to react to all of us showing up unannounced on their doorstep."

Julie reached over and gave his hand a small squeeze.

"We can only control our own reactions, not theirs. All we can do is be nice and respectful. At the very least, they'll know that you're not giving up easily. Better to know what you're facing now than to be blindsided in front of the judge."

He knew she was right and tried to relax his death grip on the steering wheel. St. Louis had its usual snarl of traffic, but thankfully, Lexi's grandparents lived in one of the ritzy suburbs outside of the city, so he was able to exit off the interstate and get out of the traffic without having to go through the maze of downtown St. Louis.

Despite how he'd tried to rehearse what he was going to say, his mind went blank when he finally pulled into their driveway in front of the massive three-car garage. The mansion where Claire had grown up loomed large and intimidating, and he had to force himself to park Julie's car and turn off the engine. Any hope that they might not be home fled when the front door opened, revealing the distinguished figure of Claire's father, Robert Donnell.

Derek shoved open his door at the same time Julie slid out of the passenger seat. Julie opened the back passenger door for Lexi, who climbed down, obviously eager to get out of the constraints of her booster seat.

"Lexi!" Claire's father called out from the front porch. "Come give your grandpa a hug!"

"Hi, Grandpa," Lexi called but instead of running over to greet him, she clung to Julie's hand.

For a moment, he thought he saw a flash of pain cross the older man's features and felt a surge of sympathy. Derek hastily came around the car and put his hand against Julie's back, gently leading her forward. "Mr. Donnell, I'd like you to meet Julie Crain. Julie, this is Lexi's grandfather, Mr. Robert Donnell."

"It's so nice to meet you, Mr. Donnell," Julie said, approaching the house with Lexi trailing along by her side. "Derek has told me so much about you."

Robert scowled at her, but Julie's smile never wavered. He had the wild idea that Julie intended to smother the old guy with kindness until he gave in and dropped the custody suit. Julie held out her hand, forcing Mr. Donnell to take it in a brief handshake before he turned his attention to his granddaughter. "Lexi, we've missed you so much," he said, reaching for her.

Lexi shrank back against Julie as if she didn't have good memories of being with her grandparents. "Can we go home now?" she asked. "I want to go for a boat ride."

Robert's eyes narrowed with anger. "You've turned my granddaughter against me," he accused.

"No, of course not. Lexi's just tired after the long car ride, right, Lexi?" Julie gave his daughter's shoulders a brief squeeze. "Lexi, it's not nice to be rude," she chided gently.

Derek took charge of the deteriorating situation. "Look, Mr. Donnell, I'm sorry to show up uninvited, but we just want a chance to discuss things with you and Mrs. Donnell. Why don't we sit down for a few minutes? Wouldn't it be better to talk now than having this conversation in front of the judge?"

"Hrumph," the older man grunted but reluctantly opened the door for them. "Gladys?" he called back over his shoulder. "Derek brought Lexi back along with his new girl-friend." There was no mistaking the snide tone in his voice as they stepped into the cool interior of the house.

He caught sight of Julie's wince and wondered if she resented being referred to as his girlfriend. The idea both-ered him, considering he rather liked the label. Their heated kiss has cost him a good night's sleep, but maybe she regretted the moment of intimacy? Too bad they hadn't had a chance to talk alone before hitting the road. They certainly hadn't discussed anything in front of Lexi.

Shaking off his disturbing thoughts, he followed Robert into the formal living room. The one where he always felt as if he had to be extra careful or he might accidently break something.

Claire's mother hurried in, looking drawn and worried despite her blindingly white linen pants and ruffled blue blouse. She was always dressed to perfection, and today was no different. "Lexi!" she gushed. "Oh, sweetie, we've missed you so much!"

Derek had to bite his tongue to prevent himself from pointing out they'd only been gone five days, not five months. But he held his silence as Lexi tolerated a brief hug from her grandmother before wiggling away.

"Mrs. Donnell, this is Julie Crain. She's an ER nurse working at the Hope County Hospital," he said, introducing Julie. "Julie, this is Lexi's grandmother, Mrs. Donnell."

"It's nice to meet you," Julie said warmly. "You have a beautiful home."

Mrs. Donnell pursed her lips together in a disapproving frown. "I'm sorry we're forced to meet under these circumstances," she said primly. She turned toward her grand-daughter. "Lexi, how would you like to play with your dollhouse up in your room?"

Lexi silently shook her head, and Derek swallowed a sigh. Lexi didn't play with dolls, at least not that he'd ever noted. But clearly, Claire's parents wanted her to.

"Actually, she'd probably love to draw a picture for us," Derek said. "Would you like to run and get your sketch-book?" he asked his daughter. "I'm sure Grandma and

Grandpa would love a pretty picture from their grand-daughter."

Lexi's eyes brightened, and she nodded eagerly.

"I'll take her out for the sketchbook," Julie offered.

"Thanks," he murmured, even though he would have liked to have Julie stay right beside him for moral support. But he didn't blame her for wanting to escape, considering the hostile atmosphere they'd stepped into. The entire scene was going worse than he'd anticipated.

Julie gave him a bracing smile as she took Lexi back outside.

But she'd barely cleared the doorway when Claire's mother made a low, hissing sound. "How dare you bring that woman into our home!"

Derek didn't appreciate the vicious attack on Julie but tried to hold back his temper. "This isn't about Julie, who has been nothing but kind to me and Lexi, so please keep her out of this."

"You claimed you loved Claire," Robert accused, siding with his wife. "But it sure didn't take you long to move on to someone else, now did it?"

He'd remained standing, facing them both and feeling seriously outnumbered. "There's no need to jump to conclusions. Julie is not my girlfriend, but she is a good friend and doesn't deserve your anger. Why on earth are you upset?" he asked, truly confused. "You know very well you didn't want Claire to marry me. I did care about Claire very much, and you know we both loved Lexi. And Lexi is the reason I'm here. I need you to help me understand why you're so determined to take my daughter away from me."

Gladys and Robert exchanged a somber look. "I'm sorry that you feel this way, but we think Lexi is better off with us," Robert said. "She needs the financial security we can offer."

Financial security? It was all he could do not to scoff at their idea of what Lexi needed. "Money doesn't automatically bring happiness. Lexi needs love and understanding more than she needs your financial security." He tried to think of a way to get through to them. "Did you ever ask yourselves why Claire ran off to the Fort Drum Army Base in the first place?" he asked. He wasn't sure how much they knew about the time he and Claire first met. "She told me she couldn't relax and just be herself around you."

"You dare speak to us like that about our own daughter?" Gladys demanded, her beautiful face, so much like Claire's, was twisted with anger. "Claire loved us and proved that by coming home to us after you left her pregnant and alone."

He hadn't left Claire pregnant and alone, he'd asked her to marry him, and she'd refused. But he knew that no matter what he said, there was no way to win Claire's parents over. Hadn't he already tried that over the past six years since Lexi was born? They refused to believe anything that didn't fit into their idea of a perfect little world. He remembered Julie's comment about how he could only control his reactions, not theirs.

"Yes, Claire loved you both very much, and I don't want to fight with you. I just want you to understand that I love Lexi. I'm her father, and she needs me, just as much as she needs the both of you. Together, we can be a complete family for Lexi, but not if you insist on tearing us apart."

They didn't say anything, and while their stern expressions didn't give much away, he sensed he might be getting through to them. At least a little. "I think that's what Claire would want," he added. "Don't you?"

—————

JULIE TOOK her time digging Lexi's sketchbook out of the trunk of her car. As much as she would have preferred to stay outside, the sun was beating down mercilessly as it was far hotter here than in Crystal Lake, Wisconsin. Within five minutes, she was sweating profusely, so she took Lexi back into the house, slipping past the three adults standing in the formal living room to make her way into the kitchen. The least she could do was give Derek and Claire's parents some privacy.

It pained her to admit that he'd been right about them. She'd never met two more miserable people. She understood they were grieving over the loss of their daughter, and truly, their hostility toward her wasn't what made her upset. It was the way they treated Lexi. Dolls? Really? They didn't know the first thing about the granddaughter they claimed to love.

Derek's assessment had been dead-on. Lexi's grandparents seemed intent on forcing the child to fit into the mold of a "perfect granddaughter."

But why couldn't they accept that Lexi was perfect just the way she was?

She sighed and shook her head. She'd sincerely believed the judge would grant custody to Derek, but now she wasn't so sure.

"Do you think my picture will make Grandma and Grandpa happy again?" Lexi asked as she worked on her drawing.

Julie was amazed at how astute Lexi was, picking up on

the underlying anger radiating from her grandparents. "I sure hope so, sweetie," she said.

Movement from the corner of her eye had her straightening in her chair. "Hi, Mrs. Donnell," she greeted the woman hovering in the doorway. "I hope you don't mind that we made ourselves at home in your kitchen. Lexi prefers to draw while sitting at a table."

The older woman gave a brief nod. "Derek tells me you're not his girlfriend."

Keeping her smile in place took considerable effort. "I consider Derek a very good friend. He's a great guy and a wonderful father. I've enjoyed getting to know him. And of course, Lexi." She gestured to Lexi's picture. "Have you seen the talent she has? I told Derek she should be in some sort of art program."

Mrs. Donnell took a step closer to peer at Lexi's drawing. "She does a very nice job," she agreed.

Nice? The woman was clueless. "I had a niece, Amelia, who was about Lexi's age before she died of leukemia. Amelia was a wonderful little girl, loved dolls and playing make-believe, but she couldn't draw anything more than stick-people. Each child has her own individual talents. Amelia's was to make people smile. Maybe Lexi's is to touch people through her art."

"I'm almost finished, Grandma," Lexi said. She made a few more strokes with her pencil before lifting up the picture and handing it to her grandmother. "See? I made a picture of Mommy. She's an angel up in heaven with God. Julie says she's up there right now, watching over me."

"Oh," Gladys whispered, her eyes brimming with tears as she gazed down at Lexi's angel, who had feather-light wings and wore a gentle smile. "That's a beautiful picture, Lexi. Thank you so much."

"Don't be sad. Mommy is watching over you and Grandpa, too," Lexi said. "Right Julie?"

She had to fight her own tears in order to answer. "Yes, that's exactly right, Lexi. Remember, we are never alone, for God is always with us."

"I...excuse me," Gladys rushed out of the room, clutching Lexi's picture to her chest.

"I wanted her to be happy," Lexi said with a frown.

"Don't worry, Lexi," she murmured, giving Lexi a brief hug. At that moment, Julie realized that Lexi's grandparents weren't trying to change Lexi into the perfect granddaughter.

They wanted Lexi to be just like Claire. Because they wanted their daughter back.

Poor, misguided souls. "Your picture was perfect and exactly what your grandmother needed."

Lexi seemed to consider this for a moment. "Okay, so now can we go home?"

"Soon," she murmured. "Hopefully we can go home soon, Lexi."

———

DEREK TUGGED at the neckline of his starched shirt, waiting for the judge to enter the chambers. Lexi was seated beside him, looking very pretty in a blue dress that matched the color of her eyes. Julie sat behind them as they waited for Claire's parents to show up.

With barely five minutes to spare, the doors of the courtroom opened, revealing Robert and Gladys Donnell and their lawyer. They sat down at the table next to him, looking impressive dressed in their formal clothing.

"Hi, Grandma; hi, Grandpa," Lexi said in a loud whisper.

The older couple looked distinctly uncomfortable as they glanced over at him and Lexi. He couldn't afford a lawyer and had refused Julie's offer to pay for one. He wasn't sure how a lawyer would help, anyway; if he couldn't convince the judge on his own, then he was in deep trouble.

Lexi moved closer, and he put his arm around her tiny shoulders. "This will all be over soon, baby-doll," he murmured.

"Then we can go home?" Lexi asked. "I really, really want to go for a boat ride."

He smothered a smile when Robert and Gladys frowned darkly. He knew it bothered them that Lexi kept asking to go home, as in back to Crystal Lake.

"All rise," the deputy said. "The honorable Judge Berkley presiding."

Since he and Lexi were already standing, he simply straightened his spine and focused on the judge. A sharp stab of panic dug deep when the judge nodded at the Donnells as if he knew them.

"Please be seated," Judge Berkley said.

Derek reluctantly sat down, drawing Lexi into the chair beside him.

"This is a preliminary hearing to determine whether or not custody of the minor, known as Alexis Claire, should be removed from her biological father, Derek Ryerson, and granted in turn to her grandparents, Robert and Gladys Donnell."

"Excuse me, your honor, but may I ask on what grounds?" Derek asked.

The judge tipped his head down to peer at Derek over

the rims of his glasses. "Based on what's best for Alexus, that's what grounds."

Derek was determined not to lose his temper. "Yes, Your Honor, I believe we all want what is best for Lexi. But I still don't understand why my custodial rights are being challenged. I love my daughter, and she loves me. I have never hurt her or failed to provide for her needs. She's been through a very difficult time after losing her mother. The last thing she needs is to lose her father as well. So again, Your Honor, I ask on what grounds is this matter being heard?"

"Your Honor, I would like to make a statement," Robert Donnell said as he rose to his feet. "We asked for this hearing because Derek Ryerson has removed our granddaughter from the private school we'd placed her in. A private school that can offer her more structure and more learning than the public school system. And we feel that Derek Ryerson was not acting in his daughter's best interests when he removed her from this highly regarded academic program."

Judge Berkley sat back in his seat and looked back at Derek. "Is Mr. Donnell's statement true?"

Derek forced a smile. "Your Honor, Lexi cried every morning that she was forced to go to that school. I fail to see how sending her there is acting in her best interest."

"That's not true," Robert said swiftly. He turned to face Derek. "You're just saying that."

"Stop it!" Mrs. Donnell's voice rang through the courtroom. "This is wrong, Robert. We shouldn't be tearing this family apart. We should be trying to hold it together."

Derek stared in shock at Claire's mother. He'd never in his wildest dreams imagined the woman would unbend enough to come to his defense. All along, he'd been banking on wearing Robert down.

"Gladys," Robert protested.

"No, will you please just listen to me for once? What we're doing is wrong. It's not going to bring Claire back." Gladys glanced over at Derek, a naked plea in her gaze. "Derek, if we drop this custody matter, will you please allow us to see Lexi on a regular basis? All we really want is to be a part of our granddaughter's life. Please?"

"Of course I'll let you see Lexi," he said slowly, his mind reeling from the turn of events. "I never intended to keep her away from you. She needs her grandparents." He didn't add that he'd only left town in the first place because they'd threatened to take Lexi away from him.

"All right, then it's settled." Apparently, Gladys had made up her mind. "See, Robert? Everything is going to be just fine."

Robert glanced over at Derek and Lexi, as if he wasn't quite ready to give in. But then Lexi smiled at him. "I love you, Grandpa," she said.

The older man crumpled. "I love you, too, Lexi." Derek gave his daughter a nudge, and she ran over to give her grandparents a hug.

Relieved, he glanced back at Julie, not the least bit surprised to see big, silent tears rolling down her cheeks. "I knew God would take care of you," she whispered.

"I know," he whispered back. The weight he'd been carrying for the past few weeks finally rolled off his shoulders, leaving him lightheaded with relief.

His nightmare was finally over.

14

J ulie smiled so much she thought her face might crack and crumble into tiny pieces. As they stood on the steps of the courthouse, she listened as Gladys talked about enrolling Lexi in an art program and enthusiastically made plans for a cookout over the upcoming weekend. Even Robert had softened toward Derek, and she wondered if the original job offer he'd taken from Derek would be reinstated.

Things were working out exactly the way they were supposed to. She was so happy for Derek.

And so sad for herself.

She slipped away from the crowd, intending to head back to her car to begin the long ride home, when Derek's hand on her arm stopped her. "Hey, where are you going?"

She closed her eyes and mentally braced herself to turn and face him. "I need to head home, Derek. It's a long drive, and I have to work tomorrow."

"The Donnells want to take us out for brunch."

"I think that's a great idea. I'm sure being together as a family will do wonders for Lexi."

His intense blue gaze searched hers. "Why don't you join us?" he asked softly.

Her heart squeezed, and she had to swallow the lump in her throat. "I think it's best if I head home," she said. "Dropping the custody battle is a big step for the Donnells, and I think the four of you could use a little bonding time together."

Without her being the unintended painful reminder that Claire wasn't here anymore.

A hint of uncertainty flashed in his eyes, but after a long moment, he nodded. "I think you might be right," he agreed. "Thanks for everything, Julie."

He drew her in for a hug, and she clung to him for a moment before gathering the strength to pull away. "Take care, Derek."

"Wait." He caught her hand before she could leave. "Aren't you going to say goodbye to Lexi?"

Her heart was breaking, but of course she couldn't leave without saying goodbye to Lexi. When Derek called his daughter's name, she came running over.

"I'm hungry, Daddy. Grandma says we're going for blunch."

"Brunch," he corrected softly, running a hand over his daughter's glossy, dark hair. "Breakfast and lunch together is brunch."

Julie smiled down at Lexi and forced a cheerfulness she was far from feeling into her tone. "Have fun. Unfortunately, I have to head home, Lexi." She wrapped her arm around the child's shoulders. "Goodbye, sweetie. Take good care of your daddy, okay?"

"Do you hafta go?" Lexi asked, returning her hug and staring up at her with a plaintive gaze that reminded her too much of Derek. "I want you to stay."

She wanted to stay, too, but she understood that staying here wasn't part of God's plan. "I'm afraid so, sweetie. I have to work at the hospital again very soon." Her vision went blurry, and she had to sniffle back her tears. "I love you, Lexi," she said huskily. She released the child and turned to walk away, hardly able to see where she was going.

It took every bit of strength she possessed not to turn and look back at what she was leaving behind.

JULIE REPORTED for her shift at seven a.m. the following morning, hoping no one would notice the puffiness of her eyes from her crying jag the night before.

But, of course, she couldn't fool her friend Merry. "What happened?" she demanded. "Did he hurt you?"

"Nothing happened." Julie couldn't have pasted a smile on her face if her life depended on it. "Derek went back home to his family, that's all."

"Oh, Jules," Merry said, giving her a quick hug. "I'm sorry."

"Don't be, it's certainly not your fault. And you did warn me, remember?" She pulled away from her friend to glance up at the patient board, desperately needing the distraction of work. "Fill me in on my patients, okay?"

She sensed Merry wanted to say more, but her pager went off, announcing the arrival of an ambulance. "I've assigned you to team three today," Merry said. "Ask Debra to give you the rundown while I go check on this new arrival, okay?"

"Sure," she murmured as Merry hurried away.

The shift started out busy, but around lunchtime, there was a definite lull, giving her far too much time to think. To wonder what Derek and Lexi were doing. To wonder if they missed her just a fraction of how much she missed them.

To wonder if she should try inviting them up for a weekend sometime soon for a picnic and boat ride on the lake.

No, don't even think about it, she told herself sternly. Derek and Lexi were back in St. Louis where they belonged. No point in dragging the agony out even further. She was happy for them and for the Donnells, who would still get to see their granddaughter.

The time she'd had here with Derek and Lexi had just been a tiny detour for them. And she had no one to blame but herself for getting too emotionally involved.

By the time her twelve-hour shift was over at seven-thirty in the evening, she was battling a wave of over-whelming exhaustion. Lack of sleep from the night before hadn't helped. She dragged herself out to her car and headed home.

When she pulled into the driveway, she heard the faint sound of laughter coming from the back side of the town-house and inwardly groaned. Obviously, the tourists were still playing out on the lake while she wanted nothing more than to crawl into bed, pull the sheet over her head to shut out the rest of the world, and try to get some sleep.

Which wasn't likely unless Derek and Lexi stopped invading her dreams.

As she climbed out of the car, she heard the front door slam. Alarmed, she whirled around and dropped her jaw when she saw Derek and Lexi walking over the front lawn toward her. Belatedly, she recognized a strange car parked along the opposite side of the street.

"Hi, Julie." Lexi greeted her with an enthusiastic hug.

"Hi, Lexi, Derek." She returned Lexi's hug but couldn't tear her gaze away from Derek. "What are you doing here?" she sputtered.

He lifted a brow. "I did a little work on the townhouse, and then Lexi and I made dinner. Hope you're hungry?"

She knew she was gaping but couldn't seem to pull herself together. "But how? Why?"

He chuckled, and she realized that, in all the time they spent together, she'd rarely heard Derek laugh. "I borrowed a car from Claire's parents and you don't lock your doors in Crystal Lake, remember?"

That wasn't what she meant, but she was so thrilled to see them she didn't care. "I'm just surprised to see you, that's all," she managed. "I wasn't expecting this."

"It's great to see you, too," he said in a low, husky tone. For a moment, his gaze bored into hers, but then he smiled and reached for her hand. "Come on, I want to show you what I managed to get done today," he said, tugging her toward the townhouse.

She didn't understand how he'd gotten anything done, considering it was a long drive up from St. Louis, but when he opened the front door with a flourish, she realized he'd completed one entire wall with new drywall. "Derek! This looks amazing!" Then she scowled. "You did this with your sore ribs, didn't you?" she demanded.

"I'm fine," he assured her, grinning from ear to ear. "But it looks great, doesn't it? If I do say so myself," he added modestly.

She shot him an exasperated grin. "Yes, it does."

"Come on, let's eat. I have some marinated chicken breasts on the grill, and hope you don't mind, but Lexi and I helped ourselves to your garden to put together a salad."

"Of course I don't mind," she said. How could she when she was still reeling from the knowledge that Derek had come back? To see her?

Or maybe just to repay a debt. As she followed Derek outside to the patio, she glanced back one more time at the finished wall and told herself not to get too excited about his being there. Now that she really thought about it, she figured he'd only returned to finish his part of the deal. Not that she'd expected anything more from him, but she sensed his pride wouldn't allow him to leave the job undone.

And if that was the case, she had no idea how she'd manage to protect her heart long enough for him to finish the stupid townhouse.

———

DEREK FOUND it increasingly difficult to keep his gaze off Julie as they ate the meal he'd prepared. The moment she'd arrived home, he'd wanted nothing more than to sweep her into his arms and kiss her soundly but had held back for two reasons. First of all, because she'd left St. Louis so abruptly, which made him wonder how she felt about him and secondly, because he knew Lexi was watching.

Hopefully, Lexi would be tired from their trip and go to bed sooner than later. He wanted, needed a little time alone with Julie.

As soon as they'd finished dinner, though, Julie jumped to her feet. "Since you cooked, it's my job to clean up," she said as she stacked the dirty dishes together. "Why don't you and Lexi enjoy the sunset? This won't take long."

Was it his imagination, or did she seem nervous? "Lexi, let's help Julie carry everything inside."

His daughter was eager to assist, and soon they had the patio table cleared off. Because Julie was so determined to do the dishes, he went back outside with Lexi.

"Did you see that, Daddy?" Lexi said with excitement. "That was a firefly!"

"There's another one," he said pointing off to the right. As darkness fell, the winking lights from the fireflies became more noticeable. He had to laugh as Lexi ran around the yard, chasing the flashes of light and trying to capture them in the palms of her hands.

"It's so great to hear her laughing," Julie said as she came back outside.

"Yes, it is," he agreed. He leaned over and captured her hand to guide her into the chair beside him. "Hopefully, all that running around will tire her out," he added dryly.

Julie gently pulled her hand away and laced her fingers together in her lap. "You didn't have to come back to finish the townhouse, Derek," she said softly.

Did she really think that was the only reason he came back? "Yes, I did, because that was a good excuse to see you."

He heard her soft gasp of surprise and grew a bit concerned. Was it possible she didn't feel anything for him after all? The morning before, when he saw her crying in the courtroom, he thought for sure she cared about him. Maybe even had started to fall in love with him.

The way he'd fallen in love with her.

"Daddy, I caught one!" Lexi shouted.

"We have to talk," he said to Julie before getting up and crossing over to Lexi. It took some finagling, but he coaxed her into letting the lightning bug go so the little guy would be free to fly through the night with his friends.

"Time for bed, Lexi," he said. "Say goodnight to Julie."

"G'night, Julie," Lexi repeated, running over to give her a hug. "See you in the morning."

"Sounds good," Julie said. "Goodnight, Lexi."

He took his daughter inside and waited patiently for her to use the bathroom, brush her teeth, and then say her prayers, a new ritual for them.

Lexi closed her eyes and pressed her hands together. "God bless Mommy up in heaven, Grandma and Grandpa in St. Louis, Daddy and Julie here in Crystal Lake. Amen." Lexi opened her eyes. "That's everyone, right, Daddy?"

"That's right, baby-doll. I love you." He gathered her close for a tight hug and a kiss. "Sweet dreams."

"G'night, Daddy."

He headed back outside to Julie, trying to ignore the sudden attack of nerves. Thankfully, Julie was still sitting right where he'd left her, head tipped back as she gazed up at the stars.

"It's so beautiful up here," he said as he sat beside her. "Lexi was not happy when she discovered she couldn't see the stars in the city."

"I'm so glad everything worked out for you, Derek," Julie said softly.

"I accepted a new job," he said.

"Really? That's wonderful! I'm so glad Robert changed his mind."

Robert? Did she really think he'd planned on staying in St. Louis? "Julie, I accepted the dispatch job here at the Hope County Sheriff's Department. I start next Monday."

"You did? But why? You promised to let Robert and Gladys see Lexi on a regular basis. It's an eight-hour drive from here to their home in St. Louis!"

"I've promised them they'll get plenty of time with Lexi,"

he assured her. "But I happen to like it here in Crystal Lake. And so does Lexi."

"I...don't know what to say," she whispered. "I never expected you to come back here permanently."

He heard the doubt in her tone and decided enough was enough. He rose to his feet and pulled her up, too, so that he could wrap his arms around her. He gently brushed a strand of hair away from her face and cupped her cheek with the palm of his hand. "Julie, tell me that what I'm feeling isn't one-sided," he said in a pleading tone. "Tell me that you have some feelings for me, too."

"Oh, Derek." She wrapped her arms tightly around his waist. "I do, but are you sure about this? I feel like I should pinch myself to make sure I'm not dreaming."

"I've fallen in love with you, Nurse Julie," he whispered before claiming her sweet mouth with his. After a long moment, he lifted his head to catch his breath. As far as he was concerned, he could stand here under the stars and kiss Julie all night long. But he still needed to know that she felt the same way. "Lexi loves you, too. Is it too much to ask that you give us a chance?"

He could feel her draw an unsteady breath and tried not to fear the worst. "No, it's not too much to ask," she murmured. "But I was engaged once before, and, well, things didn't work out. So I have to be honest and tell you that this all feels like too much, too soon. You've always lived in the city, Derek. Living out here, it's nice, but the pace is slower. The winters can be long and brutal. I don't think you really understand what you're getting yourself into by moving up here."

"Enough with the weather report," he interjected with frustration. "Julie, I've spent a long time searching for someone to share my life with. As much as I cared about

Claire, I didn't love her the way I should have. I'm sorry if some jerk hurt you, but don't make me pay for his sins. Do you really think I'd risk my daughter's future if I wasn't sure about how much I love you?"

There was a long pause before she lifted herself up on her tiptoes and wrapped her arms around his neck. "I love you, too, Derek," she confessed before she kissed him again.

"Thank you, Lord," he said when he was able to breathe again. "You have no idea how hard I've been praying for this ever since you left me back in St. Louis."

"Me, too," she whispered. "Welcome home, Derek."

EPILOGUE

Ten months later...

JULIE STOOD in the entryway of the small church, not the least bit nervous on her wedding day. The sun was shining, and there was a cool, May breeze coming off the lake. Lexi stood in front of her, wearing a miniature white gown and a ring of flowers in her hair.

"Ready, sweetie?" she asked when the organist began "The Wedding March."

"Yes, I'm ready." Lexi took her role of being the flower girl very seriously, holding on to her white basket of rose petals as if she were afraid she'd drop it. Julie smiled when she watched Lexi start down the aisle, dropping delicate red and pink petals along the way.

She glanced at Zack, who was discreetly pulling at the necktie of his tux. Her brother was escorting her down the aisle and standing in as Derek's best man. He'd come a long way over the past few months, and she was thrilled at the change in his demeanor. "Ready?" she asked.

"I'm ready if you are, Sis." Zack held out his arm, and Julie took his elbow, knowing their parents were there in spirit, gazing down from the heavens above.

She started down the aisle, not even noticing all the people who'd crowded into the small church. She only had eyes for Derek, who was breathtakingly handsome in his tux, standing straight and tall as he waited for her next to the pastor. As amazing as Derek looked in a tux, she thought he looked just as handsome in his new deputy uniform. He'd been promoted four months ago after two of the older officers had decided to step down into the dispatch positions, leaving the younger guys to the more grueling police work. She was so proud of everything Derek had accomplished in the past ten months. They'd put the side-by-side townhouse up for sale and had their eye on the perfect three-bedroom house on the lake. Plenty of room for more children, Derek had promised.

Looking at him now, she was humbled to see the love shining blatantly from his eyes.

And she knew the same expression was on her face as well.

"Take care of her," Zack said as he handed Julie over to Derek.

"I will," he promised.

She took Derek's hand and smiled up at him. She was the lucky one in this union, and as she exchanged vows with Derek, she knew that God had answered her prayers, too.

She was blessed to have finally found what she'd always wanted. A home and a family with Derek and Lexi.

COMING HOME

BOOK 3 CRYSTAL LAKE SERIES

COMING HOME

By Laura Scott
Book 3 in the Crystal Lake Series

Copyright © 2013 by Readscape Publishing, LLC

Cover art by The Killion Group, Inc.
Digital Formatting by Author E.M.S.

Please Note

1

"Merry, I'm so glad you're here!" Janelle greeted her with a dramatic sigh as Merry entered the arena of the Hope County Hospital's Emergency Room. "I've been waiting forever for you to get here."

ER Charge Nurse Meredith Haines frowned at her nursing colleague. "What's the problem? I'm not late. I'm fifteen minutes early for my shift."

"I know, but look." Janelle jabbed her finger at the large whiteboard listing all the names of the current patients in the ER. "Leonard Marks is in room ten. He's been asking for you for the past five minutes. I've been trying really hard to keep him calm until you could get here."

Merry rolled her eyes. Janelle acted as if no one else was capable of taking care of Leonard. Sure, he was a mammoth of a man with a volatile psych history, but he'd been coming to the Hope County Hospital for his medical care long before she'd moved to Crystal Lake, a little over two years ago. Surely other nurses had taken care of him before?

"Okay, I'll go and see him," Merry said. "But I'm

supposed to be in charge, so I'll need you to make out assignments while I'm talking to Leonard."

"Thanks," Janelle said with a sigh of relief, tucking a dark strand of hair behind her ear. "Don't worry, I'll take care of the assignments. Anything to help you out. I don't know how you manage to deal so well with Leonard. Honestly? The guy scares me to death."

Merry's smile was a bit forced as she walked toward Leonard's room. She wasn't about to explain that she'd had lots of practice dealing with angry, psychotic men because she'd learned from firsthand experience.

She hadn't known about her former boyfriend's psych diagnosis until he'd attacked her.

The thought of Blake finding her sent a shiver down her spine. After leaving Minneapolis, she'd covered her tracks carefully. If Blake hadn't found her in more than two years, she didn't think he'd suddenly show up now.

Unfortunately, she knew far more about the complex world of psychiatric healthcare than she'd ever wanted to know. At least, today, she could put her knowledge and experience to good use.

Moving very slowly, to avoid any abrupt gestures, Merry carefully slid open the glass door to room ten and eased inside.

———————

"HI LEONARD," she greeted him softly. "It's me, Merry."

"Merry! Where have you been?" Leonard demanded with the petulance of a small child, his gaze dark with reproach. "I've been waiting and waiting for you."

He was a full grown man of thirty-five, but his mind was that of a six-year-old. And often a bad tempered six-year-old, although she knew it wasn't his fault. Leonard had suffered a traumatic brain injury on top of his underlying schizophrenia, a combination that made him extremely difficult to manage.

Her stomach tightened when she didn't see any sign of Leonard's mother, Doreen. Had his mother dropped him off and then left? Normally, his mother stayed to help keep Leonard calm.

"I'm sorry, Leonard," she murmured, giving him a gentle smile. "But I'm here now. So tell me, what made you decide to come in to see us today?" Ironically, she'd learned Leonard didn't like the term *hospital* so she avoided using the reference if at all possible.

For a moment he looked truly bewildered. "I don't know." He rose to his feet and began to pace. "I have that feeling again. The one I don't like. The one that makes me mad. I hear voices telling me to do bad things."

Merry swallowed a knot of apprehension. The last few times Doreen brought Leonard to the ER, he'd complained of similar issues. Leonard was under a court order to take his psych meds, but his mother sometimes forgot. Merry was afraid Doreen Marks might be in the beginning stages of Alzheimer's disease. And if that was the case, Leonard would soon be too much for his mother to handle, if he wasn't already.

Without his medication, Leonard became lost in a sea of confusion. And when Leonard got confused, he got angry. And violent.

Leonard also had a medical history of poorly controlled diabetes and high blood pressure, but she couldn't even begin to examine him for his medical problems until she'd calmed him down.

"It's okay, Leonard," she said soothingly, placing a hand lightly on his arm. She was one of the few who could touch him without causing him to fly off in a rage. He tolerated women fairly well and, for once, her petite frame gave her an advantage. But Leonard didn't like men, especially those in uniform. When Leonard saw the police he went berserk, probably because he knew from several bad experiences that the arrival of the police meant he was taking a one-way trip to the mental health complex in Madison. "I'm here now. You know I'll take good care of you, right?"

"Right. Merry takes good care of me," he muttered as he pulled away from her and continued to pace. "Only Merry. No one else."

"All the nurses here take good care of you, Leonard. Not just me." She knew this odd dependence he had for her wasn't healthy. It wasn't as if she could possibly work every single day, all three shifts. "Don't worry, you're going to be fine."

The last time Leonard had come in, she'd succeeded in avoiding transferring him to the mental health facility. Once he'd taken meds to keep him calm, they'd evaluated his diabetes and his high blood pressure, making minor adjustments to his meds. By the end of the visit, he'd been able to go home with his mother, as docile as a bunny.

Maybe, just maybe, she'd be able to do that again. She wasn't sure who the doctor was on his team, but she needed to let him or her know that last time they'd started with a hefty dose of anti anxiety meds before getting him to take his usual dose of antipsychotic medication.

"Okay, Leonard, I want you to stay here. I'll be right

back. I'm going to get your favorite treat. Do you remember what your favorite treat is?"

Leonard was easily six feet tall and weighed two hundred eighty pounds, but a tremulous smile bloomed on his broad, square face. "Chocolate pudding!"

"That's right, chocolate pudding," she agreed with a smile. Sugar free chocolate pudding in deference to his diabetes, but he didn't need to know that. "Now be good and I'll get your treat, okay?"

Leonard nodded and she sent up a silent prayer on Leonard's behalf as she slid from his room. The poor man suffered more than anyone should have to. Grinding up pills and hiding the powder in the chocolate pudding was normally not an acceptable way to give patients their meds but, thankfully, Leonard's court order allowed them to do just that. During previous visits she'd been worried that he'd notice the slightly bitter taste but, every time, he'd gobbled up the pudding without detecting anything amiss.

Merry found Dr. Katy Albrecht hovering behind the desk, waiting for her. "I've ordered the Ativan for Leonard," Dr. Katy said before Merry could say anything. "The pharmacist is entering it in the system now."

"Thanks." Relieved that they were on the same page, Merry went over to the galley to grab two chocolate puddings from the tiny fridge. Then she stopped at the automated medication dispensing machine. It didn't take long to pull out the medications, crush the pills, and mix the powder in the pudding.

Satisfied, she shoved the spoon into the pudding and headed back across the arena to Leonard's room.

"Merry?" The sound of her name in a familiar, deep voice stopped her in her tracks. She braced herself before turning around to face police officer Zack Crain, who looked far too attractive in his dark blue uniform. He was tall, with short, dark hair and brilliant green eyes. Ever since she'd met Zack at his sister's wedding, her pulse jumped erratically when she was around him.

"Zack?" Her voice squeaked and she tried to get a grip. She licked her lips and tried again. "Hi. What are you doing here? I thought you worked in Madison?"

"I'm picking up the belongings from one of our car crash victims as potential evidence," he said. "Have you seen my sister, Julie? I was hoping to talk to her while I'm here."

"I'm sorry, but Julie and Derek are out of town enjoying a vacation alone while Lexi visits with her grandparents. I'm dog-sitting for them while they're gone." Merry glanced nervously over her shoulder towards Leonard's room. "Listen, Zack, I have a patient who doesn't like police, so please don't be upset, but I need to ask you to leave."

"Leave?" His eyebrows shot up in surprise, but then he scowled. "Don't worry, I'll be out of here as soon as security brings me what I need."

Merry didn't have time to argue. "Just wait someplace else, out of sight, okay?"

She turned back towards Leonard's room, but it was too late. Through the glass door, Leonard was staring in horror at Zack. There was a loud crash as Leonard slammed the bed up against the wall in a fit of anger.

"No cops!" he bellowed, lumbering out of his room, waving his arms wildly. "No cops!"

"Leonard, calm down. It's okay. I have your treat!" Merry planted herself directly in front of him, in a pathetic attempt to distract him from Zack, who she hoped and prayed was quickly ducking out of sight. "Look at me, Leonard." She captured his gaze with her own. "It's Merry, remember? I've promised to take good care of you. And I have your favorite treat!"

For a moment she thought she'd reached him, but then she saw Zack move up next to her as if he intended to protect her.

"No cops!" Leonard screamed. With a horrible keening wail, he brutally shoved Merry aside, sending her flying backward into the unforgiving corner of the nurse's station as he made a mad dash for the front door.

Oomph! She hit the edge of the counter, hard enough to steal the breath from her body, her left shoulder taking the brunt of the blow. She thought someone shouted her name over the din, but then a horrible pain exploded in her head.

Poor Leonard she thought, before darkness and pain closed around her.

ZACK STARED in horror when Merry flew into the side of the nurse's station. He heard her teeth snap together before she sailed backward, landing on the floor. Her head hit the linoleum with a sickening thud.

"Merry!" Zack was the first to reach her side, his heart thundering in his chest as he looked down at her pale, limp form. Most of the staff had gone to help bring the psychotic patient under control, and he knew he should have been helping, too, but he couldn't tear his gaze from Merry.

He forced himself to remember his basic medical training, but it wasn't easy. He gently lifted Merry's head to feel along the back of her scalp. His fingers came away wet. Stained red.

Blood. She was bleeding.

"Merry? Can you hear me?" He could barely hear himself, his heart was hammering so hard. "I'm here, and I won't leave you. Open your eyes, Merry. Can you talk to me?"

Nothing. She didn't move.

"I need some help over here," he called sharply, drawing a few stares from the group gathering around the patient who was still thrashing on the floor in spite of the pile of people trying to hold him down. He caught sight of a needle and syringe being plunged into the patient's thigh.

He couldn't suppress a flash of guilt, knowing that if he'd listened to Merry and left right away, this wouldn't have happened. But he hadn't understood the magnitude of danger. And when she faced the crazy man head on, he refused to leave her vulnerable and alone.

"Oh no, Merry!" A young female with deep red hair, wearing a long white lab coat, came to his aid. He figured she must be a doctor when she felt for Merry's pulse, and then pulled out a penlight to peer at her pupils.

"Can't we get her into a bed?" Zack asked. He didn't want to do anything that would hurt Merry, but he also didn't like seeing her stretched out on the floor.

Merry let out a soft moan and, despite her obvious pain, he was deeply relieved to know she was coming around.

"Try not to move." The female doctor's name tag identified her as Dr. Katy Albrecht. "We need to assess the extent of your injuries. Can someone get me a C-collar?" she called.

Given how hard her head had hit the floor, Zack assumed Merry had a concussion, but hopefully nothing worse. He assisted with lifting Merry's head just enough for Dr. Katy to get the cervical collar in place.

"Now we need a back board," Dr. Katy said, glancing up at the other staff members who huddled around Merry. "Which empty room can we use?"

"Room six is empty," a nurse by the name of Janelle said. "We can put Merry in there."

"Great, how's Leonard?" Dr. Katy asked in a distracted tone.

Zack assumed Leonard was the big man who'd gone crazy when he saw Zack's uniform. He glanced over the doctor's shoulder. The big man who'd been so crazy a few minutes ago was now being led back to his room by several of the staff the medications obviously working to calm him down. "He's fine from what I can tell," he told her.

"Here's the long board," Janelle said, hurrying over with a full-size plastic board with handles along the sides.

"We're going to roll Merry over on her side, and you're going to tuck the board underneath her, understand?" Dr. Katy addressed him as if he were one of her staff members.

He nodded, more than willing to help out if needed. "I have some basic first aid training, so I understand the concept of a log roll."

It took a few minutes to get Merry centered on the long board. Three other staff members helped him lift her up and carry her over to the empty room.

"My head hurts," Merry murmured, her face drawn with discomfort.

"Leonard knocked you down," Zack told her. "I'm sorry, Merry. I should have listened to you."

"Merry, I need you to stay still until we can clear you for fractures and a head injury," Dr. Katy chimed in. "Right now, we're going to get you entered into the computer system as a patient."

Merry's eyes widened. "A patient? But I have to work!"

"Not happening," Zack said, his voice harsher than he intended. He wasn't angry at Merry, but at himself. He forced himself to speak to her in a gentle tone. "You're going to do whatever the doctor tells you, okay?"

Dr. Katy nodded her approval and walked away, leaving the two of them alone.

Merry's amber gaze bored into his. "Sounds like you're not giving me much of a choice," she finally muttered.

"I know, and I'm sorry. I feel terrible about what happened, but we need to know how badly you're injured."

Zack resisted the urge to brush her reddish gold hair away from her cheek. He couldn't afford to get emotionally involved with Merry, no matter how much he liked her. Even now, well past two years after he lost his wife and daughter within six months of each other, he fought to keep his emotions in a deep freeze. Why were they thawing now, for his sister's friend, Merry Haines? It wasn't fair, since he had no intention of getting emotionally involved ever again.

"Is Leonard okay?" Merry asked.

He admired her ability to worry about the big man who'd knocked her around like a rag doll. "He'll be fine. They managed to get him medicated and back into his room."

Merry closed her eyes for a moment, and the tiny pucker between her brows made him realize she was in pain. "Poor Leonard, it's not his fault."

As a police officer, Zack interacted with many people with psychiatric issues. But he had to admit that Leonard was one of the worst he'd ever seen. That moment when Merry had stepped in front of Leonard, trying to reason with him was burned into Zach's memory. She'd reminded him of a slender David facing down Goliath, except her sling-shot was a cup of chocolate pudding. Pudding that was now splattered all over the wall.

"You should have gotten out of the way," he said in a weary tone. "The man is more than twice your size."

"Normally, Leonard likes me," Merry whispered. "I thought I could get through to him. I didn't want him to get hurt."

He wasn't sure what to say since he knew very well it was his fault that Leonard lost control.

Zack scrubbed his hands over his face. He was due to return to Madison with the evidence he'd come to collect, but he couldn't bring himself to leave Merry like this. Especially since his sister, Julie, wasn't around to help. He remembered talking to Merry at Julie and Derek's wedding and, at the time, she'd mentioned she didn't have any family in the area.

Zack pulled up a chair next to Merry's bedside and sat down. Her eyes drifted closed, deep brackets of pain pulling at the corners of her mouth. Her face was incredibly pale, each freckle standing out starkly against her skin.

As much as he didn't want to get involved, he couldn't make himself leave. At least, not until he knew she was all right. She looked far too helpless lying there on the bed.

He closed his eyes and pressed the heels of his palms into his eyes. Once he would have prayed for Merry's recovery, but not anymore.

Unfortunately, God had stopped listening to him a long time ago.

2

Merry pried open her eyelids, squinting against the pain reverberating through her skull. For a moment she had no idea where she was, though the overhead light was confusingly familiar. It took several minutes for her to realize she was on the wrong side of a hospital bed. And in the ER, the department she worked in, no less.

Very slowly, she turned her head toward the door. She was shocked to see Zack Crain sitting in a chair next to her bed, cradling his head in his hands, looking ironically vulnerable considering she was the one wearing a hospital gown.

"Zack? What's wrong?"

His head snapped up, his piercing green gaze capturing hers. A flash of relief flittered across his features. "You're awake," he said, rising to his feet.

"Barely. What happened?" she asked, putting her hand to her throbbing temple.

"You don't remember?" His eyes betrayed his concern. "Are you feeling okay?"

"Sore," she murmured, downplaying her pain as much as possible. "I remember some things, but parts of my memory is nothing more than a blur. How long have I been sleeping? Where's the doctor?"

Zach reached over to push the call light lying beside her. "You've been out for about ninety minutes or so. I'm sure Dr. Katy and Janelle will be here soon."

The image of Leonard shoving her aside flashed in her memory. "What happened to Leonard? He didn't have to go to the psych hospital in Madison did he?"

"I don't think so. He calmed down after they gave him a shot." Zack's dark green eyes reflected his guilt. "I feel awful about what happened, Merry."

She tried to smile, even though even that much movement made her head pound. "I told you it wasn't your fault."

"I should have listened to you," he persisted, his fingers tightly gripping the side rail of her bed. "I should have left the room right away."

She hated to watch him beating himself up like this. "Zack, it was probably too late. Leonard has cop radar. He can sense you guys a mile away. But it's not his fault, either. He had a bad experience several years ago and has associated police with pain ever since." She shifted in the bed, and winced. "I need to get up."

"Not a good idea," Zack said, putting a hand on her right shoulder to keep her from trying to sit up. Sharp pain stabbed the upper part of her left chest, and she vaguely remembered hitting the nursing station on that side.

"Don't move until the doctor says you can," Zack cautioned. "There was talk about a possible broken clavicle to go along with your concussion."

"Broken clavicle?" She couldn't mask her horror. A

concussion was bad enough, but a broken clavicle could keep her off work for up to eight weeks.

"They don't know for sure," Zack admitted. "They did X-rays along with the CT scan of your head."

"How's our star patient?" Dr. Katy asked cheerfully as she walked into the room.

Merry had been a patient in the hospital once before, and she didn't much care for it now. Did she sound as condescending when she talked to patients? If so, she needed to change her approach.

"Tell me about my injuries," Merry said, reminding herself that Dr. Katy was a great ER doctor, one she'd always respected. "Zack mentioned something about a broken collarbone?"

One of her colleagues, Janelle, came into the room and stood beside Dr. Katy.

"You have a cracked collarbone on your left side and a concussion," Dr. Katy informed her. "The fracture is not displaced so it should heal up fine on its own. We'll give you a sling to wear when you're up. And I'd like to keep you overnight so we can monitor your concussion."

"Overnight?" Staying here as a patient was the last thing she wanted to do. "But I'm dog-sitting Ace for Julie and Derek. He can't stay home alone."

"When did Julie and Derek get a dog?" Zack asked.

Thinking hurt, but she managed to count backwards. "About two months ago. One of their neighbors passed away so they adopted Ace rather than send him to the humane society. He's very well trained and Lexi adores him."

"Merry, being monitored here is important," Dr. Katy chimed in. "The bleeding on the back of your head has stopped and we don't think you'll need stitches. But still, you know how tricky a head injury can be." Dr. Katy raised her brow. "Are you willing? I'd like to call upstairs to reserve a bed for you."

"Stay. I'll take care of Ace," Zack promised.

Nausea rolled through her belly, a lousy side effect of her concussion. As much as she didn't want to stay, she knew that even minor head injuries could change into something worse. She needed to be smart about her health.

"All right," she agreed, swallowing hard and praying she wouldn't humiliate herself further by throwing up in front of Zack. "I'll stay."

"Great. We'll get things going on our end," Dr. Katy said in a cheerful tone that somehow managed to grate on Merry's nerves. She was really, really, going to change her bedside manner from now on. Dr. Katy left the room, presumably to get her admitted to a nursing unit. Janelle did a quick set of vitals before following Dr. Katy out of the room. Merry wasn't exactly sad to see them leave. She wanted to close her eyes and shut everyone out, but she needed to make sure Zack took care of Ace.

She glanced up at him. "I've been staying with Ace at Julie and Derek's townhouse because my apartment building doesn't allow pets. If you could stay with him there, I'd appreciate it."

"Okay. I need the key." At her blank expression, Zack grimaced. "Let me guess, the place isn't locked up."

She flashed a weary smile. "What do you think? You know there's hardly any crime in Crystal Lake."

Zack scowled but didn't argue. "Is the other side of the townhouse still vacant?"

"Yes." Merry didn't mention that she'd planned to ask if she could rent the place from Julie until her friend explained how she and Derek were putting the entire building up for sale next year. They wanted to build their own home on the lake. Not that she blamed them, but there was no way she could afford to buy the entire townhouse even if she could manage to rent out the other half, which of course was no guarantee.

"Okay, I'll check on Ace," Zack said, looking down at his watch. "I have to run the evidence back to Madison first and finish my shift, but I'll head over as soon as I'm finished."

"Thanks," she whispered. She wasn't sure she could maintain her composure for much longer. She silently prayed for strength.

"Take care, Merry," Zack said, his tone surprisingly gentle. "I'll be back later to check on you."

She wanted to tell him he didn't need to come back, but she closed her eyes, still fighting against the swirling nausea. By the time she opened her eyes again, Zack was gone.

And despite how terrible she felt, she found herself looking forward to seeing him again.

———

ZACK MADE the trip back to Madison in record time, without speeding. He reported in with the evidence he'd collected, and then went out to finish up his shift, pulling over several speeders and one OWI before heading home. It was Thursday and he was off the weekend, but he was scheduled to work tomorrow morning, unless he could find someone else to pick up his shift.

He didn't have to make too many phone calls to get someone to pick up his Friday hours. Over the past few years he'd buried himself in work, taking any and all shifts offered up so he didn't have to think about everything he'd lost. One of the guys he routinely covered for was happy to return the favor.

Swallowing hard, he steeled himself against the usual wave of anger, but surprisingly, the emotion didn't hit him with the same force it had in the past. It was a little over two years ago since he'd lost his wife and his daughter to cancer within six months of each other, and he'd hovered on the brink of despair for a long time.

It didn't seem right that he was slowly getting over the loss. Suzanne and Amelia had once been the center of his world. He had no intention of ever replacing them in his heart.

But life trudged on, and inexplicably the pain eased from sharp and breathtaking to a low constant ache. He stood in the tiny kitchen of his apartment, forcing himself to remember Suzanne's face as she held their dying daughter. The image was fuzzy, and he was irritated to realize that Merry's pale face flashed in his mind with far more clarity.

No. He wasn't going there. Merry was his sister's friend, nothing more. He'd enjoyed talking to her at Julie and Derek's wedding but was determined to keep his distance from anything remotely romantic. She was a friend, and that was the only reason he was pitching in to help out. Especially since her injury was mostly his fault.

He changed out of his uniform and pulled on comfortable clothes—well-worn jeans and a T-shirt, both hanging loosely on his lanky frame. He'd returned to the gym, trying to gain back some of the weight he'd lost after burying his family but, so far, he was still a good thirty pounds under his normal weight.

Zack packed spare clothes in a small duffel bag, tossed in his tablet which contained the latest legal thriller, and then tucked his badge and his gun inside. He hooked the duffel over his shoulder, grabbed his keys off the table and headed back outside to his black pick-up truck. Since he was officially off the next three days, he didn't want to drive the squad car. He realized it had been too long, since Derek and Julie's wedding, that he'd had some downtime. As he headed out of town, he filled up his gas tank, wincing at the ridiculously high prices, before heading out to the interstate.

The summer sun was high in the sky and a cool breeze filtered in through his open driver's side window. For a moment he felt almost happy, or at least not sad. He told himself that his lighthearted mood was probably because he didn't have to work for the next few days. He was clearly overdue for some rest and relaxation.

He tuned in the radio to his favorite country station and let the twang of music wash over him as he headed out to Crystal Lake. He and Julie had grown up there, and the small town was chock full of memories, both good and bad. Growing up they'd had a great time, waterskiing and tubing on the lake. He'd met Suzanne in college, and they'd gotten married as soon as he'd graduated. They'd made their home in Crystal Lake until cancer struck, not just once but twice, stealing the two people he'd loved the most.

He'd moved away after losing Suzanne and Amelia, but if he were honest with himself, he'd admit that Madison just wasn't home.

Of course, he'd never have a home again, so it didn't matter much that the city housing the state capitol was still as foreign to him now as it had been two years ago when he first moved. Some of the guys he worked with still razzed him when he managed to get lost.

His truck quickly ate up the miles, and he made it to Crystal Lake near dinnertime. He drove down Main Street, smiling a little when he saw Rose's Café. Josie ran the place now, and he wouldn't mind stopping there to get something to eat. But first he had to head over to Derek and Julie's townhouse to take care of Ace.

His sister's home was located a few minutes outside of town, one of the few rental properties with lakefront access. He pulled into the driveway and climbed from the truck, gratefully stretching out his legs.

He headed up to the front door, hoping that Ace would somehow recognize him as a friend rather than a foe. He could hear the dog start barking the minute he climbed up onto the front porch, and he wished he'd kept his uniform on since it was entirely possible that Merry's scent would calm the animal down.

"Easy, Ace, good dog," he called. He opened the front door, and the black lab stood his ground, barking furiously as if protecting the home from an invader.

Zack tensed, hoping the animal wouldn't leap up and sink his teeth in. He considered lowering himself to the stoop, so that his body was less threatening, but wasn't sure if that would be a good idea if he had to run.

"Easy, Ace. I'm Julie's brother, and I'm not going to hurt you." He felt a bit ridiculous talking to the animal, but he wasn't sure what else to do. He didn't dare take his eyes off the lab, and slowly lowered himself into a crouch. "I'm a friend, Ace. I'm a friend."

The dog stopped barking, and Zack let out a tiny sigh of relief. Ace came outside, sniffing the air as if trying to determine if he approved of Zack's scent. Zack wished he'd spent more time at his sister's house so the dog would recognize him. Was four months too long for his scent to linger?

"Easy boy," he said again, holding out his hand palm up. "Do you want to smell me some more?"

Ace stretched his neck out, his nose still sniffing the air. After what seemed like forever, the dog crept closer and sniffed his hand. Zack stayed still, unwilling to make any sudden moves. Maybe there was some of Merry's scent still clinging to his skin, because Ace began to wag his tail in a sign of welcome.

"That's it, boy, we're good." Zack stroked the dog lightly, and then stood up as the lab bounded out to do his business.

"Okay, I think we've made it past the first hurdle, boy," he said, still talking to the dog since there wasn't anyone else around. For the first time he thought that having a pet to come home to might not be a bad idea. He'd chosen to live a lonely life, a decision he didn't regret. But a dog would make his self-imposed isolation more bearable.

"Come on, Ace, let's go inside," he called. He stepped back up on the porch and opened the front door, hoping the dog would get the message.

But Ace ran over to the bushes around the corner of the townhouse, sniffing furiously along the ground, growling low in his throat.

"What's wrong, boy?" Had the dog found some sort of animal hiding under there? If so, he hoped it wasn't a skunk. That was a nightmare he did not need. Zack crossed over to the dog. "What's wrong, Ace? What did you find?"

No signs of an animal that he could see, but then he caught a glimpse of a footprint in the mud, almost directly beneath the bedroom window.

He narrowed his gaze, kneeling beside the footprint that looked to be relatively fresh, considering a band of severe thunderstorms had moved through just two days ago. He couldn't see the imprint of a tread, and from the shape of the print he thought it was likely a boot had made the impression rather than an athletic shoe, a size eleven or twelve at best guess. He wanted to get a ruler to use as a reference point for the footprint.

He rocked back on his heels, glancing around the area, searching for anything that seemed out of place. He didn't know for sure how long Derek and Julie had been gone, but it seemed odd that the boot print would belong to Derek anyway. The window looked to be in perfectly good shape, with no evidence of recent repairs.

"Good job," he murmured to Ace, who came up beside him. He leaned down and gave the dog a thorough rub. "Good boy."

He went into the house and searched for a ruler. Then he returned to the site, setting the twelve inch ruler against the boot print, first lengthwise, and then measuring the width, taking several photos with his phone.

While he was glad that Merry had Ace here to keep an eye on her, he didn't like the thought of someone creeping up to the bedroom window, trying to look inside.

If the mystery Peeping Tom planned to return while Zack was here, he'd be in for a big surprise. Because Zack wasn't going to take a crime like this lightly, especially if Merry or his sister, Julie, were the intended victims.

———

MERRY COULDN'T BELIEVE how uncomfortable hospital beds were. How in the world did they expect patients to get better when they were resting on a bag of rocks that masqueraded as a mattress?

She never should have agreed to stay. If she were back at

the townhouse she'd be resting in a softer bed and would have Ace for company.

"Time for your neuro check," Gail the floor nurse said as she entered the room.

Merry tried to smile, knowing her bad temper wasn't the staff's fault. All this time she thought doctors always made the worst patients, but maybe nurses ran a close second. "Okay."

Gail ran through the routine, one that had been repeated every two hours since she'd regained consciousness.

"How are my pupils?" she asked, when Gail finished peering into her eyes with a penlight.

"Equal and reactive," Gail responded. "Do you know where you are?"

"Hope County Hospital," Merry responded. "My name is Merry Haines and today is August eighth, twenty-thirteen."

"I'm sure this is getting annoying by now," Gail said sympathetically.

"Oh yeah." She preferred Gail's honesty over the false cheerfulness. Or maybe it wasn't false, but dealing with perky cheerfulness when your head felt like it was going to explode wasn't easy.

"You get to advance to full liquids for dinner," Gail said. "Let me know when you want me to call for a tray."

Her earlier nausea had faded after drinking broth and eating Jell-O, a good sign that she was getting better, not worse. "Now is good. It's already after six." And visiting hours were over at eight o'clock, not that she'd been watching the clock for Zack to show up or anything. She was grateful enough that he was taking care of Ace.

"All right. Is there anything else I can get you?" Gail asked.

"A softer mattress?" Merry forced a smile. "No, thanks. I'm fine."

"I'm sure it's not easy for you being a patient here," Gail said. "I don't think I'd like it much either."

So her bad temper was noticeable. What was wrong with her? Usually she was always the one with the positive glass-half-full outlook on life. She needed to get over herself already.

"Yeah, I wouldn't recommend it," she said to Gail. "But seriously, thanks for everything."

"You're welcome. Expect your tray in about an hour, okay?"

"Sounds good." Merry shifted in the bed, trying to find a more comfortable position. Maybe it was a good thing that Zack hadn't returned. With any luck she'd feel more human by morning and be well enough for discharge. Although what she'd do with herself for eight weeks, was something else entirely. The thought of sitting idle in her apartment was far too depressing.

There was a knock at her door. "Come in," she called, expecting her dinner tray.

Zack poked his head in. "Are you up for a wheelchair ride?" he asked.

She shouldn't be so happy to see him, but she was. She wondered if he knew she was on bed rest or maybe he just assumed she needed a wheelchair. "I guess, why?"

"It's a surprise." Zack thrust the door open and pushed a wheelchair through. "Do you need help?"

She hoped he didn't notice her blush. "I can get up on my own," she muttered.

He stood holding the wheelchair steady as she stood at the side of the bed, grateful that she was wearing a robe so that her backside wouldn't be flapping in the breeze, and then turned to sit back down. She tugged at her shoulder sling, trying to make her arm more comfortable.

"Ready?" Zack asked, grinning like a fool.

His smile was contagious. "Absolutely."

He wheeled her down the hall and into the elevator. When they reached the lobby level, he pushed her straight through the revolving doors and into the fresh air.

"This is wonderful," she said, lifting her face to the warm summer breeze and taking a deep breath, enjoying the strong scent of lilacs. "Thanks so much for bringing me out here."

He pushed her down the sidewalk until he found a shady spot beneath a tree. He set the brakes on her wheelchair. "Wait here, okay?"

"Sure." She frowned when he hurried away to the large surface parking lot. What was he doing?

A few minutes later, he returned with Ace trotting at his side, looking downright docile on his leash. She couldn't prevent the huge smile that bloomed as they approached.

"I figured you needed a friend," he said. "And I didn't want to leave him home alone, again."

Zack let go of the leash and Ace ran over to her, wagging his entire body as well as his tail in welcome before he tried to crawl into her lap.

It had been so long since anyone had done something this nice for her. And the fact that Zack had gone out of his way to cheer her up meant far more than it should have.

She knew Zack was still mourning his deceased wife and daughter, so getting emotionally involved with him was not an option.

No matter how much she wanted to.

3

M erry grimaced as the dog licked her face. "No, Ace, knock it off," she said, trying to avoid another doggie kiss.

"Down, Ace," Zack said firmly and, amazingly, the dog sat back on his haunches, his tongue lolling out of his mouth as he looked at them.

"Wow, he must think you sound like Derek. He doesn't behave like that for me." Merry reached out to scratch Ace behind the ears. "Thanks so much for bringing him. Ace is just what I needed to cheer me up."

"Pets are good at that, aren't they?" Zack bent over to pick up Ace's leash, and then looped it over the arm of her wheelchair.

"Yes, they are. I appreciate the last minute dog-sitting duty, too."

"It's no problem," Zack said. "Although I have to admit, it was touch and go when I first got to the house, while he decided whether or not I was one of the good guys."

"Oh no, I never thought of that," Merry said, battling a wave of regret. Why hadn't she considered that possibility?

Especially since she knew Ace was a good guard dog. "See? I knew I should have insisted on going home. At least then I could have made the transition easier for you."

"I'm glad you're staying," he said. "Otherwise I'd have to worry about you."

The thought of Zack worrying made her heart flip, and she took a deep breath in an attempt to hide her reaction. "I'm fine. Dr. Katy was being overly cautious."

"Smart doctor. So what time do you think they'll let you go tomorrow?" Zack asked, changing the subject.

She shook her head. "I'm not sure, but the sooner the better as far as I'm concerned. I have my car here, so I'll be able to drive myself home. Thankfully, I don't have a stick shift and I'm right handed, so driving shouldn't be a problem. What about you? Do you work tomorrow?"

"Nope, I have the next three days off." Zack looked so relaxed and content that she could barely reconcile the man sitting on the bench beside her with the man she'd chatted with at Julie's wedding. Of course, it could be that watching his sister get married, while knowing he'd already lost his wife and daughter, had been extraordinarily difficult.

"I'm glad to hear you have some time off," she said, petting Ace, who'd flopped down at her feet. "I imagine your job is stressful."

"So is yours," he pointed out. "I think you should have a cop stationed in your ER all the time, considering some of the stuff that's happened there."

She couldn't argue his logic. They had a shoot-out in the trauma room of the ER over a year ago, and now this latest issue with Leonard. Both incidents were very much out of the ordinary for Hope County Hospital.

Her stomach rumbled and she thought about her dinner

tray waiting for her. "I should probably head back inside," she murmured. "I'm so lucky, I get to eat soup for dinner."

"Just soup?" Zack echoed with a wry grimace. "Do you want me to sneak you in a burger from Rose's Café?"

She laughed and shook her head. "That's a nice offer, but no thanks. I've been feeling sick to my stomach since this morning, so going slow is probably a better option right now. By tomorrow I should be able to have normal food."

His smile faded, and she regretted reminding him about her accident. "I understand," he said. "Give me a minute to put Ace back in my truck, and then I'll wheel you back upstairs."

It was on the tip of her tongue to tell him not to bother, until she realized she couldn't propel herself with one arm. She waited for Zack, thinking there nothing worse than feeling helpless.

A glimpse of a red-haired man flashed along the edge of her vision. She instinctively froze, her heart pounding in her chest. She forced herself to swivel around in her seat to sweep her gaze over the area. Her entire body was tense, until she saw the redhead amongst a group of staff members, all wearing scrubs, walking out toward their cars. She let out a heavy sigh. It was seven-thirty, the end of shift for some of the staff who worked twelve hours at a time.

Idiot, she scolded herself. The redhead she'd glimpsed was not Blake. She'd stopped looking over her shoulder, searching for her ex-boyfriend a year ago, so why was she suddenly doing that again now? Because she'd been injured and was feeling vulnerable? Maybe. The last time she'd been in the hospital as a patient had been after Blake attacked her.

Regardless, she had to stop this nonsense and move forward with her life. She hadn't been out on a date in forever, although, between her job and volunteering in the church choir, she managed to keep busy. Truthfully, she didn't have any desire to get back out in the dating scene.

Blake had seemed so nice and normal at first. To discover his true nature had been a horrifying shock.

She didn't want to think about Blake any more. No doubt, feeling helpless had brought her old fears back to the surface. She pushed the old memories away with an effort, catching sight of Zack jogging back over, secretly relieved and grateful that he hadn't been there to witness her moment of panic.

She already felt pathetic enough, being injured and sitting in a wheelchair. The sooner she got out of the hospital, the better.

"All set?" he asked as he bent down to release the brakes of the wheelchair.

"Sure thing."

He pushed her back inside, neither one of them saying much on the trip up to her room.

"Thanks again," she said, breaking the moment of awkwardness. "Both for bringing Ace to visit me and for keeping an eye on him tonight."

"I don't mind," Zack said. "I'll see you tomorrow."

She lifted her eyebrows in surprise. "Tomorrow?"

He nodded. "I've decided to spend the weekend in Crystal Lake. I haven't been out on my boat in ages."

Merry stared at him in shock, never expecting that he'd be staying at the townhouse, too. But really, what could she say? Zack was Julie's brother, and the speedboat moored up in the boat lift was his. He had every right to stay at his sister's townhouse.

Unless he was doing this out of a misplaced sense of guilt?

"Zack, I hope you're not hanging around just because of what happened with Leonard. I've told you several times it wasn't your fault."

He shrugged in a way that made her think he was still wrestling with guilt. "To be honest, I haven't had time off in months, and I'm looking forward to spending the weekend on the lake."

Merry knew that Julie would be ecstatic to know that her brother was planning to spend the weekend relaxing on his boat. Julie's concern over her brother's emotional state was no secret. His taking time off work to play on the water seemed like a huge step in the right direction.

Who was she to argue?

"I'm glad," she murmured. "You deserve a little fun."

His gaze darkened for a moment, before his expression cleared. "Goodnight, Merry." Zack flashed a crooked smile before leaving.

She ate her cream soup, Jell-O and pudding, trying not to get too excited about spending the weekend with Zack. Not that he'd indicated they'd actually spend any time together. With her lingering headache and her left arm in a sling, she wasn't going to be up for doing much, anyway.

She had to remember that Zack needed a friend, nothing more. But to be honest, she wouldn't mind having him as a friend, too.

ZACK WOKE up the next morning with Ace nudging him, feeling oddly refreshed despite spending the night in one of the twin beds that were *not* designed for a man of his size.

He blinked and stared at the ceiling for a moment, realizing he hadn't dreamed about Suzanne and Amelia in several months. Relief warred with guilt. He didn't want to forget them.

Ace whined and yelped to get his attention.

"Okay, okay, I coming." Zack swung out of the small bed and staggered through the townhouse toward the patio door in the open-concept kitchen and living area. The moment he slid the door open, Ace leaped outside.

"Ace!" he called, hoping the dog wouldn't decide to run off. Since he was dressed in a pair of running shorts and a T-shirt, he headed outside to keep an eye on the lab.

He needn't have worried. The dog did his business, and then loped back up to where Zack stood near the front of the house. Ace dropped a tennis ball on the ground and glanced up at him with a hopeful expression in his doggy eyes.

"Why do I feel like I'm going to regret this?" he asked as he bent over to pick up the ball. He tossed it high in the air, using his former high school baseball skills to make sure it didn't drop into the water.

Ace ran, leaped up and grabbed the ball in his jaw as he landed. The dog ran around in a tight circle for a minute before dashing back over to Zack, dropping down on his haunches and keeping the ball locked in his mouth.

"Neat trick," he said, smiling down at Ace. "Obviously you're in the mood to play, but I need to shower, shave and get dressed first." The last thing he needed was for Merry to come home while he still had a bed-head.

The thought pulled him up short. Since when did he care what Merry thought of him? He shouldn't care what anyone thought of the way he looked. He wasn't here to impress anyone. Least of all a woman.

Determined to prove to himself that he wasn't vain, Zack bent down and gently tugged the ball from the dog's mouth before sending it flying up in the air again and again. On the fourth time, when he put too much muscle behind the throw, sending it out over the lake, Ace didn't hesitate to jump into the water to swim out for the ball that bobbed up and down in the lake.

The water looked cool and inviting. Zack stared at the lake for a moment. Why not? He ran down the grassy embankment and jumped off the end of the pier, grabbing onto his knees so that his bottom hit the water, making a huge cannonball splash.

The cold water stole his breath, but when he shot back up to the surface, he couldn't help letting out a whoop. "Doesn't that feel great, boy?"

Ace swam over to him, the ball clenched between his teeth. Zack propelled himself toward the pier and climbed up the short ladder. Since Ace couldn't climb the ladder, the dog headed toward the shoreline to get out of the lake. Ace stood and shook his entire body, sending droplets of water in all directions.

Zack ducked his head to avoid the worst of Ace's shower. When he turned back, he saw Merry standing on the back patio, wearing her work scrubs and the arm sling. Her wide smile spiked his pulse.

"Looks like fun," she called.

It took several minutes to find his voice. "How did you manage to get discharged so early?" he asked, striving to sound casual as he walked up the lawn, water running off his clothes, to meet her.

Her grin widened. "Special treatment and a threat to leave against medical advice if they didn't let me go."

He searched her gaze, noticing the remnants of pain hidden in her eyes. "How's your head?"

"Still attached to my body as far as I can tell." She bent down to pet a very wet Ace, grimacing when he brushed up against her scrubs.

"Have you eaten breakfast?" Zack asked, tugging Ace away from her. "I was about to make some bacon and eggs, and I have more than enough to share."

He knew he was sunk when her eyes lit up with gratitude. "That would be awesome. The hospital food wasn't exactly inspiring."

"All right, give me some time to shower and change. Ace, stay," he commanded in a stern tone.

The dog flopped down on the grass, rolling around on his back as if the ground could help dry him off. Zack shook his head with amusement and went back inside the townhouse.

He found himself hurrying through his shower, and then nicked himself shaving. He dabbed at the small cut, telling himself he was an idiot.

Merry had been home for only five minutes and already he'd offered to cook her breakfast. This was supposed to be a nice relaxing weekend, not a potential date with his sister's friend and colleague. He needed to stay focused.

Because if he wasn't careful, he was going to find himself in over his head in no time.

———

MERRY HEADED BACK inside her side of the townhouse to make a pot of coffee. She'd been up since six o'clock in the morning, having showered at the hospital. Thankfully, Carrie, her day shift nurse, had brought her a clean pair of scrubs and had helped her comb and dry her hair after her shower. Merry had been forced to ask Carrie to pull her hair back in a simple ponytail since she couldn't manage to do even that much one-handed. Luckily, her reddish gold hair had a bit of a natural curl.

The next six to eight weeks weren't going to be easy, she admitted grimly as she filled the glass carafe with water and carried it over to the coffee maker. Even the simplest tasks took twice as long as normal.

At least she had Ace to keep her company for the weekend. And Zack.

When the coffee finished brewing, she balanced her cup in her injured hand, making her way outside so she could sit on the patio overlooking the lake. Ace padded over to greet her, giving her a lick before dropping at her feet.

As she stared out over the water, she sighed, thinking that being off work for eight weeks wasn't going to help her save any money for a place of her own. She wondered if maybe she should ask Julie to rent out the vacant townhouse. A year of being on the lake was better than nothing, and maybe by then she'd have enough money saved to buy the place.

If she could work enough extra shifts. And if she could manage to save her money. Once she was cleared to return to full duty.

When she heard Zack moving around in the kitchen making breakfast, she got up and crossed over to head inside. "What do you need help with?" she asked.

"Nothing at all, just sit down and relax." He barely looked at her as he spoke, as if making bacon and eggs took all his attention.

No sense in staying where she wasn't wanted. "Do you drink coffee?" she asked.

That caught his attention. "Of course. Who doesn't?" he asked perplexed.

He made her laugh, without even trying. "I'm sure there's someone in the world who doesn't," she teased. "But I made a fresh pot next door. I'll bring a cup over for you."

Fifteen minutes later, Zack poked his head out the screen door. "Breakfast is ready."

It didn't take long to bring the plates filled with bacon, eggs and toast outside. She topped off their coffee, and then sat down and bowed her head.

"Dear Lord, thank You for providing this food to eat and guide us on Your chosen path as we enjoy this beautiful day. Amen."

She lifted her head shocked, to see Zack's expressionless face as he stared out over the lake. Her heart sank with the knowledge that he hadn't bothered to bow his head or attempt to pray.

It made her sad to realize he'd turned his back on God.

Her appetite faded, but she forced herself to eat, taking a bite of the crispy bacon. "This is delicious, thanks."

He sighed and reached for his fork. "I forgot what it was like to share a meal with a Christian."

She felt worse, knowing that Zack didn't consider himself a Christian any more. Julie mentioned that Zack hadn't been to church since his wife and daughter died. She wished there was a way to convince him that God could help support him through this difficult time in his life.

"You're still a Christian, Zack," she said. "God hasn't given up on you, even if you've given up on Him."

Zack didn't respond, eating his food as they were in a race and he wanted to finish first. The easy camaraderie they'd shared evaporated and she had no idea how to get it back.

Did she even want to get it back?

Yes. Yes, she did.

She stared out at the lake, watching the water-skiers and tubers having fun as they flew behind their respective speed boats. Zack would likely head out onto the water as soon as they finished eating, no doubt anxious to get away from her.

She told herself it didn't matter, that Zack was here to relax and have fun. If he didn't want to talk about his faith or church, she wouldn't push.

"When did Julie and Derek leave?" Zack asked.

She was startled by the change in subject. "Tuesday morning, why?"

"You've been here since Tuesday?" he persisted.

She shrugged, using her fork to toy with her eggs. "Yes, I stayed over on Monday night because they were hitting the road early. They dropped Lexi off at her grandparents' house in St. Louis before they headed for a cabin they rented in the Smokey Mountains."

"And Tuesday night the thunderstorms came through, right?" he asked.

"Yes. Why? What is this about?"

Zack was silent for a minute. "Do you see that fishing boat out there on the water?"

Fishing boat? She looked over in the direction he indicated and froze when she saw a man with a baseball cap on his head, fishing not far from the end of their pier.

Her fork clattered to her plate as her fingers went numb. Beneath the blue baseball cap, she could see the thick, bright red hair.

Blake!

4

"No!" Merry stumbled to her feet, nearly falling over in her haste to get away from the table. This couldn't be happening. How had Blake found her?

Zack jumped up to catch her, his strong arms holding her steady. "Merry, what's wrong?"

She shook her head, unable to answer. Trembling with fear, she peered over his shoulder and stared out at the lake, trying to make sure that the guy was actually Blake. But the man in the fishing boat had turned around and was moving steadily away so she could only see his back.

And another glimpse of his red hair.

"Merry, who was that guy?" Zack persisted.

"I—I don't know," she whispered. Was it Blake? Or was she imagining things again? Every guy with red hair wasn't Blake. Hadn't she made the same mistake last evening outside the hospital? Yet, despite the summer heat she was chilled to the bone.

Zack must have known she was cold because he pulled her into his arms and hugged her. For a moment she rested her head on his shoulder, grateful for his strength and his warmth. Just inhaling his musky, male scent brought her a sense of calmness.

Please, Lord, keep me safe from Blake. Please!

"Let's sit down and finish our breakfast, okay?" Zack murmured.

She forced herself to pull away from his embrace. One last glance at the lake confirmed the fishing boat was long gone. Merry sank into her seat and picked up her fork, although her appetite had completely vanished.

"Merry, you need to tell me what happened," Zack pressed as he sat down beside her. "Has someone been bothering you? Maybe an old boyfriend?"

Ace came over and stuck his head into her lap, as if he sensed she was upset. She stroked the dog's black, silky fur, trying to bolster her flagging courage. As much as she didn't like to talk about her past, she knew Zack deserved some sort of answer.

"I haven't dated anyone in over two years," she said finally. "Since I lived in Minneapolis."

If he was shocked by her lack of social life, he didn't let on. "So you haven't noticed anyone following you lately?" Zack asked.

"No, I haven't." Suddenly she was angry with him. "Why don't you just get to the point, Zack? You're the one who noticed the guy in the fishing boat. Do you think he's following me? Why do I get the feeling there's something you're not telling me?"

Zack grimaced. "You're right. I did notice that guy in the boat. I thought it was a little odd he chose to fish right here amidst the boaters, tubers and skiers churning up the water. Early morning hours are best, and any serious fisherman would know that. I thought he seemed suspicious."

She didn't understand what he was trying to say, especially since Zack couldn't possibly know about Blake. "But why in the world would you think some guy in a fishing boat is watching me?"

"Yesterday afternoon, when I came here to let Ace out, he went sniffing and growling by the side of the house. I thought he found an animal or something, but when I went over there, I saw a footprint in the soft soil beneath the bedroom window."

Merry felt the blood drain from her face. "A footprint?" she repeated hoarsely.

"Yeah. So when I saw that guy in the fishing boat right next to our pier, I became suspicious. Especially when you seemed to recognize him. So now it's your turn, Merry. Tell me who he is."

She shivered, and couldn't help wondering if the man in the boat really was Blake after all? Would he really have come to find her after two long years? And if so, why? Surely, he couldn't still be obsessed with her?

She didn't want to believe the man was Blake, but she was equally afraid to ignore the potential threat. She pushed her plate away and struggled to her feet. "Show me the footprint."

Zack stood and walked across the patio, around Julie's small vegetable garden, to the south side of the house. She followed with Ace trotting along beside her.

"Right there," Zack said, as he indicated the area beneath the bedroom window where she'd been sleeping the past few nights.

She crept closer until she could see the distinct footprint in the soil. Seeing the evidence for herself only made her feel sick to her stomach.

"I've taken pictures of the print, and I'd be happy to help you file a police report if necessary," Zack was saying.

She swung around to face him. "How can I file a police report? I didn't get a good look at the guy in the boat, so I can't describe his face."

"But you know who he is, right?" Zack said gently.

She let out her breath in a loud sigh, knowing that Zack's cop instincts were not going to let this go. "It could be a guy I once dated, Blake Caruthers. He has bright red hair, just like the guy in the boat. But he lives in Minneapolis, or he did the last time I saw him. Don't we need proof that he's really here, following me, before we go to the police?"

"It wouldn't hurt to file a restraining order against him," Zack said.

She shook her head, a sense of helplessness washing over her. "There's no point. I already have a restraining order against him and it's active for another two years. Besides, in my experience, a restraining order isn't worth the paper it's printed on."

Merry turned and walked away, unable to bear talking about Blake any more. If he was really here in Crystal Lake, then she'd have no choice but to pick up and move again.

Although that wouldn't be easy, since she wasn't able to work for the next six to eight weeks. Not to mention packing or lifting boxes. She'd have to wait for her collarbone to heal.

And by then she could easily be dead. Because if Blake was really after her all this time, she knew he wouldn't stop until he satisfied his need for revenge.

———————

ZACK FOLLOWED Merry to the patio, his thoughts whirling. Granted, he was the one who'd found the footprint and noticed the guy in the fishing boat, but he was still shocked to know Merry was really being stalked.

"I need you to tell me everything you know about this guy, Blake Caruthers," he commanded when she sat back down at the table. "I'll start investigating him, immediately."

Merry grimaced and shook her head. "I don't want to go into all this now."

Zack battled a flash of temper. "Merry, we can't just sit here and pretend this isn't happening. This guy, Blake, could be dangerous. I'll start investigating him, and once we prove he's not in Minneapolis any more, we can go to the sheriff's department here. Trust me, being in a small town will be an advantage. The Crystal Lake deputies will be far more concerned about protecting one of their citizens, especially a young woman like you, than any big city cop."

She lifted her brow. "Aren't you a big city cop now?"

"Don't try to change the subject," he warned, ignoring the light jab. "Because I can tell you right now, I'm not going to let this go."

"It's a long story and one that can certainly wait until later." She stood and picked up her plate, but when she turned to the sliding glass doors leading into the house, she stopped and let out a frustrated sound. "Will you open the door for me, please?"

"Sit down. I'll take care of the dishes. It's not like you can do much with one hand."

"Fine." She thrust the plate at him, and then went around to the other set of patio doors. "I'm going to rest for a while. My head is pounding." Merry didn't so much as glance at him as she went into Julie and Derek's side of the townhouse, the screen door snapping shut behind her.

Zack rubbed the back of his neck, knowing she was upset with him, but uncertain as to why. It wasn't his fault that Blake was here, following her. All he wanted to do was to help protect her.

He stacked their dirty dishes and carried them inside. He quickly washed and dried them before grabbing his tablet out of his room.

The glare of the sun made it difficult to read the tablet outside, so he stayed inside to begin a cursory search for Blake Caruthers. When Ace whined at the door, he stood up and let the dog inside.

"Good boy," he murmured, giving Ace a pat on the head. After seeing the guy in the fishing boat, he was even more grateful to have Ace around as a watch dog. He was tempted to put Ace in Merry's side of the townhouse, but didn't want to interrupt if she really was trying to get some sleep.

He surfed the internet for the next hour, trying to find anything he could about Blake Caruthers out of Minneapolis. He found a social media account for the name, but there was no photo attached to the page. According to the information on the social media account, he could see that Blake attended the University of Minnesota. He sat back in his seat, wondering if Merry had received her nursing degree at the same college. It would make sense that they'd met there.

It bothered him to think about how Merry had dated the guy. A man who'd betrayed her trust, doing something terrible enough that she was able to take out a restraining order against him. He knew for sure Blake had hurt her emotionally, but had he also hurt her physically? Sexually?

He felt sick at the thought.

Zack found a Caroline Caruthers linked to Blake's social media page. When he clicked on the picture he saw a pretty woman with bright red hair. Very different from Merry's reddish blonde but they shared similar freckles. Was Caroline Caruthers, Blake's sister? Did Merry know Caroline, too? Was it possible they were all at the University at the same time?

He scrounged around the townhouse to find paper and pencil. He caught a glimpse of Lexi's many sketchbooks and decided his niece wouldn't mind if he borrowed a few pages.

Taking notes helped keep his simmering anger at bay. If this Blake guy thought he was going to hurt Merry again, he was sorely mistaken. After Zack took notes on the scant information he'd been able to find, he searched on the public access simple case search function to find the restraining order. The information was there, but there wasn't much detail. Just that Blake Caruthers was supposed to stay at least twenty feet away from Merry Haines.

He stared at the computer, wishing he could find a way to prove Caruthers had already violated the court order. There were other violations in the system for Blake, too. Zack read each one, noting that Caruthers spent time in jail for possession of illegal drugs, theft, disorderly conduct, and breaking and entering. Obviously the guy didn't seem to learn from his mistakes.

Zack scowled and reached for his phone. He called his buddy, Colton Wallace, the guy who'd covered his shift for him.

"Cole? It's Zack."

"What's up? Are you enjoying the lake?"

"Sure am," Zack replied. It wasn't a lie, he had enjoyed his brief swim. "But I need a favor. There's a young woman in town being harassed by some guy, and she already has a restraining order against him. I found a copy on-line, but I need to know what kind of vehicle this guy is driving. Can you look up his driver's registration for me? His name is Blake Caruthers and he lives in Minneapolis, Minnesota."

"Sure." He could hear Cole typing on a keyboard in the background, each squad was equipped with a computer. "What's his date of birth?"

Zack gave the information he'd found on-line, making a mental note that Caruthers was two years older than Merry.

"Got it," Cole said.

"Give me the tag number of his vehicle."

Colton rattled off the information and Zack wrote everything down.

"He actually drives a minivan?" Zack asked incredulously.

"That's what's registered to his name, although I suppose he could have purchased a different vehicle without bothering to notify the state." There was more tapping of the computer, and then Cole let out a low whistle. "Wow, this guy has quite the rap sheet."

"I know," Zack muttered.

"You better watch your back," Cole warned. "This guy is no stranger to crime."

No kidding. And it really made him mad that Caruthers was likely out here, stalking Merry. "Thanks for the help, Cole. I really appreciate it."

"No problem. Let me know if you need anything else."

"I will." Zack disconnected the call, grimly realizing he might need Cole's help again.

He wasn't going to rest until he found Blake Caruthers, proved he violated his restraining order and sent him back to jail, locking him up where he belonged.

MERRY TOOK some ibuprofen and tried to rest, but she couldn't seem to get past the brief image of the red-haired man on the boat. She told herself that if that guy really was Blake, at least he knew she wasn't here alone. He would have seen Zack and Ace both sitting beside her on the patio.

But the knowledge wasn't exactly reassuring, since she knew all too well what Blake was capable of.

She squeezed her eyes shut, not wanting to relive the past. It was over and done. Zack was right about one thing—Blake wouldn't find it so easy to get to her here in Crystal Lake. She knew many of the deputies by name, since they often accompanied car crash victims or DUI violators to the emergency department. Plus, Julie and Derek were her friends, and Derek was one of the sheriff's deputies, too. Being on a first name basis with the police would certainly help.

With a rush she sat up in bed, making her head pound with the sudden movement. Wait a minute, she didn't have to pick up and move. She could ask Julie and Derek to allow her to rent the other half of the townhouse. Then for sure, Blake wouldn't be so brazen as to violate the restraining order. Not when Derek, another sheriff's deputy was living right next door.

Feeling calmer at having a rational and workable plan, she settled back down. She must have dozed a bit because when she opened her eyes, she realized well over an hour had passed.

The nagging headache lingering behind her eyes had faded, so she swung out of bed and made her way back into the kitchen. She poured a tall glass of sun tea, one of her favorite beverages, and looked longingly outside. Realizing that attempting to hide from Zack was just plain stupid, she forced herself to go outside to sit on the patio.

"Merry? How are you feeling?" Zack asked, as he came outside to meet her. Ace acted as if she'd been gone for days instead of hours, greeting her with a wagging tail and happy doggy kisses.

"Better," she admitted, giving Ace the attention he craved. "My headache is mostly gone."

"I'd offer to take you out on the boat, but I'm afraid that hitting the waves would make your headache come back," Zack said with regret. "But maybe we can go tomorrow, if it stays nice and doesn't rain."

She shouldn't have been so thrilled with his offhand invitation, but she was. "I'd like to go out on the boat. Couldn't we try this afternoon?"

"Tomorrow is soon enough," Zack said firmly. "You just got out of the hospital, remember?"

"I suppose you're right," she said with a sigh. She glanced out at the water, instinctively looking for the fishing boat. "Any sign of him?"

"No, but I've done a little research while you were resting," Zack admitted. "Do you know Caroline? Is she Blake's sister?"

Her mouth fell open in surprise. "How did you know?"

"I went through social media websites to find him and found her, too. I noticed you all went to college together."

She was amazed he'd found out so much information in such a short period of time. "Yes, we did."

Zack leaned forward, his gaze earnest. "Look, I don't want to upset you, but the only way I can keep you safe is if you tell me what happened."

Zack compassion was nearly palpable, and she knew

feeling embarrassed was ridiculous. It wasn't as if she'd asked for Blake to become obsessed with her.

Just like it wasn't Blake's fault that he suffered from a mental illness.

"Merry, please," Zack said in a low, rough voice. "I wouldn't ask if it wasn't important."

She stalled, taking a long sip of her sun tea. "I was an only child, and lived next door to the Caruthers when I was growing up. Caroline was my age and we became best friends. I spent more time at the Caruthers' house than I did at my own home, but my parents didn't seem to mind. They were older when they had me, and I think they were a bit overwhelmed by the responsibility of raising a child. And to be honest, I craved being a part of the loud, rambunctious family next door."

Zack reached out to take her hand, and the simple touch helped keep her grounded.

"I had a huge crush on Blake when I was a teenager, but he was two years older and barely noticed me, treating me like another kid sister. Caroline and I both wanted to go to the University of Minnesota and were thrilled to be accepted. We even roomed together. That's when Blake noticed me."

The knot in her stomach tightened painfully. She took a slow breath, staring down at Zack's hand holding hers, so that she didn't have to look him in the eye.

"We began dating, but Blake was different. Moody. He talked to himself and sometimes became violent. One night, he slammed his fist through a glass window and had to be taken to the hospital. His behavior became worse, paranoid and delusional. During his second trip to the hospital he was diagnosed with paranoid schizophrenia."

Zack's fingers tightened on hers, and she forced herself

to meet his gaze. "At first, it wasn't too bad. He was put on medication and seemed to be doing better. But then he stopped taking the medication, claiming he didn't like the side effects. Shortly after that, he attacked me."

"You don't have to tell me anything more," Zack protested, but she ignored him.

"Caroline came to help me and the police took him away. Blake went back on his meds, and then went off them again. Over the next few months, it became a never-ending cycle."

"I'm sorry, Merry," Zack murmured. "I'm so sorry you had to go through that."

"I tried to stay with him. I didn't want to leave Blake just because of his diagnosis. But he wouldn't stay on the meds and without them he was just too impulsive and violent. I had no choice but to break things off."

"You did the right thing."

She shrugged. "After I graduated, I started working as a nurse at one of the hospitals in the Twin Cities, and Blake would always be there, waiting for me at the end of my shift or hanging around my apartment. I moved, but he found me. He attacked me again, so I filed the restraining order. And when that didn't work, I picked up and moved to a different state without telling anyone where I was going."

"And you came here, to Crystal Lake," Zack finished.

She nodded. "I've been here for two years. And I thought I was finally safe. But he must have found me, again, even after all this time."

"I'll keep you safe. You don't have to be afraid of him."

She shook her head, battling a wave of helplessness. "You don't understand, Zack. I'm also worried about you. Blake must have seen you on the patio. He'll assume we're, um, you know." Her cheeks heated and she ducked her head. "He'll see you as a threat. I think it's best if you head back to Madison."

Zack let go of her hand and scowled darkly. She tilted her chin, not caring if she made him mad.

She would rather have him safe. And if that meant being alone until Julie and Derek returned, then that was just fine with her.

5

Zack had to work hard to rein in his temper. Did she really think he was going to leave her here with a crazy man stalking her? Fat chance. What kind of guy did she think he was? As if he cared about whether or not Caruthers came after him? Frankly, he'd welcome the chance to take him down a peg.

Instinctively, he knew Merry wouldn't want to hear that, so he took several deep breaths before turning around to face her.

"I'm staying the weekend, end of discussion. Are you hungry? We could head over to Rose's Café for lunch."

"Don't do this." Her blue eyes pleaded with him. "Don't underestimate Blake."

He narrowed his gaze. "I'm a police officer. I'm more than capable of being your bodyguard. If Blake were smart, he wouldn't underestimate me."

"Maybe we should stay here, keep a low profile."

If he wasn't so angry, he'd be touched by her efforts to protect him. "Actually, I'd like to go to town, see if we can catch a glimpse of his navy blue minivan."

She glanced up at him in surprise. "How did you find out what he's driving?"

"I have connections." He hesitated, wondering if he should tell her everything else he discovered. He didn't want to scare her, yet she needed to understand what she was dealing with. "You need to know Caruthers has done jail time. He has a rather significant criminal record. Drugs, breaking and entering, disorderly conduct."

She didn't look too surprised. "I guess that's more proof he's not taking his medication."

"Please let me take you out to lunch." The moment the sentence left his mouth, he wished he could take it back. He hadn't intended to make it sound like he was asking her out on a date. "I think it would be fun to go into town for a while," he tacked on.

"What about Ace?" she asked, rubbing the dog behind his ears. The lab's head rested on her lap, his eyes gazing up at her adoringly.

"He'll be fine inside for a bit. I'll play with him when we get back."

"All right," she agreed. "But I'll be rather conspicuous in my scrubs."

"You can change if you'd like."

She seemed to consider the idea but then shrugged it off. "I'll wait until later."

He told himself again, to think of Merry like a younger sister, but so far, that tactic wasn't working as well as it should.

"If you're sure." He was anxious to go, partially because he really wanted to see if he could get a glimpse of Blake's van. The sooner he found this guy, the better.

"I'm sure."

Zack put Ace inside the townhouse. "Guard the door, Ace."

The dog thumped his tail, and then stretched out in front of the patio doors as if he'd understood Zack's command.

Merry didn't say much on the short drive into town. He kept his eyes peeled on the road for any sign of a navy blue van with the tag number of 555VRY. They passed a blue van on the highway, and his heart leaped with anticipation, but the plate number didn't match.

Main Street was busy with summer tourists, forcing him to park his truck several blocks down from the café. As they strolled along the sidewalk, he caught sight of the modest Crystal Lake Motel. He paused, scanning the parked cars in the tiny parking lot, figuring if Caruthers was in the area, he had to be staying somewhere.

"Do you see the van?" Merry asked, catching on to what he was doing.

"No." He scowled and reluctantly began walking again. "Could be that he has it down by the public boat launch."

"Or it could be that he's not even here. We don't know for sure that Blake was the guy in the fishing boat."

He didn't bother to argue with her. The boot print beneath the bedroom window, along with the redhead in the fishing boat, was too much of a coincidence to ignore. He held the café door open, the tiny bell jingling to announce their arrival.

"Howdy stranger," Josie greeted him with a broad smile. "It's about time you came back home."

"Just here for the weekend," he pointed out with a grin, even though the word home tugged at his heart. In his mind, Crystal Lake would always be home. Josie was the café owner and self-proclaimed gossip. He knew within minutes the whole town would be buzzing with the news of the prodigal son's return.

"Nice to see you, too, Merry," Josie said with blatant curiosity in her gaze. Zack feared she was already pegging them as a couple. "Find a place to sit, and Darcy will be over shortly."

"No problem." A booth along the row of windows opened up and he nudged Merry in that direction.

"She's going to have us married off in about an hour," Merry muttered half under her breath.

Zack froze for a moment as he was sliding into the booth, and then forced himself to relax. "I could care less what the wagging tongues in Crystal Lake think, but if you're worried, I'll make sure she knows we're just friends."

Merry waved her hand. "It's fine. Hopefully, once you're back in Madison, they'll forget about this and move onto something else."

The thought of leaving Merry here alone while he returned to Madison bothered him. He stared down at the menu, wondering if he could find someone to cover his next few shifts. His boss wouldn't begrudge him the time off, but it was summer and many of the guys had plans.

Everyone except him. Until now.

Grimly, he realized he'd need to find a way to get the time off he needed. There was no way he could leave Crystal Lake. Not yet. Not until he managed to find and arrest Caruthers for violating his restraining order.

He couldn't stand the thought of Merry being hurt again.

———

MERRY ENJOYED EATING lunch in Rose's Café more than she thought she would. Although she was nonplussed to discover that Josie knew all about how she'd sustained her injuries.

"Are you feeling better, honey?" Josie asked, when she came over to refill their iced teas. "I heard you were injured by one of your patients."

Since Darcy was technically their waitress, Merry figured Josie was trying to get the scoop on details.

"I'm fine, really." Merry didn't want to talk about poor Leonard. For one thing, what happened wasn't his fault. Besides, the government expected healthcare workers to keep patient's information confidential. Obviously, someone at the hospital had talked, but she wasn't about to compound the error.

"Can I get you two anything else?" Josie asked.

"No thanks," Zack responded. She wondered if everyone else in the diner noticed how much he'd stared out the window. She knew he was still searching for the blue van, but now that time had passed since the fishing boat incident, she'd convinced herself that she'd let her imagination run away with her. The possibility of Blake actually looking for her and finding her here in Crystal Lake was extremely remote.

She toyed with her straw, thinking about how much she missed Caroline. Picking up and moving from Minneapolis had been hard, but nothing was as difficult as cutting off all ties with her best friend. And not just Caro, but the entire Caruthers family. She'd loved spending time with the noisy bunch. Had thought about having a big family of her own someday.

But, obviously, that wasn't meant to be. She knew Blake's illness wasn't Caro's fault either, but her friend had inadvertently let key information slip in the past. Blake had found the location to her new apartment in the Twin Cities, just by following Caroline to her place.

Cutting off all ties had been the best thing to do, to stay safe. Caro wouldn't appreciate it if Blake ended up going to jail because of Merry, either.

Her feelings must have been reflected on her face, because Zack reached across the table and took her hand. "What's wrong?"

"Nothing." Subtly, she removed her hand from his, knowing that everyone was already gawking at them. No reason to give them any more to talk about. "Just feeling a little tired, that's all."

"Is your headache back?" he asked with a frown.

"No, I'm fine." The ibuprofen she'd taken earlier had worked wonders. She adjusted the strap of her sling, trying to work the kinks out of her neck. "I guess I find it a little frustrating that I haven't bounced back, yet."

"Now who's doing the underestimating?" he asked in exasperation. "That patient of yours knocked you around pretty badly. I'm amazed you didn't have to stay in the hospital longer than twenty-four hours."

Zack's concern was touching, and she had to remind herself not to read too much into it. She ate the last few bites of her salad, and then pushed her plate away. "I'm ready to leave when you are."

Zack signaled for Darcy to bring their bill. Darcy's flirtatious smile grated on her nerves, but Zack didn't seem to notice. He dug his wallet out and tossed enough money to cover the tab and provide a decent tip. "Let's go."

She didn't say anything when Zack took a detour past the public boat launch, scanning the area for a blue van. And he drove up and down Main Street.

Twice. She was oddly glad that Zack hadn't found any evidence that Blake was here. She even felt a little guilty for making a big deal out of the redhead in the boat.

When they arrived back home, Ace ran around the backyard in circles, obviously excited to see them. True to Zack's word, he tossed a tennis ball for Ace, who threw his whole body into the chase, while she sat in the shade.

She gasped when Ace jumped into the lake, swimming out for the ball, and even more surprised when Zack pulled his phone and his wallet out of his shorts pockets to jump in, too.

It occurred to her that Zack seemed happier now, compared to the last time she'd seen him. She was glad he seemed to be getting over his loss. Although he still hadn't prayed with her before lunch.

Zack's phone beeped and vibrated on the table. She hesitated, and then reached for the phone, thinking she could at least take a message. "Hello?"

There was a long pause on the other end. "I'm sorry, I must have the wrong number," a male voice said.

"No, this is Zack's phone. I'm—a friend of his. He's swimming in the lake right now, but I'd be happy to take a message."

Another pause. "I'm sorry, but did you say swimming?" the man asked, incredulous.

She laughed, realizing that the caller must be a friend of Zack's. Someone who knew him well enough to know that Zack wasn't the average fun-loving guy. "Yes, he's actually swimming. With a black lab named Ace."

"I'm tempted to drive over there, just to see that for myself," the caller said with humor. "You must be Meredith Haines."

The hair on the back of her neck lifted in warning. "Who am I speaking with?" she asked sharply.

"My name is Cole Wallace, and I'm covering Zack's shift today. Have him call me back when he's finished swimming. I've been doing some digging and have a little more information on that Caruthers guy."

She relaxed, realizing that this was clearly Zack's source of information. The fact that Cole was a fellow police officer added to her relief. "All right, but my friends call me Merry, not Meredith. I'll be happy to have Zack call you back."

"Great. Well, it was nice meeting you, Merry."

"Take care, Cole." She pushed the button to end the call, glancing up as Zack approached.

"Too bad you can't swim yet. The water is perfect!" he declared.

She didn't mention that watching him had been just as much fun as swimming herself. She cleared her throat and gestured to his phone. "Your friend Cole called. He mentioned he has information about Blake."

Zack straightened, water dripping off his soggy T-shirt and shorts in tiny waterfalls. "Are you upset with me because I asked Cole to help investigate Caruthers?"

She swallowed hard and shook her head. "No, I'm not upset. But it was a little weird that he knew my name."

Zack dropped into a chair beside her. "I didn't tell him everything," he said softly. "Just enough so he could help me find this guy."

"I know." She forced a smile. "It's just that no one in Crystal Lake knows about my past problems. I guess I was hoping it would stay that way."

"I'm not planning to go around and tell people," Zack said, his gaze serious. "My only goal is to keep you safe."

She stared down at Ace for a minute, wishing desperately that Zack was here because he wanted to be. Because he enjoyed spending time with her. After everything he'd been through, he deserved some relaxation and fun.

Instead, he'd shouldered her problems. And instead of taking well needed time off work, he was having a busman's holiday.

She needed to remember that she was nothing more than another member of the public who he wanted to keep safe.

Her job would be to protect her heart.

———————

ZACK COULD TELL Merry wasn't thrilled with how he'd called Cole for help, but given the same set of circumstances he'd do the same thing again in a heartbeat.

He reached for his phone, but then hesitated when he realized he left his notes inside. He was still sopping wet, although the hot summer sun was beginning to dry him off. He stood and padded over to the patio doors, darting in and out of the kitchen so that he wouldn't get the floor too wet.

Derek had spent a lot of time and muscle refinishing the townhouse that had once suffered from a kitchen fire. He didn't think his new brother-in-law would appreciate water stains on his freshly sanded natural wood floors.

Zack returned to the patio table, wishing Merry wasn't there to listen in on his conversation with Cole. He was anxious to see what his buddy had uncovered, so he didn't want to wait until later.

Besides, the sooner Merry knew exactly what was going on, the better.

He pushed the call back button on his phone and waited for Cole to pick up. "Hello, beautiful."

Zack scowled. "Cole, what are you talking about?"

"Oh, sorry. I thought Merry was calling me back."

Zack had to grit his teeth to prevent himself from snapping his friend's head off. "And just exactly how do you know what she looks like?"

"I pulled up her driver's license photo. She's a cutie. Is she single?"

His fingers tightened on the phone to the point he feared he'd crack the casing. "Knock it off, Cole," he practically growled into the phone. "I thought you had new information for me?"

"Oooh, touchy, aren't you? What's the big deal? You're not planning to break your vow and start dating again, are you?"

Zack could feel Merry's amber eyes boring into him as she listened. He was so not in the mood to have this conversation with Colton, especially not in front of Merry. "Focus, Wallace. I need to know what you found out about Caruthers."

"Oh, I get it," Cole said. "Pretty Merry is sitting right there, isn't she? Okay, here's the deal. A friend of a friend knows a cop in Minneapolis. That cop went over to Caruthers' place and verified the guy isn't home. According to the neighbors, no one has seen him for a few days."

A few days? As in since Tuesday? "Thanks for doing that for me."

"Wait, there's more. Seems Caruthers has to check in with his parole officer once a week, and his last visit was Monday. If he doesn't check in by next Monday, they can arrest him for being in violation of his parole. Of course, he won't do a lot of time, but at least he'll be off the streets for a little while."

"That's excellent news." Zack could barely contain his excitement. "Can I get his parole officer's contact information?"

"Sure." Cole rattled off the name and phone number. "Watch your back, Crain. This guy isn't exactly known to be rational."

"I know. I need one more favor. I need someone to pick up my shift on Monday, too. Can you put the word out for me?"

Cole let out an exaggerated sigh. "I guess I can cover it for you, but you're going to owe me one. Hey, how about this? You introduce me to pretty Merry, I'll willingly wipe the slate clean. How's that for a deal?"

No way, no how. Zack was glad Colton wasn't here to see just how much that idea bothered him. "I'll pay you back, Cole. Tell me what shift you need covered, and if I'm not working I'll take it."

"Hmm, interesting that you seem reluctant to introduce me to your friend. And since I'm a nice guy, I have to think it's because you want her all to yourself."

Okay, enough already. He was finished with this discussion. "Goodbye, Colton." He pushed the end button and forced himself to face Merry as if that embarrassing conversation hadn't just taken place. "I have the name and number of Blake's parole officer. If Caruthers doesn't report in on Monday he risks being arrested for violating his parole."

Merry frowned. "I guess I shouldn't be surprised Blake is on parole. He'll keep ending up in jail if he doesn't take his medication." She tilted her head. "So what else did you discover?"

He glanced down at his scribbled notes, hoping she

hadn't been able to hear Colton's comments. "Cole contacted a friend of a friend who went over to Caruthers' apartment. No one has seen him for a few days."

"I guess that fits our timeline, huh?" Merry's expression was troubled. "I wish I would have gotten a better look at that guy in the fishing boat. For all we know, Blake is visiting his sister or his parents. He might not be here in Crystal Lake at all."

Zack knew she was holding out hope that this would just go away, but he was just as certain that Caruthers was here someplace, watching her.

He stared out over the lake, carefully examining the boats flying back and forth over the water. He was just about to suggest that he go out looking for him, when he caught a glimpse of a man in a blue baseball cap pulled low over his brow.

"You're going to get your wish, because he's out there, right now. Let's go."

Zack rushed down to the boat lift, wishing he'd put the boat in the water earlier. He spun the wheel as rapidly as possible, lowering the frame holding up the speedboat into the water. Merry climbed into the boat and Ace jumped in, too, unwilling to be left behind.

He jammed the key in the ignition and fired up the engine, hoping they weren't too late.

erry held on for dear life as Zack thrust the throttle of the boat forward, zooming over the water. She squinted against the whipping wind, trying to catch a glimpse of the fishing boat. But when she looked at the last place she saw it, the boat was nowhere to be found.

There were lots of other boats on the lake, and Zack had to be careful as he drove, keeping track of the skiers and the tubers.

The boat slowed and Zack glanced over at her. "Do you see him anywhere?"

She shook her head, slowly scanning the water. How was it possible for him to disappear so fast? Then she caught a flash of blue, way over on the opposite side of the lake. "There! Near the public boat launch."

"I see him," Zack muttered grimly. He swung the boat around to give a couple of jet skis a wide berth before heading across the lake.

Merry sat there, her heart racing. She was deeply afraid

of seeing Blake again. The last time he'd attacked her, he'd almost choked her to death.

Her hand crept up to her throat, and for a moment she could still feel the imprint of his strong fingers. Even though she reminded herself that she wasn't alone this time, that Zack was with her, she still didn't want to see him.

Zack slowed the boat as they approached the shore. She clenched her fingers in her lap, trying to remain calm.

"I think that's his boat," Zack said.

She couldn't tell one boat from another but she trusted Zack's keen observation. "Any sign of him?" she asked.

"No, I don't see him." Zack's tone was ripe with frustration. "I'd like to get out and search for him, but I don't want to leave you alone."

She didn't want Zack to leave her alone either, but told herself to stop being a chicken. She reached over and stroked the lab's fur. "I won't be alone. I have Ace."

She could tell Zack wanted to take her up on her offer, but after several long moments he shook his head. "There's plenty of time to track him down. We'll find him."

She couldn't deny feeling a wave of relief. No matter what Zack said, she was worried that Blake would see him as a rival. She'd rather the sheriff's deputies be around to take care of apprehending Blake.

"How's your headache?" Zack asked, as he put the boat in reverse and backed up.

She smiled, for the first time in what seemed like hours. "I'm fine, Zack. Being out on the water is wonderful."

"I'll try to keep a slower pace on the way back," he promised.

"Great, I was hoping you'd take the long way home," she teased.

"Happy to oblige," he responded with a broad smile.

Merry caught her breath at the way his smile lit up his entire face, and she quickly turned in her seat, so that he wouldn't notice her reaction.

She needed to concentrate on relaxing and enjoying the sunshine, not imagining what it would be like to be with Zack as more than a friend.

———————

ZACK FELT AMAZINGLY CONTENT, appreciating the sense of calmness that surrounded him when he was out on the water. He was annoyed that he hadn't been able to catch up with Caruthers but he did get the number off the boat's hull and could use that to find out who rented it.

He was confident he'd have the guy behind bars, soon.

Per Merry's request, he took the long way back to their pier, cruising along the edge of the lake. He saw several new houses along the shoreline that he didn't remember seeing before, as well as a few properties that were for sale, including a tiny cottage almost surrounded by trees not far from his sister's place. There were still a few empty lots that were also for sale, and it occurred to him that maybe he should invest in one, just in case.

He mentally rolled his eyes at his foolish thought. In case of what? He'd made a decision to move away from Crystal Lake, so there was no reason at all to consider buying a lot. What was wrong with him, today? He needed to remember that this was just a nice mini-vacation, nothing more.

Glancing over he saw Merry was relaxed in her seat, her face tipped into the wind while she rested her hand on Ace's head, idly scratching him behind the ears. He was struck once again by her beauty, and was forced to silently admit that he didn't want her to meet his buddy Cole. Because he wanted her for himself?

Yes. No. Maybe.

She was what was wrong with him today. Ever since he'd begun to spend time with Merry, his traitorous thoughts kept wondering what it would be like to spend time with her more often. Like on a date. Ridiculous to consider such foolishness. For one thing, she was a devout Christian, and no matter what she said, he knew that God had given up on him. Besides, she deserved a family of her own and that was the one thing he knew he couldn't do. No way, no how.

Tearing his gaze away from Merry, he glanced around at the other boaters, making sure that Caruthers hadn't returned. There was no sign of the fishing boat, and while he knew he should get back to his sister's place so he could start making phone calls, he didn't want to get off the lake just yet.

After a good forty-five minutes, he turned the speedboat back toward the pier. They hadn't brought any sunscreen and he was concerned Merry's pale skin would burn.

As he pulled up alongside the pier, Merry stood and reached over to grasp the side of the lift, helping to guide the boat into position. She acted like an experienced boat rider, and he wondered if that was because she'd gone out with Julie several times.

"Thanks Zack," she murmured as he finagled the boat into place. "That was a nice ride, at least on the way back."

"You're welcome." He needed to get away from her. Fast. Before he did something stupid like try to kiss her. "I have to run into town, would you mind heading inside with Ace while I'm gone? And lock the doors, too."

She frowned but then shrugged. "I guess I can do that. I wouldn't mind resting again for a little bit. Even though I haven't done anything all day, I'm still exhausted."

"You need to listen to what your body is trying to tell you," he said, taking her arm to help her get out of the boat, and then following her up the grassy embankment to return to the house. "How about I stop at the store and pick up something for dinner? I wouldn't mind grilling out tonight."

Merry kept her eyes downcast, and her cheeks were pink, no doubt from the sun. "Sure, that's fine. I'll raid Julie's garden and make salads."

He wouldn't say no to fresh veggies, but hoped that he hadn't made the invitation to share dinner sound like anything other than what it was, friends sharing a meal. It seemed stupid for each of them to make their own separate dinners.

"See you later," he said casually, as Merry went inside his sister's place, taking Ace with her. He waited until he heard the door lock click into place before he crossed over to his side of the townhouse. A little distance from Merry was exactly what he needed right now. He went into the bedroom and rifled through his duffel bag to find his badge and his gun before heading back out to the main living area. Grabbing his truck keys from the counter, he headed out front to where he'd left his pickup parked on the road.

The drive into town, for the second time that day, didn't take long. He wanted to stop at the rental place first, to see if he could convince the owner to let him know who'd taken out the fishing boat. Granted, he had his badge and his weapon but he clearly wasn't wearing his uniform, and anyone with half a brain would know he wasn't on duty.

He didn't recognize the young man behind the counter of Boats Are Us, so he pulled out his badge and glanced at the name tag pinned to the man's shirt. "Hi, Dave, I'm a cop, and I need to know who rented a fishing boat earlier today."

Dave pushed his glasses up his nose as he glanced at the badge, and then frowned. "We rent a lot of boats, Officer. I couldn't begin to tell you who rented what."

Zack nodded. "I have the number off the hull." He scribbled the number on a scrap piece of paper and slid it across the counter. "Do me a favor and check your files, okay?"

Dave hesitated, as if he thought he was doing something wrong. "Maybe I should call my boss."

Zack shrugged. "You can do that. I can also call my friends at the Hope County Sheriff's Department to rush things along, as well. What's the big deal? It's just a name, right?"

"I guess," Dave mumbled. He picked up the number and went over to the computer system. He tapped on the keys, searching for the information. "Here it is. The guy's name is Calvin Reynolds, and he rented the boat for a week."

What? Zack scowled and wished he could see the computer screen for himself. "Are you sure? Check again."

"I'm sure. It's right here." Dave jabbed his finger on the computer screen.

Zack couldn't believe it. Was it possible he'd gotten the number wrong? "Okay, try this then. Search for the name Blake Caruthers."

This time it took Dave much longer, and at one point Zack actually spelled out the last name, in case Dave had it misspelled.

"Nope, don't have anyone in the system by that name," Dave said with a sigh. "Sorry."

Zack stared at him, trying to figure out if he was really wrong or if Dave was actually covering for Blake by lying to him. He didn't want to believe he could be that paranoid, so he thanked Dave and turned away.

Then he swung back. "Tell me something, that first name you mentioned, Calvin Reynolds. You said he paid for a week. What day did he rent the boat?"

Dave went back to tapping on the computer keyboard. "Tuesday morning."

Coincidence? Zack wasn't about to leave any stone unturned. "How did he pay, with a credit card?"

"Actually he paid cash, but we require a credit card number on file in case there's any damage to the property."

Was Caruthers smart enough to get a fake credit card and driver's license? He wasn't sure. Maybe Zack was the one being paranoid. "Did you happen to catch what type of vehicle he was driving?" Zack asked.

"No. I wasn't here when he rented the boat."

"I see." Zack knew he couldn't count on Dave to describe the guy, then, either. "One last thing. Any chance you know the address that goes along with the credit card? Any chance it's from out of state? Say, Minnesota?"

Dave folded his arms over his chest. "Look, Officer, I tried to help you, but I can't run the credit card address for you. I don't even know how, even if I wanted to. If you need that information, then you may as well call your deputy friends."

Zack shrugged. "All right, I'll do that. Thanks for your help."

He turned and left the boat rental, trying to understand this latest clue. Or lack of a clue. Somehow, he just couldn't buy the idea that a red-haired guy who looked like Caruthers just happened to rent a boat for the week. Reynolds had to be Caruthers.

The scary part was that even with his psych history,

Caruthers was going well out of his way to cover his tracks. As if he had more on his mind than simply scaring Merry or just trying to talk to her.

But how could Zack prove it? He went back outside and, once again, drove up and down Main Street to look for the blue van. If he found that, he'd know for sure that Reynolds and Caruthers were one and the same.

He drove into the motel parking lot, but as before, there was no sign of the blue van. He drummed his fingers on the top of the steering wheel, wondering how many other places there were to stay in Hope County? Probably way more than he wanted to know.

It suddenly hit him that he was looking for a van, and there was a campground located not too far outside the Crystal Lake city limits. Why hadn't he thought of a campground? Caruthers could be sleeping in the back of his van or in a tent. Cheap and with easy access in and out of the city.

Zack backed out of the motel parking lot, turned around, and then headed for the highway, a keen sense of anticipation rushing through his system. This was a good lead and, with any luck, he'd have proof Caruthers not only violated his restraining order but also committed identity theft.

He dialed Cole's number as he drove. "Hey, I need you to run a check on another name for me."

Colton sighed. "You're just full of favors today, aren't you? All right, what do you have?"

Zack quickly filled him in on the boat chase, and the information he'd uncovered from the Boats Are Us rental agency. "I really think Caruthers is using this fake name, Calvin Reynolds. See if you can find out if he has any friends or known associates by that name."

"Okay, but explain why you can't do your own legwork on this?" Cole asked. "I'm the one working your shift, while you're slacking off on your boat."

"I would, but I'm heading over to the Hope County Campground. I've been driving all around town and haven't seen that van, but never considered he might be using a tent to camp out."

"Good point," Cole muttered. "All right, give me some time with this and I'll get back to you."

"Thanks, Cole."

Zack ended the call, trying not to be too disappointed. After all, Cole was working his shift. He couldn't complain about the fact that Cole had put his job first and Zack's request for information second.

The campground was only seven miles down the highway, and he slowed his truck and turned carefully onto the gravel driveway. The conditions were typical of any other campground—a building housing bathrooms and showers, with several paths winding around the area, providing many opportunities to pitch a tent or park a camper.

Zack took his time, driving super slow and checking out the area. There were dozens of campsites and he knew this might take a while. He was tempted to call Merry to let her know but held back, just in case she was sleeping. And he needed to pick up something to cook her for dinner.

Enough, already. He shook his head as if he could dislodge his wayward brain cells. He needed to concentrate on finding Caruthers rather than constantly thinking about Merry. He was helping to keep her safe, nothing more. As soon as he'd found the guy and arrested him, he'd head back to Madison, where he belonged.

The sooner, the better.

MERRY STRETCHED out on her bed, her eyelids feeling incredibly heavy. How she could feel so tired, she had no idea. She hadn't done anything even remotely physical. She hated to admit how much the concussion she'd sustained had affected her.

Ace settled down on the floor beside her bed, his tail thumping reassuringly against the floor. "Good boy," she murmured. Having Ace around helped her feel grounded and safe. Slowly, she relaxed, and eventually felt herself drift off to sleep.

Ace's barking broke through her nightmare, moments before Blake was going to kill her. She awoke with a start, her heart pounding in her chest. What was wrong? Based on the blue lights of Julie's alarm clock, almost two hours had passed.

She rolled out of bed, wincing as she moved her arm without the sling to help remind her to keep it still. She hurried out to the main living area, where Ace's barks had turned into a low, menacing growl.

"Ace? What's wrong? Did you see a squirrel?" Ace was known to take all threats, even small furry ones, seriously. He'd scared her more than once with his ferocious barking, only to discover a rabbit had ventured too close to the patio.

As she approached the kitchen area, she caught a glimpse of a face pressed against the small window above the sink.

For a moment she could only stare in horror but then she let out an ear-shattering scream.

7

Zack pulled in front of the townhouse and was walking up to the front door when he heard Merry scream. His heart lodged in his throat and he leaped up on the front porch and yanked at the door, belatedly remembering he'd locked it on his way out.

"Merry!" He shouted, as he fumbled for his keys. "It's Zack! I'm here!"

Ace's barking joined the melee, and Zack finally found the key and twisted it in the lock. He dashed inside, following the sounds to the kitchen area.

She stood, still wearing her badly wrinkled scrubs, shaking as she pointed to the window. "It was—right—there!" she stuttered.

He couldn't stop himself from wrapping his arms around her, to try and settle her down. "What was there? Did you see something?"

"A face. In the kitchen window."

Caruthers had been here? Zack thought fast, going through the options. Had Caruthers escaped down to the lake or around to the front where he may have left a car? "Stay here with Ace and lock the doors. I'll be right back."

Leaving Merry wasn't easy, but there wasn't a moment to lose. He hadn't found the blue van at the campsite, though there were plenty of tents without vehicles that could have belonged to Caruthers. He'd hated to come back without the evidence he needed. But now he had a chance.

Zack dashed through the patio door, down to the lake. He figured that since he hadn't seen any sign of the blue van when he'd returned home, Caruthers must have used the fishing boat again. But he didn't see any sign of it. How much time had passed since Merry saw the face in the window? Five minutes? Less?

He scanned the area, looking for anything remotely suspicious. But there was nothing. No fishing boat. No redhead in a baseball cap.

Could he have missed him out front? He wasn't sure how, but decided to double check. He ran around the side of the house back to the street. In the distance, he could hear the sound of an engine.

He didn't hesitate, but jumped into his truck. He didn't see anything to the east, so he grabbed his sunglasses to cut the glare and drove west, directly into the setting sun, down the road toward the highway that lead away from town.

Was that Caruthers up ahead? Zack could just barely make out a dark colored vehicle way off in the distance, but he couldn't be sure that it was a van verses any other SUV type of vehicle. Thankfully, his truck had a big engine, and he floored the accelerator in an attempt to gain some ground.

But after he came over the crest of a hill, there was nothing in front of him on the highway.

He slammed his fist on the steering wheel, venting his

frustration. He was a better cop than this. How could he have lost him? Had Caruthers gotten off on one of the side streets? And if so, which one?

Slowing down at each intersection, and there really weren't that many, he tried to get a glimpse of the dark colored vehicle. There were a few other cars, but none resembling a blue van.

Every instinct he possessed told him to keep searching, but the memory of how Merry had looked, so shattered and alone, convinced him to turn around and go back.

Was it possible she imagined the whole thing? No, he heard the car engine and Ace had been barking. Caruthers had some nerve, showing up at the townhouse in broad daylight.

And then it hit him. His truck hadn't been parked outside. Had Caruthers noticed that small detail and decided to make an attempt at getting to Merry? Or had Caruthers followed him? Had Merry's former boyfriend caught a glimpse of Zack leaving alone and decided to make his move?

At this point, anything was possible. Caruthers could have seen him in town, for all he knew. And while Zack had been checking out the campground, Caruthers had gone back to the townhouse.

Zack pulled up in front of his sister's place, grimly realizing he couldn't afford to make the mistake of leaving Merry home alone, again.

He'd have to stick to her like glue, no matter how difficult that was for him. Her safety was more important than his reluctant attraction.

He'd just have to find a way to deal with it.

MERRY BOWED her head and prayed for strength and guidance, for herself and for Zack. Feeling calmer after she'd locked all the doors, she sat on the edge of the sofa, holding Ace close to her side. She tried to remember any details from the brief glimpse of the face at the window, but already her memory was a bit fuzzy.

Zack returned about twenty minutes later, once again using his key to come in the front door. By the dejected set of his shoulders, she guessed he hadn't caught up with Blake. If the face at the window even belonged to him. Was it possible she had two stalkers in one lifetime? She sincerely hoped not.

"I'm sorry, Merry," Zack said, rubbing the back of his neck. "Somehow I lost him."

She forced a smile. "It's okay, I'm just glad Ace was here with me. His barking woke me up from a sound sleep." She decided not to mention the nightmare. After all, there was nothing Zack could do about it.

He dropped into a chair at the kitchen table. "You woke up when you heard Ace barking? And then what, you came out into the kitchen?"

She nodded. "Sometimes Ace barks at chipmunks, squirrels, or other dogs, so I didn't really think too much about it. But when I came into the kitchen he was growling, and that's when I looked up and saw the face. His hands were cupped around his forehead and cheeks, as if to cut out the glare from the sunlight so he could see inside better."

"And that's when you screamed?" Zack asked.

She felt her cheeks flush with embarrassment. "It all happened so fast, I think he may have disappeared already by that time, but I can't say for sure. I normally don't lose control like that."

"You don't have to apologize. You have every right to scream when you find someone peeking into your window." Zack sighed and shook his head. "I'm the one who's failed you. He was so close. I should have been able to catch up with him."

She hated the way he was beating himself up over this, and wished he'd share his burdens with God.

"Zack, if you were on duty you would have had backup for assistance. You can't be everywhere at one time. Did you find out who rented the fishing boat?"

He grimaced. "Another dead end. But I still need to follow up with Cole to see what he found out. And I picked up hamburgers and brats for dinner. Hope that's okay."

"It's perfect. I'll go outside and pick some veggies out of the garden."

Zack shot to his feet. "Wait. I need to look around, just in case he left another footprint or some other clue. Stay here with Ace for just a little while longer, okay?"

She nodded and didn't protest when he went back outside through the patio door. After another ten minutes, he returned and held the door open as an invitation to come outside. "I didn't find anything, but that's probably not surprising. You had the shades pulled in the bedroom, so I'm guessing he didn't bother to try to look through those windows. And of course, I didn't find anything out here on the concrete patio."

Was it possible Zack didn't really believe her? No, after all, he'd taken off looking for Blake, going as far as to try and follow him in the truck. Surely Zack believed in her.

Just as a precaution, she kept Ace next to her as she worked in the garden. While picking vegetables, she pulled a few weeds and made a mental note to water later tonight once the sun went down. Julie had encouraged her to eat the vegetables in the garden so they wouldn't go bad in the time she and Derek were gone.

Merry gathered cucumbers, lettuce, peppers, onions and tomatoes using the hem of her scrub top to hold everything together. Her shoulder was still sore, but she didn't want to put the sling on just yet.

"Looks good," Zack commented, as he held the patio door open for her. As soon as she disappeared inside, he went back to cleaning up the grill.

The domesticated scene seemed a bit surreal. If she didn't know better, she'd think Zack planned on settling down again someday.

But she didn't dare get her hopes up. Even if he did ask her out, which she could scarcely imagine, he wasn't a Christian. So there was no point in even considering getting involved with him.

Merry shook off the depressing thought and concentrated on washing the veggies and cutting them up for salads. She could hear Zack whistling as he grilled the brats and burgers, and she wondered if he realized how light-hearted he sounded. Despite everything with Blake, he seemed to be more relaxed and content than ever.

She went into the bedroom, anxious to change out of her scrubs that were now stained with sweat and soil from being out in the garden. Washing up at the bathroom sink wasn't too difficult, but when it came to pulling on a T-shirt to wear with her Capri jeans, a sharp pain zinged down her arm.

Struggling with the fabric and her limited range of motion wasn't easy, but eventually she managed, whimpering only a little when she finally got her injured arm through the opening.

She took several deep breaths, willing the pain to subside. Reluctantly, she pulled the sling back on. By the time she returned to the kitchen she was surprised to find that Zack had dinner ready. He'd taken the salads outside and had set out plates and silverware on the patio table. In the center was a large platter full of meat, buns and condiments, including several choices of salad dressing.

"Wow," she managed as she pulled out a chair to sit down. "I'm impressed."

Zack took the seat to her right, the umbrella helping to shade them from the worst of the setting sun. He glanced at her, and waited.

It took her a minute to realize he was giving her time to pray. Pleased, she bowed her head and spoke out loud, hoping to find the words that may get through to him.

"Dear Lord, we thank You for this bountiful meal we're about to eat. We also ask that You give us strength and wisdom to get to the bottom of the mystery surrounding us. And lastly, we ask for You to ease the ache in our hearts for the loved ones we've lost, Amen."

She glanced over at Zack to find him staring down at his empty plate, his hands folded loosely in his lap. Was it possible he'd been praying, too? She reminded herself not to get her hopes up.

"Did you really lose someone close to you? Or was that last part just for me?" Zack asked in a low voice.

Her heart ached for him. "I did. My parents passed away when I was in college. My father died of a heart attack. My mother died shortly afterwards and no one could figure out why. I always figured she died of a broken heart."

"If you could die of a broken heart, I'd be dead by now," Zack muttered. "Cancer is a horrible disease."

She wanted badly to reach out and hug him, but feared he'd reject the slightest bit of comfort. "I know it is, and I know that you've suffered greatly. But try to remember that as hard as it is for you, I truly believe your wife and daughter are in a much better place with God."

"I wish I could know that for sure," Zack said.

"You'll just have to find a way to believe God's word," she said. "I've worked in the ER for several years now, and I've had two different patients tell me that they saw a bright light as we were resuscitating them. I guess that's the closest thing to proof that I can give you."

"A patient really told you that?"

She nodded. "Yes, as recently as a few months ago. One of our church members was in a terrible car crash last year, and the paramedics brought him in doing CPR the entire time. Afterward, he told me that he wasn't afraid to die because he saw the light and knew that heaven would be there for him when it was his time."

Zack stared at her for a long minute before he gave a brief nod. "I always thought those were just stories."

"Many stories have a kernel of truth to them, and I promise you, this one is absolutely true. If you tried to tell Mr. Graybar that he was imagining things, he'd be sure to set you straight." She picked up her fork and dug into her salad.

Zack picked up the platter and held it out for her, before choosing both a hamburger and a brat for himself. As they ate, the conversation veered toward less intense subjects than everlasting life.

"I went through the campground off Hwy ZZ, to see if I could find Caruthers blue van," Zack said between bites.

"Little did I know that he'd end up back here, peeping into the kitchen window."

She was thrilled that he believed her. "I'm thankful Ace was there to sound the alarm."

At the sound of his name, the dog jumped up and padded over. "No begging," she said in a stern voice. Ace whirled around and plopped back down on the ground near her feet.

"He's very well trained," Zack said, glancing down at the dog. "I know you're just watching him for Julie and Derek, but I can tell you already love him. You should consider getting a dog of your own."

"I can't have pets in my apartment complex," she reminded him. "But I wouldn't mind a dog like Ace. He's been great company."

"I was thinking I might look for a dog, too."

"Really?" She was surprised to hear that. "You must live somewhere that allows pets."

He shrugged and nodded. "Yeah, I live in the upper level of a duplex. There's a nice couple living below me. I do all the heavy work, like snow-blowing, mowing, minor repairs, and they give me a nice cut on my rent. I don't think they'd mind if I owned a dog."

Merry thought that Julie would be thrilled to know Zack wouldn't be living all alone. "Would you have time to train him?"

"I guess I'd have to make the time, but I don't think it would be that difficult."

"I wouldn't have a clue where to start. I'd have to find someone to train my dog for me." Merry finished her salad and started on her burger, discovering that eating a sandwich with one hand wasn't as easy as it sounded. "This is delicious, Zack. Thanks so much."

"It's the least I can do." He seemed to avoid her gaze and she figured he was trying to keep things casual so she wouldn't misinterpret this as some sort of date.

A fact she'd be wise to remember.

———————

ZACK COULDN'T SEEM to pry Merry's story out of his mind. Of course after Suzanne and Amelia had died, the pastor of the church had tried to tell him that they were up in heaven, but he hadn't been able to believe it. Hadn't been able to believe in a God who would take two innocent lives away from him.

But now, for some reason he wanted to believe Amelia and Suz were really were up there. In a place that was bright and warm. Where they would forever be safe from harm. Close to God.

Merry started cleaning up the dishes, carrying things into the house a little at a time. He stood to help her, but then his phone rang. He eagerly picked up the call. "Hey Cole, do you have more information?"

"Yeah, I've been running the Calvin Reynolds name and guess what? There is a guy by that name living in the Twin Cities and he's done some jail time too, at the same facility as that Caruthers dude."

"I knew it!" Zack jumped to his feet, too excited to sit still. "This has to be the same guy. He's using his friend's identity to cover his tracks."

"It's a strong theory, that's for sure," Cole agreed. "And a bit concerning. What in the world is he planning?"

Good question. "I don't know but he's not going to get to

her. Now that I'm onto him, I'll find a way to bring him down."

"Hey, I believe you. How's pretty Merry holding up?"

Zack ground his molars together for a brief moment, fighting the surge of temper. "She's fine. A little on edge, which is completely understandable, but otherwise fine."

"So, still not willing to introduce us, huh?"

Zack ignored the taunt, knowing that Cole was only trying to get under his skin. "No point. She's too good for the likes of you."

"Hey, that means she's too good for you, too."

Zack rolled his eyes. "Back to Reynolds, any chance you can send someone to pick him up? Maybe ask him a few questions?"

"On what grounds?"

"Identity theft. Tell him that you discovered someone's been charging up his credit card and that you're worried about his credit rating."

"I doubt Reynolds cares one bit about his credit rating, but I might be able to use the identity theft angle." Cole sighed. "You're going to owe me big time for all these favors, you know. Although, considering you haven't asked for anything in over two years, I'm still reeling from shock."

Zack had done plenty of favors for Cole, but he knew that doing a side investigation like this was a much bigger deal than covering a few shifts. "I know, and I really appreciate it."

"All right, I'll let you know what happens."

"Thanks." Zack disconnected from the call and stuffed the phone in his back pocket. He gathered up what was left of the dishes and carried them inside.

He was in the process of setting the stack on the counter just moments before Merry turned around and plowed into him. She was knocked off balance and he lightly grasped her shoulders to steady her.

"Are you okay?" he asked.

"Sorry, I'm a klutz." Her free hand was on his chest and for several long moments he gazed into her amber eyes.

There was absolutely no rational reason or viable excuse for what he did next. His vow of remaining emotionally distant from Merry, keeping her at arm's length, evaporated in a puff of smoke.

Instead, he drew her closer, lowered his head and kissed her.

8

Merry was startled by Zack's unexpected kiss, but only for a second. He tasted wonderful, and her fingers curled in the fabric of his T-shirt to hold herself steady as she opened for him.

Zack's kiss was tender yet demanding at the same time. She reveled in the embrace, unable to remember the last time she'd kissed a man. Certainly not since well before she'd moved to Crystal Lake.

But the heated embrace was all too brief. Zack abruptly lifted his head, pulled away and stepped back. She reluctantly released her grip on his shirt and leaned against the counter for support.

"I shouldn't have done that," Zack said in a low, gravely tone. His blue eyes clearly reflected his regret. "I'm sorry. You deserve..." He shook his head. "More. I don't have anything to give you."

She wanted to protest, but before she could get the words out, Zack turned and left, shutting the patio door behind him.

For several long moments she stood there, trying to

gather her scattered thoughts. She'd reveled in Zack's kiss. Had secretly hoped he'd kiss her ever since the first night she met him. And she hadn't been disappointed.

But clearly Zack did not feel the same way. Granted, he'd initiated the kiss but considered it a momentary lapse in judgment. Something that he obviously had no intention of allowing to happen again.

She took a deep breath and turned back to the counter full of dirty dishes. Merry didn't mind washing them. Considering Zack had purchased and made the meal, it was the least she could do. Washing them one handed wasn't easy, and after a few minutes, she shucked out of the stupid sling and finished the dishes, leaving them in the sink to air dry.

There was no sign of Zack outside, so she let Ace out for one last doggy bathroom break, before calling him back in. She tried not to feel hurt that he was avoiding her.

The truth hurts, Merry. Suck it up.

Thanks to her two naps, she wasn't the least bit sleepy. She took her Bible and settled in the corner of the sofa to read some of her favorite Psalms to ease her troubled soul.

Somehow, she just knew that if she could help Zack find his way back to his faith, he'd be able to let himself find love and happiness again.

But even with that miracle, there was no guarantee that his future would ever include her.

MERRY WOKE up to Ace whining in her ear. The dog was

better than any alarm clock she'd ever owned, she thought wryly as she staggered out of bed.

"Alright, I'm coming." Why she persisted in talking to the dog she had no idea. The thought of possibly getting a dog was becoming more appealing by the day. She ignored the constant ache in her shoulder as she headed out to the living area to where Ace was already waiting rather impatiently near the patio door.

She unlocked and opened the door. Ace bounded outside, energy radiating from every pore. There was no sign of Zack, not that she was terribly surprised. She didn't anticipate any offers to cook breakfast, either.

Maybe he hadn't liked kissing her. After all, she was out of practice. No one had ever said she was good at kissing even when she had been in the dating scene. She gathered cold cereal and yogurt for breakfast and sat at the kitchen table where she could watch Ace outside.

For some odd reason, she felt incredibly lonely. Ridiculous since she'd been eating breakfast alone for years. Why did she suddenly miss Zack's presence now? A few shared meals did not make a relationship.

She shook her head at her foolishness. By the time she'd finished her breakfast, Ace was back at the door, wagging his tail as if telling her he wanted to come in.

She opened the door, sweeping her gaze over the lake. There was no sign of the fishing boat this morning, which she chose to believe was a positive sign.

"Good dog," she murmured, scratching him behind the ears. She was tempted to walk over and offer Zack the ability to play with Ace, but then realized that was just an excuse.

She wanted to see Zack. To spend time with him.

Pathetic enough to take whatever scraps of companionship he was willing to share.

Enough, she told herself firmly. Zack was right about one thing, she did deserve more than he was willing to give. Hadn't she dreamed of having a large family of her own? No point in even thinking Zack would be willing to be a part of her future.

She showered and spent far too long trying to brush and dry her hair, hampered by her cracked collarbone. Wielding the blow dryer wasn't easy, and she gave up after a few minutes. She left her hair down, and then struggled to get dressed.

Her shoulder was incredibly sore by the time she was ready, so she popped some ibuprofen, washing it down with sun tea. Glancing at the clock, she realized she'd need to leave soon if she was going to make it on time for choir practice.

Should she tell Zack where she was going? She was tempted not to disturb him, but then again, she didn't want him to worry if he happened to discover she was gone.

She decided against carrying a purse, and took Ace with her as she went out the patio door to Zack's side of the townhouse. She felt a little foolish knocking on the doorframe. "Zack?" she called through the screen door. "I'm heading out to choir practice, so I'm leaving Ace with you."

Zack crossed over to glare at her. "I don't think it's smart for you to go off on your own."

"Well, good morning to you, too." She didn't bother to hide her irritation. "I slept well, thanks for asking."

He sighed and rubbed the back of his neck. "Look, I'm sorry, but I wasn't expecting you to announce that you're leaving. Give me a few minutes to get ready and I'll give you a lift."

It was on the tip of her tongue to refuse, but there was a part of her that knew Zack would only argue until he got his way. "Okay, but please hurry. I don't want to be late."

"Come inside for a minute." He opened the door for her and Ace.

True to his word, Zack didn't make her wait long. He came out of the bathroom, the scent of his aftershave reminding her of their kiss.

She averted her gaze, hoping her blush wasn't too noticeable. With any luck, singing hymns at church would help put everything in perspective.

Because, clearly, she needed all the help she could get.

ZACK TRIED NOT to take his foul mood out on Merry. It certainly wasn't her fault that he'd been unable to sleep.

He'd kissed her, so how could he complain when she kissed him back?

She'd been in his mind before he finally fell asleep and was the first person he'd thought about when he woke up. Man, he had it bad. And as much as he tried to tell himself that he was just worried about Caruthers, he couldn't bring himself to keep lying to himself.

He liked Merry. He enjoyed being with her, even doing nothing more than sitting together on the patio watching the boaters on the lake. And he'd missed her in the measly twelve hours they'd been apart.

Get a grip, he told himself firmly. All morning he'd been trying to keep Suzanne and Amelia in the forefront of his mind, but to no avail. He forced himself to concentrate on the road, keeping a keen eye out for a blue van.

"I'm assuming choir practice is at the church?"

"Yes. I'll be there for an hour and a half, if you want to go home and come back later."

She hadn't looked him directly in the eye since snapping at him, and he wondered if she'd thought about that bone-melting kiss as much as he had. Or was that just wishful thinking on his part?

"I'll stay." The thought of sitting in the church made him antsy, but what else could he do? He'd promised himself not to leave her alone again. And the fact that she'd be with a bunch of old people singing in a church choir didn't count as adequate protection, at least not in his book. So he'd sit in the back of the church and wait for her to finish.

Thankfully, he had his smart phone to help keep him busy.

He caught sight of the white church steeple between a break in the trees. The ride from Julie's place didn't take long, and soon he was pulling into the church parking lot adjacent to the building that looked achingly familiar.

Well over two years had passed since he'd crossed the threshold, since the day of Suzanne's funeral. For a moment his hands went damp and droplets of sweat beaded along his temple. He hadn't anticipated this visceral of a reaction to being here again. It was just a structure. Nothing more. No reason to flip out or anything.

"Thanks," Merry murmured as she moved to get out of the passenger seat. The sound of her voice helped ground him, and he put his hand out to prevent her from leaving.

"Wait for me." He quickly pushed open the driver's side door and climbed out. He rounded the truck, sweeping his gaze over the parking lot to make sure he hadn't missed the blue van.

He opened Merry's door for her, and helped her out. He followed as she headed inside.

The interior of the church was nice and cool, a welcome relief from the hot sun outside. He slid into one of the pews in the back, positioning himself where he could keep an eye on the doorway.

"Merry! We weren't sure you were going to make it," one of the elderly women greeted her. "How are you feeling, dear?"

"I'm fine, and why wouldn't I be here? A cracked collarbone wouldn't keep me from singing."

Just as he suspected, the choir was made up of mostly older adults, although he frowned when he noticed a younger man, maybe a few years older than him, giving Merry a hug. Who was that guy? Hadn't she said she wasn't seeing anyone?

Zack subtly moved up a few pews, straining to hear the guy's name.

"Hi Daniel, nice to see you," Merry said, returning the hug. Daniel wasn't very tall, just a couple inches taller than Merry, but he was clean-cut with sandy brown hair and sporting a well-trimmed goatee.

Zack rubbed his freshly shaved cheek, wondering if Merry liked men with facial hair. His beard always itched, but if that was what she wanted...

He stopped himself, mentally smacking his forehead. Losing it. He was clearly losing it.

He took his phone out and searched his e-mail for any further news from Cole, trying to ignore the group milling about the piano at the front of the church. Daniel was probably exactly what Merry needed. A nice guy who'd give her the family she so clearly wanted. Not that she'd said anything, but the way her eyes had glowed as she talked about growing up next to the Caruthers had clued him in.

When the choir began to sing, he found himself arrested by the sweet merging of voices. He could distinguish Merry's voice clearly above the others and was secretly surprised at the beautiful sound.

For a moment the music washed over him, bringing back a rush of memories, and not all of them bad. He and his family had gone to church regularly. Suz hadn't been able to carry a tune, but Amelia had been a part of the children's choir, dressed as an angel during the annual Christmas pageant, her wings hanging crooked because she'd tripped and fallen on the way up the aisle.

Tears burned behind his eyes, and he held them off with an effort.

He missed them so much. But he couldn't help thinking about what Merry had said about his family being up in heaven. For the first time since burying them, he lifted his eyes to the top of the church as if seeking the answer to his unspoken question. Was there really a God? Were his wife and daughter in a much better place now? He noticed the cross hanging above the altar and a strange sense of peace washed over him.

Of course Suzanne and Amelia were up in heaven. Why wouldn't they be? They'd both been good Christians and had believed in God. Had he been selfish to wallow in their passing?

Probably. He'd wanted them to stay here with him.

The choir finished their song, discussed things for a few minutes, and then moved on to the next one. This hymn was an upbeat song meant to lift the spirits of the churchgoers, and he found himself tapping his foot to the beat.

Maybe it wasn't quite the country western songs he tended to prefer, but for whatever reason, he enjoyed the songs just the same.

He stared at his phone, wishing Cole would come up with something, anything to give him a clue as to where he could find Caruthers. Surely Reynolds would spill something useful.

And then it hit him. They were looking for the blue van that was registered to Caruthers. Maybe they should be looking for the vehicle that Reynolds normally drove? After all, Caruthers had a credit card and an ID belonging to the guy. Why not trade vehicles too?

Heart racing with excitement, he sent a quick text message to Cole. *What does Reynolds drive? Need make model and tag# thx.*

Maybe now they could get somewhere. Too bad he hadn't considered this earlier. All this time he'd been chasing after a blue van when in reality he had no clue what Caruthers might be driving.

Ten agonizing minutes later, Cole returned his message. *Ten year old black Jeep Cherokee 555-CVB.*

A black Jeep fit with the dark vehicle he'd followed last evening and was strong enough to tow a fishing boat. Armed with this new information, he itched to get back into town, to swing past the Crystal Lake Motel and run through the campground again.

Any luck getting Reynolds to talk?

He hasn't been home yet.

Zack scowled at the message, his fingers flying over the keys. *Keep trying.*

He realized the music had stopped and glanced up to see what was happening. The members of the choir seemed to be taking a break, all except for Merry and that Daniel guy who were deep in conversation.

Zack shot out of the pew and headed up the aisle before he realized what he was doing. "Merry? Do you have a minute?"

She glanced at him in surprise, and smiled. "Sure, excuse me, Daniel."

He slowed to a stop, feeling a bit foolish for interrupting them. She walked toward him, her amber eyes quizzical. "What's up?"

Zack cleared his throat. "I'm sorry to interrupt you, but I need to ask if you can recall seeing a black Jeep hanging around. Maybe in those few days before you were injured at work?"

"A black Jeep?" She frowned and shook her head. "Sorry, but that doesn't ring a bell. Why?"

"We've been looking for a blue van, but it's entirely possible Caruthers is driving a black Jeep instead."

She nodded slowly. "Okay, that's good to know."

"So who's the guy? Daniel?" he asked, striving for a casual tone. "He seems to like you."

For a moment Merry looked flustered. "Oh, no. He's just a friend. He's one of the physical therapists at the hospital."

"No reason to think he could be the one peeping through your windows, huh?"

She flashed him an exasperated glance. "Don't be ridiculous, Zack. He's been a church member here for years. We're just *friends*."

He didn't miss the emphasis on the last word. "I'm sorry," he blurted. "I'm sorry for the way I treated you last night. I was out of line."

Her jaw dropped in surprise. "Um, okay. Apology accepted."

The choir had gathered around the piano again, clearly waiting for her. "Looks like break time is over," he murmured.

"Yeah, I better get back."

"You have a beautiful voice, Merry." He flashed a smile before turning to head back to his seat.

After he sat down, he suppressed a stab of guilt. He hadn't needed to talk to Merry right then. But he'd wanted good ole Daniel to understand he was there with her.

Could he be any more obvious? He hoped Merry hadn't noticed his Neanderthal tactics.

The choir ran through a few more songs, and then suddenly Merry was singing alone, her clear voice pure and true. She sang the verse solo and the rest of the choir joined in with the refrain.

Zack was surprised when practice was over, the time going by faster than he'd anticipated. And not once had he played games on his phone.

"You didn't have to stay," Merry said as she approached. "I'm sure you were bored out of your mind."

"I wasn't bored at all," he answered honestly. "I enjoyed listening to you sing."

"Thanks," she murmured, ducking her head at the compliment, her fair skin turning pink.

He stayed beside her as they walked outside, and it took a minute for his eyes to adjust to the glare of the sun.

"Are we going back home?" Merry asked.

"I thought we'd take a little drive, first," Zack admitted. He kept his hand in the small of her back as they walked over to where he'd left his truck.

And then he saw the black Jeep.

9

"Get in," Zack urged, opening the passenger door. Merry quickly jumped in, wincing when she knocked her arm against the door frame. Zack raced around to the driver's side.

"What's wrong?" she asked as he started the truck and peeled out of the parking lot. She clicked her seatbelt into place as the truck banked around a curve.

"We need to follow that black Jeep." Zack tried to pull his seatbelt on and she reached over to help so he could keep his eyes on the road.

Merry saw the Jeep he meant, but it was already pretty far up ahead, and she found herself pressing her foot to the floor as if she had an imaginary brake. "Do you really think that's him?"

"Yes, I do. We already know Caruthers used his friend's ID to rent the boat, so why not drive his vehicle too?"

Zack pressed steadily on the accelerator, pushing the speed limit.

A chill lifted the tiny hairs along the back of her neck.

The face in the window must have been Blake's. A small part of her didn't want to believe it. Oddly enough, she would have almost preferred some other stalker rather than knowing for sure Blake was after her again.

"Come on, where did you go?" Zack muttered, as they pulled up on the crest of a hill.

She scanned the area, looking for the Jeep even though, deep down, she didn't really want Zack to find him. "Maybe he turned off on one of the other highways?"

A muscle jumped in the corner of Zack's jaw. "I can't lose him this time."

Zack sped up and she silently prayed for their safety.

"No way! You've got to be kidding me!" Zack exclaimed in frustration.

She turned in her seat and saw the flashing red and blue lights growing brighter as the sheriff's deputy gained on them. Zack's lips thinned as he slowed down and then pulled off on the side of the highway.

"Of course I don't have my badge with me."

"Maybe once we explain about the black Jeep, you won't get a ticket." She felt bad for Zack who was only going out of his way to try and help her.

"I don't care about the speeding ticket," Zack said, reaching over to open the glove box. He pulled out the vehicle registration, and then rolled down his window. "We'll have no chance of catching up with the Jeep now."

Merry couldn't help but let out a quiet sigh of relief.

"Do you have any idea how fast you were going?" the sheriff's deputy asked.

"Yes, Officer, I was doing seventy-five in a fifty-five mile speed zone."

Merry leaned forward, trying to get a better look at the

deputy. "Deputy Armbruster? Hi, it's me, Merry Haines from the Hope County ER. How are you?"

"Merry?" Deputy Devon Armbruster bent down further so he could see her. "What are you doing with someone driving so recklessly?"

"This is Zack Crain, Julie Crain's brother," she explained. "He wasn't speeding on purpose. We were trying to catch up with a black Jeep."

Deputy Armbruster glanced between the two of them and frowned. "I guess I should have recognized you, since you resemble your sister. I'm the one who was hired after you left. Aren't you a cop in Madison, now?" he asked.

"Yes, but I took a few days off to spend time on the lake."

Merry could see the indecision reflected in the deputy's eyes. "Regardless of the reason, you were still speeding. And just because you used to be a cop here, doesn't mean I can let you off the hook."

"I know."

She had to give Zack credit for not arguing in an attempt to get out of the ticket. Of course, as a cop himself, Zack had probably heard every excuse in the book, and then some. She tried to catch Deputy Armbruster's gaze. "Listen, Deputy, you might be able to help us. You see, we have a good reason to believe that one of my former boyfriends is stalking me. We think he was driving that black Jeep. Zack was only trying to get the evidence we need to prove that Blake is violating his restraining order."

"Stalking? Restraining order?" This time Deputy Armbruster's eyebrows pulled together in a deep V. "You better come with me down to the department headquarters."

Zack scowled at her before turning back to the deputy.

"Look, I acknowledged I was speeding, you can just write me the ticket and let me go."

"Zack, we need the police to help us," she said, striving to remain calm and reasonable. "We should tell them what we know."

"Yes, you should," Deputy Armbruster agreed in a stern tone. "I'd like you to come down to headquarters, now." The deputy's tone did not offer any room for negotiation.

"Fine." Zack seemed resigned to his fate.

While Deputy Armbruster returned to his squad car, she gave Zack directions. "Make a U-turn and head back toward town."

"I know where the sheriff's department is located," he said as he proceeded to make the U-turn. "I used to work here, remember?"

"You're right, I'm sorry." She sensed he was angry with her but she didn't regret her decision to speak up. "We didn't have enough proof before, but surely we do now that we've seen the black Jeep racing away from the church parking lot."

"I bet there's more than one black Jeep in the state of Wisconsin."

"Too bad we couldn't get the license plate number," she said with a sigh.

"The Jeep was perpendicular to us in the parking lot, and by the time I got out on the road to follow him, he was too far away. You can bet I wish I had the plate number, too."

She sensed Zack was still beating himself up for not noticing the Jeep sooner. "The deputies will have a better chance of finding the Jeep than we will."

"Maybe." The doubt in Zack's tone wasn't reassuring. "Or they'll think we're crazy, seeing threats that aren't there."

She couldn't argue his point, because the first time she'd

gone to the Minneapolis police they told her she didn't have enough evidence to file a petition for a restraining order. It seemed that they didn't want to be bothered with her complaint.

It hadn't been until Blake attacked her that they'd taken her concerns seriously, although, by then, it had almost been too late.

She could only pray that the Hope County Sheriff's Department wouldn't make the same mistake. Because she knew very well just how dangerous Blake could be. Especially when he wasn't taking his psych medication.

———————

ZACK TRIED to harness his temper as he drove to the sheriff's department. Merry was probably right to include them in what was going on, but he still couldn't help thinking that he needed more proof before going to the sheriff's department.

Merry kept glancing at him, clearly worried, so he forced himself to let go of his frustration. "I'm sorry. I'm not upset with you. I just wish I could have at least gotten close enough to get his tag number."

"I understand." Merry's smile was a bit strained, and he mentally kicked himself for being a jerk. "But, you have to understand that I'm worried about you, too. By now, Blake knows that you're spending time with me, and he's not going to like that. You think he'll come after me, but if that were true, he's already had plenty of time to make his move. Now that he has seen you hanging around, I'm worried he's more likely to take his anger out on you."

Zack was deeply touched by her concern for his welfare. He hadn't wanted to get involved, but he knew that he'd do whatever was necessary to keep Merry safe. "Hey, I'm happy to hear that he might come after me. As far as I'm concerned, that's way better than going after you."

Merry rolled her eyes, but didn't say anything more as he pulled into the parking lot of the sheriff's department. Deputy Armbruster was standing near the door waiting for them with a serious expression on his face.

Zack climbed out from behind the wheel and joined Merry to walk up to the building.

"Follow me," Deputy Armbruster said.

Blessedly cool air washed over him as they walked inside. Deputy Armbruster led them over to a small conference area, gesturing for them to take a seat.

"Now then," Deputy Armbruster said as he pulled out a small notebook. "Why don't you start at the very beginning?"

Zack nodded for Merry to start. She did her best to give the short version, describing how she'd dated Caruthers, but when he turned violent took out a restraining order against him.

"And what makes you think this Blake guy is in Crystal Lake?" Armbruster asked.

Now it was Zack's turn to describe how he'd found the boot print beneath the bedroom window. He pulled out his phone and showed Armbruster the photo he'd taken, and then described the redhead they saw on the lake. "We're fairly certain Blake has rented a fishing boat under the name of Calvin Reynolds, who apparently spent time with Caruthers in prison. We also believe the black Jeep we were following belongs to Reynolds as well, although we didn't get the plate number yet."

He'd caught Armbruster's attention now. "So you believe Caruthers is here, pretending to be Reynolds in order to harm Merry?"

The familiar use of Merry's first name wasn't lost on Zack. She must know him pretty well from his frequent visits to the ER. "Yes, I do. I've been doing my best to protect her, which is why I drove her to choir practice."

"I see." Deputy Armbruster turned toward Merry. "Have you been able to identify Caruthers?"

Merry slowly shook her head. "Not exactly. He has bright red hair, but he's always been too far away to get a clear look at his face. Even yesterday, when I saw his face pressed up against the kitchen window, he had his hands cupped around it, and the image was so fleeting I couldn't swear under oath that it was really him."

Deputy Armbruster slapped his notebook shut. "That's enough to convince me," he declared. "I'll see what I can dig up on this guy Reynolds. We'll be able to get his tag number from the system and from there we'll put out an all points bulletin for the rest of the deputies to keep an eye out for him."

Zack couldn't hide his surprise. "Thank you. I have to tell you that one of the Madison cops, Colton Wallace, has been helping me investigate, too. He's trying to find Calvin Reynolds to validate that he loaned his driver's license, credit card and Jeep to Caruthers."

"Good, I'd like you to keep me updated on what Wallace uncovers." Armbruster pulled out his business card and handed it over. "Call me any time."

Bemused, Zack tucked the card in his wallet. "I will."

He'd told Merry that he thought the sheriff's department would likely take her concerns more seriously, but he hadn't expected it to be this easy. Clearly Deputy Armbruster cared about Merry, although he didn't get the vibe that the deputy wanted to date her. More that he cared about her like a sister.

Zack tried to remember the last time he'd felt remotely involved with any of his victims in Madison. He always took his job of bringing criminals to justice seriously, but he'd kept his emotions deeply hidden. A much easier task in a big city like Madison compared to the small town of Crystal Lake.

"Thank you, Deputy," Merry said, taking his hand in hers. "I'm glad to know that you'll be looking out for Blake."

The tips of Deputy Armbruster's ears turned bright red, and Zack revised his previous opinion. Armbruster didn't consider Merry a sister at all. He was just too polite to flirt with her while on duty. Or in front of Zack.

Zack's gut clenched at the thought of Merry finding someone else to share her life with. There were plenty of single men in Crystal Lake, and even in Madison, who'd obviously like to date her. Colton, Daniel, and even Deputy Armbruster. Men who wouldn't balk at the idea of giving her what she deserved, including marriage and a family.

He never should have kissed her. No matter how much he'd wanted to. No matter how much he'd enjoyed holding her. No matter how much he thought about kissing her again.

Now that the sheriff's department was on the case, Zack figured it wouldn't take long for them to find the black Jeep and, hopefully, arrest Caruthers, sending him back to jail or to a psychiatric hospital where he really belonged.

And the minute that happened, he wouldn't need to stay in Crystal Lake any longer. He could return home, avoiding the sweet temptation of kissing Merry.

But for some odd reason, the idea of leaving Merry

alone, even once Caruthers was no longer a threat, didn't make him feel better.

In fact, the ache of loneliness in his chest only seemed to spread, encapsulating his heart.

———

MERRY WAS RELIEVED to know that Deputy Armbruster whole-heartedly believed them, and he'd never given Zack the speeding ticket. In fact, Deputy Armbruster seemed to be a man on a mission to find Blake and to bring him to justice.

Once they were back in Zack's truck, her stomach rumbled loud enough for him to hear, judging by the quick glance he sent her way.

"How about we eat lunch at Rose's Café?" he suggested. "It's well past noon, and I know you're probably as hungry as I am."

She was surprised by his offer and refusing seemed pointless, considering her grumbling stomach. "That would be great, thanks."

Neither one of them said much on the trip into town but Zack's previous sense of urgency to find Caruthers seemed to have evaporated. She wondered if he was secretly relieved to have handed the investigation off to the sheriff's department. After all, Zack had taken a few days off work to relax and enjoy the lake, not to work.

Merry found it hard to believe that just a few days had passed since Leonard had knocked her against the nurse's station. Being in Zack's company these past few days had changed her. She glanced at his handsome profile, remembering their heated kiss. She told herself that she had purposefully avoided relationships over these past two years, but now realized that wasn't true.

At Julie and Derek's wedding, she'd been immediately attracted to Zack, even though she knew he was still grieving the loss of his wife and daughter. But now that he'd kissed her, she understood that she wasn't interested in other men because she cared about Zack.

Far more than she should.

There was nothing she could do though, if Zack didn't return her feelings. Was this how Blake had felt when she explained she didn't love him? She couldn't help the flash of guilt. She tried to concentrate on scoping out a parking space, which were nonexistent on a Saturday afternoon with all the summer tourists flocking to the lake.

"We'll have to walk a ways," Zack said as he reached the end of Main Street. "I should have just stayed in the sheriff's department parking lot. We could have walked from there just as easily."

"I don't mind walking. I've been feeling like a slug, and I obviously won't be able to do my usual exercise routine for the next few weeks."

"All right." Zack parked the truck and pocketed his keys. They walked back up Main Street, weaving around tourists to make their way to Rose's Café.

Merry hoped it was just her imagination that made her feel like everyone inside the Café stared at them as they walked in. Having lunch with Zack two days in a row would surely start the small town tongues wagging. Then she spotted Dr. Katy's auburn hair across the room and rushed over.

"Hi, Dr. Katy."

"Merry!" Dr. Katy gave her a quick hug. "I'm so glad to see that you're feeling better."

"I'm fine. But tell me, how is Leonard? I know you managed to sedate him, but I'm hoping he didn't have to end up being transferred to the psych hospital in Madison."

Dr. Katy's smile faded. "Unfortunately, that is where he ended up. When we finally tracked down his mother Doreen, she was in the cafeteria and had no idea how she'd gotten there. I conferred with several of my colleagues and we agreed she wasn't capable of taking care of Leonard any longer."

"Oh no, that's terrible," Merry whispered. She'd been praying for Leonard and his mother, but hearing that he might have to spend the rest of his life in a psych hospital was discouraging. "I feel so awful for what happened."

"It's not your fault." Dr. Katy's smile was sad. "Most physicians across the country will agree that the current way of providing psychiatric care isn't meeting the needs of our patients. I know locking up Leonard isn't the answer, but most halfway house facilities don't want to take a chance on taking him in because of his history of violent outbursts. It's a lose-lose situation all the way around."

Merry knew Dr. Katy was right, but that didn't make her feel any better. "I know, thanks for the update."

She turned around to join Zack, only to find him right behind her. The dejected expression on his face confirmed that he'd overheard Dr. Katy's remarks.

"I'm sorry to hear about Leonard," he murmured as they slid into a vacant booth.

"It's not your fault any more than it's mine," Merry pointed out. "All we can do now is pray for him."

"Okay." Zack shocked her by bowing his head. "Dear

Lord, we ask You to heal Leonard and to provide him the comfort he deserves, Amen."

She stared at Zack in shock, awed and humbled that he'd pray for Leonard when he hadn't prayed for himself.

And in that moment, she began to hope that Zack might just find his way back to faith and God after all.

10

*Z*ack wasn't sure why he'd felt the need to pray for Leonard, other than he felt guilty for the role he'd played in the poor guy ending up locked up in a psychiatric hospital. But the pleased expression on Merry's face made him feel good. As if she approved.

However, mere seconds later, the familiar guilt began to creep in. He knew he was fast losing control of the situation, but somehow he couldn't seem to make himself stop the downward spiral. Praying had opened up a fissure in his heart he'd thought he'd firmly cemented shut. But, thankfully, he didn't feel the same deep, stabbing pain that he had during those first few months after losing Amelia and Suz.

A sign that he was finally healing, the way their church pastor had once told him he would? Maybe. But Zack wasn't certain that it was a positive sign.

Shouldn't a man who'd promised to love and honor his wife stay true to her, even after she was gone? Was he betraying Suz by wanting to kiss Merry? And what about his daughter? How could he ever bring more children into the world after losing Amelia? No child could ever replace Amelia in his heart.

He scrubbed his hands over his face, trying not to panic. Feeling was one thing, but considering getting involved again in a relationship, was something else.

He so wasn't ready for that.

"Thank you, Zack," Merry said softly, breaking into his internal monologue. "I appreciate you praying for Leonard."

He forced a smile and tried not to take his emotional turmoil out on her. "Yeah, well, he needs all the support he can get."

"So do you."

Her words were soft, but they scrapped across his skin like a wire brush. It was all he could do not to snap at her, like a wounded animal caught in a trap.

He took a deep breath, fighting for control. "Are you ready to order?" He dropped his gaze to the plastic menu he'd once known by heart. "I'm thinking of having meatloaf."

There was a long pause, and he refused to look up at her, unwilling to see the hurt reflected in her amber eyes. He was deeply relieved when their young server, Darcy, chose that moment to sashay over holding two water glasses.

"Hi, Zack. What a nice surprise to see you two days in a row."

"Hey, Darcy, how have you been?" The moment the question spewed out, he wished he could take it back, especially when her entire face brightened.

"I'm doing really well! I'm heading back to UW Madison to complete my senior year next week." She tipped her head in a move that was probably supposed to be coy. "Maybe we can catch up some time?"

"I always work a lot of hours, but we'll see." He just

couldn't quite tell her no outright, even though he wasn't the least bit tempted to see Darcy on a personal level. "Tell us what the specials are for today."

Darcy didn't seem at all deterred by his refusal to commit to a future date. She rattled through the specials, hardly sparing Merry a glance. Darcy's rudeness was so obvious, he couldn't stand it.

"Merry, what sounds good to you?" he asked, purposefully including her in the conversation.

"Um, I don't know." Merry seemed overly preoccupied with her menu, too, and he knew he had only himself to blame. "I guess I'll have the egg salad sandwich."

"Great. I'll have the meatloaf. Thanks, Darcy." Zack handed over the menus, hoping Darcy would get the hint and move on.

"Okay, let me know if you need anything." The way Darcy put an obvious swing in her walk as she went back to the kitchen to put in their order made him wince.

"What's Darcy's major?" Merry asked, breaking the strained silence.

"No clue." And frankly, he didn't care. "She's younger than Julie, you know."

Merry lifted an eyebrow as if to say so what? He shook his head and tried to think of a way to change the subject. Again.

"When is your next doctor's appointment?" Surely Merry's health was a safe subject.

"Next week Thursday, but I'm not hopeful that anything will change. I have a feeling I'll be off work for a while yet."

It bothered him to realize he wouldn't be here to find out for himself what the outcome of her follow-up appointment would be. "Check with your boss. Since you were injured at work, there's a good chance that they'll bring you back even if it means doing some sort of light-duty work."

"Really?" Merry's gaze widened with hope. "That would be awesome. I can't bear the thought of sitting in my apartment for six to eight weeks. I'll take light-duty work over that any time."

A reluctant smile tugged at the corner of his mouth. Trust Merry to be one of the few who didn't want to be forced off work.

Which unfortunately, only made him admire her more.

———————

MERRY TRIED to ignore Darcy's obvious flirting, but it wasn't easy. The only saving grace was that Zack hadn't seemed interested in her, although the way he'd totally shut down after praying for Leonard was upsetting. She had the distinct feeling that if he could take his hastily spoken prayer back, he would.

She was grateful when the meal was finally over. But before they could leave the diner, Zack was stopped by a couple of guys she didn't know.

"Zack! Great to see you're back in town, man!" A tall guy slapped Zack on the shoulder, and she wondered if they'd gone to school together.

"Are you here all weekend?" the shorter guy asked.

"Yep, here until Monday."

"Perfect," the first guy exclaimed. "We're playing softball at two o'clock this afternoon and we could use another player. Why don't you join us? It'll be just like old times."

Merry shouldn't have been surprised to hear that Zack

had once played softball. When he hesitated and glanced back at her she stepped forward. "That's a great idea."

Zack still looked uncertain. "Are you sure you won't mind sitting and watching?"

"Of course not. We could run back to the townhouse first and pick up Ace, if you think there's time."

The smile that bloomed on Zack's face warmed her heart. "All right, that would be awesome."

"So you're gonna play?" the first guy asked.

"Yep, I'll be there." Zack took a step back in order to bring her into the group. "Merry, I'd like you to meet Tony Delarosa and Kade Thompson, two guys I played ball with in high school. Tony and Kade, this is Merry Haines. She's one of the ER nurses at Hope County Hospital."

"Nice to meet you," she murmured as the two men stared at her with blatant curiosity.

"Likewise," Tony said with a wide grin. "You've been holding out on us, Crain."

"Oh no, we're just friends," Merry quickly interjected.

The way Tony and Kade exchanged amused glances made her realize they were just teasing. She blushed and realized she was way out of practice when it came to dealing with men.

"See you guys later," Zack said, putting his hand behind her back and nudging her toward the door.

She didn't need to be asked twice. Outside, the sidewalk along Main Street was even more crowded than when they arrived. Zack held her right hand and pushed his way through the mass of people, and she did her best to follow along behind him, even though she was jostled with almost every step.

Finally, the crowds thinned and they were able to walk side by side to the spot where Zack had left his truck. He didn't let go of her hand, though, until he'd opened the passenger door for her.

"Thanks." Getting into the high truck was awkward without the full use of her left arm, but she managed to ignore the pain to avoid being lifted by Zack. Her emotions were already out of whack from spending so much time with him.

"Are you sure you don't mind sitting outside to watch the game?" he asked, throwing the truck into gear and backing out of the parking space. "Because I don't have to play if you're tired and need to rest."

"I'd like to watch you guys play," she said, striving to keep her tone light. "Should be fun."

He didn't look as if he believed her, and she wondered if he was having second thoughts about agreeing to participate. Well too bad. She wasn't about to give him an excuse to back out. Zack needed this impromptu afternoon ball game more than she did.

When they arrived at the townhouse, Zack made her wait in the locked truck with the air conditioning running while he walked around to make sure Blake wasn't lurking nearby. Zack let Ace outside, and then came back for her.

"We should pack a little cooler of soft drinks, and maybe some snacks," Zack suggested. "I have a portable canvas chair for you, and we'll need to bring Ace's water dish, too. There are some shady areas, but I'm afraid he'll get too hot sitting outside in the sun."

For a guy who seemed inclined to duck out of the game, he was doing a lot in the way of preparations.

"Okay, anything else?"

Zack paused, but then shook his head. "That should do it. Stay here and I'll get everything together."

She sat in the shade on the front porch with Ace as Zack

packed his truck. When she saw the size of the cooler, she wondered if they were providing soft drinks and water for every guy on the team.

Zack glanced at her, and then snapped his fingers. "I almost forgot sunscreen." Without waiting for a response he headed back inside, returning again a few minutes later.

Merry rose to her feet. "I don't know why you need sunscreen. You're already tan from being out in the sun."

"It's not for me, Freckles, it's for you. Are you ready?"

She rolled her eyes at the unoriginal nickname. "Yes, I'm ready. Come on, Ace."

The shadows that had darkened his eyes before lunch vanished as Zack drove to the Crystal Lake Park. She'd hoped that praying would help him find his way back to God, but for some reason, it had seemed to have the opposite effect.

At times, Zack's emotions seemed to be all over the place, and for a moment she was reminded of Blake. Not that she believed that Zack had any type of psychiatric disorder, but he still went hot and cold in a matter of seconds.

She didn't understand him, or maybe she just didn't get men in general. Several of her nursing friends had complained about their significant others not being faithful, or that they were self-absorbed or just plain not very nice.

All she knew about Zack was what she heard from Julie, who was obviously biased when it came to the older brother she idolized. She had no idea what sort of a husband or father he had been.

Clearly, he'd loved his wife and daughter, but it was also possible that he was grieving even more out of a sense of guilt. Maybe he hadn't always been there for them. Maybe he had other regrets.

Blake had damaged her physically and emotionally. It had taken years to gain her self-confidence back. Did she really want to risk being hurt again by Zack Crain? A man who'd told her more than once that he didn't have anything to offer her.

No, she didn't.

Better to focus on being his friend, helping him to find his way back to God and faith, but nothing more.

———————

ZACK GAVE Tony's bat several practice swings, glad to be doing something physically challenging. He didn't have any of his gear here, so the guys had supplied him with their spare stuff.

The glove he was given wasn't nearly as good as his, but it would do. The guys had divided up into two teams and had done rock, paper, scissors to see who would be first at bat.

His and Tony's team had won.

He handed the bat over to Tony, and then glanced back to look for Merry. She'd found a shady spot beneath a tree to sit and watch the game. With the cooler at her side, a cold bottle of water in her hand and Ace curled up at her feet, she looked perfectly happy.

The guys had razzed him about Merry, but he'd repeated her story since she'd seemed anxious to make sure they knew the truth. For his sake? Or hers? There was no reason on earth that she couldn't date one of them. Except for the fact that he wouldn't like it.

Really, this ridiculous fascination with Merry's potential

love life had to stop. She deserved better than him. His head knew that, but his heart was being stubborn.

Tony hit a double and stood on second base, grinning like an idiot. Zack shook his head wryly and stepped up to the plate to bat next. He did his best to focus on the pitch rather than thinking about Merry.

The first pitch was outside, but their makeshift umpire called it a strike. Zack scowled, tugged his baseball cap down further over his eyes, and decided he couldn't afford to be too picky.

The next pitch wasn't perfect either, but he swung as hard as he could. The bat hit the ball with a resounding crack, sending it sailing over the heads of the outfielders who were scrambling to back up. A home run! Tony made it home first and when Zack rounded second base, he saw that Merry was on her feet cheering for him while Ace barked loudly, clearly not sure what was going on but unwilling to be left out.

He was pleasantly surprised and touched that she cared enough to root for him and couldn't help but grin, no doubt looking just as goofy as Tony had on his double. Zack lifted his hand in a wave as he hit third base, and then sailed over home plate.

Their brief moment of fame was quickly derailed when the other team went up to bat and hit several home runs as well. Zack played second base and made several good plays. Apparently his high school baseball skills hadn't totally abandoned him.

The game was loud and fun, both sides scoring many points before they finally called it quits after five innings and nearly a tie score. Everyone hung around guzzling sports drinks and munchies. Merry joined the group, leaving Ace in the shade of the tree.

"Nice game," she said. "I had fun watching."

Zack swiped his sweaty face with a towel, trying to keep downwind from Merry to spare her the stench. "It was a blast, although it's too bad we're not closer to the lake so I could take a quick swim before heading home. I'm afraid I don't smell the greatest."

"I'm a nurse. Trust me, I've smelled far worse."

He chuckled and glanced over at Ace. "We better get going. I think Ace is feeling left out."

"All right."

He glanced back at Tony and Kade. "Hey guys, we're taking off."

"Try not to be a stranger," Kade said, giving him a playful smack in the shoulder. "We have these ball games often during the summer and you're always welcome."

Zack couldn't remember the last time he'd hung out with any of his old friends. Certainly, they'd hung out in the early days, when he and Suz were dating. But after they'd gotten married and had Amelia, he hadn't bothered to keep in touch.

That was on him, and to be honest he wasn't sure if he had to go back in time that he wouldn't do the same thing again. He'd liked being married. He liked having a family.

But there was something to be said for having friends, too.

He followed Merry over to where Ace was standing and whining beneath the tree. When she bent down to untie the dog's leash, he noticed a slip of paper hanging out of the side pocket of her jeans.

"Look out, you're going to lose this," he said, gesturing to the slip of paper.

"I don't even know what it is." Merry frowned as she

pulled the paper out and, suddenly, the color leeched from her face.

"What's wrong?" He took the slip of paper from her fingers and had to control the flash of fury when he saw it was a note from Caruthers.

We'll be together again, soon, Meredith.

Love, Blake.

11

Merry struggled to maintain her composure as she swiped her hands on the seat of her jeans. Just touching the note Blake had stuffed in her pocket made her feel like taking another shower.

"When did he get this into your pocket?" Zack demanded.

She shook her head and shrugged her right shoulder. "No one has been anywhere near me since we arrived in the park. But when we walked through town, we were surrounded by people. I have to assume that's when he slipped the note to me.

Zack scowled and glanced around the park, clearly searching for some sign of Blake. "I don't like this," he said in a grim tone. "I think we'd better head back to the sheriff's department and see if they have any leads. It shouldn't be this difficult to find him."

Silently agreeing with him, she swallowed hard against a wave of despair. She didn't understand why Blake had remained obsessed with her, especially after all this time had passed. She closed her eyes and prayed.

Please, Lord, keep us safe in Your care. And please help heal Blake, too. Amen.

She opened her eyes, relieved at the sense of calmness that wafted over her. She turned toward Zack, who was staring at her intently. She smiled. "I'm ready to leave if you are."

"I'm amazed how well praying seems to work for you," Zack said in a low voice. "One minute I thought you were ready to fall apart, and then next you appear calm and serene."

"Praying does give me peace," she admitted. "Facing fear is easier when I remember I'm not alone."

Zack seemed intrigued by the idea, but then Ace began to bark again and he quickly looked around, as if sensing a threat. But this time Ace was only barking at another dog, a small Westie being walked by a young girl along the edge of the park.

"Not your type, Ace," Zack said wryly. He turned to Merry. "Take the dog's leash and I'll grab the cooler."

Merry took the leash and shortened it up, since Ace seemed determined to get to know the Westie better. "Stay, Ace. Stay."

As usual, the dog didn't listen to her very well. They made their way to Zack's truck, and from there drove straight to the sheriff's department.

They arrived after the shift change, so Deputy Armbruster wasn't available, but Deputy Thomas agreed to talk to them.

"Hi, Merry." Deputy Thomas had stopped by the hospital many times, so she knew him almost as well as she knew Deputy Armbruster. "I heard about your stalker, but don't worry, we're going to catch him."

"With all the guys you have looking for him, I would

have hoped you'd picked him up already," Zack said grimly. "He's already gotten too close to Merry."

Deputy Thomas frowned. "What do you mean?"

"Read this." Zack held out the note Blake had managed to stuff into her pocket.

"When did you get this?" Deputy Thomas asked in a grim tone.

"I don't know for sure," Merry admitted. "We walked up and down Main Street this afternoon and the sidewalk was jam packed with people. He must have slipped it into my pocket, most likely after we left Rose's Café."

"Look, Deputy, I don't like the way he's watching her," Zack said, his gaze troubled. "You need to find him before he escalates."

"I understand your concern, and trust me, we are looking for him. But we also have other calls we're taking as well. We've already busted up a big fight at Barry's Pub, not to mention being called out to a couple of car crashes. Weekends are busy around here, especially in the height of tourist season."

"I know you're busy," Merry spoke up, trying to smooth over Zack's rough tone. "And I really appreciate everything you're doing for me."

"We'll do our best to find him," Deputy Thomas assured her. "We take care of our own."

She was pleased he'd included her as belonging to Crystal Lake even though she hadn't grown up here the way Julie and Zack had. The moment she'd arrived, she'd fallen in love with the small town and the beautiful lake. There were acres of woods just a few miles away, and she'd seen dozens of deer in the past few years.

"Thank you," she said.

"Have you been through the campsite?" Zack asked.

"I know Deputy Armbruster drove through," Deputy Thomas admitted. "But I think that was about the time he was called away to break up the fight. I'll head over there soon, and we all have the tag number of the black Jeep."

"I appreciate that," Zack said.

"Merry, I'd like to keep the note as evidence," Deputy Thomas said. "We're not likely to get prints, but we could always have a handwriting analysis done if needed."

Since she didn't want to see the note again, she wasn't about to argue. "No problem."

"Thanks again," Zack said as they turned to leave.

Zack seemed to be deep in thought as they walked back to the truck. She found herself wishing that he'd give prayer another try, because she was convinced he'd feel so much better if he shared his burden with God.

But she couldn't force him, either. Faith was something he had to accept on his own. And she had a feeling that Zack wouldn't be able to find his faith until he finally let go of his sorrow over losing his wife and daughter.

She wanted Zack to have peace, even if he couldn't bear to open himself up to love again.

———————

ZACK KEPT a sharp lookout for any sign of Caruthers as he drove back to his sister's townhouse. He still couldn't believe that the guy had gotten close enough to Merry to slip a note in her pocket.

Thankfully, Caruthers hadn't done anything worse.

Dear Lord, please keep Merry safe!

The prayer popped into his mind almost automatically, the way he used to talk to God before he'd lost his family.

Two prayers in one day. And he didn't regret them, either. For whatever reason he found it easier to pray for others, like Leonard and especially for Merry, than it was to pray for himself.

Would God listen to his prayers? Maybe, especially since both Leonard and Merry were truly deserving of God's love and protection.

Zack was tempted to drive through the campsite himself, but at the same time, didn't want to expose Merry to any further danger. Better for Thomas to do that, so he could go ahead and arrest Caruthers if he saw him or the Jeep. At least the note provided the proof they needed that Caruthers had violated his restraining order.

He pulled in front of his sister's townhouse and decided to walk Merry and Ace up to the house before grabbing the cooler. Maybe he was being a bit on the paranoid side, but better safe than sorry.

A quick search confirmed that the house was empty. As he was dragging the cooler inside, his cell phone rang. He set the cooler down in front of the kitchen sink and reached for the phone.

"Hey Cole, what's up?"

"Just giving you a status report," his buddy said. "Unfortunately, we still haven't found Calvin Reynolds. And he didn't show up for his bartender shift at the local tavern, either."

Zack couldn't ignore the sudden chill that snaked down his spine. "Do you think it's possible Caruthers murdered him?"

"Too early to tell. For all we know the two men are

together," Cole pointed out. "But yeah, it's definitely suspicious."

Zack wholeheartedly agreed. "I don't suppose a missing persons report was filed?"

"Not yet, but if we don't find any sign of him by tomorrow, then we may do that. I'll send over a driver's license photo of the guy, just in case he is there with Caruthers."

"Thanks, I'll be sure to share it with the deputies here."

"You have the locals involved?" Cole asked.

"Yeah. I didn't have much of a choice since I was stopped for speeding while we were trying to follow the black Jeep."

Cole chuckled. "Would love to have been there to see that."

"Do you have any other information?" Zack asked.

"Nope. As soon as we hang up you'll get the photo."

"Thanks, Cole," Zack said in a serious tone. "For covering my shifts and for the help."

"You know how you can pay me back," Cole teased. "Introduce me to pretty Merry and we'll call it even."

"Fat chance," Zack said half under his breath. "Bye." He disconnected the call, the sound of his buddy's laughter still ringing in his ears.

True to Colton's word, a text message came through a few seconds later. He stared at the grainy photograph of Calvin Reynolds, trying to remember if he'd seen the guy even in passing. Judging by the size of his thick neck, Reynolds was heavier than Caruthers, and with his long stringy brown hair and black eyebrow piercing, the guy would easily stand out in a crowd.

Zack still had Armbruster's contact information so he forwarded the photo to him asking him to share it with the rest of the deputies. Satisfied that they had another clue to go on, he began cleaning out the cooler.

"I can help," Merry said, coming up to stand beside him. Her sweet vanilla scent reminded him that he probably reeked like sweat and needed to take a shower.

"I'll finish this," he said. "You might want to stand back until I can get cleaned up."

"Don't be silly," she said exasperation echoing through her tone. "How about we work together? Set the soft drinks and snacks on the counter and I'll put them away while you drain the water out of the bottom of the cooler."

For some reason her bossy tone made him smile. "Is this why you're the ER charge nurse? Because you like to give orders?"

"Absolutely." She opened the fridge and held it open with her hip as she tucked the leftovers inside.

The desire to kiss her again was nearly overwhelming, and he was glad when the cooler was finally empty and he had a good excuse to go outside.

He liked Merry, far too much for his own good. Working together with her in the kitchen only emphasized the loneliness surrounding him.

His choice, he reminded himself. Yet at the same time, he couldn't help thinking that it could also be his choice to change his approach.

He could decide to share his life with others rather than keeping himself isolated from his friends and his family. He could even go as far as to widen his circle of friends.

After dumping the cooler upside down on the grass, he glanced toward the lake to where his boat was tied up beneath the canopy of the boat lift. An evening boat ride would be the perfect end to a great day. He and Merry could pack up the leftovers from the afternoon and last night's grilling and stay out on the water long enough to watch the sunset.

Was he out of his mind to take Merry out on what any normal person would consider a date?

Maybe. But there was no denying that he enjoyed spending time with her. That he wanted to see her laugh, to watch the expression of awe on her face as they watched the sun dip behind the horizon.

And for the first time in a long time, he let go of the pain and sorrow.

———

MERRY WATCHED through the patio doors as Zack dried out the cooler. His mood had once again shifted so that he seemed lighter and happier.

She wondered how he would feel about going to church with her in the morning. Obviously, she had to go since she was singing in the choir. But would he stay again, like he did today? Or would sitting through an entire service be too much for him?

"I'll be right next door if you need me," Zack called through the screen door. "Keep Ace with you, okay?"

"Okay." Ace had settled down in front of the door, as if a bit worn out by spending the afternoon at the park.

Suddenly exhausted, Merry curled up in the corner of the sofa, rested her head against the cushion and closed her eyes. She wished she could spend more time with Zack. Sooner or later he'd open up and let God's love shine through, and she found that she wanted to be there when that happened.

Was that being selfish? She didn't like to think so. It was

just that while watching Zack play softball she caught a glimpse of the man he used to be.

The man he could be again.

It struck her that his moodiness was more likely related to his struggles with faith, rather than having anything to do with her, personally. She hoped that Pastor John's service would somehow find its way through Zack's internal barriers.

She must have dozed again because she woke up when she heard Zack calling her name. "Merry? Are you all right?"

"I'm fine," she said, putting her hand up to smooth her tangled hair. "Took a little cat nap, that's all."

He frowned in concern. "Are you still having headaches?"

"No headaches, just this weird exhaustion that hits me out of nowhere." She stood, and then crossed over to the patio door where Ace stood wagging his tail in a way that convinced her he wanted to go outside. She opened the door and smiled as Ace bounded out to do his doggy business. Zack's dark hair was damp, and he wore a clean pair of canvas shorts and a green T-shirt that mirrored the color of his eyes. The scent of his aftershave reminded her of their all-too-brief kiss.

He was so handsome, her heart ached with longing.

"Do you think you're up for an evening boat ride?" Zack asked hesitantly. "If not, it's no big deal. I just thought it would be nice to watch the sunset over the lake."

"That sounds wonderful!" She didn't even try to hide her enthusiasm. "I'd love to go for an evening boat ride."

"Great." Zack's boyish grin went straight to her heart. "I thought we'd pack up our leftovers from last night in case we get hungry later."

She opened the door to let Ace back in. "Sounds perfect. When do you want to leave?"

"Any time you're ready."

"Just give me a few minutes to freshen up." She was feeling more than a little self-conscious about her wrinkled clothes and tangled hair, especially considering how Zack had cleaned up.

"No rush. I'll use the time to pull the leftovers together."

She nodded and slipped down the hall towards the bathroom located right outside the guest bedroom. Even though she knew better, she couldn't help thinking of this little outing as their first date.

And more than anything, she didn't want it to be the last.

———————

THIRTY-FIVE MINUTES LATER, Merry settled into the seat beside Zack as they headed out over the lake in his speedboat. Zack had insisted on bringing Ace along, since the dog clearly didn't want to be left behind. Ace settled in the back of the boat like a sailing pro.

Merry noticed that Zack set a slow but steady pace, even though she'd be willing to bet he normally preferred speed. "You don't have to go slow just for me," she pointed out.

He flashed a wide grin. "Yes, I do, you're still recovering from your concussion. Besides, I don't mind. As soon as the sun goes down, it will be a no wake zone for the entire lake anyway."

She didn't understand all the boating rules, but since Zack seemed happy enough she let the subject drop. His kind consideration warmed her more than she cared to admit. He made a circle around the lake, glancing frequently at the *For Sale* signs.

"Are you thinking of buying?" she asked, when he slowed almost to a complete stop in front of one place.

He looked at her and nodded slowly. "Yeah, I've been thinking about it. Although it seems ridiculous since I can only get up here on the occasional weekend off work."

Merry tried to ignore the leap of her heart at the thought of Zack spending more time in Crystal Lake. "It's not silly at all, having both quiet time and fun time is important."

"Yeah, maybe. Although I'm not sure if I can even afford any lake property at this point. I'm sure the prices have skyrocketed over the past few years."

"Julie and Derek are thinking of selling the townhouse next year," she offered. "Maybe an investment property would help pay some of the bills?"

He looked shocked at the news. "I didn't know they were thinking of selling."

She bit her lower lip, hoping she hadn't let out any secrets. "Julie mentioned that they want to be in their own house before they have more children. Or maybe she was just thinking out loud."

"Something to consider," Zack said softly. "Although renting out the other side of the townhouse is no guarantee."

"They had a renter for a while, but then the doctor quit the hospital to move back to Madison. Apparently, the life-style here was just too quiet for him."

"Some people love it and others don't."

"I'm in the love it category," she said, enjoying the cool breeze washing over them as Zack sped up a bit. "I hope they catch Blake soon, because I don't want to have to move again."

"We'll get him," Zack said with confidence. "Don't even think of moving. Running isn't the answer."

It was on the tip of her tongue to mention that Zack had run away to Madison to avoid the constant reminder of his wife and daughter, but just then the edge of the sun touched the horizon and the bright yellow light shifted to a deep orange.

"Look, Zack, isn't it beautiful?"

Zack shut down the boat motor so that they drifted along on the waves, the gentle rocking motion more relaxing than anything she'd ever experienced before. No wonder some people slept on their boats.

For several long minutes, they simply gazed at the glorious sunset. When the boat drifted sideways, Merry stood and turned so she could better see the colorful sky.

She was so focused on the sunset that she didn't notice the larger wave from a passing boat coming toward them until it hit the boat, making the vessel rock sharply beneath her feet. She would have fallen if Zack hadn't stood up and caught her in his arms.

"Thank you," she murmured breathlessly. Being held in his arms caused her heart to race so fast it was a wonder she didn't have a full-out cardiac arrest.

"Merry," Zack whispered mere moments before he lowered his head and kissed her.

12

Merry clung to Zack's shoulder with her right arm, reveling in his kiss. He mouth was gentle yet firm, and the way he kissed her so tenderly while holding her close made her want to cry.

Zack was so different from Blake. Even though they'd only spent a few days together, she already instinctively knew Zack would never hurt her physically. In fact, she trusted Zack with her life.

But emotionally, not so much. Not that Zack would intentionally try to hurt her, but his wounds hadn't healed and the scars from losing his wife and daughter might be too deep for her to overcome.

As much as she cared about Zack, she couldn't deny that he hadn't made any promises. There was a good chance he wouldn't allow himself to have any sort of future. Not to mention, he hadn't fully embraced his faith. Merry knew she couldn't replace his wife and his daughter in his heart. Truthfully, she didn't want to. But she didn't think Zack would allow himself to care for her, either. Or for anyone else.

This time, she was the one who broke off the kiss, easing backward until he lifted his head and dropped his arms. He stared down at her in confusion, and even though she couldn't see his eyes in the dim light she sensed she'd hurt him.

"Zack, I...care about you," she said in a low voice. "But last night you told me you can't give me what I need. And I don't think anything has changed since then, has it?"

Zack let out a heavy sigh, lifted his hand to rub the back of his neck while he looked away. "Probably not," he agreed.

She tried to smile as if her heart wasn't breaking. "I didn't think so."

"Actually, that's not exactly true," Zack corrected, abruptly swinging back around to face her. "You need to understand that for the first time in years, I feel happy. The time we've spent together has been wonderful and fun. I don't understand why, but I feel as if the heavy weight on my shoulders has lightened a bit."

A fissure of hope opened in her heart. "I thought you seemed happier since the last time I saw you, but I wasn't sure if that was just wishful thinking on my part."

"It's not your imagination, it's true." He looked pensive for a minute and even though they were missing the glorious sunset, she didn't glance away from him. "I guess it's no secret that I bottled up all my feelings, keeping them locked away as if I didn't have the right to be happy after losing Suzanne and Amelia."

She nodded, encouraging him to continue.

"I guess I just haven't been able to understand why I'm here while they're gone."

"Oh Zack, I know you've suffered more than anyone should have to, but you need to remember that God has a plan for you." Merry prayed that she'd find the right words to help him understand. "It's not really up to us to question God's will, is it? All we can do is to ask for the Lord's strength and wisdom to guide us through the difficult times."

"I don't know, maybe," he hedged.

She knew she was right, but it was clear he wasn't yet in full agreement. There had to be another way. "Suzanne loved you, didn't she?"

He looked surprised. "Yes, of course."

"And I know how much you loved her. Tell me, what if the situation was reversed? What if you'd passed away and Suzanne was alone? Wouldn't you have wanted her to find love and happiness again?"

"Of course I would," he agreed readily. "But that's a completely different situation. Suzanne would deserve to have someone love her and to take care of her."

"And you don't?" She didn't understand his reasoning.

"I'm not sure I'd survive another loss," he said in a low tone. "And somehow, the thought of having a family makes me feel like I've turned my back on the one I had."

She suppressed a sigh. "I'm sure losing your family was difficult, but refusing to open yourself up to caring about someone else isn't the answer, either. Don't you see? Caring for others is part of taking care of yourself, too."

"I don't know," he murmured. "But it still seems wrong to carry on as if nothing had happened."

"No one is asking you to do that," she pointed out. "I wouldn't want you to act as if you hadn't loved your wife and your daughter. Loving them has made you the man you are today. But I think you also need to consider that love is one of God's greatest gifts. By choosing not to open yourself up to love and happiness, you're actually letting Suzanne and Amelia down."

Zack sat down in the driver's seat and gazed at the sunset, as if contemplating her words.

She sat back down, too, enjoying the rest of the sunset while hoping that somehow, someway, Zack would find his way to peace and happiness, putting the past to rest once and for all.

———————

ZACK COULDN'T SAY how long he sat there while Merry's words reverberated through his mind, but it was well after the final golden rays of sunshine disappeared behind the towering trees along the west side of the lake.

He knew that Merry's assessment was right on, but he still wasn't sure how to let go of the past. And he couldn't help wondering if Merry was right about attending church. Maybe he should try to share his burden with God.

He blinked and realized that darkness had fallen. "Sorry about that." He twisted the key in the ignition and the small lights came on in the front and the back, giving off enough illumination that no other boaters would accidently run into them.

Even in a no wake zone, two boats colliding could be trouble. He should have known better than to sit out in the lake, lost in his thoughts.

"It's no problem," Merry said. But when she huddled down in the seat, he knew she was chilled from the light breeze.

"I have a blanket you can use." Zack set the boat on idle while he lifted the seat cushions in along the back to pull out the spare blanket. It didn't smell too musty as he unfolded it and shook it. He flipped the blanket over her and she clutched at the edge, seemingly glad for the warmth.

"We'll be back at the townhouse soon," he promised. They were on the opposite side of the lake and, with the no wake rule, he figured they would be back in fifteen minutes or so.

Merry didn't say much as he steered the boat and he wondered if she was disappointed in him. Not that he could blame her. This was the second time he'd kissed her in two days and he still couldn't seem to get the tangled mess in his head straightened out.

They hadn't eaten any of the leftovers and he knew that was probably his fault, too. He wasn't hungry, but Merry was still recovering from her concussion and her cracked collarbone. She needed to keep up her strength.

"We should eat dinner when we get back," Zack said.

"I'm not hungry," Merry murmured.

Her dejected tone stabbed deep. What was wrong with him? Why couldn't he just relax and take things one step at a time?

Because Merry deserved more, that's why. She deserved a man who was serious about a relationship. She'd admitted she cared about him.

And he cared about her, too. More than he wanted to.

The last thing he wanted to do was to hurt her. After everything she went through with Blake in the past, and what she was going through again, was rough enough. Merry needed some stability in her life. A man who knew exactly what he wanted. A man who'd share her dreams.

Despite what Merry had said, she deserved the man he'd once been, not the man he'd become.

Zack maneuvered the boat around the lake, the light on

the stern of his boat flickering across a few of the *For Sale* signs. The idea of purchasing a property along the Crystal Lake shore wouldn't leave him alone.

As he approached Julie's pier, he slowed considerably and watched as Merry stood along the side of the boat, reaching for the rope to pull them in, looking as comfortable as if she'd often done the same thing.

It occurred to him that they made a great team.

Merry opened the side door of the boat so she could step out, and Ace followed her. When she was safely on the pier she reached for the bag of leftovers and he couldn't help feeling another spurt of guilt. It was his fault they'd gotten all serious, which had made her lose her appetite. "I'll get that," he called.

"It's okay," she said, turning to make her way up the grassy slope toward the house.

The darkness made it difficult to see, but he managed to get the boat into the lift. He took a few minutes to crank the wheel so that the boat was raised out of the water.

He heard Ace growl and glanced up toward the house.

"Ace down," Merry commanded sharply.

Zack frowned and quickly abandoned the boat lift to catch up to Merry.

"Hi, Meredith," a male voice said.

"Hi, Blake. What brings you here?"

Blake? Zack froze, mentally kicking himself for letting Merry walk up to the house alone, and for not bringing his service weapon. He wanted to rush over to Merry's side, but at the same time, remembered the incident with Leonard. He edged closer, staying in the shadows, searching for Blake. His heart stopped in his chest when he realized that Blake was standing just a few feet away from Merry, holding a gun.

MERRY FOUGHT TO REMAIN CALM, trying not to do anything that would set off Blake's anger. She'd learned from her past mistakes that disagreeing with Blake was the wrong approach. He would only get angry and more irrational. At the same time, she was deeply afraid that Blake wouldn't hesitate to shoot Zack, especially if Blake considered him a threat. She hoped and prayed Zack would stay back, out of sight.

"Thank you for the note," she said, trying to keep Blake's attention focused on her. She held onto Ace's collar, unwilling to give Blake the chance to shoot the animal. "What brings you to Crystal Lake?" she asked.

"I came to see you, Meredith," Blake answered in a reasonable tone, as if he wasn't holding a gun. "To bring you back home where you belong."

It took every ounce of willpower she possessed not to turn around to find Zack. Her best chance right now was to treat Blake like a friend rather than put him on the defensive. He was dressed in a pair of jeans and a denim shirt, once again wearing the blue baseball cap. In the dim light it wasn't easy to see his bright red hair.

"Is Caro with you?" she asked, trying to stall. She didn't think Blake's sister would go along with his plan, but if she gave Zack enough time, he could circle around to get on the other side of the house to call for help.

"No. But Caroline misses you, Meredith," he said in a chiding tone. "You shouldn't have left without telling us where you were going."

"I'm sorry," she murmured, wishing she knew exactly

how Blake had found her in the first place. "I miss Caro a lot, too. I miss all of you." And in a way she did, because the fun times she'd spent growing up with the Caruthers family were some of her happiest memories.

But the months she'd spent dating Blake were also her saddest and darkest memories. As nice as he sounded right now, she knew full well he was capable of killing her. Especially if he found out she had no intention of going back with him.

"How is David? And Joey?" she asked, hoping she could gain a few minutes by discussing Blake's siblings.

Blake waved the gun as if they weren't important. "There will be plenty of time for you to catch up with the rest of the family later. Right now, you need to come with me."

She tightened her fingers on Ace's collar as fear shimmered along her spine. No matter what he threatened, she couldn't bear the thought of going with him.

Help, me, Lord! Show me the way!

"You'll have to give me a few minutes to pack my things," she said, playing along with him. "If you'll wait here, I'll be right back."

"I don't think so," Blake said in a harsh tone. "Do you think I'm stupid?"

She swallowed hard and tried not to back away from him, even though he was beginning to show the depth of his mental illness. She reminded herself that it wasn't his fault that he had a mental illness. Although it had been Blake's choice not to take his medication, which brought them full circle.

"I didn't say that, Blake. You were always smarter than me in school, remember?"

Blake took a few agitated steps making Ace growl again.

"Easy boy," she whispered.

"Do you have any idea what I've gone through while you've been gone?" Blake asked harshly. "And what I had to go through to find you? And then come out here without getting caught?"

She couldn't sense Zack behind her, which gave her hope that he was on his way to getting help. How long before the sheriff's deputies would get here? She had no idea.

"That was you out in the fishing boat, wasn't it?" she asked. "And that was you I saw looking into my kitchen window, too, wasn't it? Why didn't you say something? Or come inside to talk to me, then?"

"You know why," Blake said, pacing again, back and forth in an agitated way. "Because that man was there. I thought about trying to kill him, but first I had to get away."

Her blood ran cold as Blake voiced her greatest fear. She couldn't bear to think of Zack getting hurt, or worse, because of her.

A wave of helplessness washed over her. What if Blake never got over his obsession with her? What if she ended up running away from him for the rest of her life?

"Is he your boyfriend now?" Blake demanded. "Did you move here because of him?"

"No, Zack isn't my boyfriend," she said. "He's the brother of a friend, that's all. I haven't dated anyone since you, Blake."

Blake twitched and glanced over to his right, as if seeing something that wasn't there. "I know, I know. We have to go. Soon."

Her stomach clenched with fear as she recognized the outward sign of Blake's hallucinations. At times he could seem so rational, so normal, and then suddenly he was talking to people who weren't there.

And if he was losing his grip on reality, there would be no way to reason with him.

"I'll just put the dog inside the house, so he doesn't run away," she said, taking a step sideways to get closer to the house.

"No!" Blake's sharp tone made her jerk her head backward, as if expecting a slap. "We have to go now, don't you see? Everyone is waiting for us."

"We can't take the dog with us, Blake," she said striving to sound reasonable. "I'll just put him inside where he'll be safe."

Blake mumbled something she couldn't hear as he turned and walked several steps away before spinning back around to face her. "Why do you have a dog?"

"He's not my dog," she tried to assure him. "I'm just taking care of him."

"Fine, but hurry up. We have to get out of here."

She wanted nothing more than to get Ace inside the house where he'd be safe, but something on the grass in the area behind where Blake had been standing caught her attention. She frowned, trying to figure out what it was.

A shoe? Why would there be a shoe there? As she stared at the sight, she realized the shoe was attached to a leg.

Dear Lord, was there a person lying on the ground? Had Blake already shot and killed someone?

And if so, who?

13

Z ack crept along the farthest edge of the lawn, staying in the shadows of the pine trees as he made his way around to the front of the townhouse.

As soon as he was safely around the corner, he broke into a jog and pulled out his cell phone to dial 911. The ringing on the other end of the line seemed to go on for an exceptionally long time before the dispatcher answered. "Hope County Sheriff's Department. What is the nature of your emergency?"

"I'm at 2414 South Lake Drive and there is a Blake Caruthers here threatening Merry Haines with a gun," he said in a low voice. He stopped short when he realized there was an unfamiliar car parked along the side of the road. In the darkness he could just barely make out the emblem of the sheriff's star on the side. "There may be a deputy already on the scene. There's a squad parked in front of the townhouse."

"We haven't dispatched anyone to that location," the dispatcher said. "What's the license plate number of the squad located there?"

"First I need you to send additional deputies, but no lights and sirens," he ordered. After listening to her send out the call for help, he rattled off the license plate number.

"I've dispatched two squads to the address," the dispatcher informed him. He could hear clicking of computer keys in the background. "The squad on the scene belongs to Deputy Armbruster."

Zack wondered if Armbruster had stumbled across Blake's black Jeep and followed him here. But then where was the Jeep? He didn't see any sign of it. How had Blake gotten there? The guy must have parked the Jeep further down the street and came up on foot.

"I don't see Armbruster, but I'm sure he's close by," Zack said, hoping he was right. Just knowing he wasn't alone already made him feel better. "Please tell those squads to hurry!"

He didn't wait for the dispatcher to respond, but disconnected from the call. He paused, debating between going inside for his weapon and circling around the other side of the townhouse to sneak up on Blake.

Since Blake was armed, Zack figured he needed to even the odds. Even if Armbruster was already behind Caruthers, Zack would prefer to be armed, too. He silently opened the front door and used his key to get inside. Forgoing lights, he felt along the wall until he found the hallway that lead to the two bedrooms. He found his service revolver on the top of his duffel bag, and then went back through the townhouse the same way he came in.

Zack stayed close to the house as he went around to the other side so he could sneak up behind Blake. When he reached the corner of Julie's garden, he abruptly stopped, staring at the ground in horror.

Armbruster was sprawled face down on the grass. And

there was only one explanation. Zack was very much afraid Blake had shot and killed the deputy. They hadn't heard a gunshot while out on the lake though, so either Caruther's weapon had a silencer or he used some other type of weapon on him.

He was thankful he'd gone to get his gun as he planned his next steps, knowing that backup wouldn't arrive for at least five to ten minutes.

Zack listened to Merry's attempt to reason with Caruthers and sent up a quick prayer for her safety.

Then he lowered himself to a crouch, easing into a position where he could see Caruthers. The man was pacing erratically and occasionally talking to himself.

He didn't want to shoot the guy, especially if there was any chance of hitting Merry. But he would shoot if he had no other choice.

Zack hoped Merry would keep her distance, giving him room to maneuver. But just then he caught sight of her stepping closer to Caruthers.

Where was Ace? He couldn't see any sign of the dog, which was odd since he'd heard Ace growling at the guy, earlier. He wished Merry had kept the dog close at hand, just in case. And why on earth did it seem like she was going along with Caruthers?

He wanted to shout at her to stay away, but all he could do was wait and watch for an opportunity to take Caruthers out.

———

MERRY DIDN'T WANT to walk any closer to Blake, but since he

was waving the gun at her again, didn't have much of a choice. She couldn't tear her gaze from the shoe. She'd stalled as long as possible after putting Ace inside the house, but Blake was getting more and more agitated. She felt bad for Blake having to wrestle with his demons, but she also knew he was partly responsible.

"Where have you been staying?" she asked, hoping that if Zack was nearby, he could find a way to follow them. "At the campsite?"

Blake laughed a horrible sound that grated along her nerves. "I was there at first, but for the past two days I've been staying right next door to you, Meredith."

She tried not to gape at him. "Really? Where?"

"At the house two doors down from you that's for sale," he said in a smug tone. "I jimmied the basement window to get inside. Pretty smart, huh?"

As much as it pained her to admit it, Blake's idea of staying in a vacant house was a stroke of genius. No wonder they hadn't been able to find him. And now she knew how he'd disappeared so quickly the day he'd peered in the kitchen window.

Had he laughed as he watched Zack run around looking for him? The idea made her shiver. They were so lucky that Blake hadn't tried shooting Zack back then.

"Is that where we're going now?" she asked. A brief movement from the corner of the house caught her eye, and she breathed easier knowing that Zack was nearby.

Now she just needed to think of a way to disarm Blake before he started shooting.

But how?

She stopped in her tracks and it took Blake a moment to realize she wasn't coming along. "What are you doing?" he asked.

"Did you hurt someone, Blake?" she asked. "I see someone lying on the ground over there."

Blake didn't so much as glance behind him. "He tried to stop me, but I took care of him. Let's go. Now! Or I'll have no choice but to hurt you."

It was on the tip of her tongue to point out that he had a choice, but she bit back the argument. "I'm a nurse, remember? If that man is hurt I need to go and help him."

From the corner of her eye she noticed Zack edging closer. When he scowled, she belatedly realized she should have been trying to get Blake further away from Zack's hiding place rather than bringing attention to the area.

The moment Blake's attention was diverted, Merry slid her injured arm from the sling and rushed toward him, grabbing his gun hand and pushing it upward towards the sky. As if reading her mind, Zack charged forward at almost the exact same time, hitting Blake in the back of the head.

The sound of a gunshot echoed through the night, but then Blake crumpled to the ground. Zack quickly disarmed him.

"Are you okay?" Zack asked harshly.

"I'm fine," she murmured her ears still ringing from the sharp retort of the gun. She could barely hear Ace barking madly from inside the house.

"Can you find something to tie him up with?" Zack asked, turning Blake onto his stomach and yanking his arms behind his back. Blake groaned and tried to struggle. "See if Armbruster has his handcuffs with him."

Deputy Armbruster! She ran towards the prone figure. She pulled off the handcuffs from his belt and handed them to Zack before going back to kneel beside the deputy to feel for his pulse.

Please be alive, she whispered as she placed her fingers

along the side of his neck. At first she was worried she was feeling her own racing heartbeat, but then realized the reassuring slower beat belonged to the deputy.

"Zack, he's alive!" she called out. "We need an ambulance, stat!"

"Just give me a minute," Zack said. She could hear him phoning for an ambulance. She couldn't see much, but felt along the deputy's arms and legs, searching for some sort of wound.

"Devon? Can you hear me?" She hoped using his first name would get through to him.

Deputy Armbruster began to groan seconds before two additional deputies arrived on the scene.

"Where's Caruthers?" Deputy Thomas asked.

"Zack has him handcuffed. Devon is hurt and I'm afraid to move him."

"The ambulance should be here any minute," Deputy Thomas assured her. "Ian, shine your flashlight over here," he called out to the other deputy.

She couldn't see Deputy Ian Kramer as he was holding the flashlight, but at least now she could do a better job of examining Devon. Her fingers stumbled across a huge knot on the back of his head, and she winced in sympathy knowing he was going to have a concussion or worse.

"I don't see any bullet wounds," she said half under her breath.

Devon groaned again and she decided that maybe they could log roll him onto his back. "Tuck his arm along his side," she told Deputy Thomas. "I'll support his head and his neck as we roll him over."

"You're injured," Zack said, coming over to kneel beside her. "I'll do it."

She'd been ignoring the ache in her broken collarbone,

knowing that Deputy Armbruster was hurt far worse. Besides, it was worth it to get Blake under control.

"I'm alright," she protested, but sat on her heels to let Zack and Jason Thomas roll Devon over onto his back.

"What happened?" Devon asked hoarsely. "Where am I?"

"You're at Julie and Derek's townhouse," she said. "Where do you hurt the most?"

"My head," Devon whispered. "I was following Caruthers, or at least the guy I thought was Caruthers, but I should have called for backup right away. I wanted to be sure he was our guy, first, but I underestimated him."

"It's all over, we have Blake in handcuffs," she assured him. "Do you hear the ambulance? Help is on the way."

Devon Armbruster's eyes slid shut as if the light from Ian Kramer's flashlight was too much. She knew just how he felt. As soon as the paramedics arrived, she gave them a brief summary.

"Hi, Sam," she greeted the young man who was Sheriff Torretti's son. "I'm fairly certain Deputy Armbruster has a concussion, and so far I haven't found any other injuries."

"Good to know," Sam said as he deftly started a peripheral IV. He glanced over at Deputy Thomas. "You better let my dad know about this."

Deputy Thomas nodded. "I know. The sheriff isn't going to be happy at losing another deputy, even temporarily."

Sam grimaced. "That's for sure."

Within moments Sam and his partner had the deputy bundled onto the gurney. As they whisked Devon away, Deputy Thomas and Deputy Kramer went over to take Blake into custody.

"Make them stop yelling at me!" Blake shrilled as they hauled him to his feet. "Make them stop!"

"Who's yelling at you?" Deputy Thomas asked. "What are you talking about?"

"He needs psychiatric care," Merry said as Blake continued to talk nonsense. "You'll need to take him to the hospital."

"I hit him in the back of the head, too, so you might need to rule out a concussion," Zack added. "And here's the gun he was pointing at Merry."

"We'll drop him off at the hospital first, but then we're going to need statements from both of you," Deputy Thomas said. "I know we've been looking for his vehicle, too. Any idea where it might be?"

"He claimed he was staying at the empty house a few doors down that's for sale," Merry informed them. "It could be that he's been hiding the Jeep inside the garage."

"Very clever," Ian Kramer said. "How is it that someone who hears voices screaming at him can manage to be so deviously smart by breaking into an empty house?"

"I don't know," Deputy Thomas acknowledged. "Blake Caruthers, you're under arrest for assaulting a police officer, identity theft, and violating your no contact restraining order."

Merry felt the warmth of Zack's arm around her shoulder and leaned into him as she listened to Deputy Thomas giving Blake his Miranda rights. She didn't bother to point out that since Blake wasn't psychologically stable, reading him his Miranda rights was useless.

"Are you sure you're not hurt?" Zack asked.

"I'm fine. Thank you for not shooting him."

"I couldn't believe you rushed at him like that," Zack said in an incredulous tone. "You nearly took ten years off my life with that stunt. And I wasn't going to shoot him except as a last resort. It's not his fault he's ill."

She sighed. "If only he'd take his meds."

"You can't fix him, Merry."

"I know." She couldn't believe the nightmare was finally over. At least for now. "Do you know how long he'll be in jail this time?" she asked.

"I think we can make a case that he needs a court order to force him to take his meds," Zack said. "He needs help, not jail."

She agreed, although she feared she'd never feel safe knowing Blake was out of jail and able to come and find her.

Loud yelling coming from the front of the house startled her. "What's going on?"

"I don't know," Zack said grimly.

She followed as Zack took off running in the direction that the deputies had taken Blake. When they reached the street, she stopped when she saw Deputy Thomas kneeling beside Blake's body.

"What happened?" Zack asked.

"He started fighting and head-butting us," Deputy Thomas said. "He broke free, and when Ian tackled him, Caruthers hit his head on the ground. Now he's not moving."

Merry rushed forward and felt for a pulse. "We need to start CPR!"

Both deputies worked together to perform cardiopulmonary resuscitation while Zack called for another ambulance. When they got tired, she and Zack took a turn.

They worked continuously until the ambulance got there, and once the paramedics gave him some meds, his pulse returned.

When the ambulance took off with red lights and sirens blaring, she turned to Zack. "We need to get to the hospital."

"I'll drive."

She prayed for Blake's well-being as Zack drove, regretting her earlier negative thoughts. Granted, she didn't want to have the threat of Blake coming after her hanging over her head, but she never wanted him to die, either.

Zack parked as close to the ER as possible, and when they rushed in, she couldn't tell by their serious expressions if the news was good or bad.

"Are they still working on him?" she asked.

Deputy Thomas slowly nodded. "Yeah, he's better, although they're still worried about a potential head injury.

She nodded, knowing firsthand how a concussion felt. "Why do you think he tried to run away?"

"I don't know," Deputy Kramer admitted. "Maybe the voices in his head told him to?"

"Or maybe he tried to run because he'd committed other crimes," Zack pointed out.

Dr. Gabe Allen came into the waiting room, his eyes widening when he recognized Merry. "What are you doing here?" he asked.

She couldn't seem to dredge up a smile. "The man you're working on, Blake Caruthers, was a former friend of mine. How is he?"

Gabe nodded. "He's okay. We've stabilized him. We'll need to keep an eye on him for the next few days but I think he'll be fine."

Despite her fear of Blake, she was glad he hadn't died. She hoped and prayed that this time he'd get the help he needed.

"But hitting his head shouldn't have caused a heart attack. Why do you think caused his heart trouble?" she asked.

Gabe hesitated. "We don't know for sure," he hedged. "We're checking all options."

"Likely drugs, right?" Merry knew by the look on Gabe's face that she'd guessed right. "Cocaine is known to cause heart problems, and I'm pretty sure Blake used drugs in the past."

Gabe shrugged, neither confirming nor denying her statement.

"I'm glad to hear he's okay," Ian said. "At least now I won't have to be accused of purposefully trying to get rid of the guy."

"You were only doing your job," Zack assured him. "He was mentally unstable and armed. We all did our best tonight."

Merry nodded her agreement, knowing they were right. She didn't know how long Blake would be jailed this time, but hopefully long enough that she wouldn't have to look over her shoulder and worry about him coming after her for a long time.

Still, she couldn't help wishing he'd go back on his medication. She missed the young Blake she'd idolized in high school. The one who'd been like a big brother to her.

Please, Lord, please take care of Blake. Bring him peace.

14

Zack blinked at the sunlight pouring into the bedroom and shot bolt upright, afraid he'd overslept.

He peered at the clock, relieved to note that it was still early. Merry planned on going to church and he'd promised to go along.

They hadn't gotten home from the police department until late, and then he'd gotten a call from Cole telling him they found Calvin Reynolds dead body at Caruthers' place. It seemed that Reynolds hadn't given up his identity without a struggle. He was secretly glad to know that Blake would spend a long time behind bars once the police had proved he'd murdered Reynolds.

He wasn't sure how Merry had felt about hearing the news that Blake likely killed a man. She'd been unusually quiet last night on the way home.

Still, knowing Merry, she wouldn't take the excuse of fighting with her stalker, doing CPR on him, and being up late in order to give her statement to the police to beg off from singing in the church choir.

Zack quickly showered and changed his clothes, wishing he'd brought something nicer than a simple pair of tan Dockers and a polo shirt. Still, anything was better than jeans.

He ate a quick bowl of instant oatmeal before heading outside on the patio to see if Merry was up. She was just finishing her own breakfast, and when Ace whined at the door, she looked surprised to see him. "Good morning, Zack."

"Good morning." He opened the door to let Ace outside. "Did you manage to get some sleep?"

She grimaced and nodded. "Yes. One minute I was praying for Blake and the next my alarm was going off."

He smiled, thinking it was a good thing that God was watching over her. "I'm ready to leave anytime you are."

"Are you sure? I'd like to be there early if you don't mind."

"I figured as much. You and the rest of the choir have to warm up first, right?"

She smiled and nodded. "Just give me a minute to get my purse."

"Come on, Ace," he called. The dog watered a tree, and then came bounding back to the patio. Zack rubbed Ace behind the ears while he waited for Merry.

"Back inside, Ace," he said, opening the patio door and urging the dog inside.

"Come on in. We'll go out the front door," Merry said.

He stepped inside, making sure to lock the screen door behind him. When he saw Merry dressed in a pretty blue flowered dress, he had to remind himself to breathe.

"You look great," he managed.

"Thank you," she said softly. As inappropriate as it was,

he couldn't help thinking about their kiss as he followed her outside to his truck.

He couldn't think of a single intelligent thing to say as he drove to church, not wanting to remind Merry about the events from last night. He couldn't help wondering how her collarbone was feeling, since she'd insisted on doing CPR while they'd worked on Blake.

"Thanks for coming to church with me," she said, breaking into his thoughts.

"I don't mind," he said, somewhat surprised to realize it was true. When he'd prayed last night for Merry's safety, he realized that maybe she'd been right. God hadn't given up on him after all.

He regretted the fact that he only had one more day off work. He didn't want to leave Merry and return to Madison. But he also didn't think he could give her what she deserved.

Maybe he needed to pray for God's guidance?

"I'll drop you off, and then find a place to park," he said, pulling up to the church.

"Okay, I'll see you after the service." When she climbed out of the truck he realized she was wearing her sling again. No doubt because her collarbone was hurting.

He parked his truck and walked toward the front door, trying to think of a way to convince Merry to go back to the hospital for another X-ray. What if she'd dislocated the fracture? What if she needed surgery?

He stayed outside near a group of church members who'd gathered to chat. Seeing everyone greeting each other reminded him how much he'd once liked being a part of the church community.

"Daddy," a little girl grabbed onto his pants leg, and he glanced down at her in surprise. She was a cute toddler, and when she saw him her tiny face puckered into a frown.

"Hey Kayla, that's the wrong daddy," a woman said, coming over to the rescue. "Sorry about that," she said with a gentle smile. "My husband, Gabe, is wearing the same pants, and Kayla must have gotten a little confused."

"No problem," he said, glad to see that the little girl was smiling again. When a tall man came over to join them, he recognized him as Dr. Allen.

"Hi," Gabe greeted him. "Didn't I just see you last night?"

"Yes, you did. I'm Zack Crain," he introduced himself.

"Oh, you're Julie's brother, aren't you?" Gabe exclaimed with a smile. "Of course, I should have noticed the resemblance. This is my wife, Larissa and our one year old, Kayla."

"Nice to meet you." Zack usually avoided little kids, especially those who reminded him of Amelia, but for some reason, being close to Kayla wasn't too bad. "Your daughter is adorable."

"Thanks," Gabe said.

"Let's hope she likes being a big sister," Larissa said, putting her hand on her stomach.

It wasn't until then that Zack realized Larissa and Gabe were expecting another baby. "Are you hoping for a boy this time?" he asked.

"It doesn't matter one way or the other," Gabe said. "We'll love every child we bring into the world, no matter what."

Zack nodded, and when the church bells rang they all filed inside.

As he sat through the church service, listening to Merry's beautiful voice and the pastor's sermon, he couldn't get Gabe Allen's comment out of his mind.

Why had he thought that having another child would replace Amelia in his heart? Gabe was right, each child

deserved to be loved for his or herself. Loving Suz and
Amelia didn't mean he couldn't love anyone else.

What an idiot he'd been. All this time he'd held onto his
grief and his anger, turning his back on God and the church.

He bowed his head and prayed for forgiveness as Merry
began to sing her solo.

And, finally, he embraced an overwhelming sense
of peace.

———————

MERRY COULDN'T HELP STARING at Zack during the service,
even though she should have been paying attention to
Pastor John's message.

Zack looked so handsome dressed in his nice clothes,
seated in the pew behind Gabe, Larissa and little Kayla.
Merry was surprised that Zack kept smiling at Kayla and
told herself not to read too much into his actions.

She couldn't deny she didn't want the weekend to come
to an end. Zack would head back to Madison tomorrow, and
Julie and Derek would return home the following day.

And she'd be alone, again.

Enough. She really needed to stop feeling sorry for
herself, right now. So many others had it far worse. Poor
Blake was going to jail for a long time. And Zack was finding
his way back to God and the church. How could she be sad
about that?

Very simply, she couldn't. So what if she was alone?
She'd ask Julie and Derek if she could move in next door
and maybe she'd get a dog. A black lab, just like Ace. Or
maybe a golden retriever.

She was blessed to have a good job, working with great people. She was also blessed to live in a town that felt like home in a way that Minneapolis never had. And she didn't have to run any more.

Feeling better, she led the choir in the closing hymn and couldn't help but smile when she noticed Zack was singing along.

After the service was over, she expected Zack to be anxious to leave, but found him chatting again with Gabe and Larissa while Kayla climbed up on the pew. She walked over to join them.

"How are you feeling, Merry?" Larissa asked. "I heard you did CPR last night."

Big news traveled fast in a small town. "Yes, but I'm okay."

"Hey, Doc, don't you think Merry should get another X-ray of her collarbone, just to be sure she didn't injure it further?" Zack asked.

Gabe nodded. "Yeah, that wouldn't be a bad idea."

She tried not to roll her eyes. "But my collarbone doesn't hurt that bad," she pointed out.

"But you don't want the bone to heal crooked, either," Zack argued.

"He's right, Merry," Gabe said. "Dr. Katy is on today. She'd sneak you in for a quick X-ray, no problem. You'd be in and out in a matter of minutes."

Since it was three against one, she gave up. "Okay, I'll go in and have another X-ray, but it will only prove that I'm fine."

"Good. We'll go there first, and then we can stop in at Rose's Café for lunch."

"Three days in a row?" she joked. "You're a brave man, Zack Crain."

"I can take the heat," he joked back. "Besides, we didn't eat much for dinner last night and I'm still hungry."

Her smile dimmed a bit as she remembered why they hadn't eaten their leftovers. Not just because of Blake, but because Zack had kissed her.

And she'd kissed him back.

But he couldn't give her what she wanted, a relationship with a future.

"Up!" Kayla demanded, holding her arms out to Zack.

He stared at the little girl in surprise, but then reached down to pick her up, holding her in the crook of his arm.

"You should feel honored," Larissa said. "Kayla is normally afraid of strangers."

Little Kayla rested her head against Zack's shoulder, and Merry couldn't help but think about what a great father he must have been to Amelia.

And what a great husband and father he could be again if he allowed himself to fall in love.

———

STOPPING off at the hospital for an X-ray didn't take long, although Merry quickly discovered that Devon Armbruster was still a patient up on the same neuro floor she'd been on.

"Do you think we should go up to visit him?" she asked Zack.

"Maybe we should wait for a while. I think his concussion was worse than yours. Besides, Blake might be on the same floor. He's under guard, so you wouldn't be able to visit him."

Merry nodded, thinking about how terrible she'd felt

during the first twenty-four hours of her brief hospital stay. "Your right, I'll have plenty of time to stop in to see him tomorrow or the next day. And I have no plans to visit Blake. I'm hoping at some point he'll forget all about me."

Zack frowned but didn't say anything as they walked back out to his truck.

When he headed toward Main Street, she stopped him with a hand on his arm. "Could we pick up something and eat at home?" she asked. "I'm just not up for all the questions about last night."

"Sure, what would you like? Sub sandwiches? Or a pizza?"

"Let's get a pizza." She could almost smell the tangy sauce and the melted cheese and her stomach rumbled with anticipation. "I haven't had one in ages."

"Sounds good."

Zack pulled up in front of the pizza joint in town and picked up a ready-made pizza. She held it on her lap, trying not to drool as he drove back to the townhouse.

He took the pizza from her hands and carried it inside, holding it high enough that Ace couldn't get to it. "Down boy," he said.

Ace dropped to his feet and she remembered how well the dog had listened to her last night. "Good boy," she said, giving him a good rub.

She let Ace outside and brought out paper plates and napkins so they could enjoy their meal on the patio in front of the lake. Zack put the umbrella up for shade, and then sat down next to her and bowed his head.

"Dear Lord, thank you for this beautiful day and for the food we're about to eat," Zack said. "Please heal Blake Caruthers and bring him the peace he deserves. Please help

Merry and Devon Armbruster heal from their injuries, Amen."

"And please watch over Zack when he returns to work," Merry added. She was touched by the way Zack prayed for Blake, the same way she had last night. "Thank you, Zack."

He reached over and gave her hand a quick squeeze. "Thank you for taking me to church with you. I really enjoyed it."

She wanted to ask more but he released her to take a big bite of his pizza so she helped herself to a piece too. "Mmm, pepperoni, my favorite."

"Mine, too," Zack said between bites.

Being with Zack was wonderful and she wished the day would last forever. When they'd finished the pizza, managing to eat every slice, she sat back in her seat gazing out at the lake as Zack threw the garbage away.

"It's a great day for a boat ride," she said.

"We'll go in a little while, once our stomachs have had a chance to settle," Zack said, sitting beside her.

"Well, maybe you shouldn't have eaten so much," she said.

He grinned. "You managed to eat your fair share."

She laughed softly, knowing he was right. "Zack, I feel bad you didn't get to enjoy a full weekend off work."

He looked surprised. "What do you mean? This was a great weekend for me. You're the one who didn't get to enjoy it very much. I got to swim, ride the boat, play softball and spend time with you."

Her heart stuttered and she took a deep breath, knowing he didn't mean that the way it sounded. "I had a great weekend, too. I'm just sorry about everything that happened with Blake."

"You can't hold yourself responsible for what

happened," he said gently. "Blake was a sick man who did this on his own. I'm glad he's been arrested and that he won't hurt you again."

"Do you really think he killed that other man, Reynolds?"

"Yeah, I do."

"Me too," she confessed. "And as terrible as it sounds, I'm glad he'll either be in prison or in a psych hospital for a long time."

"It's not terrible at all, I feel the same way." Zack paused. "Merry, I'd really like to see you again. After this weekend, I mean."

She tried not to let her shock show on her face. "Really?"

Zack nodded. He turned in his seat so he was facing her. "Today in church, I realized that you were right about everything. God never turned away from me. But after losing Suz and Amelia, I couldn't seem to find my way back to the church and my faith. Until now."

Her heart swelled with hope. "Oh Zack, you have no idea how happy I am to hear you say that."

"Merry, I care about you. But I need to know, do you have feelings for Devon Armbruster?"

This time she couldn't prevent her jaw from dropping open. "What? Why on earth would you think that?"

"The thought of you dating other men makes me feel sick," Zack mumbled. "You seemed so worried about him, I just thought maybe..."

"Of course I was worried about him. Blake almost killed him!" She couldn't believe what Zack had thought and, for a moment, she wasn't sure if she should trust him with her heart.

But then she realized she'd already given Zack her heart. She just hadn't told him that, yet. "I don't have any interest in dating anyone other than you. Don't you know that I've liked you since we first met at Julie and Derek's wedding? I knew you were hurting so I didn't let my true feelings show."

"I thought about you, too, Merry. More than I had any right to. And I'm relieved to know that you're not harboring secret feelings for Deputy Armbruster, and hopefully not for anyone else, either."

"Anyone else?" she echoed. "You act as if I've been dating men all over town."

He scowled. "You might not realize it, but there are a lot of men around here who are secretly dying to go out with you. But please don't. I know I'm asking a lot because I still live in Madison, and it won't be easy to mesh our schedules, but I'm asking you to give me a chance. Give us a chance."

Tears burned her eyes as she struggled to smile. "Zack, I'm not interested in seeing anyone but you."

"Really?" He looked so happy and surprised she couldn't stop herself from baring her soul.

"Zack, I don't want to rush you, and please know that you can take all the time you need. But I'm already in love with you."

His mouth dropped open and she hoped she hadn't said too much too soon. But then suddenly he was standing and drawing her to her feet. "Merry, sweetheart, I don't deserve you," he murmured before lowering his mouth to kiss her.

This time, pulling away wasn't even on the radar screen. She gave herself up to his kiss, trying to show him with actions how much she loved him.

And there was a tiny thrill when he pulled her closer, showing her how much he cared, too.

After what seemed like an eternity, Zack lifted his head, breathing heavily. She snuggled into his embrace, unwilling to let him go.

"Merry, I'm not sure I deserve your love, but I know that you deserve mine," he whispered. "You told me that love was God's greatest gift and I know that's true. I love you, too."

"I know." She lifted her head and gazed up at him. "We have plenty of time, Zack. There's no rush. We'll be together as often as possible and give our love time to nourish and grow."

He smiled and gave her another quick kiss. Ace butted his head between them, making sure that they hadn't forgotten about him.

Maybe one day, she and Zack would have a dog of their own. And a family.

But for now, she was content to wait.

EPILOGUE

Zack stood at the front of the church, tugging on the necktie of his tux, more nervous than he cared to admit. Derek, his best man, put a reassuring hand on his shoulder. "You'll be fine."

"I know." Zack wasn't worried about getting married to Merry. He was concerned that he'd somehow mess up the best thing that had happened to him in a long time. He'd spent every bit of free time he had with her, showing her how to train King, the black lab puppy he'd bought. They'd tried to take things slow, but within a month he'd applied for a job with the Hope County Sheriff's Department, and once he secured the position, he'd moved back home.

And he'd proposed to Merry the night he'd accepted the job.

He loved her more than words could say, and he was ready to have a family with her.

The music swelled and the people packed in the church rose to their feet and turned to watch Merry walk down the aisle. His sister Julie came down first, the gentle swell of her abdomen showing her early pregnancy. Behind his sister came Derek's daughter, Lexi, an old pro at being a flower girl.

And then, finally, the tightness in his chest eased when Merry came forward, escorted by Mr. Abe Caruthers, Blake's father. Zack was thrilled she'd reunited with the Caruthers family and amazingly, none of them held everything that had happened with Blake against her. Especially once they heard he was being tried for murder.

Blake's father kissed Merry on the cheek, and then handed her over to him. Zack took her hand and turned to face the pastor.

He was the luckiest man in the world to be given a second chance at love. And he silently vowed to be the husband and father Merry and their future children deserved.

If you enjoyed this story, please check out the first chapter in the next book in the series, Worth The Wait.

DEAR READER

I hope you're enjoying my Crystal Lake Series. First let me say, that Ace is a real black lab belonging to my brother-in-law's family and I enjoyed dog sitting for him while they were on vacation. Sometimes there is nothing like a pet to help break through the loneliness and that was one of the main reasons I decided to use Ace in my story.

I have another dog, a German Shepherd Duke in my next story, Worth The Wait.

Thanks to those of you who've written such wonderful reviews of my previous stories, Healing Her Heart and A Soldier's Promise. There are six books total in the series and I hope you give them all a try. Please consider signing up for my newsletter at www.laurascottbooks.com. I only send out a newsletter when I have a new release and I offer a free exclusive Crystal Lake Novella to all subscribers! I also love hearing from my readers so drop me a line if you have time.

Yours in Faith,

Laura Scott